A PLUME BOOK

MY ONE SQUARE INCH OF ALASKA

Gwen Short

SHARON SHORT is the recipient of a 2011 Montgomery County (Ohio) Arts & Cultural District Literary Artist Fellowship and a 2012 Ohio Arts Council individual artist's grant. She is "Literary Life" columnist for the *Dayton Daily News* and directs the renowned Antioch Writers' Workshop in Yellow Springs, Ohio. Short lives in Ohio with her husband and is the mother of two daughters in college. Visit her at www.sharonshort.com.

My One Square Inch of Alaska

A NOVEL

Sharon Short

A PLUME BOOK

PLUME
Published by the Penguin Group
Penguin Group (USA) Inc., 375 Hudson Street, New York, New York 10014, U.S.A.
Penguin Group (Canada), 90 Eglinton Avenue East, Suite 700, Toronto,
Ontario, Canada M4P 2Y3 (a division of Pearson Penguin Canada Inc.)
Penguin Books Ltd., 80 Strand, London WC2R 0RL, England
Penguin Ireland, 25 St. Stephen's Green, Dublin 2, Ireland (a division of Penguin Books Ltd.)
Penguin Group (Australia), 707 Collins Street, Melbourne,
Victoria 3008, Australia (a division of Pearson Australia Group Pty. Ltd.)
Penguin Books India Pvt. Ltd., 11 Community Centre,
Panchsheel Park, New Delhi – 110 017, India
Penguin Group (NZ), 67 Apollo Drive, Rosedale, Auckland 0632,
New Zealand (a division of Pearson New Zealand Ltd.)
Penguin Books, Rosebank Office Park, 181 Jan Smuts Avenue,
Parktown North 2193, South Africa
Penguin China, B7 Jaiming Center, 27 East Third Ring Road North,
Chaoyang District, Beijing 100020, China

Penguin Books Ltd., Registered Offices: 80 Strand, London WC2R 0RL, England

First published by Plume, a member of Penguin Group (USA) Inc.

First Printing, February 2013
10 9 8 7 6 5 4 3 2 1

℗ REGISTERED TRADEMARK—MARCA REGISTRADA

LIBRARY OF CONGRESS CATALOGING-IN-PUBLICATION DATA
Short, Sharon Gwyn.
My one square inch of Alaska : a novel / Sharon Short.
p. cm.
ISBN 978-0-452-29876-7 (pbk.)
1. Brothers and sisters—Fiction.   2. Families—Ohio—Fiction.
3. Sick children—Fiction.   4. Alaska—History—1867-1959—Fiction.
5. Road fiction.   6. Bildungsromans.   I. Title.
PS3569.H594M9 2013
813'.54—dc23
2012032249

Printed in the United States of America
Set in Janson Text LT Std
Designed by Leonard Telesca

To David, the love of my life

My One Square Inch of Alaska

Chapter 1

Later, MayJune would say that the biggest turns in life come when you're paying the least attention, making small choices you don't yet know will change everything.

MayJune was always saying things like that—corny and peculiar and true, all at once.

But, of course, I hadn't met her when I found Mama's clothes stuffed in suitcases with mothballs and made my first small choice: Instead of snapping the suitcases shut and forgetting my discovery like I knew I should, I counted the pieces.

Thirty-eight.

Dresses, skirts, blouses, pants, but mostly dresses—fine dresses, afternoon-tea dresses, party dresses, even costumey dresses with feathers and sequins. But not life-in-Groverton dresses.

Mama's wedding dress, a white satin and lace and mother-of-pearl-button confection, filled one suitcase all by itself.

There were also hats and shoes and a few purses, but I didn't count them.

It was October 1946 when I found Mama's clothes. I was

ten years old. Making my first trip to the forbidden base-ment, I cradled armloads of home-canned green beans and corn and tomatoes, fall harvest gifts from neighbor women who, even with the war over, still had victory gardens and made it their business to worry about us.

Fearful of slipping and dropping the jars, I stared past my arms at each step mottled with dull blue paint, remem-bering Mama's warning that it was too dark and dirty down there for Will and me. Fear crept in when the wobbly bot-tom step threw me off balance. In that moment between almost falling and not falling, I saw the suitcases lined up against the wall, in the shadowy corner behind the Singer sewing machine.

I didn't fall.

My hands trembled as I opened the big trunk first. The Mama we knew dressed in dowdy housedresses or bath-robes, occasionally some denim pants and a loose blouse, or a simple dress.

Nothing with even the tiniest downy feather or hint of sparkle.

But these clothes had to be Mama's. Underlying the mothball smell was a hint of rose and jasmine—Mama's scent. I scooped an armful of clothing up to my face and breathed, as if by inhaling deeply enough I'd bring Mama back.

I wondered where Mama might have gotten these clothes. Definitely not from Miss Bettina—even though she had been Mama's best friend—who owned her own dress shop in downtown Groverton and lived next door to us on Elmwood Street. The dresses Miss Bettina wore and sold were dark hued, proper. These, other than the white wedding dress, were all bright colors—azure, scarlet, tangerine, emerald—and featured plunging necklines, side slits, even backless designs.

I put Mama's clothes back in the suitcases. Then I went to find Babs Wickham, *my* best friend, and told her she had to come over. I showed her the clothes—all except the wedding dress—a treasure trove for dress-up.

But Babs proclaimed dress-up as babyish, and whispered that she had taken something *really* special from her own mama—a Max Factor Red-Red lipstick. Giggling at each other in my dresser mirror, we assured one another that our red lips made us, finally, grown-up.

And a grown-up would know, instinctively, that asking Daddy about those clothes would take us into territory far too dangerous. So I never mentioned Mama's mysterious clothes, never looked at them again. But I thought about them, for seven years, until I secretly began remaking those clothes, one by one, into outfits of my own creation.

Such a small choice, I thought.

In September 1953, it was the fourth day of my senior year of high school and Will's fifth grade. That morning I became so absorbed in sketching a design for a dress— sleeveless, slim lines, just right for one of Mama's old yellow prints—that I didn't notice the toast burning and the stove clock ticking, until my little brother, Will, tried to talk with his mouth full of Marvel Puffs and instead spit a gob of cereal in my ear.

I started to snap at Will about table manners. But he stared at me with his wide blue eyes and his cheeks so ridiculously bulged with cereal that I had to laugh. Softly, of course. Daddy's bedroom was just on the other side of the kitchen wall.

Will finally swallowed and said, "Your toast is burning."

I jumped up from our kitchen table and ran to the toaster, forcing up its stuck lever. The whiff of burned toast soured my stomach. I hated that bitter smell, and the sound of removing the char, but I pulled open the utensil drawer— the one that took two tugs to get past its sticking spot—got out a knife, and started scraping away.

"Donna?"

I looked over at Will. He was a little pale around his mouth. Too many servings of Marvel Puffs, instead of hearty breakfasts with eggs or sausage. And unburned toast. Another pang of guilt . . . *I should try harder to take care of Will.*

"You don't have to eat burned toast," he said quietly.

That was as close as he ever came to inviting me to eat Marvel Puffs. He was saving up cereal box tops to send in to the Sunshine Bakery Company for the prize of his wildest dreams: an official, certified deed to one square inch of the Territory of Alaska, a promotion Marvel Puffs was doing with *Sergeant Striker and the Alaskan Wild* to advertise the show's television debut and, of course, the cereal. Kids who included a 250-word essay with the box tops were in the running for having their photo with the actor who played the television Sergeant Striker featured on the front of Marvel Puffs boxes. Marvelous. Better than a peashooter, anyway.

Will's rule for earning his deed: eating all ten boxes of Marvel Puffs, not one puffed morsel left in box or bowl.

Asking for help would be cheating, as bad as bratty Howard Baker across the street, who whined until his mom bought ten boxes at once, just for the box tops, and then threw away the cereal. Daddy or I could have Marvel Puffs, but only if we asked. We didn't.

I had rules, too. I didn't spend our household money on overpriced Marvel Puffs; Will had to buy them with his newspaper route earnings. And I didn't eat cereal that looked like grubs and made strange popping sounds when milk was poured on it.

I started scraping my toast again. "This will be fine with grape jelly."

"Thought we were out of grape jelly," Will said, and popped another spoonful of cereal into his mouth.

We were. Of course we were. We were out of grape jelly and macaroni and applesauce, and had been for a week. I'd put off going to the grocery because I'd been so focused on finishing the dress I wore that morning, made for my interview after school for a secret job, one I hadn't told even Babs—still my best friend—about.

I already had two jobs everyone in Groverton knew about: doing alterations at Miss Bettina's Dress Shop and waitressing at Dot's Corner Café. But those jobs were for helping my family. Grandma Dot—Daddy's mother—said I reminded her too much of Mama, so she gave my wages and tips to Daddy. "Your mama was reckless with money," she'd say (as if Daddy wasn't), quick to add "God-rest-her-soul," just like that, like the phrase was one word, the perfect word for excusing any comment.

From sneaking back some tip money, plus just a little from my alterations work, I'd saved $83.12. But that wasn't nearly enough to fund getting out of Groverton, Ohio, for good, after my senior year. I hadn't told Babs or Will about that, either. Babs would just laugh at me—"Oh, Donna, you're such a dreamer!" And Will would look at me with fear in his big blue eyes, but I told myself that he was growing fast, that he'd be able to deal with Daddy next year.

I took my scraped toast and sat back down by Will at the table. I stared at the toast as I said quietly, "Now, tell me again what you're doing this afternoon."

"You can't walk me home after school because you have a big project you have to work on at the library. So I have to come straight home. No going with Tony to Weaver's Drugstore." Will pulled his mouth down. He loved Weaver's ice cream floats. "No fishing. Just come straight on home, and run if Howard and his gang get after me, because I'll really get in trouble if I get in another fight"—he mocked my voice, making me sound like Grandma—"and there's meat loaf for dinner in the refrigerator, and—"

"Shush!" I hissed. Will had said the last bit too loudly. We had a whole Morse code of looks and tones where Daddy was concerned. Some mornings he got up, joining us for breakfast as polite and proper as could be. Other mornings, if he'd stayed out late the night before, he'd be angry—or, worse, sullen and sad—if we woke him up.

I lifted my left eyebrow to let Will know that this was one of *those* mornings.

But then Will looked so sorry that I patted his arm. "It's OK," I said quietly, words I'd learned to tell Will even when they weren't true.

I bit into my toast, studied my sketch. Maybe if the neckline had more of a scoop . . .

Will sidled up close to me again and said around another mouthful of Marvel Puffs, "Why can't I just meet you after school and go with you to the library?" This time, he sent the moist little specks onto my cheek.

I dropped my pencil on the table and shut my sketchbook. "Because you'll just keep bugging me like you are now." I put my toast on top of the Marvel Puffs box and went to the sink to again wipe off my face. "You know, if you keep eating big mouthfuls of that stuff, your stomach might explode."

Instead of looking terrified, Will swallowed his cereal and started to laugh—but then the telephone in the living room rang. Two short bursts and a long trill, our ring on our street's party line. Will and I stared at each other. My stomach lurched. But I was in the living room answering the phone before the next long trill, my voice a breathless whisper as I said, "Lane residence." I stared at the door to Daddy's room, wondering if I'd heard restless movement.

"Why are you whispering?" It was Babs, sounding giddy and loopy, a sure sign that she was already into her mom's Dexamyl. "Oh I get it, late night for the old man, huh?"

I winced at Babs's giggly attempt at sympathy. I didn't care if Miss Bettina heard; she knew all about life at the Lane house. But I couldn't risk Mrs. Baker or other neighbors picking up the shared line.

"Babs, what is it?"

"Special project time!"

That was her code for having the family car, most likely because her mama had gone with her aunt to visit their sickly mother down in Lexington, Kentucky. Babs's daddy, who was editor of the *Groverton Daily News*, walked to his office and spent long hours there. Her code also meant she wanted to skip school with me. We'd just use the "indis-posed by our visit from Auntie Flo" excuse to avoid a tru-ancy detention. Even the most veiled menstruation reference flustered Principal Stodgill.

My heart jumped at the prospect. I would not have trou-ble talking Babs into driving over to Rike's Department Store in Dayton, and I suddenly longed to see the newest fall clothes: silk dresses, tweed skirts and velvet-trimmed jackets, fur-and-felt hats, leather gloves with lace cuffs, stacked-heel shoes. . . . I loved Miss Bettina and her dress shop, but Rike's was special.

But then I looked down at my own dress. I had to get to my secret interview.

"I'm sorry, Babs," I said quietly. "I have a . . . an actual school project this afternoon. I'm worried about a big test. In Algebra. I need to study at the library starting at four or so before I go to work at Grandma's." Babs wasn't in my— or any—math class. I was one of the few girls in Algebra, but I'd insisted on taking it instead of home economics. I liked math, while Mrs. Irvine's bad instructions on how to set a shoulder seam or insert a zipper pained me.

Babs giggled. "Since when do you have to study to get good marks? Listen, I promise we'll wrap up our school project in time for you to get back for your . . . school proj-ect." Babs giggled again, and I knew she had definitely raided her mom's Dexamyl. I worried about riding with her—I didn't know how to drive, just yet—but then I thought of those dresses at Rike's. . . .

And that's when I made my next small choice, the kind MayJune would call life-changing-once-you-look-back. I said, "I'm glad we get to work on our, um, history project."

"Wear something adorable, OK?" I glanced down at my dress. I hoped it *wasn't* adorable. I was sick of adorable clothes. I hoped what I'd made was chic and daring and . . . wonderful. "I have a special surprise for you!"

She hung up before I could protest. "Special surprise" probably meant she'd want to buy me something, and I didn't like taking Babs's charity. I decided to take fifty cents from my escape-Groverton savings to cover lunch at the Rike's sandwich counter.

I hung up and hurried back into the kitchen. Will was looking through my sketchbook. I grabbed it from him, but he just grinned teasingly. "Do you have a crush on Mr. Cahill? Tony says his big sister does."

I looked away from Will, hoping he wouldn't notice that my face had just flamed a Principal Stodgill red. "No," I snapped. "Mr. Cahill's art class is a joke. All we do is draw spheres and cones and cubes. . . ."

I suddenly noticed the time on the stove clock. Seven-fifteen. Babs would expect me to be at the corner of Water-shed and Sixth *before* school started at eight. Babs was always impatient; she'd take off without me if I was too late.

"You drew fancy clothes, but no people in them. Why not? Hey—are you doing a comic book about invisible people? Maybe they're invisible because they've been zapped by space aliens who . . ."

Will wouldn't leave without finishing his Marvel Puffs. I put my sketchbook back on the table.

"Will, you're right. I can't eat this without grape jelly." I smiled at him as I plucked the ruined toast off the Marvel Puffs box and took it over to the counter, where I left it by the foul-tempered toaster. I got out a blue Fiestaware bowl, one of the unchipped ones, and a spoon, and carried them over to the kitchen table. I sat down and poured the rest of the Marvel Puffs into my bowl, bottom-of-the-box cereal dust and all.

This time, I looked into Will's wide eyes as I quietly said, "Not much left. And we're almost out of milk." I pointed to his bowl. "May I?"

Will answered with a solemn nod. I poured the milk left in Will's bowl into mine. I brought the spoon to my mouth. The cereal smelled like wet cardboard—worse than burned toast. But Will fixed his big blue eyes on me, so I finally took the bite.

The cereal tasted like . . . nothing. Or maybe nothing with a hint of oatmeal. But as I chewed, the bite seemed to just get bigger. I thought, *No wonder the stuff is called Marvel Puffs*, and *I'll never get through the bowl*.

"What do you think?" Will asked anxiously.

I could have chosen to mutter my usual, "It's OK," but instead I made my next small choice. I said, "Will, that was Babs who just called. She wants me to meet her before school for this . . . school project."

Will scowled, disbelieving.

I rushed on. "Anyway, I'm kind of in a hurry, and not so hungry anyway, so why don't we take the shortcut by Stedman's and feed the rest of this cereal to that dog you like so much?"

Will stared at me, clearly staggered, his disbelief about Babs suddenly forgotten.

I smiled. "Shouldn't that count for your rule?"

"You said if I went there again, you wouldn't talk Dad out of giving me a whipping," he said.

I swallowed back shame. I *had* made that threat, after Mr. Stedman's last visit to our house to complain about Will feeding the dog. But Stedman's Scrapyard, down by the river near Groverton Pulp & Paper, was on a shortcut to where I was supposed to meet Babs. Will could just run down Sixth and cut over to Plum and get to school on time.

I looked away. "Go on—get your book bag before I change my mind!" I poured the leftover cereal into the Marvel Puffs box. Then I carefully tore off the box top and held it out to Will. He took it, wide-eyed, as if I had just handed him a deed to the entire Territory of Alaska.

Will hollered, "Trusty, we can trust this case is closed!" It was the cheesy closing line Sergeant Striker shouted to his dog at the end of every episode.

He clapped his hands to his mouth and gave me a look that said, *Sorry!* We froze, but Daddy's room remained silent—none of the crying out in restless sleep that usually followed a late-night bender.

Will grabbed his Marvel Puffs box top and rushed from the kitchen through the living room to the stairs, and up to the tiny second floor of our Cape Cod–style house, where we each had a bedroom.

I dropped the burned toast in the Marvel Puffs box, then quickly washed the dishes and wiped up the counter and table. I heard Will coming down the stairs—that third step from the bottom always squeaked—when I remembered one last thing.

I hurried through the breezeway to our garage, pulled the string for the bare-bulb light, and went to the freezer, from which I pulled out a chicken. It was Friday; the chicken would thaw in the refrigerator in time for Sunday's supper.

I could already see Grandma poking at the chicken, saying, *Such a luxury, having a garage AND a refrigerator AND a freezer.*

Tiny claws skittered nearby. I turned in time to see a mouse scurrying underneath the car.

Mama's car.

Every time I came out to the freezer, I tried to ignore the car, a 1946 Ford convertible, top still down, the open dash and seats covered with a picnic tablecloth with a faded red border and dull yellow ducks and lambs and farmhouses and flowers, as if the last time the car was parked in our garage we'd all returned from a long picnic by the Tangy River (upstream from the paper mill) and, too happily exhausted to put things away after our family excursion, just jauntily tossed the then-bright tablecloth over the open seats in a moment of silly abandonment—look at us! The perfect family, doing an imperfect job of cleaning up after our perfect family picnic! What a lark!

But I had no such memories, not even ones as faded as the tablecloth. At most, if I pushed myself I could summon, in a hazy, gauzy way that would surely sadden the once-bright ducks and lambs, some impression of riding in the car once or twice. But I wasn't convinced that was a real memory. I shook my head. No time for not-remembering.

Skittering. The mouse was back out from under the car, right at my feet. I grabbed the straw broom by the door and whacked the mouse, stunning it. I started to whack it again, but at its slight quiver, I opened the door and shooed it out with the broom. I waited a second, long enough to see the mouse regain its senses and run off into our overgrown

backyard. *That's right, little mouse. Run away from here. . . .
Far away. . . .*

By the time I picked up my school bag and the damp box of Marvel Puffs, careful to hold it away from my new dress, I expected to see Will waiting on the front porch. He wasn't there.

Then I saw his books scattered down the porch steps. The scruffy heels of his shoes. His long legs in the pants that I'd ordered special from the Montgomery Ward catalog, that he hated because they were too big, that I'd told him he'd grow into. His arms at odd angles pointing away from his body. His head turned so that I couldn't see his face.

Chapter 2

I rushed to Will's side, falling on my knees beside him, checking him over. I didn't see a scratch or bump on him, but he was out cold.

We needed help. I thought maybe I should go back in for Daddy . . . but then I saw his car parked at the curb, pointing the wrong direction, the driver's side front tire up on our grass.

Across the street, the Bakers were out in their driveway, about to get in their car, but all three had stopped in their tracks to stare at us. I looked over at Miss Bettina's house—*Come out, come out*, I willed Miss Bettina.

But then Will coughed. His eyes fluttered open. He stared up at me, blankly at first, and then with recognition, and he croaked, "Jeez, could you stop yelling?"

I realized I'd been hollering his name this whole time. I hushed and pulled him into my arms. He tried to push away, but I wouldn't let go of him, and so we ended up lumped together.

"What happened?"

"I must have tripped."

I almost believed him. I grabbed his chin, turned his

face toward me, put my other hand to his forehead. "Do you have a fever? Muscle weakness?"

Will swatted at my hand. "Oh, jeez, Donna, I don't have polio." He rolled his eyes.

But over the previous year, 1952, polio had fatally hit or paralyzed many children in Stackville, the neighborhood by Groverton Pulp & Paper, and in Tangy Town, across the river, and even three in our part of Groverton. We heard the reports when Daddy was home for dinner and watched the news on the television in our living room. Of course, he was watching for updates about his hero, Senator Joe McCarthy, and his search for communists—Reds, Daddy called them.

I took my hand from Will's forehead. He wasn't feverish; he felt cool and clammy.

"Fine. You don't have polio. But you also didn't trip. What happened?"

Suddenly, Will grinned impishly, grabbed his stomach, and said, "Oh, man, like you said—too many Marvel Puffs! My stomach exploded!" He pulled away from me and rolled on the ground, hollering, "Oh, the agony! Why didn't I listen to you? Now my guts are spewing everywhere—"

"Is everything OK over here?"

I looked up to see Mrs. Baker looming over us. She was wearing a black dress and gloves and holding a casserole dish, so I figured she must be going to set up a funeral lunch over at the Groverton First Church of God.

I've heard people say that there are no stupid questions, but this one truly was. Of course everything was not OK. The tight little smile on Mrs. Baker's pudgy face revealed she knew that.

I stood up and smoothed my dress. I couldn't stand the smirk on her face. Mr. Baker—still a marketing manager at Groverton Pulp & Paper, while Daddy, who had once been his supervisor, barely held on to his job at Ace Hardware—shook his head and got in his perfectly parked car. And Howard gave a smug little grin, a match for his mother's, as he watched from the driveway.

I focused on the rounded collar of Mrs. Baker's plain, lumpy, too-tight black dress. The collar was so matronly; I thought it would look much better with piping—perhaps in goldenrod for contrast—instead of lace trim.

"Will here has a bit of a stomachache. So I believe we're going to stay home today, call Dr. Emory to come to the house."

She stepped back, hugging her casserole dish as if it could protect her from whatever dread disease the Lanes might be spreading. "I hope it's nothing catching."

"I think it's just too many Marvel Puffs," I said.

"Oh, I would never let my Howard eat that—not nutritious enough."

No, you'd just buy the cereal and throw it away so the little brat could get his Alaska deed without—

"What? No! I can't stay home!" Will jumped up. He gave me a panicked look.

"Now, Will," I started.

"Good morning, Mrs. Baker." Thank God for Miss Bettina, in her fresh blue-and-white-checked dress and pretty faux pearl necklace, a dollop of hope compared to the gloom of Mrs. Baker.

Miss Bettina looked at me. "What's going on?" She knew better than to probe deeper.

"Will has a stomachache, is all, but just to be safe"—the image of Will, splayed flat on our scruffy lawn, made my heart clench—"I'm going to call Dr. Emory, and—"

"No!" Will shouted.

We all looked at him. Across the street, Mr. Baker tapped his car horn. Howard smirked.

"No, I'm fine, and I have to go to school, because, because—"

He stopped, and I watched his expression go from panicked to pleased. That always meant he had some mischievous idea. He grinned and said, "I have to get to school because of the science fair project I'm working on."

I lifted an eyebrow at him. The kid was stealing my cover stories.

"What? The science fair isn't until the spring," Mrs. Baker said.

"Oh, I know, but I'm doing some work ahead of time . . . for extra credit." He looked back at the porch and I followed his gaze, and saw that when I'd dropped everything, my book bag had spilled its contents, but somehow the Marvel Puffs box had landed neatly upright on the middle step, its soggy mix of toast and milk and cereal still inside.

Will leaped to the porch, grabbed the Marvel Puffs box, and scooped up his book bag and lunch pail. "I'm . . . testing the osmosis of various liquids on semipermeable surfaces . . . like, like milk in a Marvel Puffs box."

And then he took off running down Elmwood, rounding the corner onto Maple, in the direction of the scrapyard. And my shortcut to Waterhouse and Sixth. *Maybe I can still meet Babs after all.*

But first I'd have to catch up with Will. I couldn't

shake the image of him from moments before, still, unresponsive.

Mrs. Baker said, "Well, I'm glad I could help." She gave me a hard look. "Your grandmother will be glad to hear it."

"Yes, thank you, Mrs. Baker," I said. She turned and stomped back across the street toward her perfect family.

I put everything back in my book bag and started after Will, but Miss Bettina put her hand on my arm. "Donna."

My eyes pricked and I wanted to hug her, to let her hug me, to tell her how desperately I wanted away from Groverton, to ask her if she ever felt that way . . . but then her eyes wandered from mine, and I saw she was looking behind me.

I glanced back. Daddy. He was standing on the porch, staring out at all of us, looking confused. He wore the same pants from the day before, and a stained undershirt. I felt a surge of resentment. I'd have to get that undershirt clean, somehow.

But I saw the look on Miss Bettina's face. She never said it, but I could see it. For whatever reason, she was in love with my daddy.

"Porter." She said his name like a sigh.

She went to him, while the Bakers drove off.

I walked down Elmwood until I got to the corner. Then I turned and started running toward Stedman's Scrapyard. Away from all of them. Toward Will.

Chapter 3

I ran until I reached Stackville, gasping in great gulps of air vile with the rotten-egg mill smell from wood being boiled down to pulp to make paper. I put my hand to my mouth and nose, fighting back a gag, while running, running, until I finally saw Will.

He was kneeling by the barbed-wire fence surrounding Stedman's Scrapyard. My relief at finding him gave way to a moment of annoyance—my armpits stuck to my dress and my pin curls drooped, a damp mess. So much for looking fresh and perfect for my trip with Babs and my secret job interview.

But just as quickly, my annoyance switched back to alarm.

Will looked fine now—physically. I watched as he stared past the scrapyard's usual collection of tires and car parts and banged-up iceboxes—dumped as housewives got refrigerators and freezers—at the empty end of a chain attached to the hitch of an old teardrop camper with its door hanging open on one hinge. As he talked loudly to the empty chain, Will looked as unhinged as that camper door.

From Stedman's, Groverton Pulp & Paper wasn't visible, but its presence was palpable in the smell and the sight of the steam that plumed in endless white puffs from its smokestacks. That morning, although the neighborhood of narrow, close houses was quiet, the very air seemed tense, or at least I told myself it did; I'd overheard talk at the diner of a possible mill strike. I felt a tremble of hope at the possibility of this—of anything—bringing excitement to Groverton.

The only resident in sight was an old woman who sat on the front porch of a well-kept wooden house across the street from the scrapyard. She peeled apples, leaning forward, her ankle-length skirt, taut between her knees, catching the long strand of apple skin. Her hands moved automatically and she didn't keep an eye on her peeling—just on us, bemused by the sight of children who did not belong in her neighborhood.

Will's voice rose in an adamant cadence, like Pastor Stebbins at Grandma's church: "So tonight, Sergeant Striker and *his* Trusty are going to be on TV for the first time! Do you think they'll catch a robber or a kidnapper? I think . . . kidnapper. It's been a long time since the old gold miner's great granddaughter got held for ransom. So Trusty . . ."

Will insisted on calling the scrapyard-dog-with-no-name Trusty because the dog was a husky—just like, Will said, Trusty from *Sergeant Striker and the Alaskan Wild*. Will shook the box of Marvel Puffs. Milk dripped from the bottom.

"I wish you could watch the show with me, but Dad doesn't like dogs," Will was saying, as if this was the biggest problem in our house. "But guess what? As of this morning, I'm just three away from ten box tops! I'm gonna send in for my deed to my own land in Alaska, and then we'll go see it—"

"Will!" I went over to him, gently put my hand on his

arm. Dayton was as far as either of us had ever been out of Groverton. "Just leave the cereal for the dog—"

He jerked his arm from my grasp and went on, louder: "Did you know that Alaska has a flower even though it isn't a state? The forget-me-not. Ever since 1917! Did you know . . ."

He still looked too pale, and his babbling to the nonexistent dog frightened me. I grabbed him and turned him toward me. "Stop it! I think we should get back home, call Dr. Emory after all, have him check you—"

Will glared at me, the familiar accusation in his blue eyes: *You take everything too seriously!* "I'm fine now."

"Will, I'm sure the dog will eat the cereal if we just leave the box. Let's get back home, call Dr. Emory—"

He shrugged free. "No. I'm feeding Trusty. Then I'm going to school."

"What? You'd take any excuse to stay home from school."

"I don't like Dr. Emory. I'm—I'm just having, like Grandma says, growing pains."

Ah . . . I finally got it. If Will was home sick, and I wasn't home after school because of my "special project," Daddy would call Grandma, who called the television "one of Porter's indulgences for Rita," along with the house and refrigerator and freezer and furniture and car and everything else Daddy had bought for Mama in 1946, before she got sick, before she left, before he lost himself and his job.

I studied Will.

"Come on, then," I said. "We still have time to get to school early so I can, uh, go to the school library."

"You go on. I'm not going until Trusty comes out."

"Maybe the old lady across the street can tell us what happened to Trusty."

"Her name is MayJune," Will said. "She lives in Tangy Town." Tangy Town was a small huddle of houses and businesses across the river, downstream and downwind of the mill—to the people of Groverton, even less desirable an address than Stackville. Nobody lived there unless they were desperately poor or black (although back in 1953, everyone used the term *Negro*). Tangy Town kids went to our school, tainted with the mill's sour stench, usually dropping out by seventh or eighth grade.

It was also where Mama had grown up. But we never visited that neighborhood, or knew anything about Mama's life there. All we knew was that, like Daddy, she was an only child, that her parents were dead by the time she'd married, that Grandma said she was luckier than a four-leaf clover to have met and married Daddy. My guess was she'd met him at the mill.

"Sometimes MayJune babysits her grandkids here," Will said.

Will moved toward the gap in the chain-link fence, and I realized that he was going to wiggle through into the scrapyard to search for Trusty. I thought, *What if Trusty is in there after all and runs out and attacks Will? What if Mr. Stedman comes out with a shotgun?* I grabbed Will. He tried to twist from me, but I tightened my arms around his chest. "Will, it's got to be a quarter to eight by now. If you want to go to school—"

"Let me go! I have to find Trusty!" he shouted. And then, suddenly, he stopped screaming and writhing and went so limp that I thought he'd passed out again, but then I saw the dog limping out of the camper door, this Trusty surely nothing like the one that fans of *Sergeant Striker and the Alaskan Wild* would imagine.

This dog walked slowly, head down, to the gap in the fence. His right ear was ripped in half, the torn edges scabbed with dried blood. The dog's back was gashed; I recognized strikes from a belt buckle. A bit of chain hung from his neck, but I couldn't see the collar; it was lost in the dog's matted and patchy fur.

Will fell to his knees by the gap in the fence, reached a hand through, and petted him, saying, "Trusty, don't you worry. We'll go to Alaska, take you back where you belong. I'm going to get my one square inch, and then more and more square inches, and you and I will live there." The dog nuzzled his hand.

I grabbed Will's shoulder. Even though I knew the dog couldn't understand him, I was suddenly angry for Trusty. I shouted, "Will, stop it!" He was making promises that he couldn't keep.

Will ignored me, picked up the dripping Marvel Puffs box, and eased it through the fence. He turned the box upside down and poured out the burned toast and cereal. Trusty gobbled up the food as it poured out, and then snagged the box from Will and started eating it, too.

When the dog finished, he looked up at me. I stared into his runny, ice-blue eyes. Groverton, Ohio, was a place of beagles and German shepherds and mutts, not huskies that looked like wolves.

I felt so sorry for the dog that I reached for him—wanting to undo the collar, unmat the fur. But at the first flicker of my hand, the dog lunged, spit flying from his snarling jowls.

As I stumbled back, my heart pounding, the dog's mouth moved as if he were barking, but no sound came out. He had gone mute.

I shouted for Will to come away from the fence, reached for him, but before I could grab him, I felt a hand on my back.

"Honey, if that dog really wanted to get out at you, or out for any reason at all, it would get through that gap, even if it tore its body up even worse. Mr. Stedman's been beating the poor dog because he stopped barking," said the old woman.

I stared past the junk to the ramshackle building that was both Mr. Stedman's business headquarters and his home.

"Don't worry—he's not there. I've been a-staying with my daughter and her young'uns the past few days—my Mary, she's laid up with a pulled back so I brought my poultices to her—and I saw him leave last night, but he hasn't come back."

The dog—Trusty—finished gobbling the Marvel Puffs, box and all, and thrust his snout as far as he dared through the fence, sniffing at Will. Seeking more food? But no. Now that his hunger was sated, the dog gazed up at my brother, Trusty's icy eyes turned soft with soulful concern. I told myself I must be imagining this, but it felt as real, as palpable, as the tension in the very air of the neighborhood.

"Oh," I said. "Thank you for telling us. I'm Donna Lane. Nice to meet you Mrs.—" I held out my hand.

The old woman took my hand in a grip that was far firmer than her thin, twisted hand belied. "Just call me MayJune. I don't need any other name. Will's told me all about you."

I looked at Will stroking the wild dog's head. I wasn't the only one with secrets. Will must have been going to visit Trusty—and, I guessed, MayJune—pretty often. Enough to make the wounded, wild animal trust and care about him. Enough to befriend the oddly named woman and talk with her about me.

I took another look at her. MayJune was wearing mismatched, worn clothes—an old pink flowered blouse, a checkered blue and red skirt, a green sweater with frayed cuffs shoved up to her knobby elbows, a brown scarf tied over her head. Tufts of coarse gray hair poked out here and there from under her scarf. Her potato brown skin hung loose and wrinkled.

I felt my lips pulling together in a taut knot—and then I looked away. I was judging MayJune as surely as Mrs. Baker judged me.

She put her hand on my arm and her scent—something herblike that I couldn't quite place, maybe sage with a dash of cinnamon—was somehow forgiving, just as her nearly toothless smile was calming. So instead of pulling away, I looked back at her.

"Yes, that dog could get out," she was saying, "but some critters get so used to being penned in, they can't run even when they've got the chance. They've been trained to stay put, no matter how bad their circumstance."

The wistfulness that wove in and out of her aged, crackling voice made me think that her observation was not limited to the dog.

She let go of my arm and moved toward Will, holding something out to him. He took it—the peels from her apples. As the St. Thomas Catholic Church sounded the eight o'clock chime, I watched Will hold out the apple peels, one at a time, and Trusty gently take them between his teeth.

Chapter 4

Babs waited for me after all—but not in her daddy's car, and not by herself.

She was in the backseat of Jimmy Denton's cherry red Chevrolet, grinning at me, giggling and gesturing—*Come on, get in*—while Hank Coleman, her boyfriend, kept trying to pull her down.

Jimmy sat with his right hand loosely on the steering wheel, his left elbow on the rolled-down window, holding a cigarette in his left hand, staring ahead with a look of resigned boredom, as if he didn't see me on the corner, didn't notice Babs or Hank in the backseat.

It was another small-choice moment.

Someone in the car behind his honked. Jimmy casually took a drag off his cigarette, then gave me a long, hard stare: *Make up your mind. Are you coming with us or not?*

And so I made my choice and got in Jimmy's car.

He peeled away from the stop sign as if suddenly he couldn't get out of Groverton fast enough, as though, like Babs and Hank and me, he'd lived there his whole life, instead of just a few weeks.

I stared awkwardly ahead at the town quickly giving way

to cornfields as we drove west, while Jimmy drove and fiddled with the radio. Babs managed to push Hank off of her long enough to say something about her mother and aunt having a quarrel and not going out of town but Jimmy being willing to drive, and wasn't that a *special surprise . . . the four of us, almost like a double date*?

I wanted to yell at Babs—what was she thinking?

Then I shook my head—silly me. Hank was Groverton Senior High's star quarterback. And Jimmy Denton was the one and only son of Roger Denton—the new president and CEO of Groverton Pulp & Paper. Those facts were a good enough excuse for anything in Groverton.

I stole a glance at Jimmy, just as he stubbed out his cigarette and then ran a finger around the inside of the collar of his burnt orange turtleneck, as if he were too hot, even though wind rushed into the car through the rolled-down windows. I thought, *I make him nervous.*

I was used to everyone seeming a little sorry for me. *Poor Donna Lane*, I could sense even other kids thinking, *having to be like a mom to her little brother, and that daddy of hers, so sad. . . .*

Jimmy's Chevy hit a large rut on State Route 35 and the car's glove box popped open, smacking my knees. Out tumbled a flashlight, a tire gauge, and a *Sterry Oil Road Atlas for the United States, Canada, and Mexico.*

"Are you all right? Sorry about not noticing that rut."

With Babs and Hank making out in the backseat to the sounds of the Four Aces crooning "Just Squeeze Me" over WBEX, it took me a second to realize Jimmy was talking to me. I glanced at him. He looked truly concerned.

"I'm fine, thanks." I finished reassembling the glove box contents except for the *Sterry Road Atlas.*

"You're being awfully quiet," Jimmy said over the wind and the radio. "Worried about sluffing off?"

I didn't want to say, *No, actually, Babs and I have it down to a fine art*, so as I thumbed the atlas's frayed cover and dog-eared pages, I started to say something about there being a Sterry Motor Oil on this same route except on the east end of town, but at the same time Jimmy started speaking, too, and then we both stopped talking.

Now on WBEX Perry Como was singing "Don't Let the Stars Get in Your Eyes." *That's for you and me both, Babs,* I thought.

"Sorry, you go ahead." Jimmy said it so sweetly that— even though I was still annoyed at Babs dragging Hank and Jimmy into our day—I felt something inside me warm and soften. Maybe I'd judged him too quickly.

Or maybe you're just being silly—a money grubber like your mama was.

I tried to shake Grandma's voice from my head, but I still stuttered when I repeated, "J-just—there's a Sterry Motor Oil, east of Groverton on State Route 35, if you need a new road atlas."

Dumb. Why couldn't I think of anything smart to say?

But Jimmy's laugh was easy, not a bit mocking. "I guess I do need a new one. I pretty much wore that one out, driving cross-country to move here."

I turned in my seat, looked at Jimmy. He'd said that so casually, as if seventeen-year-old boys drove across the country from California to Ohio every day. "You mean that you drove cross-country with your parents?"

"No, I mean *I* drove cross-country, by myself. My parents wanted to sell my car in California—too much trouble to move, they said. We could just buy another one here."

Right. As if buying cars was as easy as picking up a dozen eggs at the A&P grocery.

"But I've gotten pretty partial to this car. Good memories."

Like what? I wanted to ask. Making out in the backseat? Driving up and down the coast, or through the city? The thought of all that freedom made tingles dance over my skin.

"So one morning, I threw a few things in the trunk. Took off before they woke up."

I stared down at the smiling, well-groomed mechanic on the atlas cover, thought about flipping open the atlas to the dog-eared pages to see if Jimmy had marked routes.

". . . but I can see how something like that would be frightening to you," Jimmy was saying. "It would be different for a girl to drive cross-country. Dangerous."

Suddenly, I was mad. *Pompous ass*, after all!

"That's ridiculous. Of course a girl could drive across the country. There were women aviators in World War Two—"

"Service planes. Not fighters."

"Not their choice. The point is, if women can fly planes, then driving across the country should be a breeze."

"She can't drive at all," Babs gasped from the backseat. I wondered how she'd been able to follow our conversation. "Even though she has a car," Babs added, before Hank started kissing her again.

"You have a car, but you can't drive, but you think driving across the country would be easy," Jimmy said flatly.

It sounded ridiculous when he put it like that. But I said, "Sure, driving cross-country would be fine, if I actually had a car, which I don't, really." I felt a guilty twinge—just a while before I'd thought how Will and I had never been any farther than Dayton, and how Will was ridiculous for mumbling out loud to a dog that he could take them to Alaska. But I went on. "Babs just means the convertible that my dad, well, stores in our garage."

"Your family has a convertible that just sits in your garage?" Coming from Jimmy that sounded even more ridiculous than Will's travel-to-Alaska-with-wild-dog fantasy.

And that made me want to lash out, to make him feel small. "Daddy bought it for Mama about a year before she got sick. Really sick—cancer. She went to a clinic in Florida. Daddy said there were some new treatments they could do to help her, but she died anyway. That was seven years ago. Daddy's not over it, so everything stays the way it was before she died. Like a shrine to her. Including the convertible."

Now who's being an ass? I thought. I wished I could take back my sob story, braced myself for some polite words of pity.

Jimmy said, "I bet the tires are sure flat by now."

Giddy relief at his joke made something inside loosen, start to break free, like a moth inside my chest. I looked at him just as he glanced at me, and I could see that he was nervous again.

Suddenly Jimmy swerved and drove off the road toward the sharp stubs of a plowed-under cornfield. As my books spilled out of my bag at my feet, Babs screamed and Hank cursed and I thought, *We're going right into that field.* But then Jimmy made his car skid to a stop, fast but smooth as sliding on ice, and I grinned at him, the tickly, loose feeling fluttering free once more, and I wanted to tell him, *Do that again!* But Babs was still screaming, so I turned around to see her. Her lipstick was a magenta smear up her left cheek but her hair was still intact under her scarf. Hank lifted his hand, about to slap Babs to make her shut up. But Jimmy grabbed Hank's arm. "Cool it," he said.

Who is this boy, really? I wondered.

He looked at me and said, "You're going to drive now. Can't be too hard—women fly planes all the time, right? And this is a straight, flat road. Couldn't be easier. I'll teach you." He revved the engine twice, widened his eyes at me. "Trust me?"

He waggled his eyebrows, flirty, no longer nervous, but his look was so challenging that I had to look away, across the plowed-under cornfield.

"You're going to shred my atlas," he said. I looked down. My hands clutched the book so tightly that my knuckles had gone white.

I turned to Jimmy. "I really appreciate your offer." He looked amused but I went on, even more stiffly. "However, Babs and I are eager to get to Rike's Department Store—"

He turned off the radio, right in the middle of Patti Page singing about "That Doggie in the Window" (I bet she'd never seen a dog like Trusty) and leaned close to me. I breathed in his scent—aftershave and soap, of course, but deeper than that, something else . . . something a little musky, something essentially him. My face flamed as he grinned at me and said softly, "Come on. I'm a good teacher. You know you want to learn to drive, or you wouldn't have said all of that—"

"Donna's going to drive?" Babs called from the backseat. "Take us to Dayton, Donna! No . . . not Dayton. I want to go to Paris! Drive us to Paris, Donna!"

"Paris is across the ocean, you—" Hank began.

"Hank," Jimmy warned.

"I'm not driving," I said. "We're not going to Paris."

Babs leaned forward, putting her head over the top of the seat between Jimmy and me, making him move back into his seat. "Why not? Donna used to say she wanted to be a fashion designer and live in Paris! Did you know that, Jimmy?"

"Babs, just stop. We're going to Dayton. Shopping, remember?" I looked at Jimmy, pleadingly: *Just start the car back up!*

But he shrugged and smiled. "I want to hear more about you and Paris."

"She was going to go there to study fashion, and I was going to go with her to *buy* fashion."

Hank sneered, "Like that dress she's wearing now? What is that, anyway?"

I stared out the window. I disliked Hank, but his comment still made my eyes sting. After all, I'd known him and Babs my whole life, and I still had memories of when we were kids and he wasn't such a jerk.

But the dress I wore that day *was* different—a cap-sleeved, dark gray sheath with a swirl of deep cerulean blue, a color that I imagined could only come from the deepest part of the ocean (not that I'd ever been to the ocean), that started at the hem by my left knee and swirled up around my waist and ended at the back of my left shoulder. I'd thought it was brilliant when I'd pieced it together from two of Mama's old skirts, but suddenly I knew that Hank's reaction would have been everyone else's if I'd gone to school that day.

"It *is* different," Jimmy said quietly. "But beautiful."

Then Jimmy put his hand on mine. His touch was smooth and light and sent a shock of warmth spreading up my arm, loosening my skin—well, not literally, but that's how it felt, just from him putting his hand over mine.

"Babs has talked about going to Paris ever since we read about it in third grade," I said, breaking the moment. "Her favorite perfume—Evening in Paris. Her favorite movie— *An American in Paris.* It's as crazy as my brother talking about going to the Alaska Territory."

Jimmy lifted his eyebrows, nodded like he was impressed. "The Alaska Territory . . . nice. I think I like your brother."

"He's ten, and goofy, so what does he know? But Babs should know we're never going to Paris—"

"Switch places with me." Jimmy held my gaze, steady, and I saw he wasn't joking. He wanted me to learn to drive. He wanted to be the one to teach me.

Suddenly—yes! I wanted to learn to drive. And not to go to Dayton or Paris or anywhere in particular. I just wanted to feel that steering wheel in my hands even more than I wanted to feel Jimmy's hand on mine, and so I found myself nodding.

A minute later, I was in the driver's seat, revving the engine like Jimmy had a minute before, with two quick taps of my foot on the accelerator pedal. I grinned. It was ridiculous how good this felt—I just pressed down with my foot and the engine revved, all under my control. Jimmy grinned, too, as he got in on the passenger's side.

But Hank jumped out of the car, hollering, "Are you nuts? You can't teach her to drive. I'm not riding with this crazy dame—stop messing around—"

"Then walk back to town!" Jimmy snapped.

I relished the thought of driving off without Hank, but then he got in the backseat next to Babs. I glanced in the rearview mirror, watched her resettle against his shoulder. Hank scowled but did not pull away, and Babs grinned up at him, like a whipped puppy grateful to be taken back by its master.

The image of Trusty—the real one—flashed across my mind and I shuddered, but then Jimmy said, "OK, check to make sure no one is coming up the road, then nice and easy, put her in gear."

I looked in the rearview mirror past Babs and Hank at the road behind us, then ahead. Either way, the road seemed to go on forever. We were alone, in the middle of Nowheresville, and suddenly I was anxious to get somewhere, anywhere.

While Jimmy talked me through, I eased the car onto the road and pressed a little harder on the accelerator, and then we were moving, slowly, in little jerks.

"Am I doing it?" I clutched the steering wheel, feeling my stomach fall to the floorboard as the road started to slip away underneath us. "Oh my God—I am! I'm moving the car—"

"It's OK if you outpace the field mice," Jimmy said, laughter in his voice.

So I pressed a little harder on the accelerator. The car picked up speed, the road slipped away faster, and I felt a tingle, something akin to how my hand had felt at Jimmy's touch, racing up my arms to my armpits, and something in me said, *Go—go—go—just go!* So I pressed the accelerator more.

"Now you might want to slow up, just a little," Jimmy said.

But I couldn't. *Go—go—go—just go!* pulsed in my head, and I couldn't resist the command.

Suddenly, around a slight curve, there was a tractor in front of us, growing quickly larger as we came up on it.

"Donna, slow down, OK? You want to slow way down to go around this tractor."

I fumbled for the clutch and gearshift, then for the brake. At the last second, Jimmy moved the gearshift as I hit the clutch, then I pressed on the brake, slowed, swerved around the tractor just as we were heading into the big rear tires.

But in the oncoming lane, another car came at us, head-on. Babs screamed. Hank cursed. Jimmy barked orders at me.

And I tuned them all out. I swerved between the tractor and the oncoming car, overcorrected and hit the lip of the ditch, which for just a second sent us flying. Jimmy's car skimmed the side of a wire fence, but then it landed in front of the tractor, and somehow, I shifted gears again and was driving up the road just fine.

When sound came back to me, Babs was still screaming, Hank cursing, Jimmy talking.

But that momentary sensation of flying stayed with me, and something welled up inside me and broke loose.

Laughter.

Finally.

And I laughed and laughed and laughed.

Chapter 5

A few weeks before Labor Day, 1953, a classified adver-
tisement had appeared in the *Groverton Daily News*:
*Wanted—One model, female, age 20–30, to sit for artist Nate
Cahill, 2 times a week, 1–2 hrs. per session, $2.00/session, at 325
Plum Street, phone 21983.*

The advertisement had caused a scandal in Groverton, a
distraction even from the rumblings about a possible strike
at the mill. At Dot's Corner Café, Grandma told anyone
who would listen that she thought the new art teacher should
be fired before he could corrupt the minds of Groverton's
youth, and why did the high school need an art class anyway,
when it had gotten along for years without one?

Babs told me that Mr. Cahill's ad had turned into a real
headache for her daddy. People called his newspaper office
and even their home (I suspected, but never knew for certain, that Grandma was one of the callers) to complain
about the disgraceful suggestiveness of the ad. I remember
asking Babs if she thought everyone was so fired up because
of what Senator McCarthy had to say about artists, but Babs
just rolled her eyes at me and said if I'd actually ever *read*
some of the novels she passed on to me for my *real-life*

education, I'd know that artists sometimes wanted their models to pose *nude*.

In any case, Babs's daddy had yelled at the advertising manager to actually read ads before running them, and then pulled Mr. Cahill's ad just two days after it appeared, but not before I read it and decided that I would secretly reply. I figured no one else would answer, so I'd have a pretty good chance at the job, even if I was younger than what he'd advertised for.

I really wanted that two dollars a session. At four dollars a week, by the time I graduated, I'd have enough to go somewhere far away, and then I'd send for Will when he was old enough.

After Babs and Jimmy and Hank and I got back to Groverton around four o'clock that day, I had Jimmy drop me off at the library, where I said I needed to study. I waited, then went out the back door and hurried through the drizzling rain over to the alley on Ridgeview, to a house just down the road from my grandma's—thus the need to sneak over via the alley. The house had once belonged to Mrs. Bentley, until she'd died the previous spring. Her son had decided to rent it out rather than sell it, and that's how Mr. Cahill ended up living there.

Under the back porch awning, I took a few seconds to compose myself, sweeping my hair up into a ponytail with an extra ribbon from my purse. Then I took a deep breath and knocked on the back kitchen door.

A madman version of Mr. Cahill answered.

His hair stood out in spikes, like he'd run his hands through it many times. He was barefoot and wearing jeans and an undershirt, spotted and smeared with paint. I tried not to stare at his bare, muscled arms and shoulders, or the hair at his armpits and on his chest, curling over the top of his undershirt, and the effort of not staring made my face flame.

A cigarette dangled from his lips, and he held a telephone receiver a little away from his ear as a woman's voice shrieked on the other end. He held the cigarette from his lips. "Julia," he said, then, louder, "Julia! I'll call back. Someone's at the door." Mr. Cahill hung up.

"That's a party line, you know," I said.

Mr. Cahill nodded. "I know. I'm not sure if Julia does." He squinted at me. "Let's see. You are in one of my *wonderful* art classes." Then his eyebrows went up. "Ah, yes! You're the one who sketches clothing!"

My face flamed even more hotly. "You've seen that?"

He took a drag from his cigarette. "You sketch, someone else in your class does line drawings of cars"—my guess was Hank—"and other students doodle. One is particularly good at rendering comic book characters." He shrugged.

Then why don't you actually teach us something? I thought.

But it wasn't my place to criticize a teacher, and I was there for a purpose. My secret plan.

"I'm here to apply for your modeling job."

He narrowed his eyes at me. "What's your name again?"

"Donna Lane." A gust of wind blew rain across the porch, striking my back and Mr. Cahill's face.

Mr. Cahill sighed. "Come in for a second."

As I stepped into the messiest kitchen I'd ever seen, he tossed me a dish towel—grimy, but I patted the back of my neck and arms. He shut the door, took another drag on his cigarette, and studied me with such a penetrating gaze that

I had to look away again. This time, I focused on the "Home Sweet Home" cross-stitch sampler hanging next to the wall phone. I was sure Mr. Cahill hadn't brought that sampler with him, that the home's original owner, the late Mrs. Bentley, had made it. Sad that her son hadn't wanted it.

"Donna, do you know the scandal my simple little ad caused?" Mr. Cahill said. "This town is so small-minded."

Then why did you come to this town, anyway? There were rumors he was from San Francisco, or maybe New York, or maybe even somewhere really exotic, like New Orleans. "Well, are you still working on whatever project you needed a model for?" I asked.

He lifted his eyebrows. "Yes."

"Then I'm here to apply for the job."

"Are you between twenty and thirty?"

I frowned, wondering if he was just being snippy or trying to imply I seemed so dumb that I'd been held back that much. "No. I'm . . . I'll be eighteen in January."

"Congratulations. But this is September, so you're seventeen, so no."

I looked away from him, tears suddenly stinging my eyes. I needed this job. As I tried to blink the tears back, I caught glimpses of a sink full of unwashed dishes, of a counter covered with newspapers, books, mail, and more dirty dishes, of another burning cigarette balanced on top of an ashtray overflowing with crushed-out butts. At least the burning tobacco partially masked the reek of spoiling food.

"Maybe you could just hire me as a housekeeper, then," I said. "The town would probably thank both of us for that, especially if I save you from catching this house on fire with overflowing ashtrays, or from attracting rats. And if I model while I'm here, then . . ." I imitated his shrug. "Well, then, you'd have to pay me for both." Mr. Cahill's eyebrows were now above the rim of his glasses. I crossed my arms and looked stern like I did when I was reprimanding Will. "But no funny business while I'm modeling, and I won't model naked."

Mr. Cahill stared at me for a second, then burst out laughing. I looked away, horrified, thinking I'd never again be able to look him in the eye in art class.

"Donna, first of all, let me assure you that you're in no danger of funny business with me. Trust me." I believed my safety lay in his love for the shrieking Julia.

While I considered that possibility, Mr. Cahill glanced at his watch. "Isn't there a big football game tonight? Shouldn't you be getting ready to go to that with all the other kids?"

"I don't do things like other kids. I work for my grandma and Miss Bettina—that's Miss Bettina of Miss Bettina's Dress Shop—and that money goes for my family." I paused. "Well, most of it does." I paused again, taken a little aback by the look of pity starting to cross Mr. Cahill's face. I hated pity, and suddenly the last person I wanted it from was Mr. Cahill, who was, so far in my life, the most interesting person I'd ever met. So I squared my shoulders and said something I'd never shared with anyone else—I could barely whisper it to myself. "But I have a plan. Next summer, I'm going to New York City, where I'm going to be a seamstress, working on costumes. So I need another job. Just for me. Now, do you need a housekeeper and model, or not?"

I was trembling when I finished speaking. Mr. Cahill frowned, looked like he was about to say something, and then seemed to think better of it. He shook his head. For a second, I thought I'd ruined my chances at this job.

And then Mr. Cahill (who definitely hadn't met MayJune, and never would) made his own life-changing-small-choice.

He started muttering to himself, "Well, I *thought* I could do the work for the show without a model, but maybe . . ." He shook his head, ran his hands through his hair in a gesture of frustration, and suddenly grabbed my cheeks between his hands, turning my head this way and that.

"Hmm. Good cheekbones. Too strong of a chin, but I can work with it." He let go of my face and stepped back, but still studied me as he said, "All right. I guess you'll do. Twice a week. Three dollars. Housekeeping, light . . ." He paused to gesture at the mess of a kitchen, while my heart started racing around in my chest like the mouse I'd set free that morning. And then he grinned. "And modeling. No nudity required."

"Oh, thank you, Mr. Cahill," I said, and put my book bag on the floor next to the kitchen table and rushed toward the nearest pile of dishes.

"No, no, let's start with the modeling first," he said. And then the telephone rang.

He pressed his eyes shut and groaned. "My studio is upstairs, first door on the left. I'll be right up."

He turned his back to me, rested one arm on the wall and his head on his arm, then answered the phone. "Julia," he said. But he didn't sound happy, or even wistful, like Miss Bettina did when she said Daddy's name.

I walked through the dining and living rooms, where there was just a card table cluttered with papers, two folding chairs, a worn couch and matching chair I recognized as having been Mrs. Bentley's, an old lamp, a bookshelf, and a few unpacked boxes that I guessed held books. Not much to clean in here.

I caught a faint whiff of the licorice drops Mrs. Bentley always kept in a cut glass jar, offering them to me at every Grandma-enforced visit. But the cut glass jar, the doily-covered side table that had been its home, the other good furniture—all that was gone. Her son must have taken everything he thought he could sell.

At the top of the stairs, I found the bedroom that Mr. Cahill had turned into his studio.

His easel and stool were at the front of the room. At the back was an ornate settee, the carved cherrywood worn but the fabric still a beautiful deep burgundy velvet. Another castoff from Mrs. Bentley's son.

Suddenly, the strong smell of paint and turpentine hit the back of my brain all at once, making my head spin. I stumbled over to the settee and flopped onto it, nearly upsetting a small table.

There I noticed a white bowl filled with fruit about the size of a plum, yet nothing like any fruit I'd seen. Still, my mouth suddenly watered. I hadn't eaten much that day and I liked the way the pale green and orange fruit looked in the white bowl, the shine of the fruit's taut skin, and I thought how that color and sheen would be perfect in cloth, a satin or silk, for a soft, flowing dress. Maybe, I thought, Mr. Cahill had shipped this exotic fruit all the way in from Paris, or from somewhere even more exotic, like, say, Persia . . . and I shouldn't touch it.

Then I thought that Mr. Cahill wouldn't mind if I ate one fruit—and then I thought, *Maybe I'm* supposed *to be eating the fruit; maybe he's trying to get over the shrieking Julia by painting* Young Woman Eating Exotic Persian Fruit on Settee.

Much better than my earlier real-life pose, *Young Woman Choking Down Tasteless Marvel Puffs for Little Brother's Quest for One Square Inch of Alaska*.

So I picked up a piece of the fruit. I closed my eyes so I could focus on savoring the taste of the fruit, and then eagerly bit into it. A sharp, bitter taste filled my mouth. I yelped and opened my watering eyes, desperately looking for a receptacle into which I could spit the acrid pulp.

Just then, Mr. Cahill came into the studio, saying, "Sorry, that was an important call—"

He stopped talking when he saw my face and burst out laughing. I forced myself to swallow the bite.

Mr. Cahill sat down at his easel and started sketching, staring at me, not even glancing at the paper or the charcoal in his hand, making big, sweeping strokes. My face suddenly burned and I longed for a glass of water to wash away the taste.

"Persimmon," he said.

I glanced around. Did he want me to fetch a pastel, a paint pot, a pencil?

"The fruit you just tried to eat," he said.

I glanced down at the fruit. "Persimmon is a color. Orange red. That"—I pointed at the fruit—"that is mostly green."

"It's not ripe yet," Mr. Cahill said.

"I figured that out. I also figure you didn't get them at the A and P. Or the old Pleasant Valley Orchard."

He just kept sketching. I wanted to throw the nasty green persimmons at him, like baseballs.

"Well, where did you get them?"

"From my backyard."

"I was just in your backyard and I didn't see anything but an ordinary maple."

Mr. Cahill put his charcoal down with a purposeful snap, like I'd done that morning with my pencil when Will kept asking me questions.

"I was clearing out brush and poison ivy along the back fence and came across a small tree with green fruit," he said. "At first I thought it was a plum, but then I realized that fall is the wrong time of year for plums. And then I recalled I'd had this fruit before, in Japan."

Japan! Maybe he'd been a missionary. But no, I couldn't imagine Mr. Cahill preaching the gospel like Pastor Stebbins every Sunday at Grandma's church, sin and sorrow and guilt and redemption. Maybe he'd been in Japan as part of the occupation—he looked too young to have been there in the war—and he met a beautiful woman who became his Japanese bride and she took the name Julia for her life here but now she was unhappy, torn from her native land, and they separated and—

"Different variety, of course," Mr. Cahill said. "American persimmons usually grow farther south."

He wasn't going to tell me why he'd been in Japan. Disappointment made me petulant. "Why would anyone want to grow a tree that puts out such terrible fruit?"

He looked amused. "Ancient Grecians called persimmons the fruit of the gods."

I thought, *He's going to fire me on day one if I say more.* But I couldn't stop. I said, "Pastor Stebbins would say no wonder the fruit's so bitter, coming from heathens."

"Then your Pastor Stebbins must not know that once the fruit ripens, it becomes a beautiful red-orange, sweet and tender. It just has to go through the first frost. I'm doing a series of pastels of persimmons—before they're ripe, and then again when they're at the peak of ripeness. Just for fun."

The question popped out of my mouth: "Why can't we draw something like persimmons in class? Just for fun?"

Mr. Cahill gave me a sharp look and held up his hand. "If you want to talk," he said, "we can do that, after I'm done with my sketches. But it will be about your designs—and how you should think about that instead of sewing other people's ideas."

Suddenly, I was mad. He didn't know a thing about my life, or what I wanted. "That's not enough?"

He stood up, walked over to me, took hold of my left cap sleeve and fingered the hem stitching between his thumb and forefinger. His fingertips brushed my arm, and hot redness flared up my chest and neck and face, even though I tried to will it away.

Mr. Cahill stepped back. "You want to be a designer," he said.

"No, I didn't say that, I just—"

"You do," he said. "I remember more clearly now, your sketches. They are pretty good. And this dress, it shows potential."

He turned and walked back to his easel, sat down, started sketching. "Yes," he said firmly, "we will be talking about your potential. That will be part of your job. Maybe while you're cleaning. But not while you're modeling. So now, turn your head to the left, lift your right arm over the back of the chaise longue—that's right, but a little farther back— now stop. Stay still. And be quiet!"

Chapter 6

After an hour of posing, my neck was stiff and my head heavy. Still, I washed the dishes piled in Mr. Cahill's sink. Then he insisted I show him my sketches. He demonstrated how to make thick, velvety lines with the side of my pencil to illustrate a heavier fabric, and thin, wispy lines for lighter fabric.

A few minutes after six, I ran down the alley to the back entrance of Dot's Corner Café. I'd just grabbed my smock—an awful white-and-red-checked cotton print—when Grandma emerged through the dining room's swinging door. The kitchen hushed. Big Terry, the cook, and Ralph Seward, the dishwasher, stopped their work. Even the hamburgers seemed to sizzle more timidly.

"You're late. And what on earth are you wearing?" Grandma stared with her judged-and-found-lacking gaze at the cap sleeve that Mr. Cahill had just admired.

"Home-ec project," I said. The answer was automatic, defensive—a lie.

I was still giddy from the drawing techniques Mr. Cahill had shown me, my mind buzzing with ideas about how to improve my designs. I had three dollars carefully wrapped in my handkerchief in a corner of my book bag. My only worry, flitting across my mind like a familiar dark moth, was that after my stint at Mr. Cahill's I hadn't had a chance to go by our house and check on Will.

But surely he was fine. He'd *seemed* fine after our strange visit with Trusty and MayJune. I wondered what he would think about Mr. Cahill saying I should consider fashion design school. Will—with his crazy desire to visit one measly square inch of Alaska—would probably just shrug his shoulders and say, *Sure, why not? . . .*

"Donna, I asked you a question!"

I snapped out of my reverie and looked at Grandma. She was shorter than I, and yet even in heels I felt as though she loomed large.

"Yes, ma'am?"

"Why are you wearing those ridiculous shoes?"

I thought fast. "Today we modeled what we'd made over the summer for home-ec class." I held back a smile at *modeled*. I'd definitely modeled. . . .

"In my day, we learned how to make proper items befitting a lady."

Like fussy little tea towels? But I just repeated, "Yes, ma'am," and quickly tied on the ugly smock. I started toward the dining room door, eager to get out of the kitchen, away from Grandma, but she stopped me with a hand on my arm.

"Your heels are going to be as bloody red as those shoes by the end of your shift," she said with a pleased little smile. I thought, *I don't care! I made it through the day in these shoes*—high-heeled, cranberry T-straps that had been Mama's and that went perfectly with my reconfigured dress—*driving a car, getting a job with my art teacher that will help me get away from Groverton for good, forever, and . . .*

"Yes, ma'am," I said, again fighting back a smile. Grandma interpreted all my smiles as mockery.

"Those aren't appropriate shoes for this establishment!" she hissed, a bit of spittle flying from her lips. Big Terry pressed down extra hard on a hamburger patty, making it sizzle. Ralph Seward clinked together the dishes in the sink. Those little tics of sound were Big Terry and Ralph's way— they never let me call them "Mr."—of wordlessly expressing their sympathy.

"I should send you home, dock your pay, tell your father—"

Shirley Wyland, the other waitress on duty that night, whisked into the kitchen through the swinging doors. "Mr. and Mrs. Leis are here," she said. Shirley was old enough to be my mama but had said—out of earshot of Grandma, of course—that I should just call her Shirley, because I was doing a grown-up woman's work. She grabbed two slices of pecan pie and two cups of coffee and whisked right back out.

Mr. and Mrs. Leis were regulars, and Mrs. Leis always wanted me to wait on them. *Thank you, Mrs. Leis.*

"They'll want the blue plate special," I said. "What is it tonight?"

"Shit on a shingle," muttered Big Terry. Even cooks as good as he was had prepared creamed chipped beef on toast in World War II army kitchens, and Grandma never let him forget his service. Jealous that her customers loved Big Terry's food as much as they loved her pies and cakes— delectably sweet and tender, just the opposite of the bitter person who made them—Grandma insisted that Big Terry's least favorite food be offered as the blue plate at least twice a month, just to rile him. He riled her right back by using the crude nickname for the dish.

I grinned as I poured cups of coffee for Mr. and Mrs. Leis, even as Grandma glared at me, and I kept grinning as I carried the Leises' coffee out into the dining area of Dot's Corner Café.

On that Friday night in September, most everyone in town was at the Groverton Senior High School football game, so the café's few customers were the older regulars. I hadn't been to a football game since Grandma demanded two years ago that I give up being a cheerleader with Babs and start working Thursday, Friday, and Saturday nights— the better to keep an eye on me, she'd told Daddy.

I put the cups of coffee down near Grandma's idea of a centerpiece, a pair of whimsical salt and pepper shakers. Mr. Leis was playing with the ceramic Dutch boy and girl, holding them face-to-face, muttering under his breath. He was in his eighties, but there was something lost and young in his expression as he played with the figurines costumed in native dress.

"My dear, you're looking particularly happy tonight," Mrs. Leis said.

I smiled at her. "It's been an interesting day." I pulled my order pad and pencil out of my smock pocket.

"Oh, interesting days are always the best," Mrs. Leis said. "Speaking of interesting—how is Mr. Cahill doing?"

I froze. Did she know I'd been to Mr. Cahill's house? Had a neighbor seen me coming or going?

Mrs. Leis looked perplexed. "You did say last week that you were going to be in his art class?"

Relief rushed through me. She was just making chitchat. Still, my hand shook as I finally jotted "Blue Plate special x2" on my order pad.

"Yes. We're learning about shading." My voice shook a little and I wondered if Mrs. Leis would notice, but I was saved by Mr. Leis reaching into his inside jacket pocket for the gospel tract "Are You on the Right Road to Salvation, Or . . ." The images completed the rest of message: In a wood-paneled station wagon, Dad cheerfully drove a beaming Mom, Sis, and Brother toward the lovely angel-inhabited cloud at the top of the pamphlet, while a bearded man drove his hapless companion, a buxom woman swigging from a liquor bottle, toward the flames at the bottom. Mr. Leis always left this tract, plus thirty-five cents, as the tip.

Mrs. Leis directed her attention at her husband. "Not yet, dear; Donna has just brought us coffee. She hasn't taken our order yet!" Mr. Leis was a deacon at Grandma's church, the Groverton First Church of God. The Sunday before, he'd tried to eat the flowers from the top of Mrs. Whitstone's hat, mistaking the silk rosebuds for some kind of fruit. I'd figured cherries, but I wondered—ripe persimmons?

"I'm so glad to hear that Mr. Cahill is doing well," Mrs. Leis said to me. She lowered her voice conspiratorially. "You know, I've been pushing for an art teacher to come to Groverton Senior High for years."

Mrs. Leis was on the school board, the only woman who'd ever served. Grandma said she put on airs because of it, but I think what she really meant was that a woman didn't have any business sitting in meetings with men.

"What's more essential to humans than art?" Mrs. Leis was saying, while gently moving Mr. Leis's hands apart—he was clicking the Dutch boy and girl shakers together, like they were kissing. "Even the cavemen knew that art was essential." She laughed. "Well, I couldn't exactly make *that* argument, now, could I?"

"No, ma'am." The hint of evolution wouldn't have gone over well, especially from the sole female board member. I had to smile, even with Grandma glaring in the background. I liked Mrs. Leis's pluck. I wondered if I'd ever have it . . . or if maybe I already did.

"Fortunately, the Dentons came to town."

My mouth pursed in a silent oh-no. What did Jimmy's family have to do with this?

Mrs. Leis mistook my alarm for curiosity and said, "Oh, I met Mrs. Denton at one of those boring Groverton Women's Club lunches. Luckily, we hit it off. Her love of art came up, and I pointed out that Riverdale Senior High has had an art class for three years now." Riverdale was our town's biggest football rival. "And, much to my delight, she said she knew from her college days the perfect person to fill the job of art teacher."

I stared at Mrs. Leis. Mrs. Denton—Jimmy's mom—was the reason that Mr. Cahill had come to town to teach art? I searched for a subtle way to inquire further. But Mrs. Leis was again gently pulling apart Mr. Leis's hands, in which the Dutch boy and girl shakers had heightened their ardor. Mrs. Leis distractedly ordered the blue plate specials, plus butterscotch pie for her, coconut cream for Mr. Leis. And more coffee—whenever-you-get-a-chance-dear.

I turned from their booth, stopped by one of Shirley's tables, just vacated, and gathered up the plates, glasses, and silverware. I felt generous for having taken my time with the Leises—I noticed at church that more people were starting to avoid them as Mr. Leis became more bizarre—and for clearing Shirley's table, but Grandma had a different view. As I went into the kitchen with my armload of dishes, she followed me through the swinging doors.

"What were you doing, loitering at the Leises' table?" she nagged, keeping her voice low so no one in the dining area could hear her. "And look at you, carrying a lazy man's load!"

Ralph and Big Terry stopped chatting. Shirley grabbed a cloth and trotted out to the dining area, more eager than usual to wipe down her table.

"You have too big a head on you, girl," Grandma hissed. "Just like your mother."

I looked at Grandma, this small, round, soft-featured, puffy-haired woman—everyone's idea of a grandma, if it weren't for the perpetually sharp, angry set to her mouth. Everyone made excuses for her—poor-Dot-if-only-her-lazy-husband-hadn't-lost-her-family-fortune-in-bad-deals-in-the-Depression-but-those-cakes-and-pies-and-diner-of-hers-are-so-good. . . .

Suddenly, I didn't see her as that.

I saw her as just plain mean.

Big Terry's sizzling griddle, Ralph's dishwashing clinks, the chime over the front door as a new customer entered—suddenly all of these sounds seemed muted, coming from a great distance, separate from this moment between Grandma and me.

"I don't remember much about Mama," I said quietly, "but I don't remember her having a big head. I just remember her as sad. Maybe because you always made sure to tear her down."

Grandma's hand whipped toward my face, but this time, instead of taking her slap, I jerked back. I lost my balance and my hold on the armload of dishes.

The plates spun on their edges on the hard concrete, ringing out in the split second before the crash, like the hum that comes after the last chord of a hymn on the church organ. Grandma lunged toward me, again trying to slap me as the dishware disintegrated, but I grabbed both of her wrists, stopping her hands in front of my face.

I was amazed by how thin and frail her wrists felt in my hands.

Her skinny fingers wiggled, like bird claws trying to gouge my face, even as she hissed in fear, "The good Lord punished your mama for her uppity ways—"

Shirley's voice fluted through the order window. "There's a customer here, says he specifically wants Donna Lane to wait on him."

I immediately thought, *Mr. Cahill.* My face flared. Grandma's eyes narrowed. My moment of triumph was over.

"*He* wants to see Donna?" she said, with lewd emphasis on that one little syllable. "Tell him I'm not running a brothel. If he wants that, he'll have to go to Tangy Town."

I still held Grandma's wrists, but my head snapped back as if she'd broken free and slapped me after all. *Tangy Town.*

The old chant I'd taught Will played in my head: *Sticks and stones can break my bones but words can never hurt me.* But I knew the chant was a lie.

Big Terry was saying, "Dot, now you've gone too far,"

and Shirley was saying, "But it's Jimmy Denton who's asking for Donna!"

At that, Grandma's fingers stopped writhing. Her hands went still, limp, like I'd strangled the life out of them. But she gave me a long look, reassessing me. Of course I didn't have to explain who Jimmy Denton was. Everyone in Groverton knew he was the son of Roger Denton, CEO of Groverton Pulp & Paper.

Grandma said slowly, "Well, Donna, you just go see what the young man wants."

I headed out through the swinging kitchen door, and there was Jimmy, perking up in his booth at the sight of me. But I almost stopped in my tracks as I caught myself wishing that he was Mr. Cahill.

Chapter 7

I took my time getting to Jimmy's booth.

He looked both shy and eager as he asked, "What's today's special?"

"Shit on a shingle," I blurted. My hand went immediately to my mouth, as if I wished I could stuff the words back in, and I dropped my order pad and pencil.

We burst out laughing, then went for the pad and pencil at the same time and knocked heads. That just made us laugh even more.

Finally, Jimmy quickly scooped up the pad and pencil and handed them to me. I caught my breath and said, "That's what our cook—the one besides Grandma, I mean—calls today's special. Chipped beef and cream gravy on toast."

Jimmy wrinkled his nose. "I think your cook has the right name for it."

Suddenly, something inside me tightened. *As if you've ever eaten chipped beef and cream gravy on toast. Or leftover stew on rice. Or wondered how you'd make one supper's worth of soup stretch into two watery suppers. . . .*

I pressed my pencil to the pad and snapped, "The cook makes a great club sandwich."

"That sounds fine. And coffee."

He couldn't just be here, missing the football game, for a sandwich and coffee. This had to be about that scratch on his car, after all. But I played along. "You want Sanka?"

"Regular coffee is fine. I'm going to be up all night anyway, thinking of you."

I snorted at that cheesy line. Hurt flashed in Jimmy's eyes. He forced a self-conscious laugh, as if his attempt at flirting was just a joke. But he flushed.

It hit me: Jimmy Denton, son of the most powerful man in town, who had driven his own car all the way across the country, who seemed so worldly and sophisticated, was, without Hank's bravado to hide behind, really just shy and awkward. So different than smooth, cool Mr. Cahill . . .

I flushed, stammered, "Cream? Sugar?"

"No. Just plenty of refills." He smiled, encouraged by my flush and stammering, thinking it was about him. "I'm just looking for an excuse to stay here until you get off work."

"Oh. Dot's doesn't close until ten o'clock, and then I'll need to stay to help clean up."

"Fine with me. I'm hoping I can give you a ride home—" Suddenly, Jimmy stopped talking and his flush flamed into a bright red. I caught that faint whiff of Grandma—grease, scouring powder, and too many dabs of Youth Dew perfume applied in an unsuccessful effort to cover the kitchen smells that were now part of her skin. She had just sidled up next to me.

I steeled myself for her anger, sure I was guilty of some sin or another, but not quite sure which one—saying shit on a shingle? flirting too much? not flirting enough?—but when I looked at her, I was startled to see that Grandma was smiling.

"I was just about to let Donna off work. She deserves time—with pay, of course—with her friends." Grandma gave me a chummy little pat on my forearm, leaving her thin, knotted fingers lightly on the top of my arm, while her thumb-dig into the back conveyed, *Stand up straight! Carry the Lane name with pride!* And a host of other admonitions usually reserved for Sunday-go-to-church-best. "Go ahead, dear. Sit down with your friend. I'll have Shirley bring Jimmy's club sandwich, and pie for you."

I didn't want pie. I didn't want to be shoved at Jimmy like this. *If it weren't for Will, I could just walk out of here, out of town, away from Groverton, Ohio, forever.*

With that thought, guilt swooped down on me like a heavy cape, and I sank into the booth across from Jimmy. I put my notepad and pencil next to a rooster (pepper) and a hen (salt). *Mr. Leis would have a lot of fun with those.* I smiled a little at the thought.

Jimmy mistook my smile for encouragement. He said, "I hope you won't hold it against me that your grandmother approves of me."

I *did* like him. But I wasn't about to make this easy for him. "I can think about getting over that, if you think you can get over the fact I didn't instantly know how to handle your car like a pro race car driver."

"I was a jerk, I know. That's why I came in here, to apologize. I was worried about how I was going to explain that scratch to Dad."

I could understand that—being afraid of an angry dad.

"I decided to tell him the truth—sort of. I said the accident happened after school, that I tried to teach this pretty girl who has me completely entranced how to drive, that the scratch on the car was really my fault."

Pretty girl . . . completely entranced . . . That made me smile, this time genuinely, at Jimmy.

But then fear washed over me again, and I drew in a sharp breath. "What did he say?" I held my breath, waiting for the answer. *Please don't say he's going to call Daddy.*

Jimmy shrugged. "That I'd have to pay for the repairs."

Oh. Maybe this was really why Jimmy came in, after all. "I can pay," I said, keeping my voice strong, even as tears pricked my eyes at the thought of how much that would set me back.

He frowned. "No, no. You didn't hurt the car beyond some surface damage"—he waved his hand, as if paying for those repairs was no big deal to him; and to him, I realized, it wasn't—"and even if you had . . . well, I shouldn't have been such a jerk. *That's* why I came in."

He reached into his denim jacket and pulled out a small white box, just as Shirley got to our booth. Quickly, I moved the box to my lap.

Shirley put Jimmy's club sandwich and my slice of apple pie on our table. Grandma, of course, hadn't asked what kind of pie I'd like. I thought, *I'd rather have coconut cream.* Such a simple thought, but it startled me a little, this notion that I could have opinions, and they should matter, and people should pay attention to them—even people like Grandma. Did my notion come from being around Jimmy, from my boldness in talking Mr. Cahill into a secret job, from Mr. Cahill saying I had *potential*? I wasn't sure. But I did know that I liked this notion.

"Anything else I can get for you?" Shirley asked, overly polite, annoyed that she was covering my tables—and of course Grandma wouldn't pay her double.

"Listen, I'll take some of your shift tomorrow—" I started, as Jimmy said, "No, thanks," and Shirley stalked off.

Then Jimmy said, "I hope what I got you makes up a little bit for how I acted earlier."

I looked at him. His expression was hopeful. He liked me . . . he wanted me to like him . . . simple enough. And yet it wasn't. We were at most ten minutes into getting to know each other, and already our relationship—if we could even call it that—was burdened by unspoken expectations by Grandma, by what I guessed his parents would think of me, by the secrets I couldn't share. My head suddenly whirled with all of that, plus the simple fact that I hadn't eaten anything since the nibble of persimmon.

The thought of that made me blush anew. Jimmy gave me a shy smile, encouraged again by misreading my expression. I opened the lid to the plain white box and pulled out a pink heart-shaped bottle with a blue lid. The heart-shaped label read Blue Waltz Sachet. The gift seemed strangely intimate from someone so shy.

"After I dropped you off, I asked Babs what I should get you to show I was sorry, and she said you like this sachet powder, to put in your drawer of . . ."

Poor Jimmy. As he faltered, turning red, I could just hear what Babs had said: *Now Jimmy, she loves to sew little sachets, fill them up with this lovely powder—you can get it right at the Woolworth's in town—and put the sachets in her intimates drawer. . . .*

Somehow, she'd have managed to say it so sincerely, so convincingly, that Jimmy wouldn't be embarrassed until he was actually giving me the gift, and imagining my *intimates. . . .* Bras. Slips. Panties.

I put my hand on Jimmy's, a calming gesture, like I would do with Will, but a tingle ran through me that was anything but sisterly. The feeling jolted me right out of my impending giggles.

I caught my breath but managed to say, "Jimmy, this is a really sweet gift. Thank you."

He looked relieved. "I'm glad."

I pulled my hand away, suddenly awkward. I picked up my fork, took a bite of pie. I nearly moaned at the flavor, forgetting I'd have picked coconut cream, the crust and apple filling melting on my tongue. Grandma's sweet pies would make a person nearly forget what a sour person she was.

Jimmy took the little flag—an orange paper triangle on a toothpick—out of his club sandwich, and bit in.

Somehow, quietly sharing a meal dissolved the awkwardness between us. We ate happily, without talking, until there was nothing left of my pie but a few crumbs, and nothing of Jimmy's sandwich but the little flag. I picked up the flag, twirled it between my thumb and forefinger, and giggled after all.

"Share with the whole class, Miss Lane," Jimmy said, in perfect nasal-y imitation of our English teacher.

My giggle turned into a real laugh, and I realized that in spite of all our awkwardness, I'd laughed more with Jimmy that day than with anyone else in a week. "It's just—this sandwich flag made me think of my little brother—" I stopped. *Dumb!* What boy wants to know that he's worked up the courage to give sachet powder to a girl for scenting her *intimates*, and she's suddenly thinking about her little brother?

But Jimmy said, "The one who wants to go to the Alaska Territory?"

He remembered. That made me soften even more toward him. "Yes. Will's crazy about Alaska. Last year, he even made a diorama of Alaska for class, when it was supposed to be a diorama of Ohio, and got an F! And you know the Marvel Puffs cereal promotion, for the switch to television of the radio show *Sergeant Striker and the Alaskan Wild*?"

Jimmy shook his head.

"Well, if you were a ten-year-old boy like Will, you'd know. For ten Marvel Puffs box tops, you can send in for your very own official deed to one square inch of Alaska! I guess that's all right, but he also has this crazy notion that he'll visit his claim someday. This sandwich flag"—I waved it under Jimmy's nose—"is just the right size for one square inch of land; that's how silly one square inch is."

Jimmy laughed.

This time, I didn't. "This isn't funny!"

Jimmy suddenly made his face fake serious, his lips still twitching. "You're right. There's nothing funny at all about using a sandwich toothpick flag to claim a piece of land as your own." He took the flag from me and stuck it in the corner of the Blue Waltz Sachet box.

I started to smile after all. It *was* a funny image. And I knew that soon enough, Will would see those dreams for what they were—silly and impossible—which should have comforted me. But, instead, I suddenly felt sad. And weary.

I needed to change the subject, get us back on a light-hearted tone, but the overwhelming smell of old sweat and grime hit me. I looked up. Strange Freddie was standing at our table, staring down at Jimmy. I gasped. Strange Freddie never came into the businesses in Groverton—not for long, anyway—without getting run out again.

Strange Freddie leaned over and smacked what remained of his right hand, wrapped in a dirty, cut-up flannel shirt, on the table by Jimmy's plate, making his coffee slosh. On impulse, I grabbed that silly little sandwich flag, protectively put it in the box with the sachet bottle, closed the box, and put it in my smock pocket.

Jimmy stared down at Strange Freddie's arm, and his face went from confused to horrified as he realized that the filthy wrappings didn't leave room for fingers, that this crazy man's right arm must end in a mauled stump.

"I hear you're th' son of th' new big boss at th' pulp and paper," Strange Freddie said. He gasped, like it was labor to speak at all, and I realized I'd never heard Strange Freddie say actual words before. He always sat outside Main Street businesses, muttering. Like his hand, his voice was mangled, but from lack of human interaction instead of by a machine.

"I am." Jimmy lifted his hand automatically for a handshake, then pulled it back. The corner of Strange Freddie's chapped, crusty mouth twitched. Jimmy cleared his throat. "Jimmy Denton. And you are?"

"Frederick McDonnell."

It was the first time I'd heard Strange Freddie's last

name. That made me really look *at* him, instead of past him.
I tried to see beyond the grime and shakes to the person
that Strange Freddie—Frederick McDonnell—might have
been before he became a lone wolf in Groverton. That thought
reminded me of Trusty. I immediately felt ashamed, compar-
ing a man to a dog.

"Mr. McDonnell," Jimmy was saying, "it's nice to meet
you. Is there something I—"

Suddenly, Grandma was at our booth, holding a wooden
spoon as if she might at any second start beating Strange
Freddie about the head. "Leave this young man alone! It's
bad enough I send you food outside, but coming in here,
smelling up my place—"

Strange Freddie shrank back at Grandma's shrill tone
and started to back away from our table. But Jimmy snapped,
"Mrs. Lane!" and Grandma fell silent. The whole restaurant
went silent. Even Strange Freddie looked shocked. No one
talked to Grandma like that. "I'm having a conversation
with Mr. McDonnell." He looked away from Grandma—
dismissing her—and back at Strange . . . at Mr. McDonnell. "Sir, is there something I can help you with?"

Surprise tinged with a bit of fear flashed in Mr. McDonnell's expression. He'd come in itching for a fight with the
new Groverton Pulp & Paper boss man's son. He hadn't
expected to find, instead, respect.

"Jus' . . . jus' tell yer daddy that you met a man who lost
his fingers an' most of his right hand in a conveyor at his
plant, back in forty-six, all 'cause management didn't want
to spend money on safety shutoffs."

Suddenly, he looked at me, his eyes narrowing. "We
was about to strike, but your daddy promised he'd get

management to see our side." He shook his head. "But he didn't. Porter Lane betrayed us. Nothing's changed."

Daddy hadn't kept his promise, and as a result, Strange Freddie—Mr. McDonnell—lost his hand. Daddy must have caved to pressure from other managers not to be a union sympathizer. My stomach turned at the thought: *My daddy . . . a coward.*

Then I thought, *Nineteen forty-six. The year Mama went to the treatment center . . .*

Maybe Daddy had been so caught up in his grief that he just forgot to keep his promise. Still, my stomach flipped again. *I knew Trusty, an innocent dog even if he was scary, was being abused, and I didn't want to do anything about it, because I was so wrapped up in my own problems. . . .*

Jimmy was saying, "I will tell my dad. I'm sure he'll make safety a top priority."

Mr. McDonnell nodded slowly. "If he doesn't, he'll face a strike." He leaned forward, his sour breath turning my stomach further as he added, "Talk is Local Eighty-three is thinking of letting the Negroes in." Local 83 was one of several locals of United Paperworkers International Union, most of its members being janitors and sweepers. Those were also the only jobs that blacks were allowed to have at the mill back in 1953. I suddenly understood. . . . If the white members of Local 83 who wanted to strike could get enough new members in and swing the vote to strike, Local 83 could join with the other two mill locals for a powerful enough strike to shut down the mill.

But why would Mr. McDonnell want to reveal this to Jimmy? Did he really think his testimony would be enough to get Mr. Denton to approve safety features and avoid a strike, which would cost workers a lot in lost wages? Was he trying to be a hero? Or was he trying to get back at all those who'd shunned him since his accident?

I shook my head. Either way, Strange Freddie had to be crazy. His former coworkers would only be angry with him when they learned he'd revealed the local's plans to the mill president's son.

Jimmy said, "Thanks for filling me in. Do you mind if I buy you dinner, as a thank-you?"

Strange Freddie/Mr. McDonnell squared his shoulders as best he could after years of shuffling about town slump-shouldered. "Nah. Mrs. Lane always sends out food to me," he said, and cut another look at me, but this time his watery gaze was grateful.

Then it hit me. . . . Daddy must have told Grandma that she should feed Strange Freddie whenever he showed up near her café. *Daddy.*

"It's starting to rain. Wouldn't it be nice to eat inside?" Jimmy stood up, reached in his denim jacket's inner pocket, pulled out his wallet, and got out a five-dollar bill and put it on the table. Then Jimmy smiled at Shirley, who along with everyone else had watched the exchange in stunned silence, and said, "Please clean our table and get Mr. McDonnell whatever he wants for dinner. The change is yours."

With that, Jimmy looked at me, and I knew he expected me to follow him.

"I—I have to get my things—from the back—"

I grabbed my notepad and pencil and rushed through the kitchen doors to the locker, and shoved the notepad and pencil into my smock pocket, where I felt the box of Blue Waltz. I opened the locker and grabbed my book bag, dropped in the box, then quickly hung up my smock and rushed out, resisting the thought that everything that had happened was just a dream.

But when I stepped into the diner, there was Mr. McDonnell, sitting up straight as he could at the booth where Jimmy and I had been, placing his order as if he ate *inside* Dot's Corner Café all the time. There was Jimmy, waiting for me at the front door. There was everyone else, looking at me with new approval—except for the Leises, the only ones who seemed not to have noticed the exchange between Jimmy and Mr. McDonnell.

Outside, Jimmy and I stood for a second on Groverton's Main Street.

The World War I memorial—a kneeling soldier aiming his rifle, primed to break free from his bronze pose and fire—was still in the middle of the town square. The mannequins in dresses still graced the window of Miss Bettina's Dress Shop. The red, white, and blue pole still turned by the barbershop's door, next to the Woolworth five-and-dime, where Jimmy most likely got the Blue Waltz Sachet.

Everything was the same, yet utterly changed.

I smiled at him. "What now?"

He smiled back. "Now . . . I really teach you how to drive!"

Chapter 8

And so I drove.

With Jimmy Denton patiently giving me instructions and tips, I drove.

"Give me a tour of Groverton," Jimmy said.

And so I did.

Now, fourteen years later, I still remember everywhere we went: up and down Main Street, away from Dot's Corner Café; by Miss Bettina's Dress Shop; by the Ace Hardware where Daddy worked; by the big Victorian house Grandma had grown up in, where her father practiced medicine as one of the town's doctors and where she still lived, polishing her bitterness as carefully as she did the silver she'd inherited from her own grandmother; then out to the edge of town to the Cosmic Burger and Shakes, where I carefully steered Jimmy's car up to the speaker, without adding a single scratch to the damage I'd already caused, and where we laughed at the shock on Lisa Kablinski's face when she roller-skated out to deliver our chocolate malts. By morning, everyone would know that Donna Lane, instead of working Friday night again at Dot's Corner Café, had been out with Jimmy Denton, even driving his car!

Then I drove us on out of town, passing by the Lucky Horseshoe Bar, where Daddy drank most nights, by the Groverton Cemetery, where Mama should have been buried but wasn't—her body had never come home from Florida because Daddy said it was easier to have her buried down there—and on out to Pleasant Valley Orchard, which had closed after the owner passed away, its gravel lot by the old barn becoming a favorite make-out site.

But at first, we just talked. We talked on the drive and in the orchard parking lot, talked and talked.

We didn't drive by Mr. Cahill's house. Groverton Pulp & Paper. Across the bridge to Tangy Town—definitely not there. Jimmy's house.

Eventually we kissed. My first kiss. I don't know if it was Jimmy's—probably not, but I didn't care. It was a sweet, lovely, tender kiss that lingered and that made me feel just . . . happy. Nothing like all the pulps Babs insisted on loaning me, like *Frenchie* and *Bonanza Queen*, said I would feel. But happy.

At some point, Jimmy turned on the radio, to a station playing some song with a racy fast beat and a wailing horn line.

"Is this local?" Jimmy said, sounding surprised.

"Are you kidding? No. It's out of Chicago. Every now and then, late at night, you can pick it up here. But the local station would never play this. It's jazz. Grandma says it's only fit for colored folks to listen to."

"What do you think?"

I wasn't sure how to answer, what he expected me to say. I decided to tell him the truth. After all, I'd perpetuated a lot of untruths that day.

"I like it!" I said.

Jimmy smiled. "I'm glad. I do, too."

So we listened and kissed until the old gravel parking lot filled up with too many other cars for us to really feel comfortable and then, at nearly midnight, I drove back to my house, my head fairly spinning at how much had happened since that morning, which now seemed a lifetime ago.

The closer we got to 230 Elmwood Street, the more my heart thudded. It was dark, so Jimmy wouldn't really be able to see how ramshackle our house looked compared with everyone else's. But it was also late, much later than I usually got home on a Friday night after closing up at Dot's Corner Café.

I prayed, *Please . . . let the porch light be off, the living room dark, just a glow coming from Will's room, Will reading his comic books under the bedspread. . . .*

But Dad's car was in the driveway. The porch light was on. The living room was lit up. Will's bedroom window was dark. And parked by the curb was a ramshackle truck with faded lettering on the back: Stedman's Scrapyard.

My stomach lurched. Oh God. I had to get inside, find Will. . . .

"Thanks, Jimmy, it's been wonderful," I said in a hurry, rushing out of the car.

"But I should walk you to the door, meet your dad," Jimmy said.

"Not tonight, Jimmy," I said firmly, and slammed the driver's door shut, leaving him in the passenger seat feeling, I was sure, hurt and confused.

Even before I was all the way up the porch steps, I heard the angry voices bellowing inside the living room. I glanced across the street. The curtain over the Bakers' picture window fell back in place. I rushed into our living room, still lovely with the furnishings Mama had optimistically chosen: cabbage rose rug, striped chairs and couch perfectly perpendicular to the fireplace, a pastoral painting and candles on the mantel.

Daddy and Mr. Stedman stopped shouting and stared at me. They looked so much alike in their rage, open mouths panting, bellies heaving over too-tight belts, in too-tight shirts.

I'd stumbled into some grotesque diorama, in the middle of which was Will, slumped on the floor in front of the couch. I knelt down next to him. He looked up at me, his face wide open with fear. I thumbed away his tears.

"Are you OK?" I asked softly, in a near whisper.

Will barely moved his lips: "Trusty."

He wasn't worried about himself, just that crazy, mute, wild dog. I pressed my eyes shut, forgiving my little brother his fervent passion for lost causes.

"Damned boy poisoned my dog!" Mr. Stedman yelled.

I squared my shoulders. "Mr. Stedman, how do you know your dog was poisoned?"

"Stay out of this, girl!" Daddy shouted. I could smell the booze on his breath. He toddled a little, grabbing for my arm, missing. This was the first time he'd talked to me in three days.

Mr. Stedman was no longer interested in Daddy. He gave me a long, appraising, leering look. "What else makes a dog retch?"

Gee, Mr. Stedman—how about old fluids from cars, or upholstery filled with rat poop, or starving a dog and beating it and

making it so desperate that it will eat anything—how about that,
you creepy old man?

Of course, I didn't say that. I said, "I don't know, sir, and
I'm sorry your dog is ill. But I'm sure Will had nothing to
do with it. He loves animals."

"That mongrel isn't a pet—he's a watchdog"—spit flew
from his mouth as Mr. Stedman yelled at me—"and I've
warned your brother before, but there he was this afternoon,
feeding the thing some kind of meat, but he ran away before
I could catch the little rat."

It took me a second to realize that by "little rat" Mr.
Stedman meant my brother, not the dog. But I couldn't show
my anger.

"Oh. That meat. Well, that was my fault. I let some meat
go bad, I'm afraid, and I paid my brother a dime to dump it
at your place after school."

I looked at Daddy. "So I guess you'll have to punish me,
instead."

Daddy grabbed my arm. As I stumbled toward him, I
caught Mr. Stedman's expression. He was smiling. My stomach turned. He liked the idea of seeing me get whipped.

"Go to your room," I said to Will. I didn't want him to
see this. As best I could, I'd have to mute my cries—just like
Trusty—so he wouldn't have to hear it, either.

Will was paler than ever, paler than seemed possible.
He said, "No, Donna, you shouldn't get whipped, and neither should Trusty. He's beautiful and strong and ought to
be in Alaska and—and he's just not treated right or fed
enough."

Mr. Stedman snarled. "You've given that worthless dog a
name? All it has to do is bark to keep away punks like you,

and a few weeks ago it stopped doing that. Why, I oughta put it down—"

Will jumped up, lunged at Mr. Stedman, hitting at him, but before he could even finish his first swing, Mr. Stedman had his big hand on Will's head, and suddenly instead of being angry, Mr. Stedman was laughing at my little brother's ridiculous attempt at assault, at Will's arms windmilling as he screamed, "No! No! You can't kill Trusty, you can't! He doesn't bark because you beat him, and he's hungry! No, no!"

Daddy let go of my arm and shoved me out of his way, lurching for Will. I plunged in between the men again, pulling Will away from Mr. Stedman, and as I did, the blow Daddy was aiming toward Will smacked across my face.

For a second, the room went silent and dark, but then I heard my name again—"Donna!"

It was Jimmy's voice. He was standing in the doorway between the entry and the living room, holding my book bag, staring in horror at our diorama gone mad.

"Donna," he said again.

I felt the blood running out of my nose, I felt Will gasping in sobs, pushing into my waist and chest, and I felt my arms go around him. But I was struck numb from the shame of Jimmy seeing us—seeing me—like this.

Daddy looked at me, confused, at the blood dripping onto Mama's remade dress, at the dress itself as if it was somehow familiar. And then he looked at Jimmy. "Who the hell are you?"

"Jimmy Denton, " he said as if his very name was a dare. Flashes of recognition struck both Daddy's and Mr.

Stedman's faces. Even they, in their rage, knew exactly who Jimmy Denton was, and why it was important.

But Jimmy didn't see those flashes. He was looking at me with a mix of expressions on his face—anger at my bloody nose, concern for my well-being.

But no pity. Thank God, no pity.

Jimmy spoke again. "And I am here to return Donna's book bag. She left it in my car. After our date." I couldn't repress the thought—*That was a date?*—or the tickle of giddiness that he'd called it so. He placed my book bag on the chair nearest the door. "I thought I should return it. And meet her father."

Suddenly Will broke away from me, running to Jimmy, sobbing out his words: "You have to do something! They're going to beat Donna! And kill Trusty!"

Jimmy knelt down, caught Will by the shoulders. "Whoa there, big guy. You must be Will. Donna's told me all about you. But who is Trusty?"

"Mr. Stedman's dog—"

"Dog don't have no name," Mr. Stedman started.

"Name or no name," Jimmy said sharply, shutting up Mr. Stedman, "no one is going to kill a dog, Will, and no one is going to beat Donna."

I felt a significant pause, as if something very important was being silently decided.

And then, suddenly, there was a rush of movement. Mr. Stedman muttered good night and hurried out the front door. Daddy shuffled after him, but only to take up his place again on the front porch. Will ran upstairs. Jimmy got out a handkerchief and held it gently to my nose, then pulled me to him, and after a little while he whispered, "Are you going to be all right?"

Of course I would. I'd survived such scenes before. But I waited just a second, liking the feeling of Jimmy's arms around me, before I nodded, rubbing my head against his chest.

I held the handkerchief to my nose for a long time after Jimmy left, alone and shaking in the middle of our living room, knowing that Will and Trusty and I had all been rescued. For now. Knowing that I should feel relieved.

Finally, I picked up my book bag and started up the stairs, trying to keep the third step from the bottom from squeaking, failing as usual. I just wanted to go to bed, to not think anymore about this crazy, long day, but as I passed Will's bedroom, he softly called my name.

I stopped, pushed open his door, went in. His room was, as usual, a mess—shelves stuffed with books and half-made models of cars and ships, and collections, if piles of rocks and feathers and sticks could be called collections.

He was sitting up in his bed, cross-legged, his too-small pajamas showing his wrists and ankles. In his lap, he had the Alaska Territory diorama that had earned him an F. The grade hadn't driven him to tears, but his teacher's comment had—that he was a foolish boy for thinking the territory would ever be a state.

I sat down on the edge of the bed. "Brush your teeth?"

Will nodded.

"Liar," I said, sounding harsher than I meant to.

His face crumpled a little. "Donna, I'm sorry about

taking the meat to Trusty. I just . . . felt so sorry for him. I swear I didn't think Mr. Stedman saw me."

"It's OK," I said. Who was being the liar now? But Will looked so small and pale, still scared, I supposed, from the awful scene we'd just endured.

He grinned. "It is OK now, isn't it? 'Cause of Jimmy. I promise I won't even make fun of you for having a boy-friend," he said, but he put a lilt on *boy*, and grinned wider. "Jimmy fixed everything! Mr. Stedman won't kill Trusty, and Daddy won't give either of us a whipping. Look, I made this!"

Will held out his hand, cupping a crude paste-and-paper sculpture of a tiny dog with pointy ears as big as the whole rest of the dog's body.

"Trusty," Will said, handing the tiny dog to me. "I bet Jimmy could even figure out how to get Trusty to Alaska!"

I stared into the diorama, at the brown construction paper mountains, and the cotton ball snow, and the tinfoil lake that was supposed to look like ice, and the small pine-cones painted green and glued around the lake, and the toothpick beaver dam. And then I looked at the tiny model of Trusty in my hand, and for a moment, I was tempted to close my hand over Trusty, crush the model of the dog, take the diorama and toss it to the floor and crush it, too. I didn't want the weight of this—Jimmy's presence making every-thing right—affecting my relationship with Jimmy, what-ever that relationship was now or would become. I didn't want us to be rescued, like he'd rescued Strange Freddie, turning him into Frederick McDonnell. I wanted Jimmy just for me.

And there was something else, too, I realized, as my

fingers started to curl around the silly little paste-and-paper Trusty.

People leave.

Mama left. Mama died.

I was desperately dreaming of leaving the next year, when Will would be big enough, I hoped, to defend himself against Daddy, or maybe Miss Bettina would take him in.

But in the meantime, what if Jimmy suddenly realized that he didn't really want the girl from the right side of the tracks with the wrong-side-of-the-tracks family?

Daddy had fallen apart when Mama died, and I'd been keeping us together ever since, as best I could. Not doing a great job, obviously, or Jimmy wouldn't have had to step in downstairs. But what would happen if he went away and things fell apart even worse than before? I didn't think I'd have the strength to pull us all together, not again.

I felt Will looking at me, and my eyes flicked up from the paper-and-paste Trusty model. Those wide blue eyes of his . . . he always knew I couldn't resist them.

I uncurled my fingers and placed Trusty across the lake from the toothpick beaver dam. Just to give those beavers a bit of a chance.

"That good?" I asked.

Will beamed at me, nodding.

I carried the diorama back to the bookshelf and put it next to his jar of cicadas. Then I sat back down with him, pulling him to me, and he snuggled up willingly. I wondered how much longer he'd be agreeable to snuggling with his big sister—he was ten, after all—and I said, "Did you get to watch *Sergeant Striker* tonight?"

I felt Will's nod against my chest.

"Well, I didn't," I said. "So tell me what happened."

"Well, first there was this miner," he said, with as much excitement as a whisper can bear, "and he found gold, but he didn't want the other miners to know. . . ."

And on he talked, telling me in detail each bit of the show's plot, which hadn't changed much in the move from radio to TV. Soon his voice became heavier and heavier, and he barely made it through the cheesy closing line: "Trusty, we can *trust* this case is closed!" And after that, he fell asleep, his breath slow and soft and even.

Chapter 9

The next morning, Daddy's car was gone. So I reck-
lessly banged pots and pans and spoons and spatulas
while taking my time—it was a Saturday—to fix Will a
proper breakfast: pancakes, bacon, eggs. I even turned on
the kitchen radio and sang along loudly to the hits on
WBEX and laughed when Will stumbled into the kitchen,
sleepy-eyed and grumpy at being awakened by my ruckus.
He was even grumpier when he realized that I expected him
to eat that proper breakfast. No passing out from eating just
Marvel Puffs. But he cheered up when I told him he could
also have Marvel Puffs—if he finished a plate of everything
else—and then danced him around the kitchen to Pee Wee
King crooning "Slow Poke." He seemed just fine; his normal self, full of life with rosy cheeks and a sassy attitude. I
told myself his loss of consciousness the morning before
had been an anomaly.

We didn't worry too much about where Daddy had gone.

Then, as Will and I washed up the breakfast dishes, our
telephone rang. It was Jimmy, asking if I'd go with him that
night on a double date with Babs and Hank to the Route 42
Motor-Vu, to see the *Roman Holiday* and *High Noon* double

feature. I hesitated, knowing I was supposed to work that night, but Jimmy hurriedly added that he'd cleared the date with both my grandma and daddy. When had he done that? The night before?

But I decided not to worry about that. I said yes and, for once, hoped the whole neighborhood was on our party line. Especially Mrs. Baker, from across the street.

As soon as I hung up with Jimmy, I called Miss Bettina at her dress shop and asked her if she would watch Will at her house when I went out that night if Daddy wasn't home. Or maybe even if he was home. I was relieved when she said yes.

For my first official date with Jimmy, Babs loaned me one of her Ayer's lipsticks, Roulette Red. That night at the drive-in, when Hank called Babs stupid for spilling some popcorn, Jimmy told him to shut up. After that, Hank was nice to Babs. And Babs let me keep the Roulette Red lipstick.

Jimmy took me out almost every night after that first date—to the Motor-Vu, to the Cosmic Burger, to the Pleasant Valley Orchard parking lot, and sometimes even to Dot's Corner Café. Grandma always looked so proud when we showed up there. Every now and then, we'd see Frederick McDonnell sitting there, drinking coffee.

Somehow, it went without saying that I no longer needed to work at the café. Grandma hadn't stopped passing on the equivalent of my pay to Daddy for my household allowance. She looked proud of me when I walked into church with her. Once, I overheard one of her friends—the Blue Hairs, Will called them—ask Grandma if Jimmy was churchgoing. Grandma shot her an annoyed, what-does-it-matter look and answered, "He's Presbyterian, which is good enough."

Now, like all the teachers at school, Mr. Cahill knew that Jimmy and I were dating, but unlike the other teachers, who seemed to see me with new appreciation and deference, he didn't seem affected by it one way or another. He continued our professional arrangement without comment, though he surely knew my new outfits were handmade, not special-ordered from Miss Bettina's Dress Shop, like I told the newly admiring girls at school.

On the next Saturday, I was hurrying to get dinner on the table for Daddy and Will—tuna noodle casserole, with the crunchy saltine cracker topping that Will liked. Miss Bettina was supposed to come over again for Will. I wasn't having dinner, because Jimmy had told me he had a special surprise. Babs had loaned me a small vial of her Evening in Paris. I planned to dab it on just before Jimmy arrived. I put together a special outfit, too—a sweater set, a sleek black skirt I'd refashioned from one of Mama's, and a black leather belt with a bold bronze buckle I'd found in one of her suitcases.

The belt was unique enough that I worried Daddy might recognize it, but he was sitting at the kitchen table reading the day's editorial in the *Groverton Daily News* and muttering angrily, which meant it was a rare one that didn't support Senator McCarthy's views. Will was looking at his Roy Rogers comic book just as intently. Daddy and Will's heads were tilted in the same direction, at the same angle, their mouths pursed and brows furrowed.

I spooned casserole onto Will's plate. He immediately started picking out the peas.

"Will, you have to eat those, too!"

"I'm not really hungry," he said, pushing the flakes of

tuna away from the noodles and peas. Soon he would have three islands on his plate—peas, noodles, tuna, in a sea of mushroom soup and milk.

"You have to eat something. You barely touched breakfast—"

"That's 'cause it was French toast," Will said, as if this was an affront.

"Well, you can't have Marvel Puffs every day—"

Suddenly, Daddy pounded the table so hard that I jumped, and the scoop of tuna casserole I was about to put on his plate jumped from my serving spoon back to the casserole dish. I thought he was just annoyed at our bickering, but Daddy growled, "This red commie trash! This Nate Cahill! Who is he?"

For a moment, our kitchen went silent. There was only the sound of the clock ticktocking over the stove, the tines of Will's fork on his plate as he poked at his peas, and the thin rustling of the newspaper in Daddy's trembling hands. His hands got like that if the time between drinks went on too long.

"Says here he's an art teacher at the senior high—art, of all things!" He glared up at me. "You have this red trash at school?"

I could have lied. Daddy had no idea what classes I was in. I wasn't even entirely sure that he knew I was in my senior year.

But suddenly, as boring as I found Mr.-Cahill-the-high-school-teacher, I felt angry for Mr.-Cahill-the-artist. I said, "Yes, Dad. I have Mr. Cahill for art." That was true. "He's a good teacher." Not true.

Will stared at me, his eyes wide, holding his breath. I

glanced at the clock. Jimmy would be at our house in about ten minutes.

Daddy shoved the newspaper at me. "Does he teach this trash in school?"

I took the paper, scanned the editorial that had so offended him, and quickly realized that Daddy would not be the only Groverton citizen to be outraged. The true betrayers of our country, Mr. Cahill wrote, were not communists, but those who, like Senator McCarthy, persecuted artists and musicians and writers. A truly free society, he stated, would not fear any kind of artistic endeavor, no matter how startling or odious or beautiful the ideas.

I looked up at Daddy. "No. Mr. Cahill does not discuss these ideas in class." My heart thudding, I said, "But in social studies class, we learned that Senator McCarthy supported the Taft-Hartley Act." That act, passed in 1947, made it more difficult for labor to strike after the surge of the labor movement in 1946. The year Mama died. The year Strange Freddie lost his hand, after Daddy had promised to support safety features at the mill. "So I guess that you also don't agree with McCarthy on everything. I mean, Strange Freddie told Jimmy that you'd agreed with him about safety features at the mill. Back in 1946. But I guess you didn't get a chance to speak up, like you promised him."

I swallowed hard, knowing that I was taking this risk only because Jimmy would soon be over. And I also knew that I was being cruel, striking back at Daddy for his weaknesses in this way. The color drained from his face. Suddenly, he looked so much older than his fifty years. Quietly, he said, "I've made that up to Mr. McDonnell the best way I know how."

Tears of instant regret pricked my eyes as I heard Daddy say Strange Freddie's proper name, just as Jimmy had. I opened my mouth, about to apologize, but there was a banging at the back door. *Jimmy*, I thought—hoped—even though he always came to the front door.

But when I opened the door, it was Miss Bettina standing there. "I brought your favorite pickled green beans, Porter. One for now and one for your fallout shelter." Right after Mama died in 1946, Daddy had built that fallout shelter in a rare burst of energy, saying he wasn't going to let anything happen to his children.

"We'd better put both jars in the shelter." He slapped the newspaper. "With commies like this art teacher, we'll be under attack soon."

"Now, Porter, I don't think anyone is going to seek out and attack Groverton because of the opinions of one art teacher."

Daddy shook his head, stood up, stalked off from the table.

Will pushed his plate back. "Done!" he said. He'd eaten the island of noodles and smashed up the pea and tuna islands. He grabbed his comic and ran from the table.

"Will, you get back here!" I hollered. I looked at Miss Bettina. "Maybe you could get him to eat more later. Thanks again for watching him for me."

"I'm sorry. I can't watch Will tonight. You know I'd normally love to. But I'm going to the meeting with Porter— your Dad—tonight. It's at my church," Miss Bettina said. She drove all the way into Dayton to attend the Unitarian church (which Grandma said didn't count as a real church, but Miss Bettina's kindness always seemed real to me). I was relieved; maybe they could take Will to whatever the meeting was. But then Miss Bettina added, "An AA meeting. Alcoholics Anonymous."

"Well, how wonderful," I said. "But I don't see why you have to take him. If he's not drinking, he should be OK to drive himself—not that being drunk has ever stopped him from driving before."

Miss Bettina gasped. I looked away, wishing I could snatch back the hateful words. I hated how I sounded—stiff and mean, just like Grandma—but I couldn't suddenly feel all happy for Daddy. *Well, gee*, I wanted to say, *what made him finally figure out he needed to stop drinking? All the jobs he couldn't keep, the nights he didn't come home, the money he spent, the depressed funks that made him neglect me and Will? What has changed?*

Jimmy.

I knew Daddy hadn't quit on his own because of Jimmy. But Jimmy's presence in my life definitely had an influence on how people treated us. Made Grandma less bitter. Made people treat Daddy a little more kindly at Ace Hardware.

Miss Bettina gently put a hand on mine, but I didn't look at her. "I have to go," Miss Bettina said softly. "I'm Porter's sponsor. And I never miss a meeting myself, if I can help it."

This made me look up and study her for a long moment as her meaning sank in.

I suddenly realized that as available as she was for us, most Saturday nights she wasn't.

Because she was at AA meetings. Because, she was telling me, she was an alcoholic.

Alcoholic. No one used that term back then, just like no one said *cancer.* Especially when cancer involved private body parts. The disease was half-whispered, if named at all. Like the breast cancer that had taken my mama.

Suddenly I remembered, like a photo of the moment sliding before my eyes, Miss Bettina sitting with me on her front porch, telling me how Mama had gone away to get treatment for breast cancer down at a special clinic in Florida. Later, Miss Bettina—not our daddy—had been the one to tell me and Will that our mama had died from that breast cancer and been buried in Florida.

Alcoholic. I could attach the term to Daddy, to his angry rants alternating with his sullen sorrow. But to Miss Bettina? Sweet, quiet, soft-spoken Miss Bettina, who watched Will for me, who brought us canned goods whenever she had extras, who quietly sold dresses in her shop, who sometimes slipped me an extra quarter or two when she paid me for doing alterations?

But what did I know of Miss Bettina? Only that she'd been my mama's best friend. That she'd lived next door to us for as long as I could remember. I realized, though, that I had no idea how she, a single woman, had money for her dress shop, for a house. Why she'd never married.

I studied her tired, sad face. She wasn't trying to trick me. She was telling the truth.

The doorbell rang. I heard Will's steps galloping down the stairs, the front door being flung open, and then there was Will, rushing into the kitchen. "Oh, Donna," he said, his voice singsong. Despite his promise from the week before, he made fun of me all the time about Jimmy. "Your boyfriend's here!"

Jimmy came into the kitchen right behind Will. He laughed, scooped Will up, rubbing his knuckles across

Will's head. "Yes, I am," he declared. Jimmy and Will had become fast friends, like Will was his little brother, too.

Then Jimmy stopped, still holding Will in midair, and stared at Miss Bettina and me. "What's the matter?"

"I'm afraid I can't—" Miss Bettina said, as I said, "She can't watch Will—"

We both stopped. "I need to find someone to watch Will," I said.

"I can watch myself!" Will hollered, still writhing in Jimmy's arms. "Put me down!"

"Maybe Will could see if he can go over to Tony's house—" I started.

Suddenly, Will was making retching sounds. Jimmy quickly put him down. I could tell from Will's ashen face that he was about to throw up. I hurried him up to the bathroom, held his head while he puked noodles into the toilet. Then I cleaned him up, felt his forehead. No fever.

"I'm sorry," Will said, while I tucked him into bed. Even if he didn't have a fever, I wanted him to rest. "I've messed things up."

"Don't be ridiculous," I said. But I swallowed over a lump in my throat. "You'll be fine. You just need to eat better than noodles and Marvel Puffs cereal!"

"But I'm only three box tops away!" he said. "And the deadline for sending the box tops in is September thirtieth! Just eleven days from now!"

"Hush," I said, and went downstairs.

Miss Bettina and Jimmy were talking quietly when I went into the kitchen. They stopped when I walked in, looking a little guilty. What was that about?

"He's fine," I said. "No fever or other symptoms. I think

he just got an upset stomach from running around all day and then not eating well at dinner."

"I shouldn't have roughhoused with him." Jimmy looked sad. "I'm sorry. I was really looking forward to surprising you."

"Well, if all Will has is an upset stomach from a rough day, why not take him with you?" Miss Bettina said. We both stared at her. She rolled her eyes. "Oh, I know. It's not so romantic, taking a ten-year-old with you on a date, but isn't that better than missing it altogether?"

"Ewww . . . I'm going on a date with you two?" Will was standing in the kitchen doorway.

"Will, what are you doing? You should stay in bed—"

"I was thirsty," he protested. The little brat. If he was thirsty, he could have gotten water from the bathroom upstairs. He was spying! He looked at Jimmy. "You aren't going to make out with my sister at the picture show, are you? Then I might really throw up. All over you."

I was horrified. "Will!"

But Jimmy laughed. "I was planning on taking her on a picnic. By the Tangy River. Think you can handle that?"

Will lit up. "The Tangy River? I know the perfect fishing spot! And if it's a picnic, well, just this once I could bend the rules and we could take Marvel Puffs. For a treat."

I was about to say *No, no, no* to the whole thing, but Jimmy said, "That sounds like a great idea."

Chapter 10

We went to the Tangy, high on a bluff upriver. Through the trees, we could just make out the smoke from the stacks of Groverton Pulp & Paper, but none of the sulfur smell reached us. The bluff smelled woodsy and earthy. Jimmy had to have driven up and down River Road often to have spotted the place. It was new to me and I'd lived in Groverton my whole life—but then, I'd never had Jimmy's freedom.

He wouldn't let me do a thing to set up the picnic, but he let Will, which made Will strut with importance. I sat in the car, watching Jimmy and Will spread out a classy blue-and-white-striped picnic cloth—no faded, sad ducks and lambs, like the tablecloth on Mama's old car in the garage. Then Jimmy got a picnic basket out of the trunk, and I followed him back to the cloth, where Will was sprawled. I knew I should feel glad that Will seemed better after getting sick at dinner, but I wanted Jimmy to myself.

When Jimmy came to the car, I leaned in close to him and whispered, "I don't think he's going to give us much privacy."

He smiled. "It will be fine. Trust me."

When we got to the picnic cloth, Will sat up. Jimmy sat down next to him, while I sat down across from them. "Think you're feeling better enough to eat?" Jimmy opened the basket. "I brought grapes, olives, pâté—that's a liver spread—and good, crusty bread."

All exotic food, I thought. Except the grapes. *Persimmons . . . now that was exotic fruit. . . .* I tried to shake the thought from my head. I would not think of Mr. Cahill on this date.

But I was curious. I knew Jimmy hadn't gotten the food from the A&P. Or from a tree in his backyard. "Where did you get all of this?" I asked, at the same time Will wrinkled up his nose as Jimmy spread a slice of bread with the pâté, which looked a lot like deviled ham to me.

"That stuff stinks!" Will said.

"Will!" But it did. And the olives—which were black, instead of green—smelled briny. Still, Jimmy must have spent a fortune on the food.

Jimmy laughed. "I went to a grocery in Cincinnati."

Will took a crust of bread with pâté and bit into it. He immediately looked like he wanted to spit it out. And like he might be sick again.

I felt a little sorry for him. "You don't have to eat, if you don't want to."

He started to look into the basket, but Jimmy snapped it shut. What was he hiding in there that he didn't want Will to see? "I think I'll have some grapes. And Marvel Puffs." Will looked at each of us. "You two want some Marvel Puffs, right?"

He was getting desperate. As he kept reminding me, the deadline for the postmark for mailing in his ten box tops was September 30, just four days after his eleventh birthday.

"Of course," Jimmy said. He opened the basket just enough to slide a hand in and pull out a floral-patterned china plate. Then he poured a big heap of the Marvel Puffs onto the plate.

Will grinned. "Wow! I bet we finish this box tonight. And then just two box tops more, and I can send off for my deed." He looked perplexed, suddenly. "I wonder where in Alaska the square inches are? It doesn't say on the box. But it would say on the deed, right?"

"Of course," Jimmy said again. He got out another plate and filled it with olives, grapes, the little container of pâté. He put the bread on the picnic cloth. I realized that he had only brought two plates. "And then you can look it up on a map."

Will looked annoyed. "I don't have a map of Alaska. There isn't even one at the library! I checked when I did my diorama last year—we had to do this diorama of Ohio, but I chose Alaska because it's more interesting and I know it's not a state, not yet, but it will be, even though my stupid teacher says it never will be—"

"Will!" I gave him a warning look.

He shot back a defiant glare. "She *was* stupid. She said it would never be a state—"

"That does seem kind of stupid," Jimmy said casually. "Especially since it's already in my atlas, right there with the U.S. and Canada."

Will's eyes widened. "Really?"

Jimmy nodded. "The atlas is in my glove compartment, if you want to look at it."

Will looked at me. "Can I?"

"*May* I," I corrected, immediately hating how school-teachery I must sound. "And, yes."

Will grabbed his box of Marvel Puffs and a handful of grapes and ran to the car. He yelled back at us, "Make sure you cat all those Marvel Puffs! It doesn't count if you don't!"

"What doesn't count?" Jimmy asked.

"His deed to his one square inch of Alaska," I said. "His rule is that every last puff has to be eaten, and he can't ask for help. Other people have to volunteer. Like you just did."

Jimmy looked at the plate of puffs and groaned. "We'll find a way to get rid of them without him knowing," he said.

I looked at him, not liking that, but I didn't say anything. We were finally alone—sort of. I glanced at Jimmy's car. Will was in the front seat, head bent over the atlas as if it were a treasure map leading to the most amazing thing imaginable.

"I'm worried about how disappointed he'll be if he doesn't get all ten box tops in time. He's been getting about one a week, but he needs three, and there's less than two weeks—"

"You worry too much," Jimmy said. I looked back at him. He'd opened the picnic basket and pulled out a bottle and two wineglasses.

Jimmy smiled at me. "Champagne. It'll help you worry less." He looked at the bottle. "Moët and Chandon. My dad's favorite."

A flutter of nervousness was suddenly making my forehead and upper lip tingle. Dad and Miss Bettina were at an AA meeting, and here I was, about to drink with Jimmy. I wasn't sure if I should feel guilty or amused. *What do you feel, Donna?* It was the kind of question Mr. Cahill would ask. Answer: *I feel like drinking the champagne. Seeing what happens next. . . .*

"Won't your dad miss it?" I blurted.

Jimmy laughed as he popped the cork and poured champagne in a glass. "He has plenty more." He handed the glass to me. I took a sip. I liked how the bubbles felt on my tongue and lip. Jimmy moved closer to me, kissed the back of my neck. I moaned. Then Jimmy nipped my neck a little and I winced.

We both said, "Sorry," at the same time.

"I'm just a little stiff in that spot," I said.

"Why?" he asked.

From stretching in some impossible pose for Mr. Cahill on his chaise longue. . . . But I couldn't say that. Not if I wanted to keep Jimmy's interest. And I did. I very much did.

"Doing alterations for Miss Bettina," I said, feeling a little sick turn in my stomach at the lie. "It's really a lot of close-up work, especially the hemming."

Jimmy started rubbing my neck and I gasped, both at the jolt his touch sent through me and at how his hands made my neck start to feel like warm putty.

"I don't think she likes me," he said.

"Now who worries too much? Of course she likes you. Everyone likes you." Although, I thought, she was unusually quiet and stiff around him. Why, I wondered, wouldn't Miss Bettina like Jimmy?

But then he said, "I brought you here because I wanted to ask you something. Well, three somethings. And I didn't want to ask with anyone around—"

I laughed, a little bitterly. "I guess my little brother ruined that."

"No, he's lost in looking at that atlas. Probably mapping out a route to Alaska!"

I laughed again, but not bitterly this time. I loved how often Jimmy made me laugh. I closed my eyes, nearly moaning again. I loved his touch, too.

"Would you come to dinner at my house next Friday? That means meeting my parents."

I misunderstood and stiffened. "I'll try not to be too embarrassing, although there's not much I can do about the fact my father used to be somebody at Groverton, and now—"

Jimmy stopped rubbing my neck. He twisted around on the cloth so that he was looking at me. He put his hand to my cheek. "Donna. I'm not embarrassed by you. Do all the Lanes have such big chips on their shoulders?"

"Yes," I said.

He laughed. "I just hope my parents don't embarrass me."

I frowned at that. He had the most powerful father in town.

Jimmy shrugged. "They can be . . . a bit much. But will you come?"

The next Saturday would be Will's eleventh birthday party. I had planned to spend the week preparing for that. But I told myself I could finish the yellow dress to wear to dinner the next Friday, still prepare for Will's birthday party the next day, and, of course, keep up with school and modeling for Mr. Cahill. Not being under Grandma's critical glare made me feel I could do anything. Everything.

So I nodded. He looked relieved. "Good. They want to meet you because they know about this next question. Will you go with me to homecoming?"

I smiled. "Of course."

I'd need a dress, and I knew immediately which of
Mama's I'd remake, one of the last ones left. . . . My heart
started to flip at the idea. *Maybe it's wrong, using that particular dress . . . it's definitely risky. . . .*

Jimmy leaned close, his lips nearly brushing mine as he
said, "and here's my third question." He looked suddenly
nervous as he slipped his hand into his pocket. He pulled
out a delicate chain on which he'd hung his class ring. "Will
you be my girl?"

Of course I would. It was what I wanted, wasn't it? What
any girl would want?

I blurted the first thing that came to mind. "Why me?
When you could have any girl?"

"Because you see me for who I am. You don't put me on
a pedestal." He smiled. "And I see you for who you are. *You.*
And I like what I see."

After that, of course I said yes. But as he slipped the
chain around my neck, his thumb brushing the sore spot
where I'd stiffened from posing for Mr. Cahill, something
in me fluttered that wasn't quite giddiness.

I wasn't sure what it was. It just felt like . . . something
slipping away.

A small flock of starlings suddenly rose from the tops of
the trees on the bank of the Tangy, their black bodies temporarily dotting the gray smoke puffing up in the distance
from Groverton Pulp & Paper. Even farther away, a freight
train whistled.

Be happy, I told myself, as I watched the birds fly away,
while Jimmy pulled me to him for a kiss. *Now you're Jimmy's
girl. And everything will be fine. . . .*

Chapter 11

Will fell asleep studying the Sterry Oil atlas, waking up long enough for Jimmy to tell him he could keep it, and that we'd finished off the Marvel Puffs, so now Will had eight box tops, which made Will happy. He wouldn't have stayed happy if he'd known that we'd taken the plate of Marvel Puffs down to the Tangy and dumped them for birds to eat. Even as I was thrilled to spot a colony of great blue herons across the river, I felt guilty about dumping the cereal, but Jimmy seemed annoyed—*What could it really matter?* he asked—and I stopped protesting. After all, I didn't want to ruin a nearly perfect evening in which I'd eaten exotic food, drunk too much champagne, and become Jimmy's girl.

At our house, Jimmy gently scooped Will out of the car and carried him up the walk and porch steps to our house. Daddy's car was parked in the driveway, but the living room was quiet. There was light coming from under his bedroom door, but no sound.

Jimmy followed me up to Will's room and carefully placed him on the bed. I pulled his covers over him. He moaned a little when I started to pull the Marvel Puffs box top and atlas from his hands. Jimmy whispered, "Let him keep it," which made me smile, and forgive him for being dismissive of Will's rules. On our way back downstairs, we made the third step creak, and I heard Daddy cry out in his bedroom. Another nightmare, I guessed.

So we stepped out on the front porch. Jimmy kissed me and then whispered in my ear, "My girl." He grinned, then pulled a cigarette from his jacket pocket, lighting it as he ran down the porch steps to his car. Then he hopped in and drove off.

I stood there, still dizzy from the kiss and the evening and the champagne, not wanting to go back inside and be alone, but then a faint whiff of smoke from the direction of Miss Bettina's house drew my attention. I could just make out, in the light that spilled out from the living room window onto the porch, a slim figure sitting on the porch swing. Then there was an orange flare, the tip of a cigarette. Daddy? But no. I'd just heard him inside his bedroom—the reason I hadn't asked Jimmy to stay in the house with me. For a second, a tingly feeling came over me as I briefly imagined what might have happened if he'd been able to stay. . . . I shook my head. Did I want those things to happen? Or was it the champagne?

I walked across our lawn—the grass was too overgrown and itched my ankles—and across hers, shivering. September was more than halfway over. By October, the chill of night would creep into the day. I pulled my cardigan around me, went up the steps.

I sat down in a rocker across from Miss Bettina, who held up her cigarette. "I used to smoke all the time. Now, just on meeting nights. Everyone smokes at them."

How is Daddy? What happened? What did he say? Is he really going to stop drinking, for good? The questions swirled in my mind, but I bit them back. I didn't want to care.

"Want some iced tea?" Miss Bettina asked.

"No thanks. I'm fine."

"Are you?"

My fingers immediately went to Jimmy's ring on the delicate chain around my neck. I knew Miss Bettina wasn't really asking about my thirst. "I am fine." Defensiveness crept into my voice. "Jimmy asked me to go to homecoming. And to meet his parents. And to go steady with him. I said yes, to all three."

Miss Bettina didn't say anything.

"Jimmy is good to me, to Will," I said. For God's sake, he'd even carried Will up to the house moments before. She'd just seen that!

"Oh," Miss Bettina said, exhaling the word along with her smoke. She ground her cigarette out on the porch.

"Why don't you like him?" I asked.

"I do, honey. I think he's a very nice young man."

"He thinks you don't like him."

She sighed. "I don't want him to hurt you."

Girl on chaise longue, stretching out in a suggestive pose— turning, twisting however the artist tells her to. . . . I pushed the image from my mind. I thought, *I'm more likely to hurt him.*

"Just . . . be careful. I knew another young woman, once, who thought her life would be better because of a young man," she went on. I thought she must be talking about herself. Or was she? I remembered how little I knew about her life.

And then I thought . . . *Mama.* Maybe she was talking about Mama.

I fingered the fabric of my skirt, the perfect seam that I'd been so proud of after taking it off the sewing machine in the basement. I didn't have any childhood memories of the dress I'd made it from, or of any of Mama's other garments tucked away in old suitcases in the basement. I wondered if she'd been beautiful, laughing, carefree, charming when she wore that dress.

Suddenly, I was desperate to ask Miss Bettina what she remembered about Mama. The words finally blurted out. "Miss Bettina, do you mean Mama? She thought life would be better with Daddy?"

Miss Bettina sighed. "I'm sorry, sweetie—I shouldn't have said that. Jimmy's a nice boy, but I just want you to remember who you are."

Funny. I wanted to forget who I was.

"Please, Miss Bettina, what do you remember about my mama? I mean, from before she got sick?" I stared out into the darkness of Elmwood Street, waiting for an answer.

After a long while, though, all she did was sigh. "Just be careful, sweetie," she said, and went back inside her house.

The next Monday, halfway through art class during the last period of the day, my eyes pricked with tears of boredom. I couldn't stand shading yet another sphere while the classroom clock ticked, Mr. Cahill read a book, and half the class snoozed or passed notes.

Suddenly, I ripped the page from my sketchbook, wadded up the paper, tossed it to the floor. The rustle made the other kids stir, turn, stare at me. Lisa Kablinski glared at me the hardest—word had gotten around quickly about me wearing Jimmy's ring. Jimmy turned in his seat a few rows up and winked at me. I smiled, thinking, *Take that, Lisa.*

I flipped to another page in my sketchbook and started sketching a jacket and pants ensemble, a variation on the outfit Audrey Hepburn wore in *Roman Holiday.*

"Is there a problem, Miss Lane?"

I looked up. Mr. Cahill was standing by my desk, staring down at me.

"Um, no," I said.

"Having trouble with the sphere?"

Of course he knew I wasn't.

An awful flush crept up my face when I realized that he was staring at Jimmy's ring on the slim chain around my neck. My fingers automatically, protectively went to the ring. *Jimmy's girl.* Mr. Cahill clearly didn't approve, just like Miss Bettina didn't.

He stared at me, waiting for my answer. My neck suddenly stiffened, like it had at our last session, when I'd stretched out in some impossible pose on his chaise longue. I thought about the massage and kisses Jimmy had given me on our picnic, when I'd complained about a stiff neck, not saying how I'd gotten it. My face burned even more deeply.

"She's just upset that she's in a class with a red," Hank said.

The class gasped. I knew I should have been thankful that Hank was diverting Mr. Cahill's attention, but suddenly I was scared as Mr. Cahill closed his book with a purposeful snap and turned his gaze to Hank.

"I beg your pardon, Mr. Coleman?"

Mr. Cahill's tone would have made most kids mumble a quiet "Nothing, sir," but not Hank. He said, "My old man read your editorial. Said you're one of them reds. That true?"

The class went silent and still, a sudden tension holding everyone breathlessly in place.

Mr. Cahill said, "This is art class, Hank. I will gladly answer questions pertaining to *art*."

There was something so self-satisfied in Mr. Cahill's tone, like he knew that no one was going to ask anything about art.

"I have an art question, Mr. Cahill."

"And what question is that, Miss Lane?"

"Why don't we ever draw anything except spheres and cones and cubes, Mr. Cahill?"

For too long a moment, Mr. Cahill and I stared at each other. He reached down, his hand brushing mine, as he flipped several pages—sketches of clothes and designs— and finally stopped at a random sketch of a nude girl on a chaise longue, reaching for a bowl of persimmons. He did a double-take, and looked at me with unvarnished surprise. My face flamed.

Suddenly, the drill siren went off. We all knew what to do—duck and cover.

Mr. Cahill walked past scrambling kids, hands in his pockets, like he was ambling down the sidewalk on Main Street. I caught Jimmy's confused, questioning gaze and Hank's knowing smirk as they moved to get under their desks. I grabbed my sketchbook first, and then curled up under my desk.

I didn't actually remember making that sketch.

In the event it survived an actual atomic attack and

revealed me for the scandalous girl that I was, I pulled the awful sketch from my notebook and wadded it into a tight little ball. As soon as this was over, I'd get rid of it.

After the siren stopped, we all got up from under our desks. Mr. Cahill had left the room. I didn't see Jimmy or Hank, either. I put my books in my bag, clutched my wadded-up sketch, and headed out of the classroom. Out in the hallway, Jimmy came toward me, looking anxious. Hank stood near him, still studying me.

I smiled at Jimmy and veered suddenly into the girls' bathroom. No one was there. I dropped the sketch into the special bin for menstrual pads. For a second, I stood in the bathroom, shaking. *Pull it together, Donna.*

I went to the bathroom sink, and stared at myself in the mirror. I smoothed stray hairs back into my ponytail. The door swung open. Babs came in.

"Are you OK?" she said. "You were acting weird in art class. And you just ran away from Jimmy."

I pretended to inspect a spot on my left eyebrow. "The siren went off. You know how that makes everyone jumpy. And I came in here because, you know, I needed to."

Babs looked over my shoulder at me in the mirror. Our eyes met in the reflection. "Uh-huh. You've been jumpy all day," she said. "I bought you a little time—told Hank and Jimmy you weren't feeling well." She grinned. "They took off like two terrified little boys. Said we should meet them at Cosmic Burger."

Thank you, Babs.

"Of course, you probably want to study in the library after school again," she said. She rolled her eyes. I was supposed to go by Mr. Cahill's after school for another modeling session, but suddenly, I knew I couldn't face him. Not after he'd seen that sketch.

I shrugged. "I think I'll skip studying today." A surge of disappointment shot through me.

"Good for you!" Babs sounded pleased. "You study harder than anyone. But I still want to know what's wrong with you. You should be over the moon! Jimmy is the greatest thing that could happen to you. And you don't have to work for that old shrew anymore."

I laughed. Babs knew how I felt about Grandma.

And I knew she was right. I was now officially Jimmy's girl, and I knew I *should* be over the moon. Spending time with Jimmy almost every night. Tending to Will and Daddy. Studying. Doing alterations for Miss Bettina. Posing for Mr. Cahill—and making sure not to get caught. Instead, I was exhausted. So exhausted I'd apparently sketched myself naked at Mr. Cahill's while I was half-asleep.

Babs leaned toward me. "I think I know what's wrong with you," she whispered.

My eyes went to the trash bin. Even Babs—Babs, who loved her racy novels and who had gone all the way with Hank (it wasn't nearly as thrilling as she'd hoped, she said)— would not think kindly of me if she saw that sketch.

"Come on, you can tell me," she said.

"I'm just a little distracted thinking about pulling together Will's birthday party," I lied. "It's this coming Saturday." Will would spend the night at Tony's on Friday, and then they'd both return to our house for Will's party the next day.

Babs rolled her eyes. "Oh, come on. I don't believe for a moment that you're really tense about Will's birthday party." She waggled her eyebrows. "I know what's really bothering you."

I felt suddenly ill. Did she know I'd spent the past week modeling and cleaning after school for Mr. Cahill? "What's that?"

She laughed. "Meeting Mr. and Mrs. Denton this Friday night, of course!"

I nodded, relieved to let Babs believe this. "I—I've been working on something to wear." I'd spent most of the previous night in the basement remaking Mama's yellow dress, tense that every creak in the house meant that Daddy was coming down and would find me.

Babs reached in her purse and pulled out a bottle. Her mom's Dexamyl. My eyes widened. She pressed the bottle into my hand.

"It's the Dexamyl my mom takes." She rolled her eyes. "She has plenty of bottles—she'll never miss this one. Or the one I took for myself." She giggled. "Anyway, they'll help you be more confident, more awake."

At that moment, Lisa Kablinski came out of the stall at the far end of the bathroom. I wondered how much she'd overheard. Everything, from the look on her face.

But Babs gave her a hard, daring look and said, "You didn't hear anything, right?"

"R-right," Lisa said.

"Don't be silly, Babs," I said, "regular aspirin will take

care of my cramps." I breezed toward the door, held my hand over the waste bin as if I was throwing away the pills.

But I hung on to them.

I made it through a very busy week without taking the pills, although I thought of them often, tucked at the bottom of my intimates drawer by the Blue Waltz Sachet and my stash of money.

I missed seeing Mr. Cahill, hated myself for that, hated the hurt, questioning look in his eyes, hated myself for looking away. And always, the image of the Dexamyl bottle floated across my mind's eye accompanied by the thought that taking the pills would make things so much better.

I resisted. Instead, I worked on the yellow dress, planned Will's party, and tried to escape into the comfort of being Jimmy's girl, preening just a bit too much around other girls, clinging a little too tightly to Jimmy's arm.

On Wednesday night that week, Grandma came to our house, three days before Will's party. Daddy was out at a midweek AA meeting; Will was upstairs in his room. I was sitting on the couch in the living room, carefully reading, for the third time, the Chocolate Cake II recipe in the one cookbook in our house, the *Boston Cooking-School Cook Book*. The book had been inscribed to Mama—"with many happy wishes on your wedding day"—from Mrs. Mary Lou Johnston, the wife of the then-president of Groverton Pulp & Paper. The book's brown cover and eight-hundred-plus pages looked as new and untouched as they would have when Mama opened the gift.

Hearing a knock, I put the cookbook down on the side

table and went to the front door. Grandma stood there, over-dressed in a black wool coat and matching hat. Other than at church, where we exchanged only public pleasantries, I hadn't seen her since the night Jimmy had come to Dot's Corner Café and swept me into his life. She looked too small, smaller than I remembered her seeming at her café, at least.

"I heard you're having a party for Will's birthday on Saturday," Grandma said. There was a little tremble in her voice. I couldn't help but smile. "I thought you could use some help. I could make the cake—"

"Oh, thank you, but I have that under control," I said. Her thin eyebrows went up. I'd been studying the Chocolate Cake II recipe more painstakingly than I studied for a chemistry or algebra test. I'd made the cake at least twenty times in my mind, and each time, it had come out perfectly. I pulled myself up a little taller and stared down at Grandma. "I'm baking a scratch cake. I have a recipe from Mama's cookbook."

Grandma's eyebrows heightened almost to the gray fringe over her forehead and I could just feel her thinking, *Your mama never cooked a decent meal in her life* . . . but in the next second, her face fell. She was disappointed that I was denying her the chance to do the one thing she did really well—baking—for Will's birthday.

"Very well," she said. Her voice carried no taunting, only sadness. "I came by with something else," she added. I kept my arm up, barring her from entering our home. *Leave us be*, I thought. *Just leave us be.*

Her hands shook as she unclasped her purse and pulled out an envelope. She held it out to me. "Go ahead, take it. Look inside."

I took the envelope but said, "Will can open this Saturday, with his other gifts."

Grandma shook her head, her too-big hat wobbling on her head. "It's for you. Open it." Some of the spitfire was back in her voice, and I hesitated, but then I unsealed the envelope.

I gasped. Inside was a twenty-dollar bill. A fortune.

I looked back up at Grandma, confused. Her smile was tight with grim pleasure that she'd made me lose my composure. "I also heard," she said, "that you're going to the homecoming dance with Jimmy Denton. I thought you could use some help for a dress and shoes and such. A *real* dress." Her gaze took in the remade outfit I wore that evening—a teal-and-pink-checked skirt and a white blouse to which I'd added matching trim around the collar and cuffs—and suddenly I felt as exposed as if I were wearing nothing.

She knew. She'd probably known all along that I'd been remaking Mama's clothes. Grandma never missed or forgot a detail. Especially not where her hatred of my mama was concerned.

My hand fell from the doorpost, and I hugged my arms around me, suddenly shivering on the warm, humid evening. But Grandma didn't take the opportunity to rush past me inside to see Will, or even wait to see if I'd thank her. She just turned on her heel and walked down the porch steps with that slightly-to-the-left hitch in her gait.

I shut the door and ran upstairs to my room. I pulled Grandma's twenty from the envelope and stashed it in my own envelope, with all the money I'd already set aside for the following summer, when I'd go to New York and somehow become a costume stitcher, by the Dexamyl tablets from Babs (that I couldn't quite bring myself to throw away) and the Blue Waltz Sachet from Jimmy. Of late, my only income had been a few alterations for Miss Bettina's customers. I hadn't been working for Mr. Cahill or getting tips at Dot's Corner Café, but the twenty dollars more than made up for even weeks of lost work.

I made up my mind right then, as I wadded up Grandma's envelope and threw it in the wastebasket, that I would go through with my plan. Well, not a plan, really; until that moment it had been a vague, uneasy idea that I tried to push away. But Grandma's comment, her "gift" to me, made that idea come to life with startling, sudden clarity and determination: I would remake the last big dress left in Mama's old suitcases for my homecoming dress.

Mama's wedding dress.

Chapter 12

"Oh, for pity's sake, Jimmy, is something wrong with your girlfriend?" Mrs. Denton asked.

"No, no, she's fine," Jimmy said. "Right, Donna?"

I looked over at Jimmy . . . all the Jimmys . . . desperately staring across the table at me, nervously tugging his tie, wanting me to behave properly. So I shook my head to clear it, but that only made me dizzier. That . . . and the Dexamyl. I'd finally given in to the temptation of the pills that night, hoping they'd make me as alert and confident as Babs had promised.

Instead, on top of my dizziness, everything around me seemed distant and odd.

"Then why is she giggling and staring at me and not eating and—"

"Julia!" Mr. Denton's voice was sharp, reprimanding.

I startled out of my giggles and dropped my fork, which made a ting as it hit my plate. *Julia* . . . the name of Mr. Cahill's mystery woman, the woman I imagined as his long-lost love and the subject of his mysterious project, the woman I assumed I was a stand-in for, as I posed in tiring, awkward positions on the chaise longue . . . or *used* to.

I gave my head another little shake, picked up my fork, poked at my food. "I'm sorry," I said. "It's just that that painting behind you . . . it—it's very . . ." I stopped, not sure how to describe the dark blue swirls on black.

"Oh, that. A college friend of mine did that." She spoke dismissively, as if she'd hung the painting up to cover a hole in the wall, but I heard emotion in her voice. A bit of sadness. Even wistfulness.

I looked up and our gazes locked. "Mr. Cahill?" I said, without thinking. Mrs. Denton stiffened, her fork frozen just above her plate, on its way to her lips. The bite of cordon bleu dropped off.

A memory tumbled forth, my subconscious trying to rescue me. "Mrs. Leis is a regular at my grandma's diner, Dot's Corner Café, and she asked me if I was in the new art class, and I said yes, and she said you'd met at the Groverton Women's Club this summer, when you first came here, and that she'd said she thought there should be an art class, and you said you knew a college friend who would be perfect for the job. . . ."

Finally—thankfully—my words trailed to a stop.

Mrs. Denton shuddered, like she was shaking herself back to life, and put her fork down on her plate with a purposeful tap. "Well, aren't you just at the center of this cozy little town's grapevine," she said.

Mr. Denton coughed, warningly. Mrs. Denton ignored him and went on. "You are right, dear. The painting is by my"—she paused and gave Mr. Denton a sidelong glance—"by *our* old college friend, Nate Cahill. Well, he started out as my friend." She paused. "I was an art major."

My face involuntarily twitched with surprise. Mrs.

Denton smiled ruefully while she peered at me. "That's right. Art. Not teaching or nursing." Her gaze shifted from me to Jimmy and then to her husband. "Not that I've done anything with it. Nate, of course, has exhibited in art shows and galleries in San Francisco, Chicago—"

"Now, Julia, I think you are being too modest. You've helped Nate make connections many times," Mr. Denton said, bragging about his wife, proud of her, completely unaware of the revolted look she was giving him. He looked at me and smiled. "Mrs. Denton still dabbles in art. She's even won a few club contests over the years." He sliced off a bite of cordon bleu, held it on his fork in midair. "I'm guessing the women's club here has a contest or show, and if not, of course Mrs. Denton could organize one." He popped the bite into his mouth.

"So yes, I did recommend Mr. Cahill as an art teacher," Mrs. Denton said. "Nate was looking for a place to settle, for a while, to work *quietly* on a special project, after a particularly nasty end to a relationship—"

"Julia!" Mr. Denton said in warning.

"Oh, sorry dear," she said easily. "Have I said too much in front of the children?"

"I don't think they need to hear about their art teacher's private life," Mr. Denton said.

"Or about his political views?" Mrs. Denton asked primly, then took a sip of her wine.

Mr. Denton's smile was stiff, forced as he explained, "I—we—found Mr. Cahill's letter to the editor to be . . . unfortunate. I've asked him to refrain from writing any more such letters, out of respect for the favor my wife did for him. And to preserve the *quiet* in which he wants to work."

"Now, Donna, Mr. Cahill's not filling everyone's heads with commie ideas, is he?" Mrs. Denton studied me. I wondered what she was looking for. A hint that I might be sympathetic to his ideas? I studied her back as long as I dared, long enough to realize that *she* supported his ideas, that there was more between them than the ties of old college friends.

I squirmed under her gaze, looked past her at Mr. Cahill's blue and black swirl painting. "No, no, he's said nothing of his political views," I said. "Just taught us . . . art. Shading. Shapes."

"How very un-Nate-like. He's usually so . . . vocal." Mrs. Denton said. "Perhaps the town's *quietness* is affecting him." Mr. Denton coughed. "In any case, what do you think of his painting, Donna?"

I looked behind her again. Mr. Cahill's painting was out of place in the Dentons' dining room, with its overwrought, formal Victorian dining set that included a cabinet stuffed with fragile china, the china we were eating on, the china Jimmy had brought to our picnic when he'd asked me to be *his girl*.

"It's . . ." *wonderful, mesmerizing, enchanting, captivating* ". . . interesting."

Mrs. Denton sighed, disappointment shadowing her face. Interesting, I thought, was the safest and least *interesting* word ever invented.

I looked down at my plate. I'd barely eaten any of my meal, turning it into a mashed-up mess of ham and chicken and Swiss cheese. On Jimmy's plate, the cordon bleu was still neat. He'd managed to slice off perfectly straight, even pieces, the spirals of meat and cheese intact.

Jimmy had brought me here to meet his parents, to make an impression, and I had, I was sure—but not the sort any of us had hoped for. Then again, the family home belied conflict that predated my arrival. The living room, where we'd first exchanged greetings, was filled with the newest style of furniture—all slick, clean lines, and square shapes, and bold turquoise and lime green colors—which didn't fit this house, a mansion at the top of Watershed Avenue that had been built in 1914 by the then-president of Groverton Pulp & Paper. Mr. Denton said he'd been thrilled to buy the house of a predecessor and went on about his love of legacies and history. Mrs. Denton made remarks about keeping up with the times and that she'd heard at the women's club that a new development of the most modern houses was going to be built at the old orchard.

"Would gravy help, dear?" Mrs. Denton asked.

"Pardon me?" I said, hoping I had misunderstood her intentions.

"I thought gravy might make the meal more similar to what your grandmother probably serves at her diner." Her tiny smile caught me off guard. "Dot's Corner Café . . . what a cute name. I haven't eaten there, of course, but the neighbors tell me it's good for homey cooking. If you like that sort of thing."

An image of Grandma rose in my mind, but this time instead of seeing the lines etched in her face as hateful and angry, I saw them as weary. I saw the swollen tops of her feet spilling over her shoes, like yeast dough rising.

I mustered my wounded pride. "My grandmother has worked hard all her life to make a place beloved by people from Groverton. It wasn't easy for her. She was an only child, used to fine things. Her dad was Dr. Winthrow and he treated many of the mill workers. My grandpa was a banker but he lost everything in the Depression and after he died"—driving his car into the Tangy River on purpose, some said—"after he died, she reared my dad all by herself and started baking pies and selling them to neighbors and from there she started the diner. Lots of people love to eat there. You might even like the meat loaf and beef gravy."

My voice was shaking, so I didn't go on: *Or the biscuits and sausage gravy, or a turkey hotshot with gravy; in fact you should go swimming in gravy because it might make you feel better, happier, nicer. . . .* My hands were shaking, too. I couldn't have forked up that cordon bleu even if I'd wanted it. There was a long silence.

Jimmy said, "I've been to Dot's Corner Café. The pie is really good. The chocolate cream is the best I've ever had."

Mrs. Denton sighed. "Oh, yes. Isn't that where you met that awful crazy man?"

"He has a name, Mother," Jimmy said. "Frederick McDonnell." He looked at his father. "Have you looked into the safety issues I told you about?"

"Of course, son," Mr. Denton said. Jimmy looked pleased. But I thought, *He's just being patronizing.* Then he added, "We should go to Dot's. It would be good for everyone to see us there."

Mrs. Denton arched an eyebrow. "Mix with the townspeople, Roger? Such a sweet thought. Not a requirement at your last position, though."

"This isn't San Francisco, Julia." Mr. Denton gestured for the maid, a black woman, to enter. She did so and began clearing our plates. I felt awkward, being served like this.

I looked at the woman, but she avoided looking me—or any of us—in the eye.

"Do tell us more . . . about your parents." Mrs. Denton asked as casually as if she were commenting on the weather.

"Julia, perhaps we should change the subject."

"To what? Art?" Mrs. Denton snapped. "I want to learn more about the family of the girl with whom my son is suddenly smitten!"

She smiled at me again and I realized that she already knew about my family; of course she knew. She probably already knew the story I'd just told about Grandma. She'd asked people around town and learned that Daddy had once held a job of importance at the mill, that Mama had died, that Daddy had gone half-crazy and held on to his job at Ace Hardware as much because of the pity of his manager as anything.

I realized that I had wadded into my hands the skirt of the dress I'd made for this occasion, fusing two of Mama's dresses—one a light gray, the other pale yellow, both of satin—into something new and stylish, something *wonderful, mesmerizing, enchanting, captivating.*

I tried to remember something, anything, about Mama, something that wasn't sad, that wasn't her singing along with the radio in her and Daddy's bedroom while staring past her reflection to something only she could see in the dresser mirror, or her just staring, sitting on the couch, while I cut paper dolls from her fashion magazines or, later, tried to tend to baby Will. But all I could think of was Mama's old clothing in the suitcases in our basement, dresses I'd been cutting into pieces and parts and remaking, and suddenly all I could see were those clothing pieces, all kinds of colors and textures and patterns from a life that didn't seem to bear any connection to the Mama I recalled, swirling around my head, making a strange buzzing sound as if the fabrics themselves had a voice that was trying to come to life.

"She loved clothes. . . ." That was my voice, so distant, so disconnected.

"Donna . . . Donna!"

Suddenly, Jimmy was kneeling beside me, one arm around me to keep me from sliding off the chair, holding my glass of water to my lips as I took long gulps. My vision cleared. I was still a little dizzy from both the evening's tension and my earlier dose of Dexamyl, but not about to faint. Jimmy stood up and gave me a worried look. I smiled at him to let him know I was all right.

"I'm sorry," I said, "I've just been a little . . . under the weather." Mrs. Denton's eyebrows went up. "Nothing catching," I added hastily.

"Thank goodness," she said. "Well, we do have dessert. That might tempt your appetite. It's Baked Alaska, which is ice cream that's been covered in meringue—"

"I'm sure our guest knows what that is," Mr. Denton said.

Jimmy and I looked at each other and burst into laughter.

"Who knew of the amusing properties of Baked Alaska?" Mrs. Denton said. "Did you, Roger?"

Jimmy tried to look serious. "Donna's little brother is really enthusiastic about Alaska. He's collecting the box tops from the Marvel Puffs promotion to send in for his deed to one square inch of Alaskan territory."

Mr. Denton lit up. "Ah yes, our mill makes the boxes for

the Sunshine Bakery Company. That's the company that makes Marvel Puffs cereal. It's a great campaign. I've known Harvey Kincaid for years—"

"Donna surely knows this." Mrs. Denton looked bored. "She's lived here her whole life."

Just as I'd defended Grandma, I felt a sudden urge to stick up for my dull little hometown. What was it about Jimmy's mother that made me want to defend people and places I usually couldn't wait to get away from?

I looked at Jimmy. His face was flushed with embarrassment. At school, everyone assumed he had a golden home life. I felt a tender surge of sympathy at knowing the truth. In some ways, our lives weren't so different.

"Jimmy doesn't know these things," Mr. Denton said. "And he will need to, to work at the mill after college." I frowned. Jimmy hadn't talked about that. We hadn't, I realized, talked about our futures at all.

Mr. Denton looked at Jimmy, who was staring down at the table. "Now, Harvey Kincaid is the president of Sunshine Bakery. We met at our first jobs and have stayed in touch ever since. It's important to make connections like that. I made a deal to manufacture the boxes, knowing that the Sunshine Bakery would sell hundreds of thousands of boxes of cereal to boys like Donna's little brother—what's his name?"

"Will. And he thinks he's going to go visit Alaska someday. See his land," I blurted out.

Mr. Denton beamed, thinking I was lending support to his description of the brilliance of the campaign. "Exactly! This campaign appeals to boys just like Will, to their imagination, their sense of adventure—Alaska! The last frontier!"

Chapter 13

As we hurried out of the house, down the driveway to Jimmy's car, I didn't dare ask to drive.

He steered us to our spot by the Tangy River, and there we sat, not touching, not looking at each other, not looking at anything but the darkness and the even darker swaying silhouettes of trees. I wanted Jimmy to reach over, to pull me to him, to bridge the great gap the evening with his parents seemed to have driven between us, but he hunched in his seat in misery.

So we sat while a slow drizzle glazed the windshield and the cold crept into the car until I could no longer hold back shivers. Then, finally, Jimmy moved, his hand brushing my knee as he popped open the glove compartment. He pulled out a narrow silver flask—a replacement for the *Sterry Oil Road Atlas*—and took a long drink. When he held the flask out to me, I shook my head. Even though most of my Dexamyl dizziness had cleared, I wasn't sure what alcohol might do mixed with the pills. I shrunk back in my seat, suddenly so weary that I pressed my eyes shut.

Jimmy said, "I'm not like him," and at first I thought he

meant that his drinking wasn't like my daddy's drinking, and then I realized that he meant he wasn't like his own daddy.

"I don't want to study business or come back and work for him in that damned paper mill." His voice was rough with barely contained anger. Alarmed, I opened my eyes. Jimmy smacked his hand against the steering wheel, accidentally honking his horn. Even in the darkness, I could see that his face writhed with fury. He took another long drink from the flask. In the distance, I heard the startled, deep, hoarse call of a blue heron. Jimmy's horn had disturbed her.

Suddenly, I opened the car door, grabbed my purse, and started walking up the spongy bank toward the road. My shivers turned violent in the freezing rain. Why hadn't I worn a sweater with my dress? I thought, *Because you're a stupid, foolish girl . . . and you need to get home to Will . . . and stop thinking Jimmy is going to rescue you somehow . . . and focus on getting out of Groverton and—*

"Donna, wait! What are you doing?"

I kept walking, ignoring Jimmy. The dizziness was back, the night swirling around me in blue and black, just like Mr. Cahill's painting, but I ignored it and started running. I heard Jimmy behind me, quickly closing the space between us. I picked up my pace, but the heel of one of my shoes— gray T-strap spikes that I had thought looked so pretty with my yellow and gray dress—caught in a dip as I ran, and I fell flat, the wetness of the ground immediately oozing through my dress. I felt the left sleeve of my dress—of Mama's dress—rip.

I'm sorry, Mama. . . . I struggled to get up, slipping on the muddy slope, my right ankle throbbing with abrupt, sharp pain. And then Jimmy was over me, pulling me up from the ground and to him, saying, "Hey, hey!" not unlike a birdcall of his own making, and then, "Donna, I'm sorry, I'm sorry."

I let myself melt into him, into his warmth, and he helped me back to his car. He took off his jacket and wrapped it around me. "I'm an idiot. My mom was awful to you and all I can talk about is not wanting to do what my dad wants."

"I di-didn't make a ve-very good imp-impression." Shivers and hiccups made me stutter.

"You were fine. Beautiful! Like always." He pulled me closer. "Is your ankle OK?"

The throbbing had worsened. "Yes," I said.

Jimmy gave me a disbelieving look.

"All right. It hurts like hell."

"That's what I thought." He pulled his tie off. "Lift your foot up; put it on my knee." I hesitated. "I've already got mud on my pants. A little more won't matter."

He carefully wrapped the tie around my ankle. I leaned my head back against the cold window, focused on feeling him tend to me. In spite of the throbbing pain, his touch on my leg made me moan. He pressed the flask into my hands.

"It will help with the pain," he said. "Warm you up."

I unscrewed the flask, took a small sip. The alcohol burned my throat, made my nose tingle like I was about to sneeze. But after a few seconds, I felt warmth in my stomach.

"What is this?" I asked.

"Gin," he said.

I took another drink, much longer this time, and Jimmy pulled the flask from me. "Whoa," he said. "Go easy."

He twisted the lid back onto the flask, and replaced it in

the glove compartment. "I'm sorry I scared you into running away."

I said, "Oh, Jimmy, don't you ever just want to run away? Escape from everything?"

Like Will wanting to go to Alaska? No, not like that. Will wanted to go *to* something. I wanted to run away *from* everything.

"Yes," Jimmy said. Then he smiled shyly. "Well, not everything." He put his hand on my arm, and I moaned again at the warmth of his touch, his fingers stroking my skin as he rubbed the hem of my sleeve. He looked at the rip along the shoulder. "Will you be able to fix this?"

"Yes." The word came out thickly. I felt dizzy again, but in a pleasant, melting way.

"Good. I like your dress, the clothes you make."

I smiled lazily, mumbled, "Mr. Cahill says I should be a designer."

"What?"

I startled at the sudden sharpness in Jimmy's voice, then blurted, "Why do you hate Mr. Cahill so?"

Jimmy's face tightened. "He's always been there, between my parents, even if my dad can't see it. They all went to college together. Mom and Mr. Cahill dated and went to Japan together to study architecture. When they came back, they'd broken up, and Mom married Dad. All my life, I've heard Mom talk about Nate Cahill."

I took this in, turned it over. So that's when Mr. Cahill had been to Japan, with his Julia. . . .

"When did he say that? About you being a designer?"

My face flamed and I hoped the dark masked it. "Oh, I . . . I got bored in class and sketched some designs, and he made some comment about me becoming a designer." I forced a light laugh. "I made this dress from two of Mama's old dresses."

Jimmy stared at me.

"She had so many, and remaking them saves money. The dresses aren't doing anyone any good in the suitcases."

"How . . . sweet," Jimmy reassured me. "I think she'd be pleased."

"I've never been to Mama's grave." The words just blurted out. I frowned. Why did I say that?

But he whispered, "Go on," somehow knowing I needed to say this, to get it out. Or maybe he was relieved we were no longer talking about Mr. Cahill.

"I'm not even sure where she's buried. Somewhere in Florida, near the clinic where she was treated. Daddy was gone for a few days after Mama died, so I guess he went to oversee her burial—Will and I stayed with Grandma. . . ." A flash of memory caught me by surprise: Will marching around her kitchen, banging two pots together, laughing at the loud noise he was making, but then swinging his arms so wide that he knocked a home-canned jar of tomatoes from the counter to the floor, and Grandma screaming after the jar shattered—"This is your fault! All your fault!"—and I wasn't sure if she meant just the jars, or Mama's illness and death, or something else, but I jumped between her and Will, just in time, and took the kick meant for his behind on my leg, and knew that I would always, always have to watch out for Will.

I started shaking again. Jimmy pulled me to him, held me tightly, kissed the top of my head. "Go on," he whispered again.

"I . . . I asked Daddy once, about a year after Mama died, that summer, if we could go to Florida to see her grave, and he didn't say any-anything, and I haven't asked since."

He pulled me to him even more tightly, so my head rested against his chest, right below his shoulder, a perfect fit, and he said softly, "I will take you if you want me to. I will take you anywhere you need to go."

I turned my head and looked up at him. Something about his smile, about his lips, their tender curve, stirred another kind of warmth in me that had nothing to do with his coat or his gin.

I tilted my head so that my lips were just a breath away from his. Seconds stretched toward eternity, it seemed, but finally, finally, he kissed me, and I returned the kiss, not a front porch kiss, but something much deeper, each of our tongues gracing the other, eagerness knotting us together and away from thought, time, place, everything.

Chapter 14

"Yes, Mrs. Baker, I completely understand. I hope How-ard feels better soon," I said, and then listened to her give another faltering apology about why Howard could not attend Will's eleventh birthday party that afternoon—something about a terrible headache—until she finally said good-bye and I hung up.

Howard's headache sounded like an excuse. I actually did have a headache from the night before, from the mix of Dexamyl and gin.

Still, I felt triumphant—finally, Mrs. Baker was kow-towing to me.

But in the next instant, I felt disappointed for Will that yet *another* guest's mother had called with a last-minute excuse for her son not being able to attend. Will's eleventh birthday and party were on September 26, 1953, a beautiful, warm Saturday afternoon, and even with my pounding head, I could appreciate that.

I stomped through the living room and kitchen to the basement door, through which I could hear whoops of laughter and crashing sounds, like crazed horses bouncing off walls.

I called through clenched teeth, "What is going on down there?"

Will trudged up the stairs. "We're just playing pin the tail on the donkey," he said, making his wide blue eyes wider still. "Just like you said." He tried to hold back his laugh, but it tumbled out. I finally caught a glimpse over his shoulder of the seat of his pants. Pinned to it was one of the donkey tails I'd carefully made from gray felt I'd bought at Woolworth's.

Not wild horses bouncing off our basement walls.

Wild donkeys.

I forced back a smile. "You're supposed to pin the tail on the picture of the donkey," I said. I'd finally drawn something in Mr. Cahill's class other than shapes or clothing sketches—an outline of a donkey. "You're supposed to play nice!"

"I *am* playing nice. Sometimes I'm the donkey, and sometimes I let Tony be the donkey."

I frowned and was about to reprimand that by *nice* I meant *properly*, when Will leaned toward me and whispered, "Did you know another word for donkey is *ass*?"

Will's big grin—showing gapped teeth, puffing up his freckled cheeks, crinkling the corners of his blue eyes—did me in. I burst out laughing. But I was supposed to be in charge here. I needed to take control.

"Will!" He looked a little deflated at my return to a stern tone, but I continued, avoiding his gaze. "I've just had four— *four*—of your guests' mothers call to cancel. That means it's just you and Tony now!" Tears of frustration pricked my eyes.

"Gee, that's too bad, but Tony and I are having a great time!" He followed that up with another wide grin.

But I wasn't going to let him charm his way into my good graces this time. "What did you say, or do, to keep your guests from wanting to come to your party?"

Will shrugged. "They weren't *my* guests, anyway. They were yours."

"But, I wanted . . . your first party . . . to be special. . . . I've worked so hard."

Will rolled his eyes. "You're acting like Grandma!"

I recoiled, as stunned as if he'd slapped me. His expression softened. He put his hand on my arm. "Don't worry, Donna. There will be other guests. I invited my own friends!"

He trotted back down the basement stairs. I had to smile at the silly little gray donkey tail—the ass's tail—flicking up and down on his pants seat.

I left the basement door open a crack and sat down at the kitchen table, suddenly weary. I put my head to my hands.

Miserably, I had to admit that Will was right. I had been acting like Grandma, using his birthday party—his first one ever—to try to gain social favor. I knew I could because I was, after all, Jimmy's girl. Suddenly, instead of feeling angry at Will for doing or saying whatever he'd done or said to keep the Howard Bakers of Groverton away from his party, I felt ashamed.

Not about the night before—Jimmy and me escaping from ourselves by losing our virginity to each other had been delicious, wonderful. I didn't regret it. Yet I suddenly felt fragile, as if at any minute I might say, or do, or wear just the wrong thing and send Jimmy fleeing. Or I might have already done so.

The timer dinged on the oven.

I pulled on my mitts, opened the oven door, pulled out

two cake pans, and put them on the hot pads on the kitchen table.

The doorbell rang. I hurried to the front door, my heart speeding up, nervous to see who Will had invited. There stood a woman and a girl, her hair done up in high pigtails, her white blouse and poodle skirt neatly pressed.

The woman said, "Is this the home of William Lane?"

"I told you he goes by *Will*," the girl said.

"Yes, this is Will's home," I said. "I'm Donna, his sister."

"Oh, well, I'm Mrs. Hilliard," the woman said. Then she looked down at her daughter. "Susanna, please introduce yourself, dear."

The girl looked up at me. "I'm *Suze* Hilliard," she said. "Nice to meetcha."

"Make your acquaintance," her mother whispered.

Suze sighed. "It's nice to meetcha . . . and make your acquaintance," she said. Then she peered around me. "Will said he's having a birthday party?"

"Oh, yes, he's downstairs with the other . . . guests," I said, hoping Tony wouldn't mind that I'd just multiplied him. A crash and a thud made both Mrs. Hilliard and me jump. Suze grinned. I explained, "They . . . they're playing pin the tail on the donkey."

Suze ducked around me into the house, following the noise. Mrs. Hilliard stared after her daughter as she asked, "You're not here by yourself with the children, are you?"

I started to tell her that our dear neighbor Miss Bettina was coming over in a few minutes—even though, still angry that she had judged Jimmy so harshly, I hadn't invited her.

A whoop rang from the basement.

Suddenly I really did see a woman coming up the walk to

our front porch, wearing a big hat and carrying a gift, and I thought, *Miss Bettina . . . she let one of her assistants take over at the dress shop.*

But this wasn't Miss Bettina. This woman's hips were too wide, her gait too slow, and she wore a shabby old dress that Miss Bettina would never wear. After a startled second, I realized that this was MayJune.

Mrs. Hilliard turned, regarded MayJune, then faced me with a pinched look of judgment. I felt a rush of defensiveness for MayJune. I called hello to her, realizing that when we'd met at the scrapyard I hadn't gotten her last name, and so I couldn't properly introduce her to Mrs. Hilliard. I called, "So glad you're here!"

MayJune, I realized, must have walked all the way from her daughter's house. She said, "I'm MayJune Winton. A friend of the family." And then she grinned at Mrs. Hilliard, and suddenly Mrs. Hilliard relaxed and introduced herself.

MayJune turned her toothless smile on me. "Why don't you go check on the children? I'll be glad to greet guests."

"Of—of course," I said as another crash sounded. I rushed through the living room and kitchen. Suze had dumped on the table her gift, her poodle skirt, and the ribbons that held up her pigtails. I opened the basement door and hurried down to find Will and Tony and Suze, all in blindfolds, all giggling away, trying to pin the donkey tails on one another. Suze had on long shorts and her hair was done up in a messy ponytail on top of her head. Away from her mom, she'd reverted to her natural state: tomboy.

Good for you, Suze, I thought, but I hollered, "Children!" They all stopped cold, their feet trampling peaches and green beans from jars that had been knocked from the storage shelves to the floor. "Remove those blindfolds!"

All three pulled off their blindfolds and stared at me.

"You will help me clean up this mess," I said, "and then we will go upstairs, where you can play outside until the other guests arrive!"

I looked at Will. Yes, his lopsided grin confirmed, there would be other guests.

By the time I headed back up the stairs—after a few minutes, I'd sent will and Tony and Suze outside to play—my stomach was churning. What eleven-year-old kid would invite an eighty-something woman from the wrong side of town to his birthday party?

I shook my head at myself, realizing I was thinking, again, like Grandma.

Will would, that's who.

There, at the kitchen table, MayJune and Miss Bettina sat, fanning themselves in the muggy heat, chatting away like old bird friends who have landed next to each other on the same wire time and again.

"I brought lemonade," Miss Bettina said, as easy as if our friendship had never skipped a beat. "I knew Will would want lemonade at his party. I hope you don't mind."

I sank down into a chair. I wanted to stay mad at her, knowing I couldn't and wouldn't. "Not at all. Will loves your lemonade. But your shop—"

"Oh, I have Mrs. Sherrod keeping watch for me," Miss Bettina said.

I nodded. Then I looked at MayJune. "Mrs. Winton—"

"Now, child, I told you when we met to call me MayJune," she said. "I meant it." The teakettle started singing on the stove. "Oh, the water's ready for your tea!" She rose slowly and started toward the stove.

"My tea?"

"For your headache," MayJune said.

I thought I'd hidden it well. "I took some aspirin."

"That's fine," she said, "but some black tea with peppermint will do you good. Of course, chamomile would be better."

Miss Bettina said, "She sent me to cut some of the mint that grows wild at the back of my yard as soon as she saw me!"

MayJune set a steaming mug before me. I picked it up, breathed in the vapor, took a sip. And then another.

Then I said, "MayJune, where is Mrs. Hilliard?"

"Oh, we convinced her that her little baby would be just fine here," she said. She and Miss Bettina grinned at each other, pleased with themselves. "Did you see Jimmy playing with the children out back?"

"It's my understanding that Will invited him," Miss Bettina said, her voice a little tense.

MayJune chuckled. "I'm trying to convince Bettina that your young man isn't all bad." Somehow, that, of all things—MayJune calling Jimmy my young man—made me blush.

"Now, I never said he was all bad," Miss Bettina said. "I just said I think Donna should be careful of her heart."

I stared at the two women. They'd just met, but they'd been talking about my romantic life, while I was downstairs sopping up peaches and green beans and glass with three juvenile *asses*, as if they were, what—my old aunties?

"Well, now, of course she should be careful of her heart—all womenfolk gotta be careful of their hearts—but he's not a bad drink of water to look at, and nice manners, so for now—"

I started to snap at them to please stop talking about Jimmy, but then I realized that I'd already sipped half the mug of tea and my headache was easing.

And then I noticed the cakes on the kitchen table. They'd sunk in on themselves, a gooey mess oozing up from the middle. "Will's cake . . . it's a disaster!"

"Maybe we could cut off pieces from the outer edges, ice the tops, and serve that," Miss Bettina said. "Like square cupcakes."

MayJune smiled and said, "Don't worry about that, honey. Just leave the cake be and let Will open his gifts. Things will work out just fine."

I'd failed at not just one but three attempts to make Will a birthday cake. I thought that I should at least throw away the ruined cake. Not let it sit there on the kitchen table as an embarrassment to myself, to Will . . . and then I thought, no. I was trying to do things Grandma's way again, make our lives seem perfect, pretty, unblemished. And I was tired. I'd try it MayJune's way.

So I nodded at her. MayJune and Miss Bettina smiled.

Jimmy and Will led Suze and Tony and (I later learned their names) twin brothers Herman and Harold through the back kitchen door. Jimmy grinned at me, so happy to see me, and suddenly all my fears about our relationship dissolved. He swooped me up in a hug and kissed me on the forehead, so of course Will hollered, "Ooh, yuck!" echoed by the other children. That just made Jimmy grin and kiss me again, this time on the cheek, which started another round of whooping and gagging, until Miss Bettina and MayJune shooed us all into the living room, where the gifts were neatly stacked on the coffee table.

Miss Bettina served everyone lemonade and Suze designated herself the "gift fairy," delivering one gift at a time to Will, who looked happier than I'd ever seen him.

I made mental notes about each gift so Will could write thank-yous later: from Miss Bettina, a wallet including a lucky dollar; from Tony, three new Western comic books— a Roy Rogers, a Lash LaRue, and a Gene Autrey; from Suze, a yellow Matchbox convertible. Will and the boys oohed and ahhed appreciatively, but as Miss Bettina's and my eyes met, her expression was so sad that I had to look away. From Jimmy there was a compass dedicated to "all of Will's coming adventures," a prophecy that had Will grinning extra wide; from Herman and Harold, an honest-to-goodness pin the tail on the donkey game, which made everyone laugh, including me. Will flashed his blue eyes when he opened my gift, a new copy of *The Call of the Wild*. Daddy had left a long lumpy package on the kitchen table. Will opened it, revealing a BB gun.

That left two gifts. From Grandma, two pairs of socks. He started to laugh at the humdrum gift, but I saw no need to mock Grandma, so I shook my head. Will quieted down, and turned to the last gift—MayJune's.

Will had carelessly ripped the wrapping paper off his other gifts, but this one he opened slowly and carefully, maybe because it was his last one, or maybe because it was from MayJune and he knew that it would be special.

Something small . . . like those little choices MayJune would talk about soon enough. But life-changing.

The gift was two boxes of Marvel Puffs cereal.

Will looked at MayJune, his eyes suddenly shiny, and said, "Thank you! MayJune, how did you know I was two box tops away? And the postmark deadline is in just four days—September thirtieth."

"You're welcome, Will," MayJune said. "Donna, do you think it's time for Will's birthday cake?"

A pang shot through me . . . that awful cake, both layers a gooey mess collapsed in their pans. Another flush rose up my neck and face. And then, as I looked at MayJune's kind, soft face, I realized why she'd said not to worry about the cake, to let Will open his gifts first, that things would work out just fine.

I grinned. "MayJune, I'd love to, but it seems I can't bake a cake worth eating. The one I tried to make just collapsed in on itself in a gooey mess!" I looked at Will. "Do you think, if you don't mind sharing, we could have Marvel Puffs instead?"

"Yes!" Will whooped, jumping up from the couch. He led the charge into the kitchen. I got out eleven birthday candles, gave one to each child and two each to MayJune, Miss Bettina, and Jimmy, then quickly lit each candle. Jimmy gave me one of his candles as we started to sing "Happy Birthday," and then Will closed his eyes and made a wish, blew out his candle first, and then ran to each person to blow out the other ten candles.

We used up both boxes of Marvel Puffs and all of the milk in the refrigerator. While we ate, Suze asked MayJune to explain her name. MayJune laughed and said her mama didn't get around to naming her for months, and when she did, she couldn't remember if she'd been born at the end of May or the beginning of June, so her mama named her MayJune.

That made Will whoop with delight and say that that

meant she should get to celebrate her birthday for every day of May *and* June.

But once everyone was done eating, Will became somber again, carefully tearing off the two box tops, sternly instructing Jimmy to hold them *carefully*, while he ran upstairs to collect his other eight. I found an envelope and stamps. Then everyone gathered around while Will carefully wrote out a letter giving his name and address and requesting, with a little help from Jimmy, his deed to one square inch of Alaska, "in exchange for the enclosed ten box tops." Will even included his 250-word essay about why he'd like to go to Alaska for his chance to have his photo taken with Chase Monahue, the actor who played television's Sergeant Striker, featured on the front of Marvel Puffs boxes.

After recounting the box tops three times to be *sure* he really had ten, Will carefully addressed the envelope and put on four stamps—at least twice as many as he needed—and put his letter and the ten box tops inside.

Jimmy offered to drive Will—and Tony, Suze, Herman, and Harold—to the post office so they could all put Will's envelope in the big, sturdy blue mailbox outside, where it would be in the care of the U.S. Postal Service.

The children all whooped at this prospect, as if riding two miles in Jimmy Denton's car was a grand adventure. I looked at MayJune and Miss Bettina for guidance, and they both nodded—just slight nods that said it was up to me, but that I should approve.

And so I did.

Chapter 15

For a while, life kept feeling perfect: that night after Will's party, as I curled up in Jimmy's arms in his car parked at "our" spot by the Tangy River; even on Sunday, as we went to church with Grandma and Will dutifully thanked her for his socks and told her that he'd had the best birthday cake possible; and in the wee hours of Monday morning, after Daddy and Will were asleep, as I quietly worked in the basement studying Mama's wedding dress for how I might completely remake it by homecoming.

Then came art class on Monday afternoon. Mr. Cahill paced nervously. I recognized his manic, wild-eyed manner from the moments when he got lost in his sketching.

As we settled into our seats, Mr. Cahill said, while running his hands through his already messy hair, "All right, class—who remembers Donna's question from last week?"

My heart clenched.

His gaze alighted on me. A nervous flush crept up my face, but he pressed on. "Surely you remember. Since you asked the question?"

I shook my head as I mumbled, "No, sir."

Then Lisa Kablinski raised her hand. "Mr. Cahill, I remember! I remember!"

She has a crush on him, I thought. *She likes both of the men I like, Jimmy and . . .*

Lisa repeated, word for word, with a mimicking lilt, "'Why don't we ever draw anything except spheres and cones and cubes?'" Jimmy frowned. Babs gave me a look that said, *It's OK, honey, we can beat her up in the girls' room after class.*

"That's right, Miss Kablinski! That's exactly right!" Mr. Cahill said, with excitement another teacher might have reserved for a student perfectly reciting a line of Shakespeare or an algebraic equation. Lisa sat up a little straighter in her chair, preening.

Mr. Cahill's gaze slid back to me. I stared down at my desk. "I've been thinking about your question, Miss Lane," he said, as if he hadn't been able to shake the question free from his mind, like I wished I could shake away my betraying, awful thought about Mr. Cahill and Jimmy and liking them in the same way.

"And the answer to that very insightful question of Miss Lane's, about why I haven't had you draw anything except basic shapes, is . . ." He paused, then rushed on, "The answer is that I've been lazy and assumed that no one here really cares about art or can understand it."

I looked up at him, startled. The class went completely quiet—no giggles or restless movements. But Mr. Cahill grinned, seemingly oblivious to the hurt silence, and said, "So now we must start over! We must discuss the question: What is art?"

Silence.

"Fine. No volunteers?" He gazed around the room, pausing for a second at Jimmy. *Not Jimmy.*

"Mr. Coleman, what is art?"

"Uh . . . it's a picture of something." For just a second I felt a little pity for Hank as red splotches mottled his cheeks.

"For example?"

"Uh . . . uh . . . maybe of a . . . dog?"

A few kids tittered with quiet laughter. Hank stared down at his desktop.

Mr. Cahill said, "OK, a picture of a dog. But the class laughed." He pointed at Babs. "You. You laughed. Why? Do you think a picture of a dog can't be art?"

"I guess it can be," Babs said, hedging her bet. "If it's a good picture of a dog."

Next Mr. Cahill focused on Cedric Knowles, who was known for being painfully shy and not very bright. I felt a pang of sympathy for Cedric as Mr. Cahill put his hands on his desk and leaned toward him. Cedric squirmed nervously.

"What makes a picture of a dog *good*?" Mr. Cahill asked.

"I—I dunno. I guess if it looks . . . just like a dog. Not like a stick figure dog, or something."

More chuckles.

Mr. Cahill stood up. "Cedric here makes an interesting argument." Cedric looked shocked—and pleased. "He's saying that a good picture of a dog—a picture that can be defined as art—has to look like a dog."

Babs raised her hand slowly. Mr. Cahill nodded at her.

"So, if the picture of a dog has to look just like a dog to

be art, why not take a photograph? Why would someone
have to draw or paint a dog, then?"

Mr. Cahill beamed, as if Babs had just asked the most
brilliant question possible.

"Yeah, like Ansel Adams," Hank said.

"What about Ansel Adams?" Mr. Cahill said, ignoring
the class's surprise at Hank's unexpected contribution.

Hank shrugged. "My grandma has a book with his photos in it."

"And when you look at them, how do those photos make
you feel?"

For a second, Hank looked thoughtful, but then broke
into his usual jerk grin. "Like I'd rather look at the photos
than at the doilies on Grandma's tables."

Mr. Cahill walked to Hank's desk. "Dig a little deeper,
Hank. How do Mr. Adams's photos of the West *make you feel*?"

Mr. Cahill's voice dropped to a near-whisper at the end
of the question. The class was silent as Hank stared defi-
antly at Mr. Cahill. "Like I wanna get out of this place," he
said. "See something more than the smokestacks of Groverton sometime in my life."

We all knew what he meant—well, all of us except Jimmy,
who had gone pale at the implied criticism of the business his
father ran, a business that supported most everyone in town
in some way. But Hank was saying something that all of us
had felt at one time or another.

"Ah," Mr. Cahill said, walking to the front of the classroom. "So a photo or painting or sculpture has to make you
feel something for it to be art. Touch you, move you, in
some way."

Cedric raised his hand and Mr. Cahill nodded at him. "So if that's true," said Cedric, "then is it art if the picture of the dog ain't anything like a dog, but moves you in some way?"

I thought of Trusty, Will's Trusty at Stedman's Scrapyard. Would a painting or photo of poor Trusty be art? It wouldn't be art that most people would want to see.

"Why are you asking me?" Mr. Cahill was saying to Cedric.

"'Cause you're the art teacher!"

This time, Mr. Cahill chuckled. "I may be the art teacher, but that doesn't mean you don't know something about art. It's in you." He tapped Cedric's shoulder. "*Art is in you.*" Then he tapped Lisa's shoulder. "And you." He did the same to Babs and Hank and several other students.

He looked at me, and for a second I thought he was going to come tap my shoulder and say, "And you" to me, too, like a pastor or priest giving a blessing. But then he stopped.

"Your art can touch someone else, if it comes from you, from your heart. Art starts with emotion! So today, forget cones and spheres and cubes. We're going to draw emotion! Get out your sketchbooks. Draw what you're feeling right now, or the emotion you feel most of the time, or the emotions that you don't want anyone to know, and put it in a picture. It doesn't have to look exactly like something. It can be scribbles—just show some emotion!"

The class stared at him. He stared back, for just a second. Then he said, "Oh, for pity's sake, it can even be a sphere—a happy sphere or an angry sphere—as long as it has some emotion in it. Just get started!"

And with that, he turned, went to the chalkboard, and

started sketching, his lines quickly turning into a bowl filled with fruit. *Persimmons. . . .*

I got out my sketchbook, opened to an empty page, and stared at its suffocating blankness.

I thought, *Life is perfect. I've been telling myself that ever since Jimmy walked into my grandma's diner and took me out. So I should draw "happy." But how do you draw happy? Sunshine and butterflies?*

I put my pencil to the paper, let my mind go a little blank, just like I did when I sketched clothing ideas, let my hand start moving, expecting *happy* to show up, somehow, on my page.

But my lines came out as thick, dark, angry slashes, forming the outline of a dog.

I didn't really see this, though, until Mr. Cahill was right by my desk, bending over my work, too close, too close. I could smell his scent, a mix of coffee and cigarettes and menthol aftershave, and feel his breath on my cheek, and hear him saying in a low murmur, "Donna, now you need to tap into wherever this anger is coming from and work with that."

In the next second, he was gone, at another student's desk. I looked after him, wanting to catch his eye, but instead, my eyes connected with Hank Coleman's. A mean, taut smile curved his lips.

"Donna Lane?"

It was Principal Stodgill saying my name, and the look on his face said *trouble.*

Will.

I felt like I'd been punched in the gut. *Will.* Somehow, I knew something was wrong with Will.

In the hallway, Principal Stodgill gave me the pitying

look I'd grown to resent and tolerate from Groverton adults, the only kind of look I'd gotten until I started dating Jimmy. And there it was again, as he said, "I just got a call from the nurse at Groverton Elementary. It seems your brother is very ill. We called Groverton Ace but your father isn't at work today, and there is no answer at your house. . . ."

I ran past Principal Stodgill, down the hall toward the high school's front doors. I didn't wait to hear the rest. I just wanted to get to Will.

"Flu!" Dr. Emory proclaimed Will's diagnosis with a triumphant tone and wide grin, like he had just made a major discovery.

I looked at Will, shivering under the thin blanket over his lap, his bare shoulders hunched like he wanted to curl up into a ball, bounce out the doctor's office door, and roll home. "You don't think it's . . . It's not . . ."

Dr. Emory gave me a patient, patronizing smile. "It's not polio," he said. "Will doesn't have neck stiffness or arm and leg pain."

Will gave me a *See? Told you so!* look.

I wanted to say, *But flu comes with fever, which Will doesn't have.* I wanted to say, *Flu doesn't make eleven-year-old boys pass out in the middle of a geography lesson, especially when that's their only favorite subject.*

Tears filled my eyes. I'd been so swept up with Jimmy . . . with my *perfect life* . . . I'd stopped looking around at my real life. If I had, maybe Will would have mentioned to me—as he'd just told Dr. Emory—that he'd been throwing up, off and on, for the past several weeks.

The throwing-up confession was what made Dr. Emory proclaim, "Flu!" *Who has flu for weeks? Without fever or chills?*

"Just make sure Will gets plenty of rest and fluids. He'll be fine," Dr. Emory said. "Will, go ahead and get dressed. Donna, let's give Will some privacy."

I followed Dr. Emory out into the hallway, thinking about how the elementary school nurse had told me that he'd thrown up twice at school in the past week, that he'd seemed lethargic lately. None of this made sense to me. He'd seemed fine during his birthday party, just two days before. I hadn't seen any signs of illness . . . except that morning, the first Friday of the school year, when I'd made those small choices that, even in that moment in Dr. Emory's office, I still didn't fully understand as life changing: skipping school with Babs and thus meeting Jimmy; taking a secret modeling job with Mr. Cahill . . .

Suddenly I realized that while I'd been in my dreamy relationship with Jimmy, and visualizing big life plans because of Mr. Cahill's encouragement, Will had been keeping his own secret: how poorly he felt.

In the hallway, Dr. Emory stopped and looked at me with a concerned frown. "Donna, as you were able to put together in the exam room," he said, "Will's condition probably isn't flu. I didn't want to say anything in front of Will, because I know you are trying your best, but I am concerned about not just Will, but you, too. How well your, ah, basic health needs are being met. If you have enough to eat, nutritious enough food—"

"What? No—we're fine; we're doing just fine—" The color drained from my face as I realized that what Dr. Emory was trying to say, in his roundabout way, was that

Will was sick because of neglect. "I—I make sure Will is taken care of! He eats breakfast every morning, and I pack a healthy lunch and make sure there's dinner every night. Well, I've probably let him eat too many Marvel Puffs the past few months. I—I should have convinced him that tossing the cereal and sending in the box tops was a better idea." Dr. Emory looked genuinely confused, but I went on. "Maybe now that he's sent in his box tops, he won't be ill. I'll never let him have Marvel Puffs again, and—"

Dr. Emory put his hand on my shoulder in his fatherly fashion and I fought the urge to shrug him off. "It's a big responsibility," he said, "watching out for your little brother while trying to grow up at the same time."

I arched my shoulders back, making his hand fall away from me, and said, "We're doing just fine. I make sure he gets his homework done and I'm signing him up for Little League baseball this coming spring, and—" Tears started forming again, choking my voice, and I stopped talking, because I hated that. I hated showing any kind of weakness.

"I know you're trying to do all of that," Dr. Emory said, emphasizing the word *trying*, "but as I said, that takes a lot of work, especially with your high school responsibilities and your, ah, normal teenage interests." He glanced toward the door to the waiting room.

I knew what that glance was saying. Jimmy had grabbed my books and sketchbook and followed me over to Groverton Elementary. He had insisted on driving Will and me to see Dr. Emory, and he'd insisted he'd wait for us.

"Have you thought about having your grandmother come stay with you and your dad and Will? I know she'd be glad to." Dr. Emory gave me a kindly smile, as if he could just imagine Grandma puttering about in the kitchen in a floral print apron dusted with flour, as she whipped up cakes and treats and casseroles that would ensure our wholesome well-being. This wasn't the first time Dr. Emory had made such a suggestion, and he wasn't the only Groverton adult who had done so. Grandma, I knew, had told anyone who would listen, "I tell Porter all the time that I'd be more than glad to give up my house, or have them come live with me, to help him take care of Donna and Will."

"We are doing fine," I said, my face going to stone, my tears to gritty salt. "Daddy is just busy, working extra shifts at Groverton Ace. He's joined Alcoholics Anonymous."

Dr. Emory looked stunned that I'd know about such a thing, what's more share it with him.

The door creaked open and Will came out of the examination room. From the look on his face, I knew he'd been dressed for a while, listening to my conversation with Dr. Emory. The little stinker. But his eyes looked so dark, almost bruised, and I couldn't stay mad at him.

"Come along, Will," I said, in my most crisp, motherly voice. I thought the mothers of Suze and Tony and Harold and Herman would be impressed.

In the next second, though, I thought that MayJune and Miss Bettina wouldn't be. They'd just cluck and shake their heads sadly: *Donna, Donna, remember to be kind.* . . .

So I put my arm gently around Will and said, "Come on, kiddo. I'll make your favorite flavor of Jell-O, OK?"

Will scrunched his face. "Jell-O's yucky in any flavor."

I laughed. "How 'bout toast, then? And chicken noodle soup?"

He grinned. "And . . . maybe, since I'm sick, you can read *Call of the Wild* to me."

Then he looked up at me with his wide blue eyes, and I said, "Well, all right. Just chapter one. Just to get you started." But we both knew I'd read to him as long as he wanted.

Chapter 16

By the end of that week, which ushered in October, Will was back to being his usual self. He asked me every day if he'd gotten anything in the mail—meaning, of course, his deed to one square inch of Alaska. When I reminded him that the box's fine print stated, "Allow up to six weeks for delivery," he looked sorry for me. "Sergeant Striker would tell you to have faith," he said. "That's what he always tells Trusty, right before they solve their crimes!"

I finally settled on a design for a homecoming dress— the dance was a couple weeks away, on October 17—and had started measuring and cutting pieces. I took my inspiration from 1920s flapper girl dresses and designed a simple, floor-length, strapless white sheath, which I would make from Mama's satin wedding dress after removing the layers of lace on the top and the crinoline petticoat underneath. I planned to dye the lace the bird's egg blue Mama had favored in so many of her clothes, overlay that on the white satin sheath, and add a matching satin ribbon at the drop-waist hip line.

The only material I had to buy was the ribbon—fifty-two cents' worth to get enough to form a bow on the left hip—and a package of Rit dye for the lace. I thought about replacing the satin-covered buttons up the back with a zipper, but as challenging as they'd be to close or open, I decided I liked them. And I liked the idea of Jimmy's fingertips lingering along my back to slowly undo them.

Frugality had swept the family, with Will extending his afternoon newspaper route to save for his visit to the one square inch of Alaska that he would soon own.

I told myself that the pay for modeling and housecleaning drew me back to Mr. Cahill's the Friday after Will had been diagnosed with "flu."

"I was wondering if the persimmons were ripe," I said, standing in Mr. Cahill's kitchen doorway.

He stared at me, dazed—I realized I'd pulled him from some artistic fever—and said, "Come in, Donna. Before some neighbor sees you."

I stepped into the kitchen, which was even messier than on my first visit. I put my book bag on the floor and moved toward the sink, but Mr. Cahill put his cigarette in an overflowing ashtray on the counter and gently grabbed my arm.

"Donna," he said. "You didn't come to ask about persimmons. Or clean up after a slob. Why are you here?"

I wanted to look away, but his steady, deep gaze held mine. I wanted to pull away, but, God help me, I liked the feel of his hand, however gently, on my wrist.

Brazen, I gave the most insulting and untrue answer possible, shrugging while I said it: "I still have plans to work as a seamstress in New York. And I can still use the three dollars a session—if that's what you're paying your models."

Mr. Cahill dropped my wrist. "I haven't had any other models," he said. "No one else dared answer my ad."

"So your work is going well without a model?" I said.

He shrugged. "Well enough." But then a flicker of frustration crossed his face and he stared past me, as if in his own dream, as he said, "I'm nearly done with the sketches . . . but with one more modeling session . . ."

Then he shook his head as if to clear it and gave me a stern look. "What about your work?" At my look of confusion—was he really asking me about waitressing?—he smiled. "I mean your design work, of course."

"I'm still designing," I said. "In fact, I'm working on a beautiful design for a homecoming dress to wear to the dance. With Jimmy Denton."

He looked disappointed. "You can do better, you know." Did he mean than dating Jimmy? Or than designing homecoming dresses? "But, very well. My work would benefit from having a model. Would this be agreeable to you? One more modeling session today, and after that, if you insist you want to be my housekeeper, that's fine. But on two conditions. One is that you share with me more of your clothing sketches so I can tutor you. From what I've seen in class—at least at the beginning of the year—you have a gift, Donna, and a passion for design. I'm hoping to go to New York over Christmas break, and I plan to see a friend of mine who teaches at the Parsons School of Design."

Mr. Cahill paused, watching for my reaction. He smiled with satisfaction when I gasped at his reference to Parsons.

"If we work hard enough, you could have a portfolio that I could show him while I'm there," he said softly. "What do you think about the possibility of studying to be a designer? I know you say you want to be a costume seamstress, but I think you could go farther than that with your talent. Much farther."

I swallowed hard, but my voice belied the emotion I was trying to tamp down, quivering as I said, "I—I think that would be wonderful. I could do that. Work on a portfolio. With you."

"Good. But my second condition is that I talk with your father and let him know that I am hiring you as a house-keeper in exchange for providing tutoring," Mr. Cahill said. "I will still pay you three dollars per housekeeping session. At least this way you can come to my front door and stop hiding." His mouth briefly curved into a grin, but then he turned serious. "It's how I should have handled this to begin with."

My mind was whirling. *Portfolio . . . Parsons . . . designer . . .* Then my heart fell. There wasn't any way that Daddy would agree. After all, he ranted every time one of Mr. Cahill's editorials against Senator McCarthy's views ran in the *Grover-ton Daily News*. ("Sells papers!" Babs reported as her editor father's decision to print Mr. Cahill's pieces.)

But then I thought . . . *Miss Bettina.*

Her increasing influence over Daddy would ensure that I could go, freely, to Mr. Cahill's house, and learn from him about how to improve my designs, how to become a designer. Not a seamstress. *A designer.*

"All right," I said. "But let me talk to Daddy first." Mr. Cahill didn't need to know that I really meant I'd talk to Miss Bettina. "He's not a fan of your editorial pieces."

He chuckled. "Fine." He glanced at the kitchen door

behind me. "And now, I really ought to get back to work." He glanced at the ashtray. His cigarette had burned down to ash. He picked up a pack and lighter. "After I finish my break."

I gave him a small smile. "You said you could use one more modeling session?"

"Yes, but—" He stopped. I knew what he was about to say—that he'd thought better of it. And I could also see on his face a warring thought—that he was close, so close to getting the sketches just right, but without a live model . . .

"I'm already here," I said softly.

Mr. Cahill gave me a long look, trying to decide. "You know where my studio is. I'll be up in a minute." He lit his cigarette, leaned back against the counter, took a long drag. He never smoked in his studio.

I grabbed my book bag and hurried through the living room—which still held Mrs. Bentley's old furniture and Mr. Cahill's unpacked boxes—and up the stairs before he could change his mind.

I stood for a long minute in the doorway to his studio. The walls were covered with sketch after sketch done with pastels, some in black and blue, some in yellow and red, or green and purple, as if he was experimenting with color combinations, all drawn with thick, expressive lines. I banished the thought that these aggressive abstracts had grown from the pencil sketches of me in repose on the chaise longue. Or had they?

From the phonograph set up near Mr. Cahill's easel, I heard the scratching of needle on record. The easel held nothing except a blank sheet of newsprint. I stared for a second at the slowly spinning record.

Mama would do that, I remembered. *Play some record in her and Daddy's bedroom, but let the needle scratch on the inner paper label after the jazzy, bluesy songs stopped. Daddy would yell that it hurt the needle to do that, go in, turn off the record player. So I learned that if I heard the needle scratching, I should hurry in to turn off the player before Daddy yelled. Sometimes Mama was asleep, but sometimes she was sitting, or lying down, or standing, and just staring. . . .*

I made a small choice, and put the needle at the edge of the record. I wanted to hear what kind of music Mr. Cahill listened to when he worked.

Then I crossed the tiny room, set my book bag down on the floor next to the chaise longue, and sat down on the edge, primly, just like I'd done on my first visit. The bowl of persimmons was still there, but the fruits had ripened, a dark burnt orange color. I smiled, thinking of how I'd reacted the first time I'd tried to eat the green, bitter fruit.

What had Mr. Cahill said? That when ripe, the persimmon turns sweet.

Another small choice: I let my hand drift toward the bowl, pick up a persimmon, just as the music finally started, so softly that I could barely hear it, a slow rhythmic beat just below a solo that might be a flute but that sounded reedier, more hypnotic.

The music made my mouth water, the melody over the beat, lilting yet sure, stirring an ache and a longing within me while it slowly built toward an elusive crescendo. The music changed, grew darker, and then seemed to be flowing into me, making me acutely aware of the tender softness of the persimmon in my hand, as I moved my hand so that the persimmon brushed my lips, my lips tingling, the music building, my lips parting, my teeth teasing the flesh of the persimmon until finally, I took a small bite. The persimmon was firm, yet tenderly sweet.

The music stopped. I came to myself, startling, as if waking from a dream. I had gone from sitting up to stretching out on the chaise longue. The top two buttons of my blouse had popped open. My hands and mouth were slick and sticky from the persimmon, and I'd eaten all of it, except the stem and seeds.

Mr. Cahill was behind his easel, sketching furiously. When had he come in? I didn't remember him entering the room—just being caught up in the music and eating the persimmon. My face burned with shame. I wanted to jump up, run from the room. But I stayed put, as still as I could, even though I was suddenly quivering, while Mr. Cahill finished his sketch.

He looked up, smiled at me a little cautiously, as if he'd seen an aspect that didn't fit the me he already knew. Later in life, I'd thoroughly understand the sort of sensuality that had flamed on my face, but at that moment I could only wonder what I had revealed, eating that persimmon, lost in that music.

I sat up in my primmest pose—shoulders even, back straight, ankles crossed, hands in lap.

"That was *Boléro*," he said, his voice careful and even. "The music."

I smiled and tried to say something light and witty. "Boléro writes a pretty good tune."

The cautious expression dropped from Mr. Cahill's face as he laughed. "The piece is called *Boléro*, dear." He stood up, started toward me. "The composer is Ravel."

By the chaise longue, he held a handkerchief out to me. I wiped my chin, put the stem and seeds in the handkerchief. He looked amused as he took the handkerchief from me, stuffed it back in his pocket. "I guess you figured out that the persimmons are ripe."

"Yes, ripe . . ." A betraying flush blazed up my neck. "I'm sorry—I just remembered—I shouldn't . . . I mean, I ought to go." I jumped up, stumbled.

Mr. Cahill looked confused as he grabbed my arm to steady me. But overwhelmed by what had just transpired— even though I couldn't exactly name what *had* transpired, just that I felt exposed and scared—I stumbled again, right into his chest, and he grabbed my other arm, so that he held me without meaning to, and my face upturned and my lips accidentally brushed his chin. But perhaps not so accidentally. Perhaps the fevered music of Ravel's *Boléro* rose again in my head, overpowered my senses, so that I chose to move my lips toward his. . . .

But Mr. Cahill let go of me, stepped back, a look of horror on his face. I suddenly realized that he wasn't horrified just because I was his student, but because he wasn't attracted to me as a female. I thought about Mrs. Denton's hints of frustration toward Mr. Cahill, Jimmy's revelation about his mother's trip to Japan with Mr. Cahill, Mr. Denton's lack of concern over Mr. Cahill's friendship with his wife. And in a shocked instant, I understood that Mr. Cahill was, as the saying went back in the 1950s, a "confirmed bachelor."

I knew I was supposed to be disgusted by this realization, but instead I was just surprised, and embarrassed by my action, a mistake in so many ways. Meanwhile, Mr. Cahill's mouth gaped as he looked for the right words to turn our awkward situation back into something ordinary and safe.

It was too late for that, though. I pushed past him and ran down the stairs, intending to run straight through the living room and kitchen and out the back door, never to return. But in my shameful haste I stumbled at the bottom of the stairs, and came to a full stop just at his living room pane window. At first I saw nothing in the world around me, my mind's eye a gray whirlwind, and then, all too clearly, Will, across the street, sprawled on the ground, his bike over him.

He wasn't moving. His afternoon newspapers were scattered around him.

Without thinking of anything except the need to get to my brother, spurred by the same urge that had propelled me out our own front door and down the steps to his still body on that first small-choice morning just before I met MayJune, and Trusty, and Jimmy, before I had my secret job interview with Mr. Cahill, I rushed out Mr. Cahill's front door and across the street to Will.

By the time I got to Will, he was struggling to stand up, batting away my hands as I reached to swipe away the dirt on his face, to examine his scraped elbows and knees.

"Will, what happened?" I was nearly gasping for air as I asked the question.

"Hit a rock. Tumbled," he said. "That's all. I'm fine."

I sank to my knees, relief flooding me, as Will righted his bike, put down the kickstand, then started putting the rolled-up afternoon newspapers back in his burlap carrier sack.

"Wait—what are you doing here?" I asked.

"Remember, I told you I was taking on an afternoon route? To save up to go see my land in Alaska?" Will looked at me, his face a mix of hurt that I'd forgotten and excitement at the prospect of his new goal. Then he looked confused. "But . . . what are *you* doing here?"

"I was, I was just—" I stopped, my mouth gaping, as I finally took in the whole scene.

Will, with his perfectly innocent and understandable explanation for his presence in Mr. Cahill's and Grandma's neighborhood, staring at me.

Several neighbors, out on this fine early October afternoon to do a bit of yard work, or sit on front porches with the newspapers Will had just delivered, staring at me.

Mr. Cahill, standing on his front porch, in his paint-stained undershirt and bare feet and wild hair, holding my book bag, staring across the street at me . . . but, no, not at me. He was frozen on his front porch, staring at the red car parked in front of his house.

Jimmy's car.

Jimmy, in the driver's seat, the look of hurt and betrayal on his face unmistakable, even from a distance through the car window, staring at me.

Next to him, in the passenger's seat, leaning forward so that I could see his face, too, Hank—grinning. Triumphant. Pleased.

Suddenly, I was all too conscious of how sweaty I was, the messiness of my usually neat, ponytailed hair, and—worst of all—the top two buttons undone on my blouse.

Will took off again on his bicycle, whistling the theme song from *Sergeant Striker and the Alaskan Wild*, seemingly oblivious to the tension around him, even waving at Jimmy.

I hurried across the street toward Jimmy's car, fumbling my buttons closed. He opened his door, and I had to jump back to avoid getting smacked as he got out.

"Nothing happened," I whispered, looking up at him.

Mr. Cahill walked over, held my book bag out to me, and I took it.

"Jimmy—" he started.

"No!" Jimmy snapped. "Do not talk to me right now!"

Even as his face contorted with anger, Mr. Cahill looked at me and said, "I would be glad to give you a ride home, if you need it."

My mouth gaped. I finally found my voice and spoke aloud my small choice in a creaky half whisper: "No. Jimmy will give me a ride. Won't you, Jimmy?"

"Of course," he said grimly.

"Good luck, Donna," Mr. Cahill said sorrowfully. He turned and walked back into his house, careful to shut the door quietly behind him.

I looked at Jimmy, my eyes pleading, willing the stone set of his jaw to relax. "Nothing happened," I said in another ragged half whisper, although I wished I could find the strength to shout it for him.

"Oh, yeah? Then ask her to explain *this*!" Hank jumped out of the car and shoved a piece of paper at me. I took it in my trembling hands, blinking back tears that blurred my vision. I nearly retched when I recognized what it was: the sketch I'd done of a nude girl on a chaise longue. The sketch I'd been terrified would be found last week in art class, the day that the air raid drill siren had gone off. The sketch I'd stuffed in the trash can, right after Babs gave me a bottle of Dexamyl.

I looked up at Hank, and he laughed at my confused, questioning expression. "Lisa Kablinski gave it to me. I've been trying to convince Jimmy of what's been going on, ever since. But he wouldn't believe me. Then today, he went to the library, wanted to surprise you, was surprised himself when you weren't there." Hank's mouth turned up into a sneer. "That's when I showed him this, told him he might want to look into what you've really been studying."

"That's not true! Nothing happened!" I looked at Jimmy. "You have to believe me! I was just doing some housekeeping, some modeling—but never . . . never like that." I gestured at my sketch, which now seemed like something from one of the men's magazines Babs told me her father thought her mother didn't know about, which he hid under their guest room's bed.

"Whore," Hank hissed. "Just like your mother."

"Shut up!" I said. "How dare you speak of my mother that way!" Hot, furious tears streamed down my face. Somewhere in the back of my mind a voice whispered, *He's still angry.* Angry that Mr. Cahill got him to say how Ansel Adams's photography made him wish he could go somewhere, someday, other than *here*, when he's supposed to be the big football star around town, the current pride of Groverton.

"Oh, I'm just repeating what I hear the women of town

say. That sure, it's a shame your mama got so sick and died, but before that, it was also a shame that a whore like that snagged an upstanding man like your dad—well, he *was* upstanding. Now he's the town drunk, and you're nothing more than a whore and Jimmy here—"

Jimmy unfroze and socked Hank in the nose, sending blood spurting down his face. Hank stumbled back, shocked, and put his fingers to his nose. "What the hell . . . why . . . ?"

"Walk away, Hank," Jimmy said. "Just walk home."

Hank started to protest, but then turned, stalking away, mumbling to himself.

For just a moment, I thought all might be saved. Jimmy would understand what had happened—and what hadn't happened. I'd be forgiven. Maybe, even, I could study with Mr. Cahill after all. . . .

But my heart felt like I'd been stabbed when Jimmy looked back at me. His face was as still as stone, his eyes glinting with anger and betrayal.

"Nothing happened," I said yet again. "It's not like that. . . . Mr. Cahill isn't like that. . . . He's not interested in me—"

I stopped, my hand flying to my mouth. I might understand that Mr. Cahill was a confirmed bachelor, but I realized Jimmy wouldn't.

And, after all, I hadn't said that I wasn't interested in Mr. Cahill. I could see from Jimmy's crushed expression that he understood, if nothing else, that if there had been any return interest, I would have eagerly, willingly responded.

"Jimmy," I said, tears suddenly falling down my face. "Jimmy, I—I'm sorry. . . ."

"Get in the car," he said. "The neighbors have had enough of a scene to keep them talking for weeks." It was the harshest thing he'd ever said to me.

I did as he asked, miserably holding my book bag, trying to explain between sobs and hiccups that my modeling had been purely innocent, that I hadn't ever been unclothed, that I had only modeled and cleaned house a few times, and just because I wanted to save money for leaving Groverton at the end of my senior year, for traveling to New York, to become a seamstress. I explained how Mr. Cahill had been reluctant to let me work for him, how just that afternoon he'd insisted he would only let me keep working for him if my father agreed.

All the way home, Jimmy said nothing. Finally, I was out of things to say, too.

At my house, he turned to me. "I'm sorry," he said, "but I just can't . . . we can't go out anymore."

He turned, hands gripping his steering wheel, staring straight ahead, waiting for me to get out of his car.

Chapter 17

The next morning, Daddy was at the kitchen table, reading the newspaper. Coffee steamed in a cup. A plate held a half-eaten piece of burned toast. The smell was a bitter reminder of the day I'd met Jimmy.

The afternoon before, after Jimmy had dropped me off at my house like a sack of trash he couldn't wait to dispose of, I'd made a plate of peanut butter and jelly sandwiches and put them out on the kitchen table for dinner for Daddy and Will. Then I'd gone to my room and cried myself to sleep.

"Come sit down, Donna," Daddy said.

His voice was even, steady, and his calm command scared me more than any drunken rant.

I tried to compose myself by squinting my blurry eyes until I could make out the headlines on the front page of the *Groverton Daily News*—MCCARTHY CONTINUES ARMY SIGNAL CORPS INVESTIGATION—ALLEGES SPY RING LED BY JEWISH ENGINEERS—and below that, FIRST CHURCH OF CHRIST PIE SALE SETS RECORD. But then Daddy lowered the newspaper to the table and looked at me.

I didn't expect to see that his eyes were red and puffy too. Another bender, I thought. But no. He'd been crying.

For a selfish second, I thought, *He's crying because I've so shamed the family.*

His first words seemed to confirm it: "Word travels fast in this town." But then he went on. "It's not in the newspaper yet, but Frederick McDonnell was found dead last night."

It took a second for me to make the connection. Daddy meant Strange Freddie. It was the news of his death that had moved my father, at last, to tears.

"Why—how—" I stuttered.

Daddy shook his head. "No one will know for sure. He was found just outside of town, along the road. Looked like he'd been beaten. But who knows if it was a routine fight? Or because some union men got word of Freddie letting it slip to the boss's son that Local Eighty-three was planning to expand and then join with the other locals to strike."

Of course, I thought. *Daddy was management. He'd blame the union men.* I had a different view of "management" since working for Grandma.

Then he muttered angrily, "More likely, it's old management tricks, bringing in thugs to scare people, send a warning, and things went too far." He shook his head. "Things are about to get ugly in this town," he said. "We'll never know the exact circumstances of Mr. McDonnell's death, but one thing is certain: It will frighten some, anger others, and I can't see how a strike will be avoided."

My eyes pricked, hearing Daddy call Strange Freddie by his proper name just like Jimmy had. Daddy mistook my expression. "Ah, but you have troubles of your own, don't you?"

Daddy was right, I thought. Word traveled fast in Groverton.

"Donna, baby girl, there is no man—or boy—worth your tears if he purposefully makes you cry."

I stared at my father, even more stunned than I'd been by his news about Mr. McDonnell. I looked for something, anything, I could say . . . but the gulf between us was just too great.

"Your grandmother needs you back at the café," he said in a tone that now offered no sympathy, no opening for discussion.

He lifted the newspaper back up.

That was my punishment, then. I was being sent back to work for Grandma, supposedly to help our household, but really so that she could torment me.

I stood up, moved to the counter, and began fixing French toast for Will.

Later that Saturday night, Grandma stopped me as I came out the swinging doors at Dot's Corner Café, nearly knocking the blue plate specials—turkey hotshots, green beans, applesauce, roll and butter—from my hands.

"What do you think you're doing?" she snapped, her face a tight clot of tension.

"Taking Mr. and Mrs. Leis their dinners," I said. I'd arrived at work just ten minutes before, while Grandma was still in her tiny office in the back.

I looked past Grandma to the dining room. Mr. Leis was again busy with the Dutch boy and girl salt and pepper shakers, while Mrs. Leis smiled and waved at me. She had been happy to see me, said she'd missed me.

"I was reluctant to bring you back," Grandma said, "but

your father begged me to so I can keep an eye on you while the poor man works himself to an early grave for you and Will."

I wanted to interrupt and say, *You mean while he goes to AA meetings with Miss Bettina so he won't drink himself to an early grave.* Even though Grandma knew that Ace Hardware closed promptly at six o'clock, she always referred to Daddy's evening activities as "working." She could no more admit that he was going to AA than she had admitted he was drinking before that.

But of course I didn't say any such thing. I said, "Ma'am, Mr. and Mrs. Leis's dinners are going to get cold if I don't take them—"

Grandma snatched the plates from me. "I will take their dinners! Your scandalous behavior is not going to cost me business. Go back to the kitchen."

She put a big, fake smile on her face, turned, and headed to the Leises' table.

I stood in the kitchen, trembling, annoyed because if I couldn't wait on tables, I couldn't hold back a little tip money. I was planning more than ever my escape from Groverton as soon as I graduated high school. I wasn't even sure I wanted to wait that long. My long night of crying over Jimmy—and over Mr. Cahill—had also included bouts of anger, when I'd counted and recounted the money I'd saved, nearly seventy dollars. I figured if I could get to about two hundred by the end of my senior year, I'd have more than enough to buy a one-way Greyhound ticket to New York, find a boarding room, cover cheap sandwiches and bus fares while I went looking for seamstress work. . . .

I hadn't seen Miss Bettina since the previous day's drama. Maybe she would give me extra work if I wasn't going to get tips at Grandma's café. I had to believe some of Daddy's new, softer attitude came from her.

My eyes started to fill again, as I wondered how disappointed Miss Bettina might be in me. It didn't matter that nothing had really happened between me and Mr. Cahill; by now, with Hank's big mouth, the whole town thought it had.

Grandma came back into the kitchen, the smile falling away from her face as soon as the doors closed behind her. She reached up and plucked the cap off my head. "Ralph, you can wear Donna's hat."

She walked over to Ralph and held the cap out to him. He stared at her, gaping.

"You've said for years you'd like to be a waiter. Well, here's your chance. I'll train you."

"But—the dishes—"

"That's Donna's new job."

Ralph looked at me, pain in his eyes.

I nodded. *It's OK.*

He said, "Well, just let me see if there are some dishwashing gloves for Donna—"

"No need for that!" Grandma snapped. "You don't use them."

"But, she's a young girl, and the water is—"

"Not hot enough!" Grandma turned the tap all the way over to hot. Ralph jerked his hands out.

I went over to the sink. I nodded again at Ralph, who turned his eyes from me. *For just a little while longer,* I told myself, *until I have the money to leave, keep the peace.* I plunged my bare hands and arms into the sink, biting back the urge to cry out as the hot water scalded me for my sins.

By the time Dot's Corner Café finally closed that night, my hands and forearms burned with pain from the hot water. I yearned to get home, to carefully slather Jergens lotion over my red skin.

But Grandma found me, grabbed my arm, her nails digging into my tender skin, and said, "I guess you won't need to buy that homecoming dress now!"

Of course. She wanted her twenty dollars back, now that I obviously wouldn't be going to homecoming with Jimmy.

My response was automatic: "I've already bought cloth and supplies to make the dress, and cut up the cloth. I can't return it." I smiled.

My victory was short-lived.

"Fine," she said. "I'll just let your father know that I need to hold your pay until you've earned the twenty dollars back."

It had finally turned cold, a swift rain pummeling me on my walk home. Inside our house, I shed my raincoat and hung it on the coat tree. I walked as quietly as I could up the stairs, longing for the warmth of my bed. Of course, the third step from the bottom creaked. Still, I tiptoed past Will's room but stopped as I heard his voice call my name. I pressed my eyes shut and thought about going on past, but he called again.

I went in. He sat cross-legged on his bed, fussing with

something inside his Alaska diorama. He held it out to me. "Hey, Donna, guess what? I've added one of the Matchbox cars I got the other day for my birthday, and some people— that's me, and you, and Jimmy—" He stopped, a look of worry coming over his freckled face. "What's the matter? Did you have a crappy date with Jimmy?" Then he waggled his eyebrows and grinned, the boyish tease in him coming back. "Did he try to get to second base?"

I grabbed the diorama from him, holding either end like I was holding an accordion. "No," I said. "Jimmy and I broke up." I sounded hateful, even to myself, but I went on. "I guess the news didn't make it down to your little set of friends just yet."

Will looked hurt and confused. "You're not going steady with Jimmy now? But—why?"

And even in my little brother's voice I heard—or thought I did—that he suspected the breakup must be my fault, that somehow I was to blame, and all the anger I'd pushed down came welling up in me, and my hateful voice went on: "Because, Will. Your big sister is a whore. That's what every-one thinks, anyway. Including Jimmy. And guess what else, Will?" I was pressing too hard on either end of the shoe box, but I couldn't get my hands to stop, couldn't let go, couldn't get myself to shut up, even though by then Will was staring at my hands and arms, fear on his face, saying, "Donna, stop, don't say that; Donna, your arms, what hap-pened to your arms and hands?" while I said at the same time, "Guess what, Will? You're not going to Alaska. I'm not going. Trusty isn't going. Dreams don't come true for people like us, Will."

Suddenly, the shoe box diorama crumpled between my

hands, just like an accordion, but of course it didn't make a sound like a chord or like music, just made a crunching sound, like air whooshing out, at the same time that Will's eyes widened and his mouth opened as if he wanted to scream. But like Trusty, he'd been struck mute.

Chapter 18

The following Friday night, October 9, while Daddy and Miss Bettina were at an AA meeting and Will was at Tony's to watch the next episode of *Sergeant Striker and the Alaskan Wild* and then spend the night, I went down to the basement to finish my homecoming dress.

Of course, I knew that I wasn't going—not with Jimmy, not with anyone, not even in a group of friends or by myself.

Earlier that week, the first day back at school after my breakup with Jimmy had been painful, although Jimmy was the only kind soul, saying hello to me, making it clear to everyone that I was not to be pestered. And other than judging looks, I wasn't. I was left utterly alone. Even Babs avoided me and my teachers didn't call on me as they normally would have.

By art class, I wanted to break out of my own skin, run away from being Donna Lane, somehow ostracize myself from *me*. If I could have willed my chest to crack open and release my soul to fly away, I believe I would have.

But Principal Stodgill waited for us in the classroom. He announced that Mr. Cahill had resigned and left town but had left behind a letter that he requested the principal read to his art class: "Dear students—as you may know, I have written several letters to the editor of the *Groverton Daily News* in which I expressed my concern about our current political climate, in which the persecution of those with different ideas—or even the hint of ideas contrary to what our fine government would have you believe is the norm—is deemed appropriate and patriotic. I have been told by your school board that I must refrain from expressing my views, either in the newspaper or in person, if I am to retain my position as your art teacher. I cannot continue to serve under these terms, and so have tendered my resignation. I am moving to New York, where I will pursue completing several projects for submission to an important art show. Should my work be accepted, this will be a dream come true. I hope that I have taught you enough about art and expressing yourself that you will all continue to think about your own dreams, and pursue them. Sincerely, Mr. Cahill."

At first, my classmates tittered with laughter. Such formal phrasing sounded funny delivered in Principal Stodgill's dull, wispy voice. But then the class became quiet; those same words and phrases would have sounded so eloquent, so *right*, delivered in Mr. Cahill's voice. But he wasn't here. He was gone.

Whatever his letter said, everyone, thanks to Hank, knew why.

Everyone turned and looked at me, suddenly angry and sad. The most interesting teacher most of us had ever had was gone, and it was my fault.

Principal Stodgill called out our seventh-period reassignments; I was relegated to home ec, where I'd have to make fussy little tea towels. At least school was a little better than work at Miss Bettina's Dress Shop, where women gave me disapproving stares, or at Dot's Corner Café, where I kept dishwashing. At home, Will wouldn't speak to me because of what I'd done to his diorama, but Monday afternoon, he came home from school with a black eye, explained when Mrs. Baker came to our house to complain that he had fought with her little Howard when Howard had called me a hussy. Daddy simply listened, nodded quietly, and shut the door (with Mrs. Baker still talking). I was so relieved that I nearly cried when Daddy didn't whip Will but simply sent him to his room without supper. The next morning, when a box of Playtex rubber dishwashing gloves appeared at my place at the kitchen table—a gift from Daddy—I cried after all.

And then attention turned away from me. On Wednesday, the locals of United Paperworkers International Union at Groverton Pulp & Paper joined together to strike for better safety measures.

I found guilty relief in my sudden obscurity, even though I, too, was caught up in the tension the strike had suddenly spread over the town, as thick as the sulfur stink that spewed from the smokestacks. I'd never seen Groverton so divided, its social niceties cracked open, the underpinnings of fear and resentment laid bare.

Still, my personal drama hadn't ended. Where I had been annoyed that Will called me into his room night after night, I now missed that. I missed talking with him and fussing over him.

I missed Jimmy. I missed talking and laughing with him. I missed his touch.

And I missed Mr. Cahill. I missed art class and cleaning

his messy kitchen and his lectures about my potential. I also yearned for what I knew I had missed out on, his guidance about my designing.

On Thursday afternoon, Miss Bettina looked at me sadly as I was leaving to go to Grandma's diner and said if I ever needed to talk, she'd be glad to listen.

I nodded silently. I had said so little all week that I thought perhaps I'd go mute, like Trusty. I finally understood how the spirit could have been beaten out of the big dog to the point that he no longer bothered to make a sound.

Late Friday night, after getting home from the café, I slipped down to the basement, unable to resist the solace of working on my homecoming dress. In the basement, I turned on the bare bulb light. I opened one of the suitcases, which now just held the dress I was working on. I remembered that when I first counted them, years ago, there had been thirty-eight pieces.

Thirty-eight—it struck me for the first time that Mama would now be thirty-eight years old if she'd lived. She'd been so young, compared with Daddy, when they married. . . .

That thought made me stop, go still, and in the complete silence, I thought I heard something behind me.

I pulled my scissors from the suitcase where I stored my sewing supplies, my hand closing around the handle like I was holding the hilt of a knife, and I tried to go still again, even holding my breath.

In that complete silence, I realized that I didn't *hear* anything, but somehow I *felt* sound, like a low vibration, and my skin went cold, the hairs on my arms lifting, my scalp tingling, my throat tightening. Then I had to breathe again, and with my next sharp inhale I smelled something fecal and foul. I held the scissors tight and high, like a dagger, my hand shaking, and turned slowly, preparing to face a hidden attacker. That week Daddy had filled the void of Mr. Cahill's riles-town-but-sells-newspapers letters to the editor with crisply worded letters of his own, but his were in support of the union's demands for better safety, even citing safety concerns from his management days and his regret over not taking Mr. Frederick McDonnell's complaints more seriously. We'd received nastily threatening anonymous letters, and a man from Tangy Town—one of the perpetually unemployed who, Daddy said, management sometimes quietly hired as threatening thugs—even came into Ace Hardware and punched Daddy, cutting his face and bruising his eye. I couldn't find a way to say it to Daddy directly, but for the first time I could recall, I was proud of him.

So I had reason to fear the possibility of some madman in our basement.

Instead, I faced a mad dog.

The no-name dog from Stedman's Scrapyard.

Trusty.

The dog looked even mangier than before, with gashes in his paws and scrappy fur, his ribs prominently sticking out. He snapped and snarled mutely.

Strings of drool hung from his jaws. The dog's coat looked like a matted old fur rug thrown over a rack of shaky bones, but his teeth and jaws still glinted and snapped with enough strength to rip into me. I put down the scissors. They'd be no defense against those teeth. But I wasn't sure what to do—grab the old dress form in the corner and throw it at him? Try to dash past him to the stairs?

Suddenly Trusty lunged at me, snapping and snarling, and I threw everything I could grab at him—the scissors, spools of thread, a pin cushion—which slowed him down but didn't stop him, and I ran to the dress form, desperately using it as a shield, and then I heard Will screaming, "Trusty! Trusty!" and suddenly Will was there, throwing his body over Trusty's, and I was no longer frightened for me, but instead terrified for Will, and I rushed to him with no real plan except to grab the dog by its loose, ratty fur and pull it away from him.

But in the few seconds it took for me to get to them, Trusty had calmed to panting. Will, who was hugging the dog, murmured, "Trusty, it's OK, it's OK."

Then they both stared up at me.

"Will," I said as calmly as I could, "get away from that dog. It's wild and crazed and—"

"No," he said. "Trusty would never hurt me. He's just hurt himself, and scared. That's why I had to bring him here."

I studied the dog, how he pressed close against Will. I had to admit that while my safety might be in danger, Will was right. Trusty would never harm him, would only protect him.

"What happened to him?" I asked.

"Mr. Stedman realized he could get away with beating Trusty after all."

At first, this didn't make any sense to me, but then I realized—of course. Jimmy had told Mr. Stedman to leave the dog alone. But Jimmy and I had broken up. I . . . my family . . . my family's interests, including this dog, were no longer under the protection of the son of the new president of Groverton Pulp & Paper, especially with Daddy writing pro-union letters.

I shook my head. I was sorry for Trusty. But I could not—would not—take that blame. Trusty's condition was the fault of an angry, mean, small man. And I wouldn't be making things better for us if we kept his dog.

"We can't keep Trusty here," I said. "Sooner or later Daddy will find out—"

"I'm not taking Trusty back to Mr. Stedman," Will said, his voice thick, his eyes brimming with tears. "He'll die from another beating like this one!"

I looked at the dog. I knew he couldn't live much longer in that condition, even without another beating. "How, and when, did you get him here?"

"Just tonight."

"You said you were going to Tony's to watch your show and spend the night."

Will stuck out his chin. "Yeah. That's what I said. But I didn't. I went and got Trusty and told him to stay down here. I figured you'd just go on to bed like you always do, and not stop by my room, after you got home."

My heart clenched when he said the part about me not stopping by his room, and then, ridiculously, clenched further when I realized that he had missed *Sergeant Striker and the Alaskan Wild* to go rescue his own Trusty. After all we'd been through this past week, *that* realization made me tear up.

I blinked back my tears, though, as Will stared past me at the open suitcases and said, "Donna, what have you been doing?"

"Never mind that," I snapped. "You're in big trouble if Daddy finds out you stole Mr. Stedman's dog. You got off lucky when Mrs. Baker came over."

"I only punched Howard because of mean things he said about you," Will said.

My heart cracked at the thought of my little brother, whom I'd always taken care of, having to defend me, but I gave Will a stern look. "We have time to get Trusty back over to Stedman's. Maybe he hasn't noticed the dog is gone—"

"No! I will run away with Trusty to Alaska, which is where he belongs!"

"Don't be ridiculous," I said, and started to move toward Will. Trusty immediately lunged and snarled at me. I jumped back. Clearly, I wasn't going to be able to persuade Will to return the dog, and I wasn't going to be able to take Trusty back myself.

I sighed. "Look, Trusty needs help or he's going to die. I guess we could take him out to the country vet—" I stopped. How could we get that far without a car?

And then I thought of Mama's old car, in the garage.

"I will drive us!" I said. "In Mama's old car!"

"That'll work?"

I wasn't thinking as clearly as I should have, so I said, "Why not? Jimmy taught me to drive. The keys are probably in the glove compartment or under the floor mat."

"Not to the country vet, though," Will said.

"What? Why not? Where else—"

"We can't trust anyone not to call Mr. Stedman! Except MayJune. We could take Trusty to MayJune's!"

I started to protest, but then I thought, why not? If we could get the dog there, then he would be off our hands. Mr. Stedman wouldn't think to look there. Our house was the first place he'd come when he realized his mute dog was missing.

"Well, come on, then," I said.

But when Trusty tried to stand, his front right leg buckled. I looked down. His paw was a bloody mess, like it had been mangled on some piece of junk at the scrapyard. I could just imagine the poor animal trying to run away from Mr. Stedman's blows and cutting his paw.

Anger rose within me. That awful man. I looked at Will. "Can you keep Trusty calm enough for me to bandage his paw?"

He stared down at the paw, tears finally spilling over and running down his cheek. "I felt so bad, making him walk on that paw to get here."

I kept an eye on the dog but put my hand on Will's shoulder. Trusty looked at me warily. "It's OK, Will. You did the best you could." Another surge of anger rose within me at the injustice of Trusty's fate. "You did the right thing."

Will stroked Trusty and said, "See? She's not that bad. Let her help us. . . ."

He kept murmuring like that the whole time I tended to Trusty, my heart pounding while I swallowed back gags at the dog's awful smell. I wrapped his paw in a scrap of bright yellow cloth left over from the dress I'd remade to meet Jimmy's parents.

By the time I was done, Trusty was panting, his eyes closed.

If we didn't hurry, the dog was going to die in Will's arms. Still, a tiny sliver of hope broke through. Maybe MayJune really would know how to help Trusty.

"Come on," I said. "Let's help Trusty up the stairs."

Chapter 19

Of course, I couldn't get Mama's car to start.

In my rush to get Trusty over to MayJune's, I didn't think about all the reasons why a car that had sat idle for seven years under a stupidly cheerful red barn and yellow duck tablecloth would not start. While Will gently urged Trusty through the kitchen and breezeway, I rushed out to the garage, whipped off the tablecloth, and tossed it in the backseat, then pushed up the garage door. I checked the glove compartment and found, miraculously, the car key. For the few seconds before I put the key in the ignition, I felt a giddy relief that this would all work out easily, simply.

But the car only made a clicking sound when I turned the key. Still, I turned it, over and over. Maybe, I thought desperately, the car just needed new oil. I got out of the car to see if there was a spare can in the trunk or on a shelf. Then I remembered, from all the times I'd put mousetraps under the car, that the tires were flat.

I popped the trunk anyway. If I could just get the car started, get it to Sterry Oil, surely someone like the cheery Sterry Oil man from the cover of Jimmy's atlas—or at least grumpy old Mr. Phibbs—would put air in the tires, put in oil and gas.

There was no oil in the trunk.

I slammed it shut, got back in the car, and tried starting it again. Click, click. Maybe, I thought, I could put the car in neutral, push it out of the garage and onto the street, and then roll most of the way to Sterry Oil.

I kept turning the key, but there was, of course, no starting the car. (Later, I'd know enough about cars to realize that the battery was dead.) Finally, I gave up, put my head on my hands on the steering wheel, fought back tears, tried to convince myself that we could make a sling out of the tablecloth, somehow get Trusty in it, and between the two of us manage to walk, with Trusty in the sling between us, over to MayJune's house.

"Donna."

Jimmy's warm voice, wrapping around and through me. I thought I was dreaming.

"Donna, Will called me. I'm taking him and Trusty to MayJune's."

I didn't move, suddenly angry and shamed that Will had realized I couldn't help him after all, that he had called Jimmy, of all people.

Who else should he have called?

My anger and shame gave way to fear—how had Will phrased things on the telephone? Who might have heard him on our party line?

"Donna, you can just sit there or get up and come with us."

"I'm not letting you take Will anywhere," I said.

"And I'm not letting Will down just because you're stubborn."

He turned and walked out to our driveway. I jumped out of the car, ready to shout at him that he had no right to call me stubborn, that he hadn't really listened or been forgiving.

But he had, as much as he could. And I saw Will already in the front seat of Jimmy's car, holding Trusty.

I was shaking violently, from tension but also because of the early October cold. I grabbed the ridiculous red barn and yellow duck tablecloth from the backseat of Mama's convertible and ran out to Jimmy's car. At least I could wrap Trusty in the tablecloth and keep his blood and fur from getting on Jimmy's upholstery. Somehow, seeing him come to our rescue—just like a hero from one of Babs's lusty novels—didn't please me. It infuriated me; I did not want to be beholden to Jimmy.

MayJune opened the front door to her Tangy Town bungalow even before I finished knocking. Her expression was solemn, but welcoming, as if she'd anticipated us, but Will hadn't said anything about calling her. He'd just trusted that she'd be home, willing and ready to help.

And he was right. MayJune nodded as Will said, "Trusty's hurt real bad!" and turned and walked through her house, expecting us to follow, which we did, passing through a very tiny and tidy front room and into her kitchen, where a copper kettle on an old gas stove was starting to hum. She walked out to a screened back porch.

On the porch was a picnic table covered in drying leaves and grasses and flowers. MayJune pointed to a corner near the table and said to Jimmy, "Put Trusty right there."

As Jimmy knelt slowly, carefully, with Will hovering

beside him, I saw with a start that there was a quilt, already folded into a small pallet, in the corner. Will sat on the porch floor next to Trusty, who had gone from panting to slow, labored breaths, his eyes squeezed shut. I couldn't imagine that the dog would live, and I wanted to spare Will the pain of seeing him die—and the danger of the dog possibly lashing out in a last-minute protest against death.

"Will, we should go—" I started.

But MayJune gave me a sharp look. "Come with me," she said. "Will's fine out here with Jimmy and Trusty."

Jimmy had sat down on the floor next to them. I wasn't going to get him and Will away from the dog.

MayJune had already started back to her kitchen, and I followed her. She moved swiftly, gathering up items, disappearing briefly somewhere else in the house, coming back with other objects, all the while giving me orders, but not like Grandma did, not in a mean, threatening way. MayJune simply knew what she was doing and expected me to follow her instructions, and so I did, getting various canning jars of home-dried herbs from a cabinet, MayJune rattling off the names of the ones she wanted me to get down: chamomile, comfrey, lavender. I did as she said, putting two heaping teaspoons of each herb in its own bowl, then pinching the herbs into powder between my fingertips. The display of flowers and grasses and herbs on her back porch no longer seemed odd; I realized that MayJune was a healer, growing and preserving herbs for home remedies that she no doubt administered to the people of Tangy Town, who wouldn't find it so easy to get help from a doctor as those of us on the other side of the river.

Finally, she examined my work, putting her face down to each bowl, taking a small sniff, and then nodding, satisfied. She poured a bit of the hot water from the kettle over the crushed herbs, then spooned some of the chamomile back into the kettle, which she returned to the stove. Then she filled a cup with cold water from the kitchen sink, and drizzled each bowl of crushed herbs with a bit of it, just until they stopped steaming.

"It's a poultice," MayJune explained. "The herbs are healing, and they'll draw out the infection of Trusty's wounds."

I followed her out to the porch. MayJune knelt slowly next to Jimmy and Will and Trusty. "Ach—my old joints aren't what they used to be."

"Should I keep talking and humming to him?" Will asked, his voice strained with worry.

"Yes, and stroke his head," MayJune said, "but be careful. He might snap when I put the cider vinegar on his paws." She carefully removed the strip of cloth I'd wrapped around Trusty's paw.

"Maybe you should come over by me, Will."

"He'll be fine," MayJune said. "Will knows to be careful." Jimmy stood, came over beside me, put his arm around me. I didn't pull away, but I didn't move toward him, either. I crossed my arms. He kept his arm around me anyway.

I strained to hear Will's low hum. I should have recognized it—I knew I'd heard it before—but I couldn't quite place it.

MayJune opened a bottle. "Cider vinegar," she said. "To disinfect Trusty's wounds." She glanced at me as she poured the vinegar on a washcloth. "You did a good job binding his paw, but his wounds were already starting to get infected."

Trusty startled and then mouthed mute yelps as May-June pressed the vinegar-soaked cloth to his wounds. Then MayJune scooped the poultice onto them, one by one, rebinding them with fresh strips of cloth from a cut-up sheet while Will kept humming.

She stopped about halfway through, out of breath, her forehead glistening with sweat, and looked at me. "Donna, go pour the chamomile tea in the kettle into four separate cups. Then pour what's left of the tea into a bowl with water, and bring the bowl with a spoon out here. The watered-down tea is for Trusty."

"We're having the same tea as the dog?" Jimmy asked.

MayJune smiled. "Chamomile is a safe herb. It calms upset stomachs and nerves—I think we can all use that. Trusty is dehydrated, so he needs water, but a bit of the chamomile will settle his system so he can eat a bit, too."

When I came back out with the bowl of watered-down tea and the spoon, MayJune was sitting next to Jimmy on a yellow glider rocker, and Will was still sitting on the floor next to Trusty, humming, MayJune singing along with him:

All through the night there's a little brown bird singing
Singing in the hush of the darkness and the dew.
Would that his song through the stillness could go winging,
Could go winging to you,
To you . . .

The bowl and spoon fell from my hands as I recognized the words and the memory came back to me in a flash: Mama had sung that to us, as a lullaby.

"I don't understand. How can Will remember Mama singing that song—the melody, at least—but I can't?"

"He's younger'n you," MayJune said, then took a sip of her chamomile tea. She sat in a rocker by the fireplace. "So he's closer to his earliest memories."

I glanced at Jimmy, on the opposite end of the wooly red couch from me, the space of the worn cushion between us summing up the awkwardness of us being around each other, now that the drama of Trusty's injuries seemed to have passed.

I looked back at MayJune. "But Will was just four when Mama died," I insisted. He was out on the porch with Trusty, spooning watered-down chamomile tea to Trusty from a new bowl. "I would have been ten—just shy of Will's age now! How can he remember? Why don't I?"

MayJune gave me a sympathetic look that made me stare down into my mug. I didn't want sympathy—I just wanted to *understand*. "You've had so much on your mind, honey, so much to take care of, since your mama died."

To my dismay, my eyes welled up with tears. I blinked them back, but some moisture still crept out of the corners of my eyes. "But I should remember more than just . . . just snatches of things. And then there are things I've found that don't make sense with what I do know about her life."

I stopped, suddenly worried about saying too much. The sense that talking about Mama was taboo came over me again, but then I thought, *Grandma and Daddy and Miss Bettina aren't here*. Will was out on the porch. And what could I say in front of Jimmy that would make him feel worse about me than his feeling of betrayal over me and Mr. Cahill?

"I found Mama's old clothes—clothes that must be from before she became our mother—in our basement," I said quietly. "Packed away with mothballs in suitcases. They're all so elegant. Outfits for a fine lady. And there were costumes, as if for someone in a stage show. But it doesn't make sense. Daddy must have kept those clothes after she died— but why?" I paused. Then again, why would he keep her car? The house with the exact same furniture and appliances as right before she died? We'd grown up living in a shrine to our long-lost mama, Will and I. "But from what little I do remember of her, she wore dowdy housedresses, or robes, and—"

I stuttered to a stop, looked up at MayJune, ready to apologize. MayJune, after all, was wearing a dowdy housedress, a pale green with a faded pink floral print. But she didn't seem to mind my comment at all. Instead, she smiled as she put her cup of tea on a small side table, grasped the arms of her rocker, and pulled herself up to stand, then hobbled slowly, with that hitch in her left hip, over to a china cabinet that was squeezed into the space to the right of her fireplace.

She carefully knelt, mindful of her creaking knees, opened a drawer meant to hold napkins and silver, and then stood as upright as she could, holding a scrapbook. I stood, taking a few steps to meet her. MayJune handed me the scrapbook, then collapsed back in her rocker, her weight tipping it against the wall. All of the hustle she'd had upon our arrival was gone.

I sat back down on my end of the red couch. Jimmy glanced over, curious. I ran my hand over the worn, dark blue leather cover of the scrapbook.

"Go to the middle," MayJune said. I carefully opened the scrapbook. There were photos of people I didn't recognize, clippings from the *Groverton Daily News*: obituaries, birth announcements, an occasional article. MayJune saw my look of confusion and added, "Keep going, another page or two."

Slow understanding showed on my face. MayJune sighed with satisfaction. "There," she said. She picked up her cup from the side table and took a long sip of tea.

I stared at the photos of a young woman, painfully beautiful, a firm set to her jaw, but something uncertain in her smile, something sad about her wide eyes. I wondered what color those eyes were. In all the poses, she was onstage, singing behind a microphone, wearing dresses with too many ruffles, or with feathers, or boa trim.

The photos were sepia, so the dresses were, too, and it was hard to tell type of fabric or trim details like sequins, but still, my heart clenched as I thought, *I recognize that dress . . . but I can't recognize that dress. . . .*

Jimmy, overcome by curiosity, had scooted over beside me. He gently tapped his finger next to a photo that focused most closely on the young woman's face. "Is that your mother?"

"What are you talking about? Mama was never a singer, she was—" I stopped. Yes, Mama had been a singer. Will remembered a specific song she'd sung well enough to hum the melody. I remembered it, too, once MayJune sang the words—then explained that the song was a mournful ballad or shanty song, written by Haydn Wood and Royden Barrie and popular in the 1940s. And I had other memories, vague though they were, of Mama singing to her records, even after they stopped, in her and Daddy's bedroom, brushing her hair, gazing off into space, lost in some world that was hers alone, nothing to do with the reality of being a wife and mother in Groverton, Ohio.

"But you look just like this woman," Jimmy was saying.

I studied the photo and wanted to say, *No I don't*, to deny that I looked remotely like this beautiful, this *sexy* young woman, who despite the hint of doubt in her smile stared with an openly lusty expression into the camera, as if she was half-wooing, half-daring the photographer to come a little closer, to capture in full measure the desires of her being.

Surely, I wanted to say, in my most prim Grandma voice, I don't ever look like *this*. But then I realized . . . I had. When I was posing for Mr. Cahill, the last time, my senses lost in the Boléro music and to the taste of the persimmon.

And that expression, when I'd run out to check on Will, hadn't entirely faded from my face, even in my panic. That's what had scared Jimmy—that I'd somehow tapped into something so primal that revealed itself on my face, while alone with Mr. Cahill, even more freely than when Jimmy and I made love. A schoolgirl crush he might have forgiven, but that look, just as I came out of Mr. Cahill's house . . .

"It's your mama, all right," MayJune was saying. I opened my eyes, coming back to the moment. "She had Joey, my oldest boy, whose passion is photography even though he works over at the mill—well, now, of course, he's on strike—" Jimmy blushed. He represented the epitome of what Joey and the others were striking against. But MayJune went on. "Anyway, she had him take these photos of her, first week she sang over at the Pinewood Club on the corner. Still there. You probably passed it coming here. Anyway, she said she needed some publicity photos. Sure enough, the club used them in their newspaper ad. Turn the page in the album—you'll see."

But I couldn't bring myself to move. Jimmy reached over and carefully turned the album page. I stared down, saw the photo again, but printed on yellowing newspaper this time. My eyes darted to the *Groverton Daily News* masthead, the date—June 18, 1934, just two years before I was born— the photo, the ad copy that read, "The Pinewood Club, featuring new singing sensation Rita McKenzie."

McKenzie. Mama's maiden name.

I looked up at MayJune. "I don't understand. How did you know my mother well enough that she'd ask you, ask your son—"

"Honey, your mama grew up just a few houses down. I knew her from the day she was born and I can tell you stories about her singing in the neighborhood, and singing in church, and—" she gestured at the china cabinet where she kept framed photos instead of china, and albums instead of silver, and the loose flesh of her arm wobbled. Something in her voice told me that she had known my mother very well, and liked her. "I have photos of her scattered in among my own family photos. I can show you pictures of her as a little girl, and from when she was your age, from her singing days, right up until—"

She stopped. Her soft look of sadness flashed into some-thing sharper. "Well, up until she met your daddy."

MayJune had taken a liking to Will and me, and was willing to watch out for us and help us, because we were the children of a woman she'd known as a child, a woman who had maybe been like a daughter to her. I understood that while she was helping us at that moment because by then she liked us just for us, her interest in Will, in us, had started because of knowing our mother. Which had to mean our mother had mattered enormously to her.

What about our mama's family? Why did she stop sing-ing, if she loved it so much, when she met Daddy? And how did she meet Daddy? I was trying to figure out where to start, what to ask first, when Trusty limped into the parlor.

"Wow!" Jimmy exclaimed. "Whatever you did sure worked. Trusty is walking already!"

But MayJune and I shared a quick, knowing glance—Trusty was not miraculously well. He'd forced himself to limp in here, his jaw stretching in a soundless howl, to get us.

I shouted my brother's name, shoved the album at Jimmy, and jolted up from the couch, and I rushed to find Will.

Chapter 20

Four days later Dr. Marshall said, "Acute lymphoblastic leukemia."

At the new wing of Miami Valley Hospital in Dayton he'd ordered a test of Will's white blood cell count. He'd assessed Will's symptoms. And his diagnosis was that Will had too many white blood cells. The most common kind of childhood cancer. The kind that was survivable for five years, at most.

I looked at Daddy and said, "But what about that clinic that Mama went to, in Florida?" Out of the corner of my eye, I saw confusion snap Dr. Marshall's face out of tightness back into sloppy folds, and a little voice in my head said, *Dr. Marshall doesn't know what clinic you're talking about.*

I pulled my hand back from Daddy's, stared at him, saw in his face the truth I should have known all along—*there was no clinic in Florida.*

After I put Will to bed the night we returned from the hospital, I went into the kitchen and lined up his medicines. There seemed pitifully few for such a dire diagnosis. I put them in front of that broken-down toaster: the bottle of methotrexate tablets. Antacid for nausea. Aspirin for achy joints.

Will was to start with a week's dose of pills: three on Monday, then one for each of the next six days. The pills, Dr. Marshall told me, were to block the body's stimulation of folic acid, believed to promote the growth of leukemia cells, and might worsen Will's nausea and appetite. I picked up the bottle of methotrexate again, rubbing my thumb over the label, reading and rereading "Lederle Laboratories Division, American Cyanamid Company, Pearl River, N.Y.," telling myself that the name sounded important and serious, a place that could surely make pills that would help Will, that would buy him time during the clinical trials for new medicines that Dr. Marshall had described near the end of our meeting, after the awkward silence when I brought up Mama.

I heard a knock at our door. On our front porch, shivering even though she wore a thick, oversized sweater, stood Miss Bettina. Of course she'd come; I should have known she would. My heart jumped to my throat, but I pushed it down, down back under the ice floe that seemed to fill my chest since hearing Will's diagnosis. Still, the cold October air made me gasp a little for breath.

That was enough for Miss Bettina. She pushed herself through the door, pulling me to her in a hug.

"Oh, Donna, I just want to talk to you, to explain. Porter told me you know that Rita—your mama—didn't go to a clinic." She guided me into the living room.

I sat in the chair across from the couch and folded my arms.

Miss Bettina sighed. "You're not going to make this easy, are you?"

Even with all that was happening with Will, I wanted to hear about Mama. The truth.

"Rita loved to sing. She always loved singing. . . . When we were little girls, growing up in Tangy Town, she'd sing while she was hopscotching. Sing while she was jump-roping. Sing in church. It's the only thing that made her happy. You remember her singing—I know you do."

She cleared her throat a few times. "Well, you remember her singing sad songs. But I remember when she sang happy songs, too. Songs that made people forget their own sadness. She sang at church. And then she started singing at the Pinewood Club. After a while, I made her outfits for her performances."

All those fancy dresses in the basement . . .

"One night two men came in: Porter Lane and Roger Wilkins. We learned later that Porter was twelve years older than we were, that he'd returned to Groverton to work as an executive at the paper mill after college, and moved back in with his mother after her father died. Roger was closer to your mom's and my age, and your dad had just hired him as an accountant. But all we knew that night was that they were handsome and interested in us. Your daddy, like every man in the place, was enchanted by her beauty and her singing. She laughed off those men—except Porter. They started dating, and so did Roger and I. We had a lot of good times. . . ."

I pressed my eyes shut, trying to imagine a younger version of her, of my parents, of this Roger that I'd never heard of until now, trying to think of them laughing and talking . . .

but I realized that I was just pulling scenes from movies and books. Stock photos. As much as I wanted to, I couldn't imagine them in this happy past Miss Bettina described.

"Then Harold Litchfield showed up." Miss Bettina's voice steeled. I opened my eyes and looked at her. "He was a producer, he said, from Chicago. Wanted to take your mama with him, make a record with her. And so, Rita had a choice—go with Harold, make that record, see what might become of her life if she focused on singing. Or marry your dad."

"He'd already proposed? Or did he ask her after this Harold showed up?"

I'd meant to stay quiet while Miss Bettina talked, but I had to know.

"He proposed after Harold showed up, told her she had to make a choice, that if she left and came back, it would be no good between them." Miss Bettina shook her head.

Another question popped out: "Why couldn't he just go with her?"

Miss Bettina gave me a long look, and we both knew the answer: Grandma.

"He should have," Miss Bettina said quietly. "But Rita didn't hesitate a minute. She chose your father; they married. And Roger and I married. Eventually, we moved into these houses, two happy couples." She paused, then chuckled. "Your grandma sure didn't like her son moving out with his new bride. But your mom was so happy then. Your father gave her everything she'd dreamed of, talked about as a little girl. The best furniture. The best clothes."

Now the furniture seemed faded and worn, out of fashion.

And the clothes, well, of course I'd remade those clothes, along with Miss Bettina's costumes.

Miss Bettina's tone became somber again. "Rita had you, and I—well. Roger died in France in the war. He left me well-set, and I stayed put and opened my dress shop. For a long time, I think your daddy felt guilty that because of his age he was enrolled for military service but never called up.

"Your mom was kind to me, a good friend. I had trouble with drinking, and she stood by me. She was the only one who did, really. And she encouraged me to get help with a new group she'd read about—your mother was always reading the local newspaper, and papers from other cities, at the library. Alcoholics Anonymous was new here, and I was the only woman who went, so that got some tongues going, I can tell you, but it saved my life. I have your mother to thank for that."

Tears pricked my eyes and my nose filled, but I refused to sniffle. I blinked back those tears as fast as I could, determined not to cry. Or to care. This was just information. Filling in the blanks. Blanks that Daddy, or Miss Bettina, or someone should have filled in long ago.

"And she helped me even though she really struggled after having Will. She had some difficulty after having you but snapped out of it quickly. With Will it was different."

"What do you mean—she struggled?"

"Sometimes, honey, women get, well, blue after they have a baby. That's how your mama was. She always did chafe a bit, after settling down. Truth be told, looking back, I don't think she really had settling down bones in her. She thought she wanted this perfect life she'd imagined—house, husband, children—but she always seemed . . . restless. It just got worse after Will. Porter thought it would make her feel better to get out, to go back to the old club, to dress up, hear the music, even to sing again on Friday nights. I watched you and Will those nights."

"You mean Grandma didn't want to babysit so Mama could sing in a Tangy Town bar?"

I'd meant the words to sting, but to my surprise, Miss Bettina chuckled. "No, your grandma didn't like that one bit."

Daddy could stand up to Grandma for Mama. But after she was gone, he couldn't stand up for us. . . .

And then it struck me. Yes, he had. By not letting her move in and take over, or moving us in with her. He'd let me be a mom to Will, let us stay here, next to Miss Bettina, because he'd seen that was the best thing for us. In his own way, Daddy had done the best he could by us.

Tears stung my eyes again. I dashed the back of my hand to my eyes, wanting to smack away the wetness.

"And then," Miss Bettina was saying, "Harold returned and your mama left with him. Your daddy always believed that she would come back, and it seemed easier to tell you kids that she was sick. He thought that when she came to her senses, he could tell you that she was better."

"But he told us she died!" My voice was shaking.

"I know, honey. Not too long after she left, he got a letter from Rita, postmarked from Shelby, Montana, Harold's hometown. They'd gone there until Harold could get some money together to go back to Chicago to produce records. And Rita wanted a divorce. Your daddy went to see her. You and Will stayed with me."

I remembered staying with Miss Bettina off and on, when Mama had sick spells, and while Daddy was supposedly visiting her in the Florida clinic.

"When he came back, Porter told me it was over. The paperwork was filed. Their divorce would soon be final. He said she didn't want anything from him, but he kept sending her some money for a few years until she called him and told him to please stop . . . that she really didn't want to hear from him, from anyone in Groverton."

"Not even from Will. Or me." My voice was taut, cold. I felt numb all over.

"Oh, honey, your dad feared you'd feel that way, that you'd think you'd done something wrong. But it was just . . . who your mama was. She was never going to be happy settled down. And I don't think she was particularly happy running off. Even if the singing had worked out, I don't think she'd be happy."

I thought of the photo of Mama from MayJune's album, how her eyes seemed haunted and dreamy and distant, all at once. I knew Miss Bettina was right.

"And I guess to Porter, she really did die, in a way."

"Abandoned us, you mean."

Miss Bettina gasped.

"No! Let's just say the flat-out truth. Mama didn't die of cancer. She never had cancer. She wasn't physically sick. She was just sick of her life, of us—me and Will and Daddy. And never once in the past seven years did you think it might be a good idea to tell me?"

"Oh, Donna," she said, crying softly. "But in a way, she *was* ill."

I wanted to lash out. So I said, "I found suitcases of Mama's clothes. Dresses. Suits. I've been ripping apart those clothes. Ripping them apart and making new clothes—"

"Donna," Miss Bettina was saying softly, "I've admired what you've done with the materials. Making something new out of those old clothes—honey, that's a good thing. You've got a real talent."

Great, wrenching sobs shook me then, and in the next instant, Miss Bettina was kneeling beside me, holding me, pulling me to her. I didn't resist this time. I leaned forward on the edge of my chair, and then fell to my knees and melted into her embrace, letting her take and absorb all the pain that rattled through me.

We didn't hear Daddy come into the room.

But when we finally pulled apart, wiping our eyes and noses, there he stood in the entry to the living room, staring at us. Well, there he *weaved*, barely upright on his feet. Even in the dim living room light, we could tell that his eyes were glazed.

"Donna," he said, "you look like your mother, an angel—"

"Porter, shut up and go to bed," Miss Bettina snapped.

Daddy looked at Miss Bettina pleadingly. "I can't do this. I can't watch Will suffer. . . ."

I stood, walked over to my father, and stared up at him. There was nothing in his face of the man I'd been proud of only days before, the man who'd rallied enough to speak up for the union's campaign for safety. I felt pity—the one emotion I hated to see people feel for me. I smelled the alcohol and cigarette smoke rolling off his breath, off his skin and clothes.

"Daddy, you look at me. This is Donna. Donna! Do you understand?"

He nodded slowly.

"What is going to happen is this: You will get Mama's old car fixed. You will sign whatever paperwork it takes for me to get a license. I will drive Will to Miami Valley, and you will let the high school know that I will need time away for this. You will tell Grandma that I'm no longer working for her because Will needs me around. I've been taking care of Will since he was four. I will take care of him . . ." I paused, and finally my voice did falter, cracking, as I made myself finish, "for as long as it takes."

Chapter 21

On the Friday of the homecoming football game, October 16, I was at home after school, pulling chocolate chip cookies out of the oven. Will and Tony were tossing a football to one another in the backyard. Will had invited Tony to spend the night. And I was planning a night in, too. I told myself I didn't care that I was missing the game, or the dance.

I put the chocolate chip cookies on a plate. I was getting better at baking—this time, they were only a little burned on the edges. Then I poured two glasses of milk and called Will and Tony.

The boys rushed in, Tony devouring several cookies and gulping his milk, Will going a little slower, but still, eating. He looked at me, gave me a mouth-full-of-cookies grin. I groaned, rolled my eyes, which made him laugh. I noticed the tiredness around his eyes, tried not to let my concern show. I said, "It's getting chilly out. I think you boys need to play quietly, maybe up in Will's room, until dinner."

"Aw, come on, Donna, we're fine—" Will started, but then we heard the bang of the mailbox lid from the front porch. The boys jumped up from the kitchen table and ran to the front door.

I picked up a dish towel and started wiping up the cookie crumbs. In an instant, Will and Tony were back in the kitchen, Will clutching two envelopes. He tossed one on the damp table.

"That one's for you!" he hollered at me. "And this . . . this is from Marvel Puffs!"

"Open it, open it!" Tony shouted.

I looked down at the envelope, stared at my name and address neatly printed in block lettering.

Will and Tony whooped over the long-awaited prize from Sunshine Bakery Company, but I didn't hear.

I picked up the thick envelope and studied the two three-cent stamps to cover extra postage, the blank spot where the return address should have been, the New York postmark. My heart leapt to my throat. *Mr. Cahill . . .*

Casually, as if opening a bill from the milk delivery company, I turned the envelope over, slid my index finger beneath the flap.

I pulled out two pieces of paper and a stapled packet. The first piece, on top, was a note, written on a page of plain stationery:

Dear Miss Lane.

I hope this finds you well. Enclosed please find a copy of a letter I recently sent to the Parsons School of Design—unsolicited, I realize, but I hope it will encourage you in the dreams you should no longer deny.

Sincerely,
Mr. Cahill

How would I ever figure out exactly where he was in a city as big as New York? I shook my head at myself for even wondering and then shifted the handwritten note behind the second page, a carbon copy of a typewritten letter that Mr. Cahill had addressed to a Mr. George Worthington at Parsons.

Dear George:

So nice to meet for cocktails last evening; as I said then you and your lovely Sarah are looking more wonderful than ever. Evidently, administration and teaching suit you—something I've always wished I could find stability in, but given my attempt at the high school I mentioned, I've realized I'm not suited. I forget about boundaries too easily, it seems.

And yet I'm crossing another one here, but I wish to reiterate my recommendation of a budding young designer, Donna Lane, who I hope will be sending you pages from her design portfolio and an application this coming spring, for consideration for the entering class of 1958. While lacking in confidence and, of course, formal training, Miss Lane possesses that rarest combination—a natural eye for design, a native creativity, and passion. Her artistry bursts forth, in spite of herself. It's worthy to consider what she could achieve with an education at Parsons.

I know it is customary for applicants to request letters of recommendation and send them along with their applications—but when have you ever

known me to follow what is customary? So I'm
sending this letter of recommendation in advance
of Donna Lane's application, and without her
having requested it. I think you do know, however,
that I have an unfailing ability for knowing talent,
grit, and potential when I see it.

Sincerely,
Nate Cahill

And behind that letter was the application packet for Parsons School of Design.

For a second, I was too shocked to know what to think, to feel, to do.

"Um . . . Donna?"

Tony's voice pulled me from my thoughts, back to the kitchen table, to the moment.

I looked around. Will was gone.

I looked at Tony. "What's wrong? Did he throw up? Faint?"

"I think he's just upset. 'Cause of this." He pointed at a wadded-up piece of paper.

I picked it up, smoothed it out, laid it over the top of the pages Mr. Cahill had sent me.

Will's letter lacked a personal greeting, or even a signature. The form letter blandly read:

We are sorry to inform you that the response to our
One Square Inch of Alaska Territory deed
program exceeded expectations. We have exhausted
all the deeds available, and unfortunately, cannot
send you said deed. However, please make sure to

> *watch for more fun promotions from Marvel Puffs*
> *and the Sunshine Bakery Company, coming soon*
> *on a cereal box near you!*

Later that night, as I cleaned up from dinner in the kitchen, I had my transistor radio on and tuned to WBEX. The Four Aces were again crooning "Just Squeeze Me"—the song that was playing the first time I'd met Jimmy, only five weeks before. But it seemed like a lifetime.

I had the radio turned low, because Daddy was reading the newspaper in the living room, which really meant that he was napping. I hummed along, trying to tell myself that I didn't care that I wasn't at the game, wasn't going to the homecoming dance the next night.

As I finished drying the plate I held, a brief flash of Mr. Cahill's letter—carefully refolded and tucked at the bottom of my lingerie drawer, next to my stash of money, the Dexamyl from Babs, the Blue Waltz Sachet from Jimmy—went off in my head, and with that image came a guilty pang. Of course I couldn't apply to Parsons the coming spring. Even if Will were fine, that seemed so ridiculously out of reach. My plan now was clear—I'd stick with Will through to the end. And then I'd go to New York with my original plan to be a seamstress. But I hadn't quite brought myself to throw away the note, and letter, and the Parsons application.

I heard a knock at the front door. My heart leapt for the second time that day, this time at the thought, *Jimmy!* Maybe he'd decided to leave the football game, to come see me. . . .

I hurried through the living room. Sure enough, Daddy

was asleep in his dark blue chair. When I opened the door, there stood Grandma, looking nervous, like she was afraid I'd slam the door in her face. Had those tired lines around her eyes, her mouth, run so deeply before? I almost felt sorry for her.

But then she said, "Well, Donna, are you going to stand there gaping at me like you're trying to catch flies in your mouth, or are you going to ask me in?"

I sighed. "What are you doing here? Friday nights are the busiest—"

"Between homecoming and the strike, the café is nearly empty. I left the staff in charge. And I came by tonight because I figured—in spite of how you messed up with that nice Jimmy Denton—that you'd be at the homecoming game trying to hold your head high, instead of skulking around here. Don't you know that just makes you look even guiltier? Why—"

"Come in, Mama," Daddy said. I didn't move. "Donna, let your grandmother in."

Grandma gave me a triumphant little smile. I moved aside and she rushed past me, and plopped down on the couch. "Porter, I'm so glad you're here. I came by tonight figuring Donna would be at the game because I wanted to talk with you alone." She looked at me. "Don't you need to go tend Will?"

"He's fine," I said. "Resting."

Actually, I'd found him in his room, where he'd retreated after reading the form letter that denied him his much-longed-for deed. He refused to come down, refused to talk to Tony, refused to have dinner. I'd told him that he could not watch tonight's episode of *Sergeant Striker*—no sir, young man—until he came out and had dinner and stopped pouting.

The show would be on in ten minutes. While cleaning up from dinner, I'd envisioned him rushing down the stairs at the last minute, wolfing down his dinner, then sitting cross-legged in front of the TV, his head tilted to the right like it always was when he watched, his untamable cowlick sticking up at the back of his head.

"Is he not feeling well?" Grandma pressed.

"He's fine," I snapped. "He's just pouting because he didn't get his deed to one square inch of Alaska."

"Well, that's ridiculous," Grandma said. "If he's feeling well enough to eat, then you must demand that he do so! How else can he build up his strength, fight off this illness?" She looked at Daddy. "Porter, how can you stand for this? Clearly Donna doesn't have the strength of character to make the boy do what he needs to do."

"Donna is doing the best she can," Daddy said. "One late dinner isn't that important."

"Why, I'll just get him down here myself!" Grandma exclaimed, jumping up.

But I was already standing, and before she could take a step toward the stairs, I was in front of her, blocking her way. "No. Leave him be. I will go check on him in a minute." *After you leave.*

"All this foolishness over a cereal box promotion? How are you going to care for him if his illness gets worse?" Something in her eyes made me realize that she didn't believe that Will's illness was as mild as Daddy had made it sound. And she was, I realized, still hurt and angry that Daddy had refused to bring her to Miami Valley.

"You need me here! You need me taking care of you, of all of you, and you've needed me ever since that conniving, money-grubbing, loose woman skipped out on you, and—"

She stopped and gasped, realizing as her words rang out that she'd gone too far. She didn't know, after all, that I finally knew the truth. I heard the third step on the stairs squeak and my heart dropped. Will. He'd heard every word.

Suddenly, Daddy was out of his chair, standing in front of his mother. I watched in wide-eyed horror and fascination as he grabbed her wrists, just as I had weeks before, and said in a dangerous, low voice, "You will never, ever speak of Rita again like that. In fact, I don't want you to ever speak of her again. She was hurting and she made the choice to run off, but I never wanted to look at how much she was hurting, never wanted to see—"

Daddy's voice strangled to a stop. Grandma stared up at him, her chin suddenly quivering.

"But, Porter, you need my help; you've always needed my help. If I'd have been here running things all along—"

"No, Mama," Daddy said softly. "No. Donna is in charge. She always has been, which isn't right. But now is not the time to change it." He let go of Grandma's wrists and shook his head. "Now isn't the time."

Rage flashed across her face, but Grandma didn't say a word. She turned, squared her shoulders, and walked out of our house.

I rushed to the stairs as if I'd been released from a spell.

Will sat on the top step. His face was blotchy, tear-streaked.

"What did she mean, about Mama running away?"

"Will . . . don't worry about that. I'm not sure what she

was talking about." The words came out of my mouth before I even thought about what I was doing—perpetuating the lie that Mama had died.

Was it better for Will to learn—then, of all times—that Mama hadn't died, but had simply walked away from her family? That it was partly because of baby blues brought on by his birth? Or would he be better off thinking what he'd thought all along—that our mama had died of cancer at a clinic in Florida? The truth, and what we'd been told, and what we were now telling Will were all jumbled up in my head.

"Listen," I said, "*Sergeant Striker* is just about on. You don't even have to eat dinner, if you don't want to. I'll let you watch it, watch it with you—"

"Don't care. They lied. They said I'd get my deed if I sent in those box tops." He started crying again. "I wanted it and worked for it and dreamed about it and followed the Marvel Puffs rules. It's not fair."

"Oh, Will. Few things in life are."

"Some things ought to be, though," he said softly. Then he stood up, turned, and headed down the hall to his bedroom.

I turned, too, but went to the kitchen, suddenly understanding, suddenly knowing what I had to do.

The first step: Dig that Marvel Puffs form letter out of the kitchen trash can, smooth out its wrinkles, and wipe off the stains as best I could.

Chapter 22

"Smile!"

Babs urged me on, the following Tuesday, from the passenger seat of Mama's convertible. My eyes were focused on the road before me, my hands clamped on the steering wheel. I had the top up because it was a chilly, rainy morning. I was nervous, both because of our mission and because I hadn't driven on such slick pavement before. Babs would keep insisting, so I clenched my teeth and smiled.

"No, silly, look at me and smile!" Babs said.

"Do you mind? The road is slick and I'm trying to keep the car—"

A flash of light shot in my eyes. Babs giggled while I tried to slow the car and stay steady on the road. By then, I was so familiar with the road between Groverton and Dayton that I knew there were no curves up ahead. I was more irritated than scared that for the moment all I could see were white spots from the bright flash in my eyes.

"Why do you keep doing that, Babs?" This was the third time she'd taken my picture since we'd left Groverton.

"This is a momentous occasion—*you* talking *me* into skipping school! And besides, I'm supposed to be the photographer, and you're the reporter, so I need to practice, right?"

My eyes had cleared enough for me to glance over at Babs. She was grinning, putting on her usual larger-than-life, sassy attitude, even though there was a hint of sadness and weariness around her eyes. And a bruise on her left cheek, not quite covered by her thick pancake makeup. Something she'd done at homecoming—she wasn't sure what—had irritated Hank, and that night after the dance, after they'd parted from Jimmy and Lisa, he'd gotten rough with her. But, she told me, she must have brought it on herself—she'd had Dexamyl while getting ready, and then the vodka Hank had brought in a flask, so she didn't quite remember—and besides, Hank was touchy because Groverton had lost its homecoming game 21–7, and he'd apologized so sweetly later.

I told her the sweetest apology in the world didn't change the fact that Hank was an ass and she didn't deserve to be treated like that for any reason, certainly not because Hank was upset over a football game score. Babs had gotten mad and not spoken to me for a whole day after that. But then she'd forgotten all about it and agreed gleefully to my plan.

"Come on, you owe me a real smile and photo!" Babs said.

"Why?"

"You've got a free pass to skip school anytime now," she said lightly. I didn't find her comment insensitive. She was, I knew, upset about Will, but Babs always thought if she could be lighthearted enough, all problems would go away—no matter how many bruises gave evidence to the contrary. "What am I supposed to tell Principal Stodgill?"

I looked at Babs and gave her a full, wide smile. She snapped my picture. I looked back at the road even though I was temporarily blinded. "Just mention Auntie Flo's visit."

"How many times do you think I can use that excuse before he catches on?"

My vision started to clear. "About once a month."

Babs laughed and I was glad to hear that carefree sound—and annoyed in the next minute when she said, "We'll have time for shopping, right? And lunch at the Rike's counter?"

I sighed. "I don't know, Babs. It depends on how things go at the Sunshine Bakery."

Babs turned on the radio—WBEX—and fished a cigarette out of her purse. She popped open the ashtray and lit her cigarette. When had she added smoking to her list of unladylike sins? "I just don't see why it matters so much. What's one little square inch? That far away? And when he's so sick?"

"I don't understand it either. But it matters to Will," I said. "He's been so blue ever since he got that awful form letter. I have to try to get it for him. I know it doesn't make any difference in the long run, but for now . . ." My voice trailed off and my eyes pricked. I told myself it was from Babs's smoke. "We'll get to Rike's if we can." In spite of everything, a little part of me was eager to see what was new in the dress and hat and glove departments at Rike's. But even with Miss Bettina tending Will, a bigger part of me wanted to get back home as close as possible to the end of Will's school day.

Babs put a hand on my arm, gave me a little reassuring pat. "It's OK if we don't get to Rike's."

That was a somber statement coming from Babs. The

general atmosphere, in fact, was too somber. So I gave the car a little swerve. Babs yelped. Her pat turned into a playful swat. "You did that on purpose!"

I giggled, immediately grateful for a moment of laughter. I was about to tell her that of course I had purposefully swerved Mama's car—I was such a good driver by now that I could do little tricks like that without fear—when suddenly we heard a loud pop and the car swerved against my will, careening side to side. Babs—of course—started screaming. I took my foot off of the accelerator and slowly pressed down on the brake, easing the car off the road. At the edge of the road, I turned the car off, got out, and inspected the tires.

Babs rolled down the window; she was not going to get out of the car and let her hairdo go flat in the drizzling rain. "What happened?"

"Flat tire," I said.

"Well, what do we do now? I'm sure not walking to the next town, not in these new shoes." Babs had on red high-heel pumps, just like the peep-toes Jane Russell and Marilyn Monroe wore in their big dance number in *Gentlemen Prefer Blondes.*

I poked my head in the car and looked evenly at Babs. "What we do is change the tire. There's a spare in the trunk." Daddy had had new tires put on Mama's car, so I must have hit a nail or something sharp in the road. The spare was new, too. "All you have to do is hop out of the car and keep an eye out just in case another car comes along. The flat is on the front driver's side, so I'll be right by the road—"

Babs's eyes widened. "What? You can't do that! We

should wait for some nice strangers to come along and help us." She grinned. "Some nice, strong, handsome *male* strangers. . . ."

Hank would kill her for even saying such a thing. Babs put her cigarette in the ashtray, then opened her purse and fished out a compact and her new Roulette Red Ayer's lipstick. She opened her compact, then the lipstick, and peered in the compact's tiny mirror to reapply her lipstick—just in case those handsome strangers came along to rescue us. I rolled my eyes. I knew better than to wait for rescue.

"Fine. You sit there, and try not to scream when you feel the car lifting up."

Babs swiveled her lipstick back down, put on the lid, closed the compact, put both back in her purse, and glared at me. "You can't change a tire."

"Yes, I can. Daddy showed me how."

Her eyebrows went up. "Well, you're going to get filthy. And wet."

"My butt's already getting wet." I started to pull my head out of the window and stand up.

"Wait!" Babs said. She pulled a clear rain bonnet, folded into a tidy little rectangle, out of her purse. She held the bonnet out to me. "At least protect your hairdo!"

I had spent a lot of time on the pin curls, trying to make my hair look like I imagined a lady reporter's might. I stood up, unfolded the bonnet, and carefully tied it over my do. Then I opened the trunk, pulled out the jack, and positioned it carefully under the car.

"Girls aren't supposed to do things like that!" Babs hollered as I jacked up the car.

I was already breathless, but I called back, "Girls

aren't supposed to do lots of things . . . but that's never stopped you."

"Oooh—you're being such a bitch!" Babs laughed. "I like it!"

I used the wrench to loosen the nuts on the tires. "Enough to get out here and help?"

"Of course not," she said. "I'm busy watching for some big, handsome hunks of male to come along."

I was right; male rescuers never showed up. But I changed the tire just fine by myself.

Babs was also right—my coat ended up a smudged, tarry mess, and the hair bonnet was a good idea. My makeup smeared in the drizzle. I fixed that, though, in the parking lot of the Sunshine Bakery Company. And as soon as we were inside the lobby, I pulled off my coat and folded it so the stains didn't show. I hoped no one would notice the run up my stockings, or the scuffs on my shoes.

Of course, as soon as Babs started talking to the receptionist, I knew that I should have realized that all eyes were going to be on flashy, outgoing Babs anyway. She confidently showed her press pass, and jabbered charmingly while I pulled mine out of my briefcase—Daddy's old one, from his mill management days, that I'd found in the basement. Our photos had turned out a little blurry, but Babs said that was OK; the blurriness made us look older. Then she'd typed our fake names on the press passes—of all things Kelly Dare for me and Lolita LaPerone for her. I suspected she'd borrowed the names from her trashy novels. Babs confidently gave our cover story—that we were journalism interns from Ohio University, working at the *Groverton Daily News*, and doing a story on major Midwest businesses.

The passes and cover story and Babs's unfailing confidence got us past the receptionist and into the Sunshine Bakery's president's office—but no further. Mr. Kincaid's secretary, Miss Brewer, eyed us suspiciously, told us to take a seat and that we could wait if we liked, but Mr. Kincaid was in a meeting in another part of the building. Then she went right back to typing and answering the phone, seemingly forgetting that two young women were sitting on the leather couch in the waiting area.

I studied her beehive hairdo, her prim, tight lips. She couldn't know, but just the day before, I'd pretended to be her on the telephone in order to obtain information Sunshine Bakery would soon wish I hadn't.

"These magazines stink," Babs whispered. We'd already been waiting a half hour, and she'd thumbed through all the issues of *Bakery News* on the coffee table.

"What did you expect?" I whispered back. "*Vogue?*"

"At least *Good Housekeeping.*"

Miss Brewer cleared her throat and glared at us over her reading glasses. She poised her hands over her typewriter's keys to underscore her annoyance at the interruption in her typing. She sighed and pulled out a spool of correction tape, but by the time she was getting it in position, Babs had jumped up from the couch and rushed over to her desk. She smacked the typewriter with the offensively boring *Bakery News*.

"Look, I don't mean to be rude here, but my colleague and I don't have all day. After this little interview, we're going shopping, and the stores close by five, which only gives us four hours if we want to have lunch at Rike's counter, and—"

I groaned, jumped up, and rushed over to the desk, giving Babs the stink-eye—who was going to believe we were really reporters if she talked about shopping and lunch?—while smiling at Miss Brewer. "What my colleague is saying, actually, is that we're on deadline, so if you could please check Mr. Kincaid's schedule and let us know when he might wrap up his meeting."

"Is this some kind of college prank?" Miss Brewer demanded. She picked up the handset of her telephone and started dialing numbers with the eraser end of her pencil.

"Of course not," I said. "We're doing this series of articles about Ohio businesses for *Groverton Daily News*, and we're interns from Ohio University, and—"

"I'm calling security!" Miss Brewer said, and started to dial another number.

I reached over the desk and pressed down on the button on the receiver cradle, cutting off her call. "You don't want to do that," I said. She gasped, pulled back, suddenly looking afraid as I held up Daddy's briefcase, like a big fish I'd just caught, and shook it. "I have proof that the 'One Square Inch of Alaska Territory' promotion is a big hoax! Now, we can publish that story, and it will get picked up on all the newswires—I'm talking AP, UPI—without giving Mr. Kincaid a chance to respond to the evidence I have in here"—I gave the briefcase another shake, and Miss Brewer squealed—"or he can talk to us."

Babs stared at me with surprise and frank admiration. But the determination I'd had—and still had—to get out of

Groverton was only a fraction of the determination I had to make Will's last wish, to get his deed, come true.

Miss Brewer reached a shaking hand toward her phone. "I can try to track him down for an appointment, later today, maybe after lunch. . . ."

The door behind her opened. A middle-aged man with a gut that strained the buttons on his double-breasted suit jacket came out. "That won't be necessary, Miss Brewer." He gave me and Babs an amused smile. "I've heard the whole discussion through the door and I have to admit that I'd rather talk to two pretty coeds than keep poring over budget reports."

Babs smiled at him playfully. I was starting to wonder if there was any man she wouldn't encourage—even if he were old enough to be her father. I lowered Daddy's briefcase.

"I am quite serious about this," I said.

"Of course," Mr. Kincaid said, so patronizingly that I wanted to smack him upside the head with the briefcase. He looked at Miss Brewer. "Keep holding my calls. And no need for security."

A few minutes later, Babs and I were seated across from Mr. Kincaid's desk.

"I have a letter, sent to a young man of my acquaintance. It is a form letter from your company stating that all the one-inch plots of Alaskan territory have been distributed," I said, putting the letter that Will had received on Mr. Kincaid's desk.

"Uh-huh," he grunted, staring pointedly at Babs's

cleavage, even though it was partially covered with the bulky camera she wore on a strap around her neck.

"Given your advertising, I found this rather incredible. So I tracked down the deed office in the town of Tok, in the Alaska Territory."

Mr. Kincaid pulled his eyes from Babs and stared at me, clearly surprised. His expression turned to concern that this wasn't some prank after all. He had to know how hard it had been to locate the Tok deed office.

The day before, I'd missed school and gone to the Groverton library and found a reference book on real estate law and read everything I could find in it about deeds. From that I learned that deeds had to be filed with a county's property records office. Since Groverton was our county's seat, I went to the county building and the property records office. I said I needed some information for a school project and asked how I might find out the locations of deed offices in the Alaska Territory. The secretary—a customer of Miss Bettina's who had heard about Will's "blood disease"—took pity on me and made a few phone calls. An hour later I had the information that I should contact the Department of the Interior general land office in Sitka. I had a phone number and an address.

I knew it would take weeks to send a letter and get a reply, and I also knew I didn't want to take that much time. So I swallowed my pride and asked for Jimmy's help. That evening, while his parents were out, he took me to their home and let me use their private line to call the number. He said he'd come up with some explanation for what would be a huge phone bill. It took a while, but finally I was talking to an employee of the general land office in Sitka, and over the scratchy line I got my answer: There were several deed offices, but the deed office I wanted was in Tok, so I had the operator put me through to that number. When I reached the deed recorder, I pretended to be a secretary for Mr. Kincaid interested in acquiring more land for more deeds. That was enough to get me the basic information I needed.

"It turns out that your company, Mr. Kincaid, only bought two acres—enough for approximately twelve million square-inch deeds. That should have been enough . . . but of course, you didn't put a limit on how many deeds each person could acquire—which is great for cereal sales, I'm sure, but not exactly fair." I pulled a box of Marvel Puffs cereal out of the briefcase and tapped the picture on the back of the box. "Not only that, but the land you bought is just some rocky shore off the Tanana River, and flat land covered with pine, not exactly like the majestic mountains pictured here."

I stopped. Instead of looking horrified, Mr. Kincaid looked tickled.

But I went on. "So . . . so . . . you've been misleading the public! You should have bought more land, or at least not led the public to believe there were endless square-inch plots to be had."

Mr. Kincaid's eyes had already wandered back to Babs's camera-covered cleavage. "This has been an amusing diversion," he said. "But I really don't think your raising this fuss in your little article will get much notice. Especially not with a strike going on at the company that makes our boxes—the strike is much bigger news. The simple truth is, if you look closely at the fine print on the bottom of the box, our advertising does state 'while deeds are available.' And beneath that wonderful picture of the mountains is more fine print—'Not actual land; representation of Alaskan territory.' So I don't think you have much of a story. So you'll have to tell the little boy who tipped you off on this scandal"—he paused to laugh—"that he should do as the letter says, and watch for the next promotion—"

"Not just a little boy!" Babs snapped. Her expression had hardened with fury I'd never seen her express. Her voice pulled Mr. Kincaid's eyes up to her face, and he looked startled. "Her little brother. Who was really looking forward to that deed to one square inch. And found out that he wasn't going to get it"—I was shaking my head at Babs, *No, no, please don't drag Will's illness into this. There has to be another way, even if I just beg Mr. Kincaid for a sample copy of the deed from the advertising department . . . or break into the Bakers' house and steal theirs*, but she was staring down Mr. Kincaid, who suddenly sensed danger and was turning red—"right after he found out something else. That he has cancer. Lymphoblastic leukemia."

Babs leaned forward, her breasts almost spilling out from her bra under the camera. But Mr. Kincaid didn't even seem to notice. "So you're going to buy up another tract of land and make sure that all the kids who thought they'd get their square inch of Alaska actually do—including my friend's little brother."

She tapped the box I was still holding with her perfectly polished fingernail. "If you don't, my daddy, who is editor of the *Groverton Daily News*, will write a scathing editorial about your misleading advertising practices and how they feed the dreams of little boys, only to destroy them when it suits your bottom line."

A smile slowly filled Mr. Kincaid's face and he narrowed his eyes. He got a distant look like he was suddenly getting a fantastic idea—fantastic to him, anyway.

A chill crept slowly over my skin.

But Babs had gone back to her usual self and didn't seem to realize that Mr. Kincaid's smile wasn't for her. She smiled right back at him and added, "And Daddy always does what I want."

Chapter 23

Two nights later, October 22, Will stood next to Sergeant Striker by the makeshift podium that had been set up in the lobby of *Groverton Daily News*. He looked completely miserable.

Sergeant Striker was being played by Hugh Garvey, the actor from the radio show, whose career had suffered when his part was recast for television. Mr. Garvey wore the identical costume to television's Sergeant Striker, except that his hat was ridiculously large, his suit was too tight, and his smirk a blight on the character.

Will himself all but disappeared into a pinstriped, gray flannel suit Grandma had insisted on buying two sizes too big at Rike's Department Store. Maybe she didn't understand that acute lymphoblastic leukemia was not a growth opportunity. Although everyone, even Will, now knew the name of his disease, no one had been blunt enough to translate: *terminal*.

Indian summer had arrived in Groverton, making the lobby close and stuffy, the weight of the flannel unbearable to Will. I was wearing the homecoming dress I'd made from Mama's wedding dress, modifying it one more time for this event, taking the hem up from floor length to mid-calf, and even though it was sleeveless, I felt suffocatingly warm, standing at the front of the pack of people crammed in the lobby, most of whom were watching newspaper photographers and even television crews from WLWD in Dayton and WCPO in Cincinnati capture the event, rather than the event itself. As for me, I focused on Will, his big blue eyes holding me, begging me to get him out of there, my gaze telling him, *You'll be OK; just a few more minutes.*

I wished I'd insisted that he wear a comfortable short-sleeved shirt and pants. I wished I'd never agreed to this event in the first place, seeing how small and miserable Will looked in his suit, between the smirking "Sergeant Striker" and the podium, where Mr. Kincaid rambled about how he and Mr. Denton (who stood on the other side of the podium) were so inspired by "this brave young man" that they'd decided together to buy not just one more tract, but *two*, of Alaskan territory so that the square-inch campaign could continue.

"Not only that," Mr. Kincaid said, "but each company is donating a thousand dollars to Will's family to help with his medical costs!" The audience broke into applause.

I looked around, taking in familiar faces of people who seemed genuinely happy for Will—Big Terry and Shirley and Ralph from Grandma's diner; Mr. and Mrs. Leis (her face was wet with tears, and I thought, *She understands how serious Will's condition really is*); Will's fifth-grade teacher; his friends Tony, Suze, and Harold and Herman, and their parents. Of course Grandma, Daddy, and Miss Bettina were there, and Jimmy and Babs, both of whom kept looking at me apologetically.

Small ceremony. What a joke—on us. When I'd agreed to it, I hadn't understood that Mr. Kincaid and Mr. Denton were going to turn Will's condition into a promotional opportunity for both of their companies.

I looked back at Will. He gazed at me with his wide blue eyes: *Get me out of here.*

Suddenly, Mr. Kincaid stopped talking and hoisted Will onto a stool hidden behind the podium. Will's face peered over the top. He stared out at the crowd, his wide eyes darting back and forth, with a growing look of panic on his face.

Will, who with all his shenanigans seemed like the most confident, outgoing boy, had never spoken in public before, and it was clear that this was going to be expected of him—but he hadn't been forewarned. Neither, of course, had I.

But then Mr. Kincaid was finally thrusting a frame at Will, saying, "On behalf of the Sunshine Bakery—"

"And on behalf of Groverton Pulp and Paper," added Mr. Denton, beaming at the cameras.

"We are pleased to present to William Everett Lane an official deed to one square inch of the Territory of Alaska!" Mr. Kincaid concluded.

The crowd applauded. Will snagged the framed deed from Mr. Kincaid and held it to his chest, hugging it tightly, as if he was afraid it would be snatched back from him.

As the crowd started to quiet, Mr. Kincaid said, "Now, I'm sure you're excited to get your picture taken with the radio Sergeant Striker here"—the actor in the bad costume gave a cheesy smile at the cameras and a little wave of his hand—"but we have an even bigger surprise. In a few weeks, we'll arrange to fly you out to Hollywood to have your photo taken with Chase Monahue, the television Sergeant

Striker, so your photo can be on boxes of Marvel Puffs! What do you think of that, young man?"

The radio Sergeant Striker actor looked angry.

"Did I . . . did I win the essay contest?" Will asked. "I barely get C's in English."

All the men at the podium laughed and some of the audience tittered nervously. "No, but that's OK," said Mr. Kincaid. "After all, you're a *special young man.*"

Will frowned. "But that's not fair to whoever wrote—"

Mr. Denton cut him off with an overly hearty chortle. "Of course it is." Then he gazed out at the crowd with a somber expression. "But it also takes a long time to make these boxes, and of course, while there's a strike, the boxes can't be made." Mr. Kincaid nodded solemnly. Babs's father, Mr. Wickham, looked pleased as his reporter took photos of the stunned faces in the crowd. "Now, I'm sure we'd all love for this *special young man*, one of Groverton's own, to be on those boxes, especially in his *special condition*, but first the United Paperworkers International Union locals . . ."

Will looked confused, not understanding the nasty trick Mr. Kincaid and Mr. Denton had just pulled, or the angry murmurs starting to grow in the crowd. I started toward Will, but Daddy was quicker, shoving past a startled Mr. Kincaid and radio Sergeant Striker to Will's side. Daddy grabbed the check for medical bills from Mr. Kincaid's hand and tucked it inside his jacket pocket.

Then he nudged the evil Sunshine Bakery man out of the way, and said into the microphone, "Will says thank you for the deed and for the check." He gently lifted Will off the stool. Will ran to me, and I clasped him in my arms. Miss Bettina put a hand on my shoulder.

"But now there's something I have to say," Daddy went on. The crowd hushed, nervous but eager to hear. "And that is my boy will not be a pawn in some tricky game to end this strike! I should have spoken out years ago, when I was management and Mr. Frederick McDonnell came to me about safety issues. I'm sorry I didn't."

He looked at me, Will, and Miss Bettina. "I'm sorry about a lot of things. But now I say, as I've written in letters to the editor and will keep writing, the majority of workers at the mill need and deserve union protection, including safety measures. And it's in all of our best interests for the mill management to—"

Suddenly, someone ran into the lobby. Mr. Baker, our neighbor from across the street, shouted out his news. "I just came from the mill. There's a fire in the storage yard!" The crowd gasped. Most of the workers typically crossed through the storage yard to clock in through a back entry, and that's where most of the picketers were marching. "People are trapped. We need as many volunteer firefighters as we can get!"

The crowd broke up, people shoving and hurrying to exit the newspaper lobby. Daddy came down from the podium to us.

Grandma glared at him. "Porter, what was all that about? Turning a shining moment for the Lanes into—"

Miss Bettina interrupted. "Oh, shut up, Lorene. This wasn't about you to begin with."

"Daddy," I said quietly, as Grandma, thankfully, walked away, "I'm really proud of you."

He looked at me, a smile starting to form on his weary

face . . . but then he stared at the shoulder of my dress again, at the lace. He touched it gently and the smile vanished.

He knew. The other dresses were one thing, but I should have let Mama's wedding gown be.

Daddy's hand dropped from the lace. He looked at Miss Bettina. "I'm going to go help."

"I'm going with you," she said.

Will looked up at me. "I want to go to MayJune's," he said. "I want to see Trusty."

MayJune was waiting on her front porch swing, with Trusty at her feet. I'd barely pulled the car to a stop on the dirt and gravel road in front of her tiny house when Will jumped out and ran up her small, hilly patch of front yard to the porch. Dusk softened the scene, as if I were already immersed in a gauzy, distant memory: Trusty jumping up, tail wagging, to greet Will; Will sitting down beside MayJune, making the porch swing sway; MayJune pulling the afghan on her lap over him, then leaning over to gaze with admiration at his deed to his one square inch of Alaska.

That moment is one of my favorite memories of Will and MayJune.

I looked away from the porch scene, tears suddenly pricking my eyes, and took my time putting the top back up on Mama's convertible. By the time I joined them on the porch, I was dry-eyed. MayJune and Will were sipping tea. I sat down across from them on a turquoise metal porch chair. MayJune pointed at a mug, steam still rising from the top, on a small table.

I picked up the mug, inhaled the steam—lemony and sweet smelling all at once—and took a sip, mm-mmming my approval. This was a new concoction.

"Lemon verbena, sassafras, and honey," MayJune said, smiling so that her eyes crinkled up in that familiar, comforting way.

I took another sip, suddenly parched for the comfort and ease that the tea offered, and thought, *Of course MayJune didn't come to the ceremony at Groverton Daily News.* Somehow, she'd known that we'd need to take refuge at her small house, with her and her strange herbal teas, had even surmised when we'd come by so that our hot tea would be ready. That was MayJune's way.

She looked down at the deed and put her arm around Will and gave him a squeeze. "My, my, look at that! Our Will is a landowner!" Will beamed. Trusty bumped his head against Will's knee and Will laughed, then reached down to scratch him between his ears. His tail thumped even harder against the porch.

The dog looked mostly healed, a crookedness to his right ear and a slight limp the only signs of how badly he'd been hurt. And, of course, he still didn't bark. I wondered if he'd ever get his voice back. Or if he'd ever trust me. But I was glad to see him getting better.

Will and I filled MayJune in on the goings-on at the news conference and the fire at the paper mill. She shook her head and clucked and said, "Oh my." Then, for a little while, we all stayed comfortable in our quietness, because with MayJune, it was easy to just . . . be.

But then behind MayJune and Will, a few yards from the porch, an impossible sight caught my eye. I pressed my eyes

shut, opened them again, stared, and sure enough, its outline barely illuminated by MayJune's porch light, was a teardrop camper. I knew in my gut that it was the camper Trusty
had been so cruelly chained to in Stedman's Scrapyard the
first time I'd seen him.

"Is that . . . ?" I pointed at the camper. Will twisted
around to see where I was pointing.

MayJune chortled. "Got it last Tuesday. 'Course, my
daughter's car doesn't have a trailer hitch, so I thought about
calling you, since your mama's old car does have a hitch that
would haul that little trailer just fine." *It does?* I thought, and
then realized that, yes, there was a round hitch on the back
bumper. MayJune went on. "But I figured it was better if
Mr. Stedman didn't see anyone from the Lane family. I
couldn't have him haul it here; then he might see Trusty.

"So I got Lenny—that's my neighbor next door—to go
get it with me. Mr. Stedman was happy to let it go for next to
nothing. He said his old guard dog had fouled it." MayJune
shook her head. "Took all the doin' I had in me not to tell
him, well, you can't chain up a dog and not expect him to go
a little wild trying to get away."

MayJune took Will's empty mug and put it on the table,
and Will leaned forward and hugged Trusty.

"Anyway, Lenny helped me get it home and clean it up.
You can't tell in the dark, but it's a right shiny little camper
now, good as new, inside and out. Lenny even found some
new tires for it."

I stared at MayJune. "But . . . why?"

She smiled. "Well, my traveling days are over. But I figured someone I know might need it."

Suddenly, a look passed across Will's face and I knew, my

stomach sinking, that he had a crazy idea. "I'm taking you home, Trusty," he said.

"Will, what are you talking about? We'll find a good home for him later . . . after . . . if MayJune—"

He looked up at me, anger pinching his tiny face. "No. His home is in Alaska. I'm going to go see my land there, and bring him along."

My heart clenched. "Will . . . I don't think—"

A sudden keening noise stopped my lecture. There was a quiet moment—just the cicadas' slow chirp from somewhere in the dark—and then the keening squeal again. Will and I stared at Trusty. The sound had come from deep within him. MayJune laughed away our disbelief.

"I don't think he likes quarreling," MayJune said. "Come on in with me, Donna. You're shivering. Let me get you a sweater."

I wanted to make sure Will understood that he was definitely not going to Alaska. I'd set him straight, I thought, on the drive home.

MayJune rose stiffly and then hobbled through her front door. Trusty jumped up to take her porch swing seat and Will put his arms around him. "You made a sound," Will said, his own voice filled with wonder at the small miracle. "Just a little sound, but it was a sound."

I suddenly realized that MayJune was right—I was shivering. I went into her house and didn't see her anywhere. I sat down on the couch in the tidy front parlor. My eyes went right to the photo album that MayJune had left out, the album I'd carefully ignored because Will had been with me.

I picked up the album, opened it again, my hands quivering.

"Wasn't she a beauty?" MayJune said.

She held a sweater out to me. I wondered how long she'd let me sit like that, alone with the photos. I'd started at the front, and was on the last page.

"Yes," I said, as she settled next to me on the couch. "You said she grew up loving to sing, but there is so much I don't know about her."

"Like what, child?"

The words spilled out of me. "Miss Bettina has told me the truth—that Mama was unhappy, and ran away with a man who promised to help her make a record of her singing. But I don't know anything about *why* she was so restless. Was she always like that?" My voice knotted up with emotion and my struggle to hold back my tears. MayJune pulled me to her.

"She was an only child. Her own mama was always sickly and unhappy. I don't know why. And her daddy didn't handle it well. There were a lot of quarrels in that household. So I think your mama sang to try to make herself happy, and it worked while she was singing. And she saw she could make other people happy.

"As for her running away . . . well, honey, the biggest turns in life come when you're paying the least attention, making small choices you don't yet know will change everything. That's the way it was with your mama. She made what she thought were small choices—being nice to your daddy at the club, just to be sweet and maybe get a drink or tip. Same with going back to the club, just for old times' sake, and then taking up with that producer man. Before she knew it, she was in over her head, her choices changing her life and the lives of people around her."

I swallowed hard. I'd done that. Made small choices. Answering Mr. Cahill's ad and thinking I could get away with keeping my modeling job with him secret in a town like Groverton. Skipping school with Babs and meeting Jimmy. Even making Mama's clothes over, deep down knowing Daddy would eventually see what I'd done and be hurt by it.

I sat back up. "Thank you, MayJune." I closed the photo album. "I guess I'd better get Will on home." I stood up and stepped out onto the porch.

Will and Trusty were gone.

I found them a half hour later, walking on the dirt and gravel road along the Tangy River.

"Will Everett Lane!" I hollered from the car. "What are you doing?"

He ignored me and kept walking, his framed deed tucked under one arm, Trusty trotting along by his side.

"Come get in this car now! You scared the living daylights out of me!"

He kept on walking.

I slammed the car to a stop, turned off the ignition, jumped out of the car, and ran over to him, grabbing him by the shoulders. Trusty jumped on me, knocking me down, his body on top of mine, his teeth bared over my face. I could feel the growl deep in his body, his willingness to tear into me to—as he saw it—protect Will.

"Trusty, get off of her," Will said. He grabbed Trusty by the scruff and gave a little yank.

Reluctantly, Trusty crawled off of me, but kept guarding

Will. I sat up slowly. My back was already hurting where I'd hit the ground. I rubbed the back of my head. "You didn't sound too worried about Trusty ripping my face off."

"Don't be silly," Will said. His voice was tired. "He wouldn't really hurt you."

"Uh-huh. What are you doing, running off like that?"

"I'm going to Alaska. With Trusty," he said.

I stood up, felt my back. The lace on my dress was ripped. I hoped I could fix it—a trivial thought, I know, in that moment, but somehow it *mattered* to me.

"By walking?"

Will stuck out his chin. "I was going back to our house, on the other bridge, 'cause I figured you wouldn't think to come this way, and then get my money. I could buy a bus ticket."

"All the way to Alaska?"

"Well, part of the way. And then we could hitchhike. Or walk. Trusty would protect me."

"You know the bus driver wouldn't let a dog on the bus. Not a scary one like Trusty."

"Well, then we'll just hitchhike and walk all the way." Even with the tiredness, Will's voice was defiant.

"Will," I said. "You got the deed. Trusty is safe at MayJune's. Why are you doing this?"

"Because," he said. "I want to. I want to see my land. I want to get Trusty back home."

"You're tired, and so am I. Let's get Trusty back to MayJune's, and go home. We'll talk about this in the morning—"

"No! You'll just try to talk me out of going to Alaska!"

I didn't say anything. Will knew me well. He was right.

"Donna, I need to ask you something, and you have to swear to tell the truth."

I gave him a little smile, thinking I knew him well—that he was going to ask me how I found him, and that I would say that after searching around MayJune's house, I knew him well enough after all to realize he'd take this route home. "Sure," I said.

"Do you swear?"

"I swear."

"Cross-your-heart-and-hope-to-die swear?"

I winced at his use of that phrase, but said, "Cross my heart and hope to die, I swear I'll answer your question with the truth."

And then Will asked his question, proving that I didn't entirely know him as well as I thought.

"Donna, am I gonna die soon?"

When I could breathe again, each word came out painfully, like I was spitting up shards of glass. "Dr. Marshall says it's hard to know how your blood disease—how the leukemia—will progress, that sometimes miracles can happen, and—"

"I want to know! I want someone to tell me the truth! Am I gonna die soon?"

I stared past him and noticed, for the first time since I'd frantically started driving around to find Will, the harvest moon hanging full and orange over the river and trees, so big that it looked like we could just reach over the river and pluck it down.

Like a ripe persimmon.

I pressed my eyes shut.

The truth.

All our lives, we hadn't heard the truth.

We'd heard what people wanted us to hear. That Mama had died, when she hadn't. She'd simply chafed, like a trapped animal, at the life she'd thought she should want, until she couldn't bear it and ran away.

That she was to blame for Daddy's drinking problem and fall from power and status at the paper mill and in town, when she wasn't. He'd chosen how to react, to tend and nurture his hurt instead of really taking care of us, or noticing how much Miss Bettina loved him, or putting his life back together.

That people like Mr. Cahill were dangerous and wrong in their opinions and how they lived their lives and who they loved. And people like Mr. and Mrs. Denton were perfect and admirable.

That cereal companies and TV shows would tell the truth in their promotions and not just prey on the dreams of little boys.

That workers didn't have the right to expect safety measures.

I knew what I was supposed to say—that it was hard to say what would happen, that maybe the clinical trials Dr. Marshall talked about would turn up a treatment for Will's type of cancer sooner rather than later, that maybe if we prayed hard enough and long enough and purely enough, then God in his heaven would see fit to bestow us with a miracle.

But I couldn't do it. I couldn't be one more person telling Will what he was supposed to hear. So I opened my eyes and looked at him. As always, his big blue eyes got me. And I spoke the truth.

"Yes, Will, you are dying. I don't know how long you

have. A while, before you become weak and feel really ill, and then Dr. Marshall will add to the medicines you have to keep you comfortable—"

"I don't want to be comfortable, Donna. I don't want to win something just 'cause I'm sick, and I don't want to go to Hollywood. I don't want to stay here and have people moon over me and stare at me like they did tonight. I don't want that to be the last thing I do, Donna," Will said. "The last thing I'll be thinking about—all these people staring at me like I'm an exhibit from *Ripley's Believe It or Not* for kicking the bucket as a kid. But there is something I *do* want."

I knew what he was going to say. He grinned at me. "I want for you, me, and Trusty to go visit my land!"

He wanted us to trek across the entire country, part of Canada, and into the Alaska Territory, to see one . . . square . . . inch . . . of . . . land.

His one square inch of Alaska.

Impossible. Completely, fully, totally impossible.

And yet I knew that no matter what I said, Will would keep trying, would keep running away, just like he always did to get to his favorite place at the river, only this time, my ridiculous, stubborn, ill little brother would try, and try, and try again to get to Alaska to see his land, no matter that it wasn't much bigger than a postage stamp.

Because he didn't see it as ridiculous. Or illogical. He saw it as adventurous.

Even as all this turned over in my mind, he said, "We have a car! And we can borrow MayJune's camper—you know she'll let us. And we can take some food from Daddy's fallout shelter—he'll never miss it. And I have Jimmy's old atlas. I've already figured out two routes to get there. Both look pretty good."

The way Will put it, it seemed so easy. I thought about the money I'd pulled from tips at Grandma's, the money I'd saved from work for Mr. Cahill, from working for Miss Bettina, from making clothes from Mama's old things instead of buying new. . . . Instead of using that money for a bus ticket to New York to be a seamstress, I could use it for gasoline to go to Alaska. . . .

I shook my head. No. No. This was beyond impossible. It was insane. "Will . . . I don't think . . . in your condition—"

He put his hand over my mouth, thrust his face in mine. "My condition isn't ever going to get better. And I want to see my land in Alaska before I die."

Then he moved to stand beside me and pointed at the harvest moon . . . the persimmon moon. "There's still time," he said. "The *Farmer's Almanac* says it's supposed to be a mild fall and winter. By the time another full moon comes around, it will be too late to drive in Alaska."

Maybe, I thought, just trying would take Will's mind off his illness. We had more than a month's worth of his medicine, and we could probably get to the Alaska Territory in ten days if things went our way, if the weather held, if the car didn't break down. And Will's condition wasn't going to worsen if he rode in a car. In fact, I told myself, being made into a local oh-poor-dying-boy celebrity would run him down far more quickly.

We'd have to sneak off, without anyone knowing our plans—except MayJune, of course. Could we really leave . . . that night?

Suddenly, Trusty was looking up at us intently, his jaws open, miming barking. Male voices quickly approached. Maybe the voices belonged to the kind of men Babs had hoped would come along when I'd changed that flat tire. But Trusty wanted us off that road. Still, I knew Will wouldn't budge until I gave him an answer.

"We'll do it," I said. "We'll go to Alaska. You, me, Trusty. Now, get in the car!"

Chapter 24

By the time we got back to MayJune's, Will was fast asleep in the front seat. Trusty stood in the back of Mama's car, his head thrust between me and Will. I could hear his breathing, smell his doggy breath, feel his warm, moist exhalations on my cheek on the entire drive back to MayJune's, as he guarded Will and kept a wary watch on me.

As uneasily aware as I was of Trusty's sharp teeth, ready to snap at any second if he decided I wasn't Will's ally, I was even more nervous about what I'd just promised Will.

A trip to see his one square inch of Alaska.

Already the what-ifs were flooding my mind.

But then, how could I look at Will and take back my promise, especially after I'd told him the truth about his dying?

If Mama's car broke down, I'd fix it or find someone who could. After all, I'd changed a tire easily. If Will started getting sick, we'd find help. Or turn around and come back. In any case, I'd rather be with him if he needed help. I knew he'd just keep running away, no matter what I did or said, and that I couldn't stay awake and watch him every hour of every day.

At MayJune's, I tried to rouse Will, but he was deeply asleep. Trusty bared his teeth at me when I tried to shake Will awake.

I looked at the dog. "Fine," I said. "You stay here and watch Will."

Then I walked up the small slope of front yard to May-June's house. This time, I wasn't the least bit surprised when she opened the door before I could knock and had two fresh mugs of steaming tea waiting for us.

She took her time settling in her chair and then picked up her cup and took a sip. "Mmm-mmm. Ginger root, willow bark, chamomile. Good for my stiff old hips, at least until bedtime. I'll be stiffer than a wet sheet left on the line in winter when I wake up, though."

I smiled and picked up my cup, sniffing the aromatic steam.

"Now, honey, your tea is just ginger root. Good for soothing the stomach. And for energy." She lifted her sparse eyebrows at me. "I have a feeling you're going to need it."

I sipped my tea and then said, "I don't suppose you have a tea or poultice or broth for Will that will make him . . . better?"

For the first time since I'd met her, MayJune looked truly sad, her face and mouth drooping. "Honey child, I wish I did." She shook her head. "I wish I did."

I stared down into the amber liquid in my cup, focusing on the scent and feel of the steam, forcing my tears to retreat, to seep back in deep down with all the hurt I was holding back. If I was going to do what I planned to do, I had to be steely and not let that hurt out, not while Will was still here on this earth, needing me.

And then I looked up at MayJune, and told her my plan.

She didn't show any surprise or judgment as I told her that I'd been honest with Will about his approaching death, or that I'd promised to take us to Alaska. She just nodded like it made perfect sense. When I finished talking, she said, "Well, you know, tonight your daddy and Miss Bettina are away, helping with that terrible fire. Who knows how long they'll be?"

I stared into my now empty mug and turned this over in my mind, understanding what MayJune was suggesting. What better time than tonight, while everyone was distracted?

"Lenny's still up," MayJune said softly. "He could hook up that teardrop trailer to your mama's car right fast, while I get together some teas and herbs for you and Will and Trusty."

I looked up at MayJune.

And then I nodded.

Back at our house, Will and I worked quickly, assembling what we needed on the back porch.

Our blankets from our beds would go in the trunk, but first, we spread them out on the back porch and yard, so we could drop other items on top, to be bundled up and dragged to our car through our yard and the neighbor's behind us. (I'd parked on Maple, not wanting our nearby neighbors who might not be at the plant to see a trailer hitched to Mama's car.)

Our winter coats and hats and gloves from the front closet, even though they hadn't been aired out for the season and would smell like mothballs.

From the kitchen, two each—plates, spoons, cups, knives, forks. A saucepan and a frying pan, a spatula and a wooden spoon, and a box of kitchen matches. Bread, crackers, peanut butter.

From the basement fallout shelter, jars of home-canned peaches, apples, strawberry jam. Jars of green beans (including one jar of Miss Bettina's pickled beans), corn, carrots, tomatoes, beets, potatoes, and vegetable soup made from a little of all the leftover vegetables whenever there wasn't enough of any one type to fill a quart jar.

All the foodstuffs would go in the trailer.

All of Will's medicines in a pillowcase on the passenger's side floor.

Will's Sterry Oil United States and Canada road atlas, the one he'd gotten from Jimmy and had already marked with two possible routes to Tok, Alaska—that would go in the glove compartment.

And from the basement, we got the empty suitcases that had once been filled with Mama's old costumes and clothes—one for each of us. I told Will to pack two pants, two shirts, a spare pair of shoes, one pair of pj's, his toothbrush, and as many pairs of socks and underwear as he could fit in.

Small choices, I thought as I quickly started packing my suitcase. All that time I'd been slowly taking Mama's clothes to remake for myself, I hadn't known that I was emptying the suitcases so that we could fill them again for this adventure.

It all seemed so easy in the minutes I spent filling my suitcase with a skirt and peg-leg jeans and two blouses and pajamas—as if all the difficult events of the past months had happened so that in that moment we'd have everything we needed: the trailer from MayJune, the car and suitcases from

Mama, extra food for the taking from Daddy's bomb shelter, even the atlas from Jimmy. As if the trip was meant to be.

I sent a quick prayer up to God—in case he was listening on that warm, Indian summer night—that the trip would be as easy as our hasty packing. Then I hurried over to my dresser and opened my lingerie drawer. I pulled out several bras and undergarments, and then reached to the bottom for the envelope that held the money I'd been saving to go to New York to become a seamstress.

I'd like to say that I felt no reluctance about getting out that money, knowing it would be gone by the time we got back from Alaska, but I'd be lying. My heart clenched, knowing how hard I'd worked to save it.

As I pulled the bills out, my fingers brushed the letter Mr. Cahill had sent the week before. On impulse, I decided that I'd take the letter with me. I put half the money on one side and half on the other, telling myself that the letter was just a handy divider, that I'd take money from the front of the envelope on the way to Alaska, and that way I'd know we'd have enough for the return trip.

I hesitated just a moment, studying my other hidden items—Jimmy's Blue Waltz Sachet and the bottle of Dexamyl from Babs. I left the sachet but took the Dexamyl, deciding that if I used them carefully—maybe just taking half pills—they'd help me stay awake for long stretches of driving. I put the money envelope and the pills in my purse, dropped the lingerie in my suitcase, and then shut the suitcase.

I was about to leave my room when I thought that we should leave a note for Daddy. I picked up my sketchbook from the top of my dresser, and on a page in the back, scribbled a hasty note: *Daddy—Will and I are fine. I just needed to get him away from all the hullabaloo over him getting his deed. I have his medicines. We will call soon.*

I hesitated. I'd never written a note to my daddy before. I wondered if I should sign it "Love, Donna," but then thought that that didn't really fit how we were with each other, even with our new, careful peace. So I signed it "Sincerely, Donna."

I felt a little pang as I pulled out the note and started to put my sketchbook back on my dresser, so I opened my suitcase and tossed in the sketchbook and my pencils.

Then I picked up my suitcase and the note and stepped out of my room. Will's room was quiet and dark. He and Trusty were, I knew, waiting for me at the kitchen door.

I went down the stairs, through the living room, and to Daddy's bedroom. I put my suitcase on the floor. In one hand I held the note I'd just written. My other hand shook as I took hold of the doorknob. My heart pounded. I had vague memories of being in that room, with Mama, while she sang and stared into the mirror and brushed her hair, but I hadn't been in there since she'd died—if not literally, then to us—not even to clean.

A memory, flimsy and unprovable as a ghost, flitted across my mind's eye, of watching Mama apply makeup over and over, because she kept crying and ruining it, then wiping it off, while her handkerchiefs piled up on my parents' bedroom floor beside me like little drifts of sullied snow.

I turned the knob, and returned to the present with a switch of a floor lamp. The bed was neatly made with a chenille bedspread. Daddy's work clothes were thrown over the back of a small chair. His dresser top was empty.

I started to leave my note there, but then I saw, in the

corner opposite the chair, Mama's dressing table, undisturbed after all this time.

I drifted over to it and stared down at the photos clustered around a small glass tray covered with perfume bottles, their bottoms stained dark with dried fragrance. Still, the air in this corner of the room was heavy with familiar scents—tea rose, jasmine. Mama.

All the photos were of her.

All from before Will and I were born. Photos of Mama singing in the Tangy Town club where she and Daddy had first met. Mama in the outfits I'd cut up. Mama in her wedding dress—not Mama with Daddy—just Mama, with a careful, composed smile, perfectly beautiful in the dress I'd cut up and remade into the dress I was wearing. I picked up the photo, the note dropping from my other hand, my fingers then wandering to the lace on my shoulder. . . .

In that instant, I stopped worrying or caring about what Daddy would do or think about us going away. I knelt, swept the note up in my hand, and crushed it in my fist. Then I put it in my purse. Somewhere en route to Alaska, I'd throw it away.

I still held the photo of Mama in her wedding dress. I should replace it, I knew, but in a cruel impulse, I added it to the contents of my suitcase. I shut the bedroom door. In the kitchen, Will and Trusty waited for me.

Will held his framed deed flat, like a platter, on top of which was a box.

"What's that?" I asked.

He revealed the Alaska diorama that I'd crushed. He'd straightened it out as best he could. He shone a flashlight inside the diorama. "I added you!" he whispered.

I stepped forward, peered inside. There I was—a construction paper, glue, and toothpick version of me. Right by the toothpick flag from my first date with Jimmy.

"We don't need . . ." I started to say that we didn't have room in the car or camper for anything but necessities. Instead, I said, "Just carry it on your lap."

Will grinned, and I opened the kitchen door. We stepped out on the back porch and stared at everything we'd assembled. It seemed overwhelming, but I took a deep breath and started, "First, we'll get the suitcases out to the car, and then we'll bundle everything else up in the two blankets and drag them to the car, except the food; that we'll—"

Suddenly a figure stepped out from behind a sycamore tree. I grabbed Will and pulled him toward me. Trusty lunged, knocking the figure to the ground, standing on him.

"Get him off me," Jimmy gasped.

I let go of Will and rushed over. Trusty looked up at me and bared his teeth.

"Trusty, come here, boy," Will called quietly. "It's OK."

Trusty stepped off of Jimmy. The dog trotted over to Will but kept looking at Jimmy.

"Why'd he do that? He knows me," Jimmy said.

"Because you jumped out of the shadows and seemed like a threat," I snapped. "What are you doing here?"

"I couldn't stand to go home after what happened at the news conference. I had no idea that Dad was going to use Will like that. I knew my presence wouldn't be welcome at the mill, as much as I would like to help with the fire. So I drove around awhile and couldn't stop thinking about you and Will. So I came over to check on you, and saw your car when I drove down Maple, and a trailer attached to it. I figured you were up to something and wouldn't come to the front door, so I decided to come to the back and . . . What are you up to?"

"Nothing," I said.

He looked past me to the suitcases and blankets covered with food and coats on the porch. Then he looked back at me.

"We're going to spend some time at MayJune's, is all," I said.

"Then why the trailer? And where did you get it?"

"It's MayJune's trailer. You know how tiny her house is."

"We're going to Alaska!" Will said. I groaned. He went on. "We're leaving tonight, and we're taking Trusty, and we're going to see my land." He sounded giddy at the prospect.

"I want to go with you," Jimmy said.

My heart fell. "That's . . . that's not a good idea. Your parents . . . school . . ."

"What about your dad? And school for you?"

I thought about the photos—all of Mama—on the dresser in Daddy's room. "Daddy won't care," I said. "Your parents will. And we have a reason for missing school anyway. You don't."

"Donna, I want to do this. I want to help you. I know I . . . I was too harsh to you about Mr. Cahill. It was just that . . . when I thought . . . when I saw that sketch—well, I should have talked to you, should have listened to you more, but I didn't. I was an idiot. So I could make up for it now, by going with you. I could help drive and pay for gas. We'd get there sooner."

I hesitated. I didn't want Jimmy with us. I wanted this to be just my and Will's trip.

On the other hand, Jimmy made a good case. Plus he knew we were going. I wasn't sure I could trust him not to tell anyone.

"You don't have anything packed," I said.

"I can buy a few clothes somewhere along the way," he said.

Suddenly, the light inside the kitchen of the house behind us went on. I held my breath and thought, *Please don't come outside*. After a minute or so, the light went out.

As I slowly exhaled, Jimmy said, "I can help you get all this to your car."

"What about your car?" I asked, still reluctant to let him come with us.

"Follow me to my house and wait on the corner. I'll park my car where I usually do and then come back to your car. Deal?"

"Sure," I said. After all, we could use his help in quickly packing Mama's car and the camper. I wasn't sure, though, if I'd wait for him at the corner down from his house, or drive off without him.

Chapter 25

I didn't drive off without Jimmy.

I waited for him at the corner, just as he'd asked, studying the route in the atlas Will had marked out. By the time Jimmy got to my car, Will and Trusty were curled up, asleep, in the back, Will clutching his framed deed like it was a teddy bear, the diorama on the backseat floor. I'd kept out the blankets after we'd gotten everything loaded into the camper and car. One blanket was folded beneath Will's head like a pillow, the other covering him up, Trusty covering his legs and feet.

Jimmy got in the car and we didn't say anything. Late on the night of October 22, I just started driving to Alaska, heading out of town on State Route 35, as if we were going to Miami Valley Hospital in Dayton.

As I drove through Dayton and continued on 35, my heart pounded so hard that I could barely breathe as we crossed into Indiana. This was the farthest Will and I had ever been from home and the first time we'd been out of Ohio.

As we passed through Richmond and then Muncie, the road seemed less and less like a thread tying us back to

Groverton, until finally it was simply a road. What lay behind us suddenly didn't matter, just the next mile and the next and the next.

I drove until 35 intersected with U.S. Route 30 and then, just as Will had marked out in the atlas, I headed west. By then we were relaxed, making quiet comments every now and then about some small hamlet we'd pass by, or a farmhouse with lights still on. In Joliet, Illinois, south of Chicago, we found an open gas station—a great relief, since the gas indicator showed we only had an eighth of a tank left. Will stirred awake while the attendant filled the car. Jimmy took him to the men's room and I studied the map of Illinois, mostly to distract myself from Trusty, who was standing up, his ears perked forward as if he were on full alert, staring after Will, even though Will had told him to stay.

The atlas page showed that in Joliet, Route 6—the Roosevelt Highway—and Routes 30, 66, 52, and 31 all intersected, which explained the gas station open past midnight. I stared at the tangle of roads outlined around Chicago, and felt a pang of curiosity. *Chicago.* That's where Mama had wanted to go to record her music. Had she ever gone? Ever tried? I thought of the bridal photo of her I'd impulsively stuffed in my suitcase, the strained expression on her face, how different it was from the mischievous, carefree look she had in her old singing photos. Were there photos of her in the years after she'd left us, singing and laughing and carefree?

When I returned from my turn in the bathroom, Will and Trusty were settled down again in the backseat. Jimmy sat behind the wheel, and when I started to tell him to get out of my seat, he said, "It will go faster if we take turns driving and sleeping. I also bought two extra canisters of gas—they're in the trunk—for when we get out where there aren't many gas stations."

I started to argue with him, but I realized he was right. After all, he'd already driven across the country once, so he knew tricks like staying well supplied and ahead of fatigue. So I settled in the passenger's seat and helped Jimmy navigate to Route 52, and then stared out at the dark as we continued west on 52 out of Joliet.

For the next four days, we followed Jimmy's plan, taking turns driving, stopping just to stretch and eat and have bathroom breaks and sleep for just a few hours at a time, following Route 52 across the Mississippi River and into Iowa on the toll bridge near Savanna, Illinois, then staying on the route through Dubuque and Minneapolis and from there taking Route 12 across South Dakota and the southwestern corner of North Dakota and finally into Montana.

So on October 26, it felt like waking up when Jimmy pulled into the parking lot of the two-story Sunrise Motel in Helena, Montana. For just a second, I stared at the sign on top of the motel's flat roof—the word SUNRISE in red capital letters filled a white triangle, above which peeked a neon yellow half circle. SUNRISE MOTEL, again in red capital letters, was repeated on the side of the turquoise building, on the second story above the motel office, the letters askew as if a big wind had blown through, picked up the letters, and tossed them back onto the building, right above the entrance overhang.

I looked at Jimmy, who had been driving for the past four hours. "Why are you stopping?" I didn't want to wake from the travel dream trance. So far, we'd had good weather—just a few rainstorms—and no car trouble other than one incident of overheating in South Dakota, but we'd had that fixed quickly enough at a gas station.

"I don't know about you, but I need a shower and to just stop being in a car for a night," Jimmy said, flashing me a smile.

"All right," I said, "but we just passed a campground coming into town. We could just spend the night in the camper—"

"Let's treat ourselves," Jimmy snapped. "I'm going to check us in."

"But Trusty—"

"No one will hear him barking through the walls," Jimmy said.

I frowned, suddenly feeling defensive of Trusty's impediment. "Sure, but we can't sneak him in like a toy poodle, either—"

"Hey, Will, can you make sure Trusty keeps his head down until we can check in?" Jimmy asked.

Will looked up from his new *Sergeant Striker and the Alaskan Wild* comic book. I glanced at the comic book, already a little frayed around the edges from Will handling it so much, and tried to pull from my blurry on-road memory a specific recollection of when and where he'd gotten it. Then it came back to me: Jimmy had bought it for him the day before, while the car was being repaired at the service station in Aberdeen, South Dakota. While Will, Trusty, and I walked around the town for a little while, Jimmy went to a hamburger stand and picked up a bag of burgers for our lunch. When we met up with him again at the service station, he looked upset, but wouldn't say why. He just said he had a stomachache and wasn't hungry after all, and fed his burger to Trusty. He stayed quiet after that, but I didn't think much about it until that moment in Helena, in the parking lot of the Sunrise Motel.

"We're gonna stay in a motel?" Will asked.

"If your big sister gives us her approval," Jimmy said.

Will looked at me, wide-eyed. "Can we, Donna? Can we? We've never been in a motel before!" I looked at the white doors to the units. There were only a few other cars in the parking lot. This did not, I thought, look like a particularly wonderful first experience. But then, this might well be Will's only chance to stay in a motel. And getting out of the car for a night did sound heavenly.

Of course, I'd stuck to a strict schedule of giving Will his medicine, just like we were at home. But there was a paleness to Will's mouth and a pastiness to his skin that I didn't like. Every time I asked how he felt, he said, with some annoyance to his voice, that he was fine. Maybe, I thought, the constant car motion just worsened the side effects of his medicine. While Jimmy went to the office, I walked to the end of the motel parking lot, beyond which was nothing but wide open field that went on for miles. To the west, I saw other buildings—stores and shops—that led into Helena proper. To the north, far beyond the plain, mountains, part of the Rocky Mountain range, rose into the wide open sky. It was cool—not quite freezing—and dry, and it felt so good to be out of the close, warm confines of the car. I found myself luxuriously stretching my legs, arms, shoulders.

How many miles to those mountains? I wondered. Twenty? Forty? More? It was hard to estimate distance in this wide open land that looked like an odd mix of prairie and mountain. We'd already come about two thousand miles, and we had about that many more to go before we reached Tok in the Alaska Territory. The chance to say, *Ah, well, we can just turn around and go back* was long behind us.

Maybe, I thought, it would be good to rest for a full night, and let the car rest, too.

"We're really close to the Continental Divide!"

I startled and saw that Will and Trusty had gotten out of the car and quietly walked up next to me. Will was holding the atlas open. Trusty wandered a little way into the plain behind the motel and squatted.

I looked at Will. He'd been making such pronouncements off and on during the trip—most recently informing us that we weren't that far from Yellowstone National Park and Custer Battlefield National Monument—but Jimmy and I had just kept driving. I could sense Will's disappointment, especially about the Custer monument. He'd talked for a good fifteen minutes about the Battle of the Little Bighorn, between General Custer's 7th Calvary and Arapaho and Cheyenne Indians, and how Custer himself had been buried at the site, but his bones had been dug up and moved to West Point, and how there was a big granite memorial on top of the bones of all kinds of unknown soldiers, and also individual marker stones where soldiers had fallen.

Part of me had been aghast—how could he want to see a cemetery? And part of me had been amused. Will had always been bored in school, and yet so smart about the things that interested him, picking up knowledge from library books.

And atlases.

And the *Ripley's Believe It or Not* comic strip.

I took the atlas from him and peered at it, studying the little upside down *V*'s that marked the Continental Divide. For the first time, I felt some excitement about the journey itself, and not just an urgency to have it over with so that I could get Will back home where he'd be safe, at least for a while.

"We'll cross it tomorrow, following your route," I said.

"'Course, if we wanted to go another way, we could see Glacier Park," Will said, slyness creeping into his voice as he tapped the top left corner of the page. "We could cross the divide *and* see glaciers!"

I listened to Will go on as I stared at the map. Just east of the area labeled "Glacier National Park" was Shelby, Montana—the town where Miss Bettina said Mama was last known to live. Suddenly, I couldn't hear anything but buzzing. My vision fuzzed and the atlas fell from my hands.

"Donna!"

I looked up. Jimmy was standing over me, saying my name. I'd sunk to my knees. Will picked up his atlas and then stared at me, worry furrowing his brow. My head was still spinning, but I made myself get up, made myself smile at Jimmy and Will. The last thing I wanted Will to think was that I couldn't take care of him. I had to put the idea that we were only a few hours' drive away from Mama out of my head.

"I just got lightheaded, that's all," I said. "I'm fine."

Will ran over and threw his arms tightly around my waist. I returned the hug. "Hey," I said, "I am fine. I guess I just need dinner more than I realized."

Jimmy held up a motel room key. "How about we go see our room and get Will and Trusty in there before anyone sees Trusty, and then worry about dinner?"

"All right," I said. Will unclenched himself from me and began softly calling for Trusty to come back from the field. "I can make sandwiches in the room—"

"Actually, there's a diner across the street," Jimmy said. "I was thinking just you and I could go, and bring back something for Will later."

I frowned at the notion of leaving Will alone.

"Trusty will probably tear the room up if we take Will away from him, and I was kind of hoping to talk to you alone." Jimmy gave me a pleading look.

I looked across the motel parking lot to the diner across the street. We'd only be a few yards away. Dinner wouldn't take long. I gave Jimmy a small nod.

"How 'bout it, Will?" Jimmy called to Will, as he and Trusty walked back toward us. "You want to stay in the motel room with Trusty while I take your sister on a little dinner date across the street? There's a TV in the room and we can bring you back a burger—"

Will wrinkled his nose. "You're going on a date? Leave me out!" Then he paused and thought a second before adding, "Can I get a malt and fries, too?"

The Golden Gulch—named, according to the blurb on the front of the menu, after the discovery of gold in a gulch in 1864 that led to Helena's founding—was a lot different than Dot's Corner Café, with its polished wooden booths and ceiling lamps wired around hanging antlers. Grandma would have frowned with disgust at the spittoons beside each booth. Finally, something Grandma and I could agree about.

Still, the grilled cheese sandwich and fries were good, even though Jimmy and I ate in awkward silence. I was three spoonfuls into my hot fudge sundae when he suddenly looked up from the apple pie he'd barely touched and said, "Donna, we have to go back."

I slowly lowered my spoon to the sundae dish. "Go back? What do you mean? We're halfway to Tok!"

Jimmy looked away from me, down at his pie. "Look, I . . . I wasn't completely truthful with you about my driving from California to Ohio."

"You mean, you never made the drive? You just made that up to impress me?" I gave a little laugh, wanting to believe that Jimmy's tension was over nothing more than this. "Aw, I forgive you. It's kind of sweet and you've been so great on this trip—"

"No! The part I made up—or at least let you believe— was that my parents were OK with that trip. And they weren't. They were furious."

I stared at him. "If you want to go back, that's fine. I'm sure there's a Greyhound station here. After all, there's one in Groverton, and Helena's five times as big. I'll buy your ticket to repay you for the gas—"

Suddenly, Jimmy leaned across the booth, grabbed my hands, pulled me roughly toward him. "No, listen, we need to go back together! Plus Will is looking tired and I'm not sure it's a good idea—"

I pulled my hands from his grasp. "Don't try to use Will to make me feel guilty enough to go back with you! Yes, he's tired. But he's doing as well on his medicine as he would at home, maybe better, because he's so excited to be on this trip. Making him turn around now would just be cruel." I stopped, studied Jimmy for a long moment, and then said, more quietly, "Are you really just worried about what your parents will think? They're not going to be less mad at you if you go back now, and I don't see why Will and I need to go back—"

"Just—just—because—" Jimmy dropped his head to his hands in frustration.

"What's really going on, Jimmy?"

After a long pause, he finally said, "I got worried, OK, about what my parents are thinking, what they're planning to do when I do get back. So yesterday I made a collect call to Hank's house, but no one answered. I collect-called Babs and talked to her." Jimmy took a deep breath, exhaled slowly. "It's bad. Several people were injured in the fire. One died—Joey Winton."

Winton . . . MayJune had mentioned just once, at Will's birthday party, that that was her last name. And that she had a son named Joey. Tears stung my eyes. "MayJune's son?"

Jimmy nodded. I swallowed hard. MayJune's son had been dying at the same time she gave us the camper.

He went on, "The fire started because an incinerator door hadn't been fixed. That fire—it was because of ignoring safety practices, just like your dad said. Which means in the end it's my dad's fault for turning a blind eye. The strike is over and management is finally doing a safety review with workers, getting their input, but that doesn't change where everyone is putting the blame."

"I'm sorry, especially about MayJune's son," I said. "But I don't see why this means we—any of us—have to go back."

"Donna, I know that right now my parents—whatever their public face—see me as running away with the enemy's daughter. Babs overheard my dad rant at hers that if he hadn't printed all those letters from your father, then people wouldn't blame my father as much for what happened—the fire could just be seen as an accident."

I looked at Jimmy, horrified. "People are injured, May-June's son is dead, and your dad is worried about his reputation. And you want us to go back to make it look better for him?"

He said softly, "If you go back with me, we can convince them the trip was . . . done out of an emotional reaction. The stress of Will being sick. Even my parents could understand that. Donna, I love you. We can get back together. I can be free to go to college and figure out what I want to study and then, after a few years, we can get married."

I could see that he meant what he said, that he really *believed* it.

And I could also see a possible path for him . . . me . . . us. Jimmy Denton would—after playing at, say, philosophy and literature—take the business route his father wanted for him. And maybe, just maybe, by then we would still be together. I could become Mrs. Jimmy Denton. Have the safe, comfortable life as a woman that I'd never had as a girl. All I had to do was go back with him. No one—except Will, and maybe MayJune and Miss Bettina—would blame me. I could hear everyone saying, in a chorus of voices like Grandma's, *Why yes, Donna did have that emotional breakdown and*

*ran off foolishly with Will when he was sick, God-rest-his-soul,
but then she did the right thing, the practical thing, and turned
around and brought him home despite his protests—but what did
he know? He was sick and young, after all—and look at her now!
Nicely settled in as Mrs. Jimmy Denton. . . .*

Were those the kind of voices Mama had heard, urging
her to make the safe, practical choice of marrying Daddy,
instead of running after her singing dream?

"Look, there's another thing you should know. Babs told
me that she—" Jimmy paused, lowered his voice. "She's
pregnant. Hank hit her when she told him. Now, thank God,
Babs's dad won't let Hank anywhere near her. Her dad's taking her to a doctor he knows in Cincinnati. She's going to
be really sick for a while after—you know. She could use
your support."

I shuddered. Poor Babs. Then my stomach turned. I'd
lost my virginity to Jimmy. What if I'd gotten pregnant? I
felt sorry for Babs, wanted to be there with her through
this, but . . .

"Look, are you really going to throw over me and comforting MayJune and helping Babs because of this silly trip?
Thrown together at the last minute?"

I gasped. *Silly.* Suddenly, I saw Jimmy for who he was—a
nice boy. In over his head. Not sure what he wanted. Nice—
but not strong. Nice—but not someone who understood
me, after all. If he did, then he would never have asked me
to give up on this trip for Will when we were halfway there,
not for the reasons he'd given.

And, I thought, this trip—Will's trip to see his one square
inch of Alaska—didn't seem silly at all. And yes, MayJune
and Babs might want my help and support . . . but I knew

they'd both want, even more, for me to see this through. Maybe not my plan. But some plan—fate's. Or God's.

In that moment, I knew there was no way I would turn back.

I also realized that Jimmy had stopped talking and was staring at me, waiting for some kind of response.

"I'm going back to the motel room and, I hope, get a long, good night's sleep. And in the morning, Will and Trusty and I are going on to Alaska. You're welcome to come with us."

Jimmy stared at me a minute longer, got out his wallet, put down enough to cover our meals and a generous tip. He pulled the Sunrise Motel room key out of his pocket and shoved it across the table at me.

"I'm sorry," he said. "But I have to go back. I'm going to walk to the Greyhound station."

I swallowed hard. "I can drive you—"

He shook his head. "No. I think this is easier, if I just walk away. Tell Will I said good luck to him, OK? And to you, too."

I nodded. "You, too, Jimmy," I said.

Then he stood up and walked out of the Golden Gulch.

When I got back to the motel with a bag of burgers for Will and Trusty, Will asked, "Where's Jimmy?"

All the possible explanations I'd come up with swirled in my head. But then I shook my head to clear it. Will had wanted the truth about his dying. He could handle this truth, too.

"Jimmy got scared about his parents being mad at him for leaving suddenly, and so he's going back on the bus."

For a long minute, he was quiet. And then he said, "Well, we've always done better on our own anyway, huh, Donna?"

Tears pricked my eyes. I swallowed hard and said, "Not sure how Trusty feels about that."

"Awww, he knows I don't mean him," Will said, laughing. "Right, Trusty?" He knelt down and rubbed the dog's neck. "Hey, buddy, tomorrow we cross the Continental Divide! And then we'll keep getting closer and closer to your home!"

I'd long given up on trying to explain to Will that just because Trusty was a husky didn't mean he'd been born in Alaska. Will believed that's where the dog belonged, and maybe he was right.

Instead, I thought about those upside down *V*'s on the map, and how there was an alternate route alongside them that also went to Alaska, and took us near Shelby, Montana.

"What would you think about taking that alternate route of yours?" I said. "And maybe seeing a little bit of Glacier Park?"

"Really? That would be great!"

I had to smile at Will's enthusiasm. "All right, then. But on the way, there's something I have to tell you. And I'm going to need you to listen really carefully."

Chapter 26

The next morning, while I drove up Route 91, I told Will what Miss Bettina had told me about our mother—everything, except I softened the part about her getting the baby blues after he was born. I told him how MayJune had known Miss Bettina and Mama for a long time, from when they were even younger than Will, and that MayJune said Mama had always been looking across the horizon, wanting to get to the other side. And I told him how the last time anyone had heard from Mama, she was with Mr. Litchfield in his hometown of Shelby, and when Daddy knew she wasn't coming back, he gave her the divorce she wanted, and told us she'd died.

It felt odd, telling this story to Will, like it wasn't really about Mama, like it was something from one of Babs's overwrought romance novels. While I talked and drove, Will stared out at the wide blue sky, and cattle, and the white, jagged mountains rising in the distance, and for long stretches I wondered if he was listening to me at all. When I finished, I was quiet, waiting for his reaction.

But he didn't react. He didn't get upset or angry. He just

stared at the scenery rolling by as if he wasn't surprised that this was the actual truth about our mother. That she hadn't died; she'd simply left us.

The gorgeous Montana countryside blurred in my tears of frustration. I was, I thought, being selfish. The truth was, I wanted to see if I could find Mama. To confront her. To ask her how she could have left us like that.

"Will, maybe I shouldn't have told you. I don't think this side trip is a good idea after all. Why don't we just go on to Glacier National Park instead?" I glanced at him. He was giving me a look that said, *Don't try to bribe me*. His face was so puckered up with annoyance that I had to laugh, even while feeling miserably unsure about whether I'd done the right thing.

And so I drove on to Shelby, both of us silent for the rest of the way, Trusty with his head thrust, as always, between us. Occasionally, Will scratched the top of Trusty's head. I turned on the radio. We no longer had the station out of Helena, but after a while, we picked up KIYI in Shelby, which was on a Hank Williams kick; I tuned in to the middle of "Your Cheatin' Heart." I almost snapped off the radio; the song was too close to what our mama had done . . . and what I'd been willing to do with Mr. Cahill . . . plus it was sad to think of Mr. Williams's death at the beginning of that year. But then the next song was "Move It On Over," and Will turned up the radio, and by the end, we were crooning together. That song was also about cheatin', but it was a lot more fun to sing as loudly as possible to a rocking beat and funny words about the woes of a man in the doghouse—literally—for his sins: *Came in last night about half past ten. That baby of mine wouldn't let me in. So move it on over . . . move it on over. Move over little dog 'cause the big dog's movin' in.*

We were singing to Trusty, giving him a little nudge every time we repeated the refrain. He perked up, panting, and I realized I'd nudged and petted him several times and he hadn't silently snapped at me even once. Maybe, I thought, by the end of the trip, Trusty and I would come to a peaceful understanding.

Then the song was over and we were on the outskirts of Shelby, just a few houses on either side of a narrow strip of road.

Quickly, we went farther into the heart of the town, passing storefronts—drugstore, barbershop, "nite club"—that weren't much different from the ones in Groverton. I turned down the radio and we were silent again, staring at each place we passed as if Mama might just pop out of one of them and recognize us and of course want to run to us and embrace us. Suddenly, my heart flopped right down into my stomach, and I felt sick. Even in a place this small, how would we find her—if she was still here? It had been seven years since she'd left Groverton, and probably five since Daddy had last had contact with her, according to Miss Bettina. I'd been a fool to tell Will what I'd learned, to waste precious time on this trip to stop here.

"Wait—slow down, stop there!" Will said.

I stepped too hard on the brakes, making us lurch to a stop. A car behind us, which I hadn't even noticed, braked and honked. "What?" I looked around anxiously. "Do you see—"

I stopped, seeing that Will was pointing at a building ahead of us, the Lone Star Diner.

"What, you're hungry?" It was nearly three. We'd had breakfast early that morning in Helena and I'd insisted we stop for a snack around lunchtime—peanut butter and crackers from the camper—but I was happy to hear that Will was hungry, even if the urge seemed oddly timed. He'd shown little appetite on the trip so far.

But he rolled his eyes at me. "No, you goober. What is it you always complain about when you come home from Grandma's diner?"

The car behind us honked. I took my foot off the brake and let us coast forward, looking for a place to park—not easy with a camper in tow. "That my feet and back hurt," I said.

"Besides that."

I spotted a stretch of empty curb ahead of us, and eased us alongside it, exhaling with relief and not caring that the driver who'd been behind us lurched past in his pickup truck hollering something crude at me.

"That Grandma's a witch?"

Will laughed. "That everybody knows everybody else's business in Groverton and always talks about it at the diner, and that you have to smile like you care to get a tip."

He opened the door and got out of the car, Trusty following him. "Come on!"

I made him wait while I opened the trunk and awkwardly leaned in from the side to pull out my suitcase. I opened it, dug past my clothes to the framed bridal photo at the bottom. My fingertips also brushed the bottle of Dexamyl from Babs.

Oh, Babs, I thought, *such a mess you're in now.*

But I shook my head. I couldn't worry about her, about

Jimmy, about anyone in Groverton. I just had to focus on Will and on wrapping up this side trip as quickly as possible, so we could get on to Alaska.

My hand closed around the bottle of pills. Jimmy wasn't here to help with driving. But the pills could keep me going for hours. . . .

"Here," I said. "I brought this, Mama's bridal photo. I'm not sure why I grabbed it, except I was going to leave a note for Daddy, and—"

Will took the picture and stared at it. While he wasn't looking at me, I slipped the bottle of pills into my purse.

"Maybe someone will recognize her photograph at the diner," I said. My voice was shaky.

Will looked up at me, his eyes wide. "You look just like her," he said.

I looked over his shoulder at the photograph. There was, I thought, more sadness to her eyes and mouth, and she had a finer nose—I definitely had inherited Daddy's rounder nose—but I had her heart-shaped face, her brow, her eyes and mouth and chin.

Will sat on a bench near the Lone Star Diner, and Trusty settled down by his feet. I went inside, clutching Mama's bridal photo to my chest like a notebook of secrets.

The place was nearly empty—just a man at one end of the counter and an older couple (who reminded me of Mr. and Mrs. Leis) lingering in a booth. I took a stool at the counter on the opposite end from the man.

A waitress who was not much older than I came out of the kitchen. She gave me a bored smile but avoided looking me in the eye—end-of-shift weariness. The waitress, who wore a name tag labeled "Joanne," dropped a one-page menu in front of me and said, "Besides what's there, our blue plate is chicken-fried steak, mashed potatoes, lima beans, and your choice of pie. Personally, I recommend the club sandwich."

"Actually, I'm here looking for someone."

Joanne gave me a one-sided smile. "Aren't we all, honey. But this ain't the best place for that. Now, over at the Mountain View Nightclub—"

I smiled, partly because I instantly liked this woman's sassiness, and partly at the image of Grandma if I'd ever said such a thing in her diner. All her tight curls would have sprung right off her head. "Not that kind of someone," I said. "I'm looking for someone who came here about seven years ago with a man named Harold Litchfield. Her name is Rita. Rita Lane. Or she might go by Rita Litchfield." I thought for a second. What if she'd broken up with Harold Litchfield? Maybe she'd taken back her maiden name. "Or Rita McKenzie."

Joanne's eyebrows lifted. "What is she, some kind of fugitive? On the lam?" Her eyes narrowed. "You some mole sent in by the FBI? I've read stories about this kind of thing."

Despite the somberness of Will's and my situation, I had to laugh. Babs would love that, I thought, the idea of me as an FBI mole. I thought about our attempt at undercover sleuthing at the Sunshine Bakery, and even as I felt another pang of worry and sadness for Babs, I had to smile. "No, nothing like that," I said. "Rita was—is—my mother. My little brother and I are . . ." I paused, thinking, *Well, Will and I are on the lam, in a way*. Except I didn't think Will would see us as running *from* something. He'd say we were running *to* something. I liked that better. I straightened my shoulders, started again. "My little brother and I are on a trip and we found out our mother came here about seven years ago. And we thought we'd . . . well, we thought we'd look her up."

Look her up. As if this were as casual as dropping by for a Danish and coffee.

"Huh. So she was a kind of fugitive," Joanne said.

I started to argue. But I realized that, in a sense, Joanne had it exactly right. Mama was a fugitive from all that had made her sad and restless back in Groverton, Ohio. She'd been running *from* something. I wondered if, nevertheless, she'd found peace in Shelby, Montana.

"Well," Joanne said, "truth be told, I came here just two years ago myself. Getting away from a nasty boyfriend who liked to pop me a few." She pumped her fist in the air.

"Oh, no, it wasn't like that. My daddy didn't . . ." My voice trailed off. Then I settled for, "Daddy didn't hit her. She just . . . got weary."

Joanne nodded like that made perfect sense. "The name Litchfield rings a bell." She gave a little frown. "Not sure why."

My heart gave a small squeeze. I turned the bridal photo so Joanne could see it. "That's her. It's an old photo. Before I was born. About twenty years ago."

Joanne gasped, then looked up at me. "Why, honey, you're the spittin' image . . . except the nose." She stared at the photo again. "This is her wedding day?"

I nodded.

"But she looks sad," Joanne said, as if it were impossible to imagine someone looking sad on her wedding day.

"Jean will know who she is and where to direct this young lady."

Both Joanne and I looked up, a little startled, at the man from the end of the counter. He'd gotten up and walked over to us.

Joanne snorted. "Billy, why are you always listening in to other people's conversations?"

"'Cause you talk so damn loud," he said. He plunked down some money. Joanne grabbed it from the counter and put it in her smock pocket. The man made a shooing motion with his hands. "Go on back. Tell Jean there's a young lady here—" he grabbed the photo, looked at it. He went a little pale. Then he swallowed hard and said more softly, "You're right. She's the spittin' image of a younger Rita." He shook his head. "Anyway, go tell Jean that Rita Litchfield's daughter has showed up in town looking for Rita. Jean will know what to do."

"Jean won't do anything but yell at me if I don't go back there with an order."

I was hoping to spend as little money as possible, in case of some future emergency, but I didn't see that I had a choice. "How about two bottles of Coca-Cola?"

Joanne lifted her eyebrows at me.

I sighed. "And a club sandwich."

She jotted those items down on her order pad—like she wouldn't remember—and went through the swinging doors back to the kitchen.

Billy was still staring at the photo.

"Do you know her?" I asked softly.

He startled from his reverie and looked up at me. Then

he shoved the photo back at me. "No," he said. "Just heard her sing a few times."

"Well, where was that? At the Mountain View Nightclub? Maybe someone there—"

He shook his head. "Some things are better off not knowing, kid." He put some bills on the counter. "That's to cover your sodas and sandwich. You can always walk away before Jean comes out."

My heart started pounding. "Why? Why would I want to do that? If she knows my mama, she can tell me where to find her. Or maybe you—"

"She was a wonderful singer. Haunting." With that, Billy turned and walked away, hurrying as best he could given the hitch in his step, going out the front door just as another couple came in. The couple that had been here earlier was gone. I could see the back of Will's head through the diner's big front window.

She was a wonderful singer . . . was . . .

Why had he said "was"? Had she left town? Stopped singing?

"So you're Rita's young'un." I startled, turned, saw standing behind the counter the woman who had to be Jean. I'd expected some Montana version of Grandma, but this woman was plumper, taller, younger—and definitely more pleasant looking, although she growled at Joanne, who was standing right behind her, eager to hear what we'd say. "Get over there and take the Mitchells' order!" Joanne looked disappointed, but hurried out to the couple.

Jean sat two Coca-Colas and two wrapped sandwiches on the counter. "Joanne says you and your brother are on a

trip and just happened through here, asking about Rita."
She pointed to the sandwiches. "If you're on the road, figured you might want to take your food."

"Thanks. Um, Billy, he paid for the colas and one sandwich," I said, pointing to the money he'd left. Then I started
to open my purse.

"Don't worry about it. Where are you headed?"

"Alaska," I said.

"Alaska?" she said. "Why?"

"It's a long story. It's just . . . something I have to do for
my little brother. He's ill. Not contagious ill—that's not
why he's waiting outside. We have a dog with us—" I stopped.
This was sounding more convoluted the more I tried to
explain it. "Look, he's OK now, but he wants to go to Alaska
while he still can, so I'm taking him. That's the simple
truth. And we found out that our mama is living here. At
least, that she was as of about four years ago. We thought
she'd died seven years ago."

Jean studied me. I could tell she was deciding if she was
going to help us or not. Finally, she shook her head and said,
"I can't believe I'm doing this, but—wait here a moment,
child."

She disappeared into the kitchen. Joanne came back
behind the counter and whispered, "What did she say?
Does she know your mama? Is she going to help you? Why—"

Joanne hushed and stood up straight as Jean came back
out of the kitchen with a pie.

She set it on the counter. "Apple," she said. "Noah's
favorite." Then she looked at Joanne and demanded, "Give
me a piece of paper and pencil."

Joanne pulled a sheet off the order pad and her pencil

out of her smock pocket. Jean snatched both from her, as if she were in a hurry to do this before she changed her mind. She started scribbling and said, "This is the way to Noah's place. Just head out on Main Street, on through town, then turn right at County Road 152. You'll see his place on the right. Just tell him you're bringing a pie from Jean Garfield and that she said he should talk to you."

She shoved the little map at me and gave me a look like she wished I'd hurry up and go before she snatched the pie back and changed her mind.

"Who is Noah?" I asked.

"Noah Litchfield. My sister—God rest her soul—was married to him. She passed last spring. Anyway, Harold Litchfield was their son."

Joanne was staring at the map. "But that's—" she stopped. "Oh." She gave me a sorrowful look, then looked at Jean. "Now I remember some customer telling me the story. . . ."

Jean gave her a look. "Shush up, Joanne."

Will and I sat in the car on the gravel path that led up to Noah Litchfield's small wood frame house. To the west of that house, along the county road, was a cemetery. "Piney Woods Cemetery" was the name spelled out on a sign over the wrought iron gate, and in fact, the cemetery was amply filled with pine trees among the headstones.

I looked at Will, who was holding Jean's pie in his lap. He looked a little pale.

"We don't have to do this," I said.

"I want to know. Don't you?"

Sitting in Mama's car, staring at the ramshackle house

where supposedly lived a man who had the answers about her last years, I wished I hadn't brought up the possibility of finding Mama in Shelby. But now not knowing what had happened to her would weigh us down for the rest of the trip. I couldn't do that to Will.

I opened my car door. "Come on," I said.

Will followed me, carrying the pie, Trusty trotting along beside him. We went up the rickety steps, knocked on the front door, waited.

"Maybe he's not home. Maybe we should—"

"His truck is by the house, so he's home," Will said.

I glanced off the side of the porch at a red, rickety pickup truck. "I'm not sure that truck even runs. He could have another truck or car and be in town, or away—"

But of course Will ignored me and knocked again, harder.

A second later, the door creaked open. An old, skinny man peered out at us. He looked at me for a second, did a double-take, then started to shut the door.

"Mr. Litchfield, Mrs. Jean Garfield said if we brought this apple pie that you would talk to us!" Will said quickly.

The man peered out at us again. "Then you might as well come on in. If Jean sent you out here to talk to me, and I don't, she'll never let me hear the end of it."

We followed Mr. Litchfield into his front parlor—even Trusty, who Mr. Litchfield liked immediately. Trusty was wary of the elderly man kneeling beside him, but Will cooed at him until he let Mr. Litchfield pet him. After we settled into the dim parlor—the only light came from a fire in a buck stove—Mr. Litchfield took the apple pie to his kitchen. I looked around, noting carved wood figurines—of animals, people, trees—dotting every surface from windowsills to the fireplace mantel. The figurines reminded me of the salt and pepper shakers in Grandma's diner, except Mr. Litchfield had made these pieces, not just collected them. He came back from the kitchen with several slices of bologna for Trusty, who gobbled them up and then settled in front of the fire.

Then Mr. Litchfield asked us what we were doing in Shelby, Montana. I started to ask, right away, about Mama, but Will interrupted and said we were on a road trip to Alaska to see *his* land. When Mr. Litchfield laughed and looked skeptical, Will went back out to the car to get his framed square inch deed. As soon as Will went out the front door, Trusty was at the screen door, watching him.

"You look just like Rita," Mr. Litchfield said.

I made myself hold his gaze. "I've been told. Except for my nose. Like my daddy's."

Mr. Litchfield nodded. "I only met him once. He came here, looking for your mama. She and my son were staying with us then. I want you to know that Rita never mentioned that she had children. Or a husband back in Ohio. If we'd known that, we'd have never let her and Harold stay here. He told us they'd met and married before getting here."

My throat tightened. *She never mentioned us.* And then I thought, *Daddy must have come here when he said he was going to Florida to check on Mama.*

"Is she . . . does she . . . live nearby still?" I asked as Will came back in, holding his deed.

Mr. Litchfield studied me for another long moment.

"Darlin', this isn't a pretty tale. Are you sure you want to hear it? Or have your little brother hear it? If you think that you're going to meet your mother and she'll pull you both into her arms and tell you she loves you and that there will be a sweet reunion, I have to tell you that that is not how life works."

Will came back in as Mr. Litchfield was talking. "We know that," he snapped.

Mr. Litchfield stared at him then. *Assessing*, I thought. Deciding.

Then he sighed. "All right. We hadn't seen our son, Harold, in years, not since he shipped off with the army in World War Two.

"And then, about seven years ago, he showed up with Rita McKenzie. Said he'd met her in Ohio, before the war, scouting talent for the Chicago record company where he worked. On a road trip, he happened in to where she was singing—the luckiest day of his life, he said. After the war, he got his old job back and he looked her up again. They went to Chicago for a while, and he set up a few singing sessions for her, but things didn't work out. Then he lost his job. We never heard why, but I'm guessing he had too many wild nights and didn't make enough money for his company.

"He told us that they were married and that they were going to be in Shelby just for a little while, stay with us until they got back on their feet. Then her husband showed up— that was a shock. She'd written him, asking for a divorce because she wanted to be free to marry Harold. I only met your dad once, but I felt sorry for him. He begged her to come back with him, talked about the two of you, but she said no. She'd rather die, she said, than go back to Ohio. She was staying with Harold, and soon they'd go back to Chicago, where she could sing."

Mr. Litchfield shook his head. He picked up a figure of an owl from the end table, thumbing the top of the owl's wooden head as if it were a worry stone. "It about broke my wife's heart, learning that our only son had taken a woman away from her husband and children. Mine, too. I wouldn't talk to them after that. Or give them money. I kicked them both out."

I swallowed hard. "Did they go back to Chicago, then?"

Mr. Litchfield stared into the fire for a long time. I looked at Will, tried to read in the dim light how he was taking this news. He looked tired but then he turned his gaze to me. *I'm fine*, his expression said. I nodded.

"Mr. Litchfield, please tell us the rest," I said. "Did they go back to Chicago?"

Finally, he shook his head. "No. Harold worked here, odd jobs. Rita sang at several different clubs. I never heard her, but I heard talk that she had a lovely voice. I also heard talk that they really did get married. That's when my wife wanted me to go see them, talk to them, but I was having none of it. Then one day the sheriff came out here, told us they'd been out driving in Harold's truck. The sheriff said it was hard to tell from what was left, but it looked like your mother was driving, tried to cross the railroad track, even though the guard crossing bar had come down, but they didn't make it across in time. They died instantly."

He looked up at me, said softly, "Rumor has it that Rita had just found out she was, well, expecting a child. But no one seems to know if that's true."

Then Mr. Litchfield stared out the window. "They're

buried out there. Maureen, my wife, insisted on it. And now she's buried there, too. I don't think she ever forgave me for not speaking to Harold and Rita after your father was here. I think she always thought if I had, they'd be alive. Maybe if I had, she'd be alive. Doctor said last year she died of emphysema. I think it was mostly from a broken heart, though."

He looked down at the wooden owl, as if just then aware that he was holding it. I wondered if he'd started carving after Maureen had died.

Will and I walked to the cemetery before nightfall. We asked Mr. Litchfield if he'd like to go with us, but he told us no.

We followed the directions he gave us, winding our way, Trusty by Will's side, along the tidy gravel paths. Mr. Litchfield kept his cemetery neat and orderly, just like his house.

Then we found the headstones—Mama's, and Harold Litchfield's, and Maureen Litchfield's. Will and I studied them quietly in the cold wind barreling across the fields and cemetery. I'd like to say I felt something strong— sadness, anger, something—when I stared at Mama's headstone, reading over and over the simple epitaph: "Rita Litchfield, 1915–1949, Rest in Peace." Had she found peace? Had the wreck been an accident . . . or on purpose? Had she killed herself, and her new husband, because she couldn't stand the thought of being tied, again, to a family? Why was she so restless, so sad?

There were some questions I'd never quite find the

answers to. I suppose that I should have felt frustrated, at least.

But all I felt was nothing, except cold in the howling wind.

"I think Mr. Litchfield blames himself," Will said. "But he shouldn't. I don't think his wife is right, that it's his fault they died."

I pulled him to me, wanting to protect him from the sharp wind. "I think . . . sometimes, people just do what they think they have to do. And Mama was unhappy with us, but it sounds like she was just as unhappy without us. And that misery had nothing to do with us. We didn't cause it, and we couldn't fix it. It was just . . . hers."

As soon as I said that, I felt something after all, staring at her grave. Relief. And release. At last, I could let Mama go. I didn't need to understand everything about her. I just needed to understand that her choices weren't, in the end, about me, or Will, or even Daddy.

"Do you think we should tell Mr. Litchfield that?"

"I think he's starting to understand that, and that's why he told us everything he did."

Will frowned. "But I don't understand why his sister-in-law would just send us out here, to remind him. Do you think she blames him, too?"

I shook my head. "No. I think she wanted him to see that the children his son's wife left behind turned out OK anyway."

"We did?" Will said. "Well, maybe I did, but you can be pretty annoying sometimes."

Even standing at Mama's grave, my little brother made

me laugh. For a long time after that, we stood quietly, hugging each other in the harsh Montana wind.

Finally, we made our way back to Mama's car—no, *my* car now—and our camper. There was a note under the car's windshield wiper from Mr. Litchfield: He was cooking dinner, which we were welcome to share with him, and we could also camp there for the night, if we wanted to.

Chapter 27

Will and I took Mr. Litchfield up on his offer.

Mr. Litchfield made bologna and cheese sandwiches, and pork and beans on his wood-fired stove. The kitchen just had one small table and two chairs, so we ate the sandwiches and beans in the parlor, balancing our plates on our laps. The room was lit by the fire and a kerosene lamp on a side table next to Mr. Litchfield's easy chair.

After dinner, I washed up the bowls and stew pot in the kitchen, and when I came back out to the parlor, Trusty was settled in front of the fire again, and Will finally showed Mr. Litchfield his deed and said that we were on a trip to see his land, and taking Trusty with us, because Trusty really belonged in Alaska. He talked about how he wasn't sure how Trusty had ended up in Groverton, and about how we'd rescued him from a mean scrapyard owner, and how Trusty didn't bark but made a good watchdog anyway. He didn't say anything about being sick or how we had left in the middle of the night.

Mr. Litchfield hung on to every word Will said, even as he got a length of wood from his back porch and a whittling knife from his pocket and started working the wood. I wondered what he was making. *He's lonely*, I thought, watching him whittle as Will talked. Then Mr. Litchfield put his whittling aside and the two of them pored over the deed and atlas in detail. Finally, Mr. Litchfield stood up stiffly from his chair and lit another kerosene lamp sitting on a quilt chest.

"Will, all this talk of this trip of yours has made me hungry again," he said. "Would you go slice us up some of Jean's pie? Rattle around in the kitchen and it won't take you long to find plates and such. And get a few more slices of bologna from the icebox for Trusty, here. There's milk in the icebox if you want it."

Will looked at me and I gave him a little nod. He put his deed and the atlas on the quilt chest, next to the kerosene lamp, and headed back to the kitchen.

Mr. Litchfield picked up the deed, stared at it, running his thumbs over it. "That's quite a sense of adventure the two of you have," he said. "Makes me long for my younger days—but I'm content, I reckon, to live out what's left here. Maureen and I had a lot of good years here—and some tough ones, too."

He put the deed back down on the quilt chest and gave me a hard look. "Is Will strong enough to finish the trip?"

I shifted uncomfortably in my chair. "Of course."

"He's sick. I can tell. I've gone to see plenty of sick folk, to make arrangements before they die, and I've learned to recognize the look, even in a young one's eyes. I've been the undertaker for Shelby for near on four decades." He pointed his pipestem at Trusty, who hadn't followed Will to the kitchen, but who had perked up and was on alert for his return. "Some animals, particularly dogs, can sense it, too. It's almost like they smell it in a person. If they like the person, they'll get very loyal and protective."

That sounded crazy, I thought, the idea of Trusty sniffing cancer in Will. But then I thought of MayJune and her crazy homespun remedies and way of seeming to know when we were coming, or when we'd need something—like a camper.

I blinked back the sudden moisture in my eyes and said quietly, "Yes, Will is sick. Lymphoblastic leukemia. He's on medicine that's maintaining him for now, but in a few months . . . well. That's why we're on this trip." I blinked again, but it was too late. The tears rolled down my cheeks anyway.

Mr. Litchfield nodded. "It's good," he said. "Good you're on this trip." He paused. "Good you came by."

At that moment, Will came in, three plates of pie and a glass of milk and bologna on a tray. He distributed the food, Trusty gobbling his bologna quickly. Mr. Litchfield and Will dug into their pie, and Mr. Litchfield said, "Mmmm-mmm. That Jean's a nag, but she can bake."

I was full, but I took a bite of the pie anyway, just to be polite, and before I knew it, I'd eaten the whole slice. Mr. Litchfield was right. His sister-in-law could bake a wonderful pie. As good as Grandma's.

That night, Will and I slept in the camper in Mr. Litchfield's front yard. Trusty was still wary about the camper, so he slept up on the porch. I was worried he'd be too cold, but Will told me I was being silly, that after all, the dog was a *husky*.

For a long time, I lay awake, cuddled down under my

blanket, listening to the soft, even rhythms of Will's breathing. I thought about everything we'd learned, everything Mr. Litchfield had said, and finally I decided that he was right—it was good we were on this trip. It was good we'd come by to see him.

Then, at last, I fell into a long, deep, dreamless sleep.

When we woke up the next morning and crawled out of our camper's tiny sleeping area, we saw that the red rickety truck was gone. But Mr. Litchfield had popped open the back hatch of the camper, where there was a small workbench and above that built-in cabinets.

He had left a paper sack on the workbench. We opened it and sorted through the contents: bologna, cheese and bread, two slices of the apple pie wrapped in wax paper, and two maps, of Glacier Park and British Columbia. There was also a tiny wooden figure, a likeness of Trusty.

There was a note, too: *These maps are from my and Maureen's honeymoon, so they're old, but they have some more detailed roads than your atlas. If you can make it to Dawson Creek, you should be able to take the Alaska Highway up to Tok. The carving of Trusty is my thank-you for listening to an old man. Good Luck. Noah Litchfield.*

"The maps are good," Will said, closing his hand carefully over the wooden figure of Trusty and putting it in his pocket. "The atlas just shows the main roads in Canada."

Disappointed that Mr. Litchfield had taken off that morning before we awoke, I looked to the place his truck had been parked. "He must have had some errand or appointment in town. . . ."

"Nah," Will said. "Lots of folks just don't like saying good-bye."

Like Mama. And Mr. Cahill and Jimmy . . .

Will grabbed a slice of bologna to take to Trusty, who was stretching himself awake on Mr. Litchfield's porch. A little later, on the morning of October 28, we set off. It took us just a few hours to get to Glacier National Park, and we spent the day there, exploring as much as we could before nightfall, driving along Going-to-the-Sun Road, stopping at St. Mary Lake, Logan Pass, and Lake McDonald Valley. We didn't talk much, just stared at the lakes and majestic mountains and forests and fields as if we had been starving for these sights our whole lives and couldn't take in enough fast enough. Will wanted to see a bear. We didn't, but he seemed just as pleased by seeing elk and deer and fox, and a bald eagle swooping down from the sky to land at the top of a soaring pine tree.

Part of me wished we could stay there forever, making time stop.

But inevitably, dusk fell, and I hurried us to our car. At the back of the camper, I made bologna and cheese sandwiches for us to eat while I drove. There was one slice of bologna left.

"Go on," Will said. "Give it to Trusty."

My heart was pounding as I walked up to him. He stared at me warily. I held out the bologna, bracing myself for Trusty to jump me as he had in our basement, to snap up my fingers along with the bologna. But he gently took the bologna between his teeth and gave the slightest tug. I let go, and he ate it.

That day, after studying Mr. Litchfield's maps, we decided to abandon our plan to go over the mountains through Calgary and instead mapped out a more direct route on smaller roads. So we drove west out of Montana across the tip of Idaho into British Columbia and stopped at Kootenay Bay, where the ferry was closed for the night, so we spent the night in the camper alongside the road. The wind and rain rocked the camper, so Trusty crawled in with us, falling asleep between us.

The next morning, we crossed on the ferry. I noted the signs saying the ferry closed after October 31. It was October 29. I figured we needed at least another four days to get to Tok, another day or two at best to find that square inch. How would we get back? I pushed that worry from my mind. I'd figure that out later.

That night, we pulled off to the side of the road and made a small fire. I heated vegetable soup for supper. When I started the car back up, Will frowned. "Aren't we spending the night in the camper?"

"I feel fine. How about you nap, and I'll just drive?"

He looked wary, but didn't argue. I took one of the Dexamyl, washing it down with strong coffee. Soon Will was sleeping in the front seat. Trusty was relaxed in the back, apparently no longer thinking he needed to keep a vigil over Will. I drove, drove, drove, the car lights picking out the road.

The darkness seemed perpetual. I popped the Dexamyl, snatching a few hours' sleep here and there. I vaguely remember at some point asking Will why it was so dark all the time if we were heading toward the land of the midnight sun, and him rolling his eyes and pointing out that midnight sun happened in the summer, and above the arctic circle—and that we were traveling in late fall. I remember thinking how smart my brother was. I remember, vaguely, a surge of joy at making it at last, on November 1, to Dawson Creek, and cheering in the town's center at the 0-mile marker for the Alaska Highway.

"We're almost there," Will said, grinning. "All we have to do is stick to the Alaska Highway now!"

We had 850 more miles to go.

Sometime later, I startled awake. I could barely see for the snow swirling down in the night, but I felt our car going too fast, swerving, and I was screaming something. The head-lights picked out the edge of the road. We were on a curve around the side of a mountain, but I had us heading off an embankment. I swerved, jerking our car back to the right side of the road, but hit something—maybe a rock tumbled down from the mountain, or a chunk of ice. After the thud, the front driver's side tire blew. We started careening again on the slick road. Somewhere in the midst of this, I slammed on the brakes. A few seconds later, our car came to a stop.

I sat for a second, shaking all over except in my hands, which were clenched around the steering wheel so hard that they felt fused to the plastic.

I looked over at Will. He was staring, wide-eyed, at me. "That . . . that cougar . . . I don't think you hit it."

I nervously pulled my hands away from the steering wheel. "What are you talking about? I hit a rock or chunk of something, Will. Your imagination—"

He looked at me disbelievingly. "You don't remember swerving around that cougar in the road? Just seconds ago?"

I put my head to my shaking hands. My head was pound-ing and my heart racing. My hands were sweaty. The

Dexamyl had kept me awake so that I could drive for hours at a time, but now my body was taking over, demanding sleep in spite of the drug, and I knew I must have fallen asleep while driving. I didn't remember seeing a cougar, but in my glazed-over state I must have, and reacted instinctively. In fact, the last I distinctly remembered, it was twilight, not night. And it was clear, not snowing.

"Where are we?" I asked quietly.

"We passed through Whitehorse a little while ago."

"Show me the map," I said.

Will turned on the flashlight and focused it on the map, already spread out over his lap. It looked like we were about twenty miles out.

"We passed a roadhouse, a little ways back," he said. "We could walk back there—"

"With a possible injured cougar on the prowl?"

"I think you just clipped it. If you hit it at all."

"Will, was there a cougar or not? Did I hit it or not?"

"I—I'm not sure—it was all in a flash . . . and I was sleeping, and your swerve woke me up . . . and suddenly you were screaming about a cougar. You said you saw a cougar!"

Suddenly I understood. I was the one . . . not Will . . . who'd supposedly seen a cougar. But had I seen it? Or just hallucinated it?

"I'm sorry, Will," I said. "I think I'm just . . . too tired. But the fact is, we have a blown tire now, and we can't just stay here in the middle of the road. Give me the flashlight."

He handed it to me and I opened the door.

"What are you doing?" Panic edged his voice.

"Changing the tire. So we can go back closer to Whitehorse for the night. Camp there." Truth be told, I wanted to

keep driving, but now I didn't trust myself. Not with drift-
ing off, and the snow, and the darkness.

"But what if the cougar—"

"Will," I said, "I don't think there is a cougar. And if
there is . . . well, we'll just sic Trusty on him, OK?"

He calmed down, as if Trusty could take out a cougar.

I checked over our car and didn't see any dents or blood
or fur like there should be if I'd hit a cougar. And then I
nervously set to changing the tire, shaking in the cold and
snow. And out of fear of how I'd just nearly plunged us to
our deaths. And fear that maybe I *had* seen a cougar and not
just hallucinated.

Eventually, I swapped the blown tire for our spare—our
only spare. I had to smile, thinking, *What would Babs say
now?* I was changing a tire again—and not on a rainy day in
Ohio, but on a slick, cold night with possible cougars roam-
ing about in the Yukon Territory. She'd say, *Well now you
really need some nice young man to come along and rescue you.*

But I didn't. I just needed some real sleep. And a place in
Whitehorse where we could buy another spare.

Finally, I finished the tire change, and then got back in
the car. It took me a long time to maneuver the car and
camper around on the road so that we were headed back to
Whitehorse.

By the time we were nearing the roadhouse, though, I
could tell something else was wrong with the car. The
engine temperature gauge needle was edging toward "H"
and the engine was knocking. I pulled to the side of the
road just past the roadhouse.

"I'm going in to see if anyone there can help us," I said.

"I want to go with you."

I looked at Will. His face was drawn up in concern. I looked back at the place. It didn't have a name, just a neon "open" sign flickering in the window next to the door.

"No, you stay here. I'll just be a few minutes."

I got out of our car and made my way across the road and parking lot, leaning forward into the bitter wind and snow. I pulled open the tight door and stood shivering for a moment, trying to regain my breath, which the wind had snatched away.

When I did, I looked around, and instantly wished that I hadn't come in here. A few men sat at tables and at the bar. The bartender stared at me. I swallowed hard and went up to the bar, feeling curious eyes on me. When I got to the bar, I saw that the bartender was actually a short, squat woman, her hair slicked back in a rat-tail-thin ponytail, wearing a flannel shirt and jeans just like the men in the bar.

The woman stared at me, waiting for me to speak. I was trying to think of what to say. Suddenly, explaining that my car was broken down out front and that my only companions were my little brother and a mute dog seemed like a really bad idea. My mouth gaped and closed, and finally the woman said, "Yeah?"

"Um . . . my husband and I are, ah, traveling on our honeymoon, and he sent me in to, ah, see if we could get some . . . some sandwiches to go."

I was startled by rough laughter and glanced to my left. There were three men at a table just behind me. Two of the men were laughing, but one was staring at me. My skin suddenly crawled with a sick, clammy feeling. One of the laughing men said, "Your husband sent you in here? What, he didn't want to come in for a pint?"

"Shut up, Hector," the woman snapped. She looked back at me. "Does this look like a drive-in to you?"

I swallowed hard. "No, ma'am."

"If you and your husband want food, the general store back in Whitehorse might be open for a little longer."

"OK, thanks, that's good to know," I said, backing away from the bar.

Then I turned and hurried back out. I heard the scrape of chair legs on the rough wooden floor, the tread of someone following me to the door, the creeping sensation of being watched. I ran to the car and looked back. I didn't see anyone in the doorway. In my car, I started it up and turned it back around, keeping my eye on the engine temperature gauge heading quickly again toward "H."

"Why are we going back this way?" Will said.

Because all those men in there think I'm heading toward Whitehorse, I thought. *So I'm going the opposite direction.*

"I think we're better off camping tonight after all. In the morning, we'll get help in Whitehorse."

I drove slowly, praying for the gauge to stay below the "H" until I got to the crest of the hill we'd just driven up. We almost made it. I held my breath, gunned the overheated engine to pull us to the top, and then put the car in neutral and took my foot off the accelerator to let us coast down the hill, around the curves, past the place where I'd nearly driven us off the road. I spotted a clearing to the side of the road and slid over to it.

"We'll be all right here tonight," I said, praying that I was right. "We'll just cover up in the camper with everything we have."

That's what we did. I pulled all our clothes out of the

suitcases and piled them on top of our blankets in the camper, and we burrowed underneath those, snuggling together, with Trusty—who finally seemed to have overcome his nervousness about the camper—between us. For dinner, we ate crackers under the covers, and I giggled at Will's silly jokes.

What did the fish say when it swam into a wall?

Dam!

What happened when the goose flew upside down?

It quacked up!

Finally, Will sank into sleep. I lay awake, wide-eyed in the dark, startling at every small sound, wondering if I'd done the right thing by having us spend the night here. What if the snow was so heavy that I couldn't dig us out in the morning? But our car wouldn't have made it back into Whitehorse, and the men—and the woman bartender—hadn't been too friendly. I'd been stupid to go in there at all. It wasn't like walking into a diner in the middle of the day. . . .

My eyes grew heavy, and as much as I fought staying awake, my body yearned for sleep. I was tempted to take another Dexamyl, just one more, to stay awake for the night and watch over Will, but . . .

When I woke up, I was outside the camper. I looked around, startled, wondering why I was out, and then I realized I was hunkered down, peeing behind a shrub. I could just make out the shape of our car and camper in the dark. I must have half-woken up and half-sleepwalked out.

I finished my business and started back to the camper, shivering. The snow, thankfully, had stopped, and I guessed there were only a few inches on the ground. If our car was still overheating in the morning, we'd just walk back to Whitehorse, I thought, and—

Suddenly, rough hands grabbed me from behind. I started to scream, but then a hand moved to clamp over my mouth. I bit down, but my teeth just grabbed glove leather. I started flailing and then felt something sharp next to my throat—a knife. I went physically still, my mind scrambling for an idea of how to get away, how to get to Will. . . .

"On your honeymoon, little missy? Don't scream, or I'll slice your pretty little throat."

The hand over my mouth moved to my hair, jerked my neck back. I felt cold lips on my neck, then smelled foul breath as my attacker said, "You aren't on a honeymoon; you're by yourself. I've been looking in the little window. Just you and some kid." Another kiss. My stomach roiled and I fought back a retching gag, fearing that if I flinched at all the knife would slice across my throat. "And the kid can't help you. You're going to be mine, my . . ."

My brain turned to Will, away from the nasty things the man was muttering. How long had I been away from the camper? What if he'd already hurt Will? My shock and terror started to tinge with anger. The first thing I had to do was get the man to move the knife from my throat.

"I won't scream," I said. My voice was ragged, shaking. "But I can't go anywhere with you with the knife—" I stopped as he pressed the knife more tightly against my throat, then moved his hand from my hair to my arm, clenching it in a painful grip.

"I will let you turn so I can see you, but one scream and I'll run this knife through your tender little belly and then do the same to the kid in your camper. Understand?"

That threat means Will must still be all right. "Yes," I said.

The man moved the knife from my throat, then scraped

its edge over my coat, over my breast. I swallowed hard, fighting the instinctive impulse to scream. I prayed. *Please God, let this be another hallucination, like the cougar might have been. . . .*

But the man's hand was still on my arm, jerking me around. This was real; all too real. The first edge of sunrise was bringing our spot of the world out of darkness. I could see only the man's size and shape. He was huge. My stomach roiled again.

I told myself, *You got him to move the knife from your throat. Now get him to let go of your arm.* Then . . . what? Run to the car? Even if I could get there without him catching me, I wasn't sure I could get it to start, and he could easily break through the window. Maybe I could break a window, grab a piece of jagged glass to use as my own knife, but I'd need a piece of cloth around my hands. I suddenly realized I didn't have gloves on, that my hands were numb.

"Let her go!" Will stood in front of us, aiming his Red Ryder BB gun—his birthday gift from Daddy—over my head at the man. His hands were shaking.

The man laughed. "Go back to your sweet dreams, son. This doesn't concern you."

"Will, I'll be OK. Go to the camper—"

"No, I'm not letting him hurt you!" I could hear anger in his voice and also that he was crying.

The man laughed, nastier this time. He pressed the knife to my throat. "Go, or I'll slice her throat before you can pull the trigger, and—"

Suddenly, a beast came howling and running out of the darkness. The man startled, dropped my arm. "What the hell?" he yelled.

The animal ran past me and lunged at the man, snapping and snarling. I stared in disbelief.

The beast was Trusty. The man screamed and tried to hit Trusty away, but the dog sank his teeth into the man's arm, making him scream in agony. In the bare light, I saw that the man had dropped his knife and was reaching for it, about to stab Trusty. I ran over and picked up the knife, and in so doing, knelt right by Trusty and the man. For a second, I wasn't sure if Trusty knew who I was, if he was trying to protect me or if he'd just suddenly gone wild and happened to jump the man instead of me. But when the man grabbed for my arm as I picked up the knife, Trusty moved his muzzle right over the man's face, snapping and barking wildly.

I stepped back, shaking. One bite and Trusty could rip most of the man's face off. Trusty had known I was in trouble, and to protect me, he had somehow found his voice.

I felt a touch on my arm, jumped, and saw that Will was beside me, staring at Trusty pinning the man to the ground and snarling in his face. Will's BB gun still shook in his hands.

My hand tightened around the knife. "Tell Trusty to back off him," I said. "I think we can make him go away now."

Will looked up at me. His face was tight with fear. "Are you OK?"

Suddenly, I started shaking, but I said, "Yes. I'm fine."

Will nodded. "All right, then." He stepped closer to the man and Trusty, and called Trusty's name.

Trusty stopped snapping and snarling but stayed on top of the man, growling.

"Get him off me, get 'im off!" the man begged.

"Why should I?" Will asked, his voice amazingly steady. "You were hurting my sister."

"Aw, now, boy, I was just going to have me a little fun— why, your sister sashayed into the roadhouse and—"

"Attack!" Will snapped.

Trusty started snarling and snapping in the man's face again. I'd never heard Will teach Trusty any such command, but something in his voice cued Trusty that it was all right to start barking again. Strangely, I almost laughed, out of both relief and lingering fear. What if Trusty really did rip the man apart? And if he didn't, what were we going to do with this man? Now that the light was growing, I could see his truck, parked just across from our car and camper. If we let him go, he could run us down. I wasn't sure it made sense to try to march him at knifepoint in front of us. If we left him here and took his truck back to town, he could hurt our car and camper before running away.

Maybe, I thought, I could drive and Will could keep him under control with Trusty, but then how would we all fit into the cab? And what about the knife?

I tensed, sensing someone coming up behind me. My hand tightened on the knife.

"Shoot 'im! Shoot the dog!" the man started screaming.

I knew he couldn't be talking to Will, so I whirled around and saw the woman from the roadhouse just a few feet from me, holding a rifle, aimed right at the man and Trusty.

"If I'm shooting anything, it's you, you son of a bitch," she said.

Chapter 28

The woman had us all get in her car, handed me the rifle to train on the back of the man's head (which I did with quivering hands, even as Will kept his BB gun out, too), drove us back to the roadhouse, and called for both a police officer (to haul off my attacker) and a tow truck (to haul off our car and camper). Will and I learned that the roadhouse bartender was Molly Donovan. Her father owned the place, but ever since his health had failed and her husband had died, Molly had run it. She and her dad lived in a small house behind the roadhouse.

The man who had attacked me was Charlie Rickman—the only one in the roadhouse who hadn't laughed in disbelief at my claim that I was traveling with my husband; the one who'd stared after me, making me feel nasty and exposed. That night, he'd stayed until the roadhouse closed in the early hours of the morning. When Molly a little while later had let her own dog out, she'd seen Charlie sitting in his truck in front of the roadhouse. She'd heard him talking about me after I'd left, and knowing Charlie's reputation, she suspected he was deciding whether to follow me into Whitehorse or go home.

But Charlie had guessed I might go the opposite direction and had gone up the road and found us. Molly had let her dog back in the house, and followed.

Back in Whitehorse, while Mr. Luke Randall fixed my car (a radiator hose had a leak, causing the engine to overheat) at Luke's Body Shop, Molly took us over to have breakfast with Mr. Randall's wife and children—all four of them under the age of six. Mrs. Randall, though, seemed glad for the company, happy to make extra pancakes and thick rounds of bacon. Will told everyone how we were on our way to Tok, Alaska, so he could see his land. The little Randall children were fascinated by Trusty, who occasionally gave a bark, testing his reclaimed voice, and was as gentle with the children—letting them pull on his ears and roll around with him—as he'd been terrifying with evil Charlie.

After our car was fixed, Mr. Randall charged me far less than I'd expected for both the radiator hose and a new spare. Molly insisted we go back by the roadhouse. We sat at one of the tables in the empty place, playing Go Fish with a deck of cards she'd given us, while she went out the back to her and her daddy's house. By the time she came back out to us, Will had put his head on the table and fallen asleep. Molly handed me a sack of sandwiches along with a piece of paper.

"Names of people you can trust, and directions on how to find them, between here and Tok," she said. "I've contacted them on ham radio. If you want, you can check in with them at Haines Junction, Burwash Landing, and Northway. In Tok, if you run into trouble getting to see that land of yours, look up Sol Capputo—"

"Thanks," I said, "but I think we'll be fine." I didn't want to stop and check in with people. I wanted to get to Tok, see Will's land, and then figure out the best way to get us home.

Molly lifted her eyebrows at me. "You're a young woman traveling with your little brother, with only a dog for protection—no real gun, no means of communication— through some of the toughest terrain in the world at the start of November, in a yellow convertible with a tiny camper. For one thing, that'll make you stand out to the worst kind of predator—human, as you've already found. And for another, I figure you all must have some kind of story that's more than just following up on that cereal box deed." She paused, studying me, but I didn't get the feeling she really wanted or needed for me to give any more detailed explanation.

I waited, and finally she smiled at me for the first time since we'd encountered her. "One thing I've learned out here—it's all right to let people help you." I smiled back.

We had about 390 more miles to go.

By the time we left Whitehorse, it was late afternoon on November 2. After the previous night's events, I decided we'd stop for the night in Burwash Landing, especially since the Burwash Landing Resort—really a low-slung building that looked like a motel without any neon signs, just its name in simple brown wood letters—was open and had plenty of rooms available; it was closing up in a week. The woman who checked us in cheerfully told me that we were at "historic mile 1093" on the Alaska Highway, that the Jacquot brothers had opened a trading post at the site in 1904, and that in 1944 the lodge had opened.

The cafeteria was closed for the season. I asked her if we could have a campfire near the lake and cook some food, and she said that was fine, although she warned me of strong winds coming off of Kluane Lake.

"We have a dog with us," I said. "We can leave him in the camper, but he's really attached to my brother."

"Bring him in and let me see him," she said.

Will, who had been staring at the woman the whole time we chatted, ran out and soon came back in with Trusty. The woman knelt before him and stared into his eyes. I held my breath nervously as she cupped her hands under his chin and brought her face right to his muzzle. But Trusty just stared into her eyes, while she stared into his.

Finally, she looked up. "You have a very special guide here," she said somberly.

After we stepped out of the lodge, Will said, "She must be part of the Yukon First Nations! Did you see her cheekbones? And her hair? She kind of reminds me of MayJune!"

I realized for the first time that MayJune had Indian features. I felt badly for MayJune, but knew that somehow she was handling Joey's loss, while comforting others.

"The Yukon people helped the first miners and settlers. . . ."

And on he went, while we got our clothes into our room. He'd read up more on the history and people of this area than he had about the history he was supposed to study in school. He'd done so well on this trip that for just a fraction of a second I forgot how sick he was. We gathered up armloads of wood from the designated pile behind the resort and then carried it down to Kluane Lake. We found a fire ring and made a fire, then spread out our now filthy bed-spreads to sit on. I heated up the last home-canned jar of vegetable soup. We ate that, along with the sandwiches Molly had packed us, and stared at the still, blue lake and the mountains beyond it, until night fell.

With the darkness came cold and a swift wind, but our little fire, shielded by a large rock, kept going. Without talking about it, Will and I snuggled up together, our backs against the large rock, one of the comforters pulled over us and Trusty under the cover and resting on top of our legs. Trusty gave little kicks and sighs every now and then.

Finally, though, as my cheeks began to feel numb, I was about to tell Will that we should go into our room for the night, but then he softly said my name.

"Yes?"

"What do you want to be?" he asked. "I mean . . . later."

I stared at the fire. Any words I spoke would acknowledge a time after Will, a time *without* Will.

I thought, *How can I answer "fashion designer"?* That answer was the truth, but suddenly the truth seemed so stupid, so shallow, so trivial. Now I understood why Daddy hadn't wanted to tell us the simple truth about Mama. Sometimes the truth just doesn't seem to be . . . enough.

So I cleared my throat and said, "Dr. Emory says there are clinical trials for new medicines for your type of cancer." I paused. Each word sounded, in the clear, cold air, like a little bell ringing and then whisking away on the wind. "I'm going to be a doctor, of course. A medical researcher—"

Suddenly Will twisted away from me and then punched me in the chest with all of his might. I gasped as he pummeled me until I finally grabbed his arms and held him still. Trusty howled. In the flickering light from the fire, I could see that Will's face was scrunched up with anger.

In fact, I'd never seen him angrier. He'd never gotten this angry at Daddy and his drinking.

Or Grandma and her hatred of us.

Or Howard and his taunting.

Or the evil man who'd attacked me the night before.

Or even the terrible, unfair diagnosis he'd been given.

This was the angriest moment of his life, and his wrath was directed at me. "Bull!" Will screamed. Spit flew from his lips. "You hated biology class last year. I heard you talking with Babs about how dissecting the frog made you want to puke! You would be an awful doctor and you don't want to be one at all!"

"Will, calm down! Get back under the blanket." I started pulling him back toward me.

He pushed away from me, sobbing. "No!" He looked frantic. "I don't want your help with the blanket! I want you to tell me the truth! I want you to tell me what you really want to be when you're a grown woman! And don't you dare say a mama, either!"

His sobs quieted, settled into hiccups that punched in between every third word or so.

"But what if that is what I want to be, really?"

Will looked stunned at this idea. "But why? After all of—this—" He flapped his arms out, and I knew the gesture meant himself and his sickness and this trip and the mothering I'd done long before he became ill.

"Come here," I said. "By me."

He did, butt-scooting back to me, and then I held him,

his body pressed to mine for comfort and warmth, my arms around him, his head against my shoulder. I leaned my frozen cheeks against the top of his head, covered in a knitted cap.

Will was still hiccupping, but less often, when I finally sighed and said, "All right. The truth. I want to be a fashion designer."

I waited for a second, for another outburst, for him to ask how I could want something so trivial. But he didn't. He just said, "Ah," hiccupped again, and waited for me to go on.

And so I did. At first I talked reluctantly—about designing, and techniques, and some of the clothes of Mama's I'd remade—but then my voice picked up strength and speed, and I got lost in talking about how much I loved designing, and my ideas for designs, and my wish to study at the Parsons School of Design, and how Mr. Cahill had already written a letter recommending me, and my dreams of living in New York and working in Paris and Milan. . . .

Finally, I stopped, and the second I did so, shame washed over me again. How could I speak of such future dreams to Will? His breath was slow and even. I wondered if—half-hoped that—he'd fallen asleep and heard little of what I'd said.

But then he said, very quietly and softly, "Thank you. Now you have to promise me that you will really do it. You'll really do everything you can to make those dreams come true."

Tears welled, stinging my eyes in the cold. "I promise," I said.

"Cross your heart, hope to die promise?"

I swallowed hard, then chanted the old schoolyard oath:

"Cross my heart, hope to die, stick a needle in my eye . . . I will follow my dreams. And make them come true."

"Good," Will said as if that satisfied him and settled my future.

I pressed my eyes shut, felt the sting of cold tears on my cheeks.

Now I realize that Will *needed* to hear what I wanted from life, my plots and plans. He had known that I needed to remember my own dreams. He needed to know that I wouldn't lose sight of them.

It struck me, even then—and I still think about it—how many people we knew who had lost their dreams, and lost their way. Mama, desiring to sing. Miss Bettina, loving Daddy, but afraid to let him know. Jimmy, wanting to break free from his parents' rigid expectations.

And then there were those who had followed false dreams for so long that maybe they didn't know what they really wanted. Babs, grasping for love and attention, even from abusive boys like Hank. Daddy, clinging to an image of Mama that was really a mirage. Grandma, wanting status and approval so badly that she couldn't even see how wonderful it was that she'd created a gathering place like Dot's Corner Café. Mrs. Denton, wanting Mr. Cahill to be someone to her that he never had been, and never could be.

And finally, there were the people we knew who had quietly made peace with who they were, and their dreams, however they worked out. MayJune. Mr. Cahill. Even Mr. Litchfield. And Trusty, who had found his way back to his voice.

Suddenly, Will gasped. I opened my eyes, alert, ready to snatch him up and run if we were being threatened, but then I saw what had snatched breath from him and woven it into a sigh of wonder. The sky was alight with draping, weaving swaths of jade and magenta and azure. The northern lights. We watched together silently, even after the fire burned out.

Then Will said, "Donna, what do you think happens after we die?"

For a second, my throat closed. I stared at the dancing display of light as if I might find an answer in a swirl or turn of color. Finally I said, "Well, at Grandma's church, the pastor always said if we've been faithful, then we get to be in heaven, with God and the angels—"

Will sighed, his deep exhale asking if I'd never learn. "Not what we were taught. What you think."

I pulled him closer to me, watching the lights turn and dance. "Truth be told—I don't know, Will. I really don't. Except I think whatever it is must be amazing and beyond anything we could imagine, beyond words."

"Like this!" Will sounded pleased. I know he meant like the northern lights, draping the night sky with great sheaths of dancing gossamer, like angel wings . . . beyond words.

"Yes, Will. Like this. Just like this."

Chapter 29

The next morning, November 3, when I opened the door to our room, a blast of icy wind stung my face. I started to hurry to the office to turn in our key, and nearly tripped over two pairs of boots. Rolled up in one was a note. "These are mukluks, which will keep your feet very warm. I couldn't help but notice your thin shoes. Velma."

Guessing that Velma was the woman who had checked us in, I smiled at her generosity.

We had 214 miles to go.

Sometime after we left Burwash Landing, we realized that our car's heater wasn't working. We stopped long enough to put on our coats, hats, gloves, and our new mukluks, which wrapped our feet in a cocoon of warmth.

Trusty curled up in the foot well at Will's feet, filling the whole space.

Will held in his lap the atlas and his framed deed to his one square inch of Alaska, ready to proudly show it at the deed office in Tok.

We had 130 miles to go.

For miles after Burwash Landing, we didn't see anyone else on the road, just stunning views around every curve. I drove slowly, mindful of the patchy road, just gravel and dirt in places, and the sharp drop-offs around curves. Our breath puffed in little white clouds. We joked about making enough breath clouds to cause it to snow in the car. Then our breath started fogging the inside of the windshield, so we lowered our windows and stayed quiet, until we saw the tiny sign indicating we were crossing from the Yukon Territory into Alaska Territory. At that we cheered so loudly that Trusty barked, and his barking made us laugh.

Soon after, we rolled slowly through the tiny settlement of Northway, but didn't stop.

We had fifty-five miles to go.

About an hour and a half after we left Northway, a fierce wind began blowing snow across the roadway. I picked my way carefully, slowing to just ten miles an hour, the swirling snow blurring the edge of the road.

But as I came around one curve, I hit a patch of ice. Suddenly, our car was sliding off the road, over the edge of a sharp drop-off, plowing through brush. I slammed on the brakes, which did no good. I braced myself and held my right arm across Will's chest, as our car and camper careened, finally slamming into a stand of pine trees partway down the steep incline.

My head jolted forward and I hit my lip on the steering wheel. The metallic taste of blood filled my mouth. I gagged, about to throw up, but swallowed back the bile. I looked over at Will, who wasn't moving. My arm was still across his chest; Trusty was already half out of the foot well, his paws on Will's lap, licking at his face.

"Will! Are you all right?"

"Fine." His voice was soft, tiny. "You?"

The car slid a little. I wasn't sure how long the small trees would hold the weight of our car and camper. The only reason we were all right was because I'd been driving so slowly to begin with, and we hadn't slid that far. But with the snow blurring my view, I wasn't sure how much farther down we might go. I thought quickly, *Get Will out of the car. Get his meds out of the glove compartment.*

"I'm fine," I said, trying to keep my voice even. "But we have to get out of the car. You and Trusty go first."

"But you—"

"Don't argue! Just get out! For once, just listen to me."

He started to open the door. The car skidded a little.

"Open the door slowly," I said. "Get out carefully. Then run up the hill!" I didn't want the camper to whiplash around and hit Will.

He did as I asked, easing out of the car. Trusty followed him out. I reached over and popped open the glove compartment. I could hear Will screaming, "Hurry, Donna, hurry!" which made me think the car was barely hanging on to the side of the drop-off, but still, I moved carefully, mindfully, as I first got my purse from the backseat and then pulled the bag of Will's medicine out of the glove compartment.

Then I struggled to open my door. I realized that the

angle of the car—my door must be facing up—was making it hard. The car slipped a little. I heard the trees creaking from the weight of the car and camper.

I shoved the door as hard as I could, scrambling out as it opened, barely getting my leg out of the way before it slammed shut again. Then I half-crawled, half-ran up the incline to Will and Trusty.

We stared at our car and camper, creaking against the thin stand of pines. Then there was a sharp crack as several of the trees gave way to their weight and our car and camper skittered out of sight, crashing through other brush and small trees. After that, the moan of the wind took over again as the only sound filling the air.

I looked at Will. His eyes were wide and dark, his face pale, his breathing jagged. I knew he was scared about what had just happened, about our situation, but I also knew that he was weak from his illness and the side effects of his medicine.

I clenched the bag of medicine in my hand. At least I'd saved that. I shoved it into my purse, which held the rest of our money in the letter from Mr. Cahill.

Will hugged his deed and atlas to his chest. Trusty stood staring at us.

I guess I had every right, in that moment, to be upset and angry.

But instead, in that cold, terrifying moment after we'd lost our car and camper, I felt a warm peace rise through me. We'd nearly lost our lives—but we hadn't. We had each other and the few things that were necessary for our survival.

"Come on," I said. I scrambled up the hillside, sometimes pulling Will to help him over the steepest parts. Trusty crawled up beside us.

Finally, we made it to the top, back to the snow-swept road.

There, a gift awaited us: the fold-down hatch from the back of the camper. It must have bounced open as we went over the side and cracked off in the cold.

Despite everything, I smiled, an idea forming. I knelt down and called to Trusty.

"Go on," Will said, his teeth chattering. "Go to Donna."

I pulled the scarf from around my neck, stared into Trusty's pale blue eyes. Then, slowly, I reached for the dog. For just a second, my terror of the beast came back . . . but then I let it go, let it sweep away with the wind. Gently, I closed my arms around Trusty's neck, buried my face in the fur of his scruff, breathed in his deep, musky scent.

"I know you can't understand me," I whispered. "But I need to say this. I don't think Will can walk the rest of the way, and I'm not sure I can carry him. So I need you to help me. Help me help Will."

Then I gently tied one end of the scarf around Trusty's body. I tied the other end to a jagged piece of metal sticking out from the broken-off hatch. Will stared at me, then slowly nodded and lay down in the hatch, curling up for warmth against the wind.

I started walking down the road, along the edge against the rising hillside, as far away from the drop-off as possible. Trusty moved forward, beside me, and on the slick road, the lightweight hatch slowly began moving with Trusty's effort.

Based on how fast we'd been going and how long we'd been driving since leaving Northway, I did a few calculations in my head.

We had four miles to go.

I don't remember a lot of detail from those four miles. I remember just in snatches—cold, snow, at times helping Trusty pull the makeshift sled, other times pushing it, Trusty howling and howling and howling. I remember spotting a cabin in the distance, wondering if it was a mirage . . . a truck pulling up to us, Trusty howling some more, then calming . . . a steady, commanding male voice . . . coming to a cabin . . . a calm, soothing female voice . . . my own voice, trying to explain . . . getting out of cold clothes into warm ones and a warm bed. . . .

I remember waking up in a haze of warmth, under a thick blanket in a dark room. I remember somehow knowing that we were safe, in the cabin of Ray Martin, a sergeant in the Alaska Territorial Police, just outside of Tok, Alaska—but not knowing how I knew that.

Tok, Alaska!

Somehow, we'd made it the last few miles.

Slowly, stiffly, I got out of the bed, and was struck by the chilliness of the room. I was wearing a thin, too-large nightgown and a pair of socks that weren't my own. I was confused for just a second, before remembering that our car and everything we'd packed were gone. The nightgown was a loan from Josie, Ray's wife. Draped over the end of the bed was a robe, which I put on. My and Will's clothes were folded up neatly on a wooden chair near the door.

I stepped out of the bedroom and into the parlor and took in the scene before me. Will was curled up in a chair in front of the fireplace, napping, Trusty on the floor by his chair. Closer to the fire was another dog, also a husky.

Sergeant Martin and his wife sat at a small table, quietly sharing a meal. The aroma of the food—some kind of stew—was intoxicating. My stomach rumbled.

Mrs. Martin looked up and smiled. "Good evening, Donna!"

I realized I must have slept the night before, after Sergeant Martin found us, and through the whole day. A little flush of shame crept over my face. I'd never slept that long before, never left Will unattended that long. I looked at him, a lurch of worry replacing my hunger pangs.

"Will is fine," she said. "He's had dinner. And his medicine."

I looked back at her. She smiled. "Last night, you told us about his condition and the dosage of medicines that he needs. It was one of the first things you told me when Ray brought you both here."

Thin, filmy memory washed over me. What else had I told them? Or had Will told them? I wasn't sure. But suddenly, I felt weary again, and in the next second, washed over by not only the physical warmth in the cabin but by a calm, steady knowledge that we were all right here, and that whatever came next would be all right, too.

Mrs. Martin stood up. "Come to the table. I'll get you a bowl of stew. Venison. I hope that's all right."

Sergeant Martin looked up from his bowl and touched her hand. "Let me get it—"

But she gently, playfully swatted his hand away. "You

worry too much. I'm fine to walk two steps from the table to the stove!"

She turned toward the stove, and I studied the profile of her large belly. She was going to have their baby any day now.

"Venison stew sounds wonderful," I said, and walked over to the table. By the time I sat down, Mrs. Martin had placed a steaming bowl of stew before me. I breathed in the heavenly scent, and then I started eating, lost in the wild, rich taste of the meat and savory broth, which I sopped up with a chunk of tender bread. Without asking, Sergeant Martin refilled my bowl, and I devoured that, too.

I finally looked up from my meal, feeling a little embarrassed at how much and how quickly I'd eaten, but I'd never been hungrier in my life, or felt so nourished in appeasing my hunger. "That was good," I said.

Mrs. Martin smiled. "I'm glad you enjoyed it. Last night you were too exhausted to eat."

Sergeant Martin gave me a long, penetrating look. "When I found you, you were carrying your brother piggyback."

I frowned. "What happened to our sled?"

"You were muttering something about that. But I didn't see a sled."

"It was from the back of our camper, the pull-down hatch in the back, which broke off when our car and camper went off the road. I made a sled out of the hatch and my scarf, and Trusty pulled Will for a while."

Sergeant Martin lifted his eyebrows. "Clever. But I didn't see a sled. Where did your car and camper go off the road?"

"A few miles outside of Northway."

He studied me for a long moment. Finally he said, "Do you have any idea how lucky the two of you are?"

"Yes," I said immediately. And then, "No."

"I got a call from Molly Donovan in Whitehorse to watch out for you. And your father placed a call to the deed office in Tok, to watch for you. He'd learned from a friend of yours, who I guess was with you part of the way on this crazy journey of yours, that you were headed here."

Sergeant Martin didn't seem like Sergeant Striker from the show—all hearty and adventurous and ready to face a challenge in the Alaskan wild, no matter how dangerous. Sergeant Martin was a much more practical man. "Your father was beside himself with worry about you, as he should have been. You could have been attacked by wild animals. Probably the only thing that kept them at bay was your dog, who was howling more fiercely than our Skipper ever has, even when he's seen bear or wolf. You could have wandered off the road, into wilderness. You could have—"

Mrs. Martin stood, put a hand on her husband's shoulder. "Ray! But they didn't. They made it here."

"Lucky," Sergeant Martin grumbled. "Foolish—and lucky."

I looked at him. Lucky? Will was dying. We'd made this trek to fulfill his last wish. "I don't remember everything I told you," I said. "My brother—"

Mrs. Martin moved her hand from her husband to me, patting me gently on the back. "You told us, sweetheart."

Sergeant Martin shook his head. "I understand why you two came here. But I'm sorry. Getting to that land is too hard, too dangerous. Even if I wanted to take you, I can't leave my wife to go on such a trek. Your father has already made arrangements for the two of you to fly by bush plane to Fairbanks, and from Fairbanks to Seattle, and take a bus back to Ohio—"

"What? Wait! Have you told Will this?"

Sergeant Martin finally looked away from me. Then he nodded.

I looked over at Will, curled up in the chair, and suddenly knew that he wasn't resting peacefully and deeply, as I had been. He was curled up in defeat.

I looked back at Sergeant Martin. My voice grew thick and shaky. "We have to see that one square inch of his land before we go back. We have to. He's dying and this is his last wish, his dream, and I'd rather die myself trying to get him there, than"—suddenly, tears streamed down my face—"than to come this far and disappoint him, and—"

Sergeant Martin shook his head. "I'm sorry," he said softly.

My mind raced. Surely there was someone, somewhere in or near Tok who could help us. . . .

"Sol Capputo!" I exclaimed.

Sergeant Martin and his wife suddenly stared at me as if I'd gone mad.

"Back in Whitehorse, Molly Donovan said that once we got here, if we needed help, we should find Sol Capputo. Maybe he knows someone who could get us out to that land—"

"Why, he could get you there himself!" Mrs. Martin said, excitement growing in her voice. "He was a miner and still is a tracker . . . and didn't he help that man who came here from the cereal company go see the land before he bought it?"

"Yes, Josie, but he's also half-crazy! I've had to throw him in lockup—"

"Ray!" Mrs. Martin snapped.

I thought I saw just a bit of amusement around the corners of his mouth.

She smiled at him. "They've come this far," she said softly. "Let Sol take them the rest of the way."

Chapter 30

The next morning, November 5, 1953, Will, Trusty, and I set out with Mr. Capputo in his old, jittery blue truck. The windows didn't go up all the way, which helped with breathing in spite of eau de Capputo. I thought he might have last bathed to celebrate the end of World War II.

At the deed office, we learned that all the deeds to the square inches were numbered consecutively. Will's was lot number 13,532,181, so we'd have to start in the northwest corner of the land, walk east about 7,993 inches, and then south 1,862 inches. The man at the deed office told us that there are 63,360 inches in a mile, so once we got to that northwest corner, we'd walk east about a tenth of a mile, and then a little ways south.

My heart fell. There was no way, I realized, that we could be sure of finding Will's exact inch. And Will was smart. He had to know that, too, yet there he stood in the deed office, clutching his framed deed, grinning ear to ear.

And Mr. Capputo was going right along, making a production out of double-checking that he had the surveyor's map, and a compass, and even a measuring tape.

From there, we drove down to the Tok River, and set out

in an open flat-bottomed boat that Mr. Capputo called a skiff. Huge pads of ice whisked by on the swiftly flowing river. The wind cut into our cheeks and eyes. I was glad we had on all of our warm clothes, plus fur hats that Mrs. Martin had insisted we wear.

"Don't fall in," Mr. Capputo said cheerfully. "You won't last more than two minutes."

Will laughed . . . then scoffed when I insisted on holding him close to me.

Finally, Mr. Capputo got us across the river to a rocky shore, hopping out in his thick leather boots and chaps to tether the boat to a huge spruce. Water splashed into the bottom of the boat and froze. Then Will and Trusty and I got out of the boat.

It took a few hours, but finally . . . finally . . . we were all standing by what Mr. Capputo proclaimed to be Will's one square inch of Alaska. Will dropped to his knees and stared down at the tiny patch of frozen earth, covered in pine needles.

"This is it?" he asked—but not with even a hint of disappointment at that measly little dot of land, on which nothing grew, not even a whisker of grass.

"Yes, sir!" said Mr. Capputo heartily, as if it were truly possible to find the exact square inch.

It was close enough for Will. "It is. It's . . . mine." His voice quivered. Somehow, though, it sounded strong, shot through with conviction, awe, and wonder, as he claimed aloud his one square inch, seeing only it, blind to all the nearby square inches that were just as barren as his.

But Will, I knew, did not see hopelessness or barrenness.

He saw a little bit of land that was his, and he stared at it with such fierce intensity, like finding this one square inch, and claiming it for his own, was enough for him. Enough for a lifetime.

I blinked hard. Swore at myself—*I won't cry.*

Won't think about how I taunted him about his desire to claim that one square inch.

How I crumpled his diorama.

I blinked again, looked away, but then felt Will's intense blue eyes on me, pulling me to him as they always did. I saw the bright spots of fever in his face. I knew that the day's trip had exhausted him, that he was burning up from the inside out. There would be no miracle. All the miracles the universe had for us had been spent on getting us here, to this one spot.

Will's eyes grasped mine just as firmly as they'd grasped the land. "Is it mine just on the surface," he asked, "or all the way down to the core?"

I managed to speak around the enormity of it all, to answer, "You own it, all the way down to the core."

Just like, I thought, Will had a bit of me, all the way to my core, and always would.

He pulled off his glove, and I started to tell him, no, no, put it back on, but then he reached in his pocket and pulled out the little sandwich flag, the one I'd gotten so long ago, it seemed—an eon ago—from Jimmy.

"But—I thought—it was in the diorama—"

Will shook his head and grinned. "I took it out for good luck, right after we found out about Mama. Kept it in my pocket, like a rabbit's foot. Same pocket where I have the carving of Trusty from Mr. Litchfield."

Then he looked at Mr. Capputo, who seemed to understand perfectly. He opened his rucksack and pulled out an ice pick and mallet.

Then Will nodded.

Right in the middle of his square inch of land, Mr. Capputo drove a hole.

And in that hole, Will planted his little flag.

Claiming his land.

Claiming a miracle—his one square inch of Alaska.

Epilogue

October 26, 1967

Waiting on the kitchenette table is a letter addressed to me, postmarked from Tok, Alaska. It bears a stamp commemorating the one hundredth anniversary of the Alaska Purchase. I run my thumb over it, smiling at how Will would be able to tell me and anyone who would listen the details of that 1867 purchase. And then I swallow, blink hard. I would be glad, so glad, to listen.

In the bedroom of our tiny New York apartment, I hear Adam moving about, getting ready for dinner out with me and a few friends, some from his law practice, some from my office. I'm home late from work and need to hurry to get ready.

But I sit down and carefully open the letter. I know I'll only think about it during dinner if I don't read it. It's another newsy missive from Josie Martin. All these years, she's sent me updates, letting me know sad tidings (Mr. Capputo's death a few years before, not long after Trusty died of old age), and, more often, happy ones, usually news about her and Ray's oldest son, William—yes, named for Will—and their three younger children, and about fun things like their big celebration when Alaska finally became a state, as Will always trusted it would, in 1959. This letter is about Josie's new job as a teacher, about William's big win in an ice-fishing contest.

I set aside the letter, go to our tiny refrigerator, and pull out a bottle of white wine. I pour two glasses, start to carry them back to the bedroom, but the beautiful design of that stamp—a totem etched on a brown background—catches my eye again. I sit back down at the table, admiring and studying that stamp.

I'm thirty-one, a '58 graduate of Parsons School of Design, working for designer Mollie Parnis at Parnis-Livingston and making plans to launch my own line of purses. Adam is the love of my life. Eventually, I know, we'll marry and make beautiful babies, but in the meantime, we're content to be together, sharing our hopes and dreams, exploring passion without inhibition.

And yet, there's one way in which I've not opened up to him. All I've told him about Will is that he was obsessed with Alaska. That he died when he was eleven, on April 3, 1954, four months before I left Groverton for good to attend Parsons School of Design. He knows my full life story since I arrived at Parsons, but nothing else from before. Adam is curious to know more, and I know I'm not being fair, holding back like this, especially when I know his childhood stories so well that I can laugh at the inside jokes he and his parents and siblings, whom I love, make about their history together. But Adam never asks, never presses, not even when these letters arrive, just leaves them on the table for me, trusting that when I'm ready, I'll tell him the full story. It's one of the many things I love about him.

But I always wonder, where would I begin? With that fateful morning, when I made a small choice to take Will by Stedman's Scrapyard just to get rid of Marvel Puffs, so he'd be one box top closer to his deed to one square inch of Alaska?

Or should I fast-forward to visiting that square inch, and what happened after? I replay those events for the first time, until now keeping them tucked at the back of my mind.

Will asked the man at the Tok deed office to officially mark the deed as going to me. After we were home, Mr. Capputo sent a photo of him and Trusty—Mr. Capputo proudly holding up a huge salmon by his skiff, Trusty happily at his side. When Will started truly getting ill, the leukemia rapidly taking more and more of his strength, he'd stare for hours at that photo of Trusty. When he died, I insisted that the photo be buried with him. But I kept the wood carving of Trusty.

Later that spring, I graduated. Grandma held a party at Dot's Corner Café for me—after all, her granddaughter was very important! Going to a fancy school in New York City! And on a scholarship, at that! Now I think about the people who were at that party.

Mr. Leis—by then completely confused by his surroundings—and Mrs. Leis, doing her best to take care of him. Mr. Leis died a month later and, to everyone's surprise because she seemed so healthy, Mrs. Leis followed about a half year after that. I wasn't particularly surprised. Mrs. Leis never liked being anywhere without Mr. Leis.

Daddy was at that party, his eyes still sunken and haunted both by the news about what had happened, in the end, to Mama, and by the death of his son.

MayJune was there, of course. Still grieving Joey, but smiling and kind and quietly wise as always, and chatting with Miss Bettina—birds on a wire, just like I'd thought of them at Will's birthday party.

Babs and Jimmy were at the party. Babs looked sad, her eyes almost as haunted as Daddy's. She'd come back to school in February, after a long stay with her grandparents in Virginia to recover from the "pneumonia" she'd had treated in Cincinnati. Jimmy and I talked and laughed, friends now and comfortable knowing that's all we'd ever be.

Mr. Cahill, of course, was not there, but somehow he'd heard of it. (I suspect MayJune and Miss Bettina had something to do with that.) He sent me another letter, congratulating me, finally giving me an address and phone number and telling me to look him up once I got to New York. I did, and even attended the opening of his show "Persimmon Girl," secretly smiling at being the inspiration for the abstract prints that looked nothing like me or any other girl, or even persimmons, but that received rave reviews from critics. We've stayed good friends ever since.

I've been back to Groverton twice since I left—once about a year after my move to New York, for Daddy and Miss Bettina's wedding. For the first time I could remember, Daddy finally looked happy. Miss Bettina—who has told me repeatedly to call her Bettina, but I can't quite drop the Miss—beamed. Grandma, of course, looked put out by the whole affair, especially with MayJune as Miss Bettina's matron of honor and me as maid of honor. ("Who has both?" Grandma groused.) But none of us paid any attention to her grumbling.

I did not go home for Grandma's funeral, a few years later. Daddy and Miss Bettina understood. But a few months ago I went home for MayJune's funeral. She died in her sleep at age 102. I stayed with Daddy and Miss Bettina in the little house on Elmwood, and I was happy to see that Miss Bettina had completely redecorated and refurnished it to her own taste.

While I was back, I visited with Babs. She had attended Kenyon College for two years before marrying an older man, who moved his medical practice to Groverton just for her. She says she's happy, with her lovely home and husband and three children, but I didn't see the glow of joy about her that I saw in Josie Martin. We talked about Jimmy, always sharing news whenever one of us received it. He's happily married, an attorney at a nonprofit focusing on workers' rights issues in Washington, D.C.

At last, I pick up the glasses of wine, head back to my and Adam's bedroom. Adam is in our tiny bathroom; I hear the sounds of shaving, him humming, and this makes me happy. I put the wineglasses on the bureau, slip out of my pumps, open the top bureau drawer to select a fresh blouse . . . and then something moves in me, a little voice saying, *Now . . . now is the time. You can be late for dinner . . . but now is the time.*

I close that drawer, kneel, open the bottom drawer—still where I keep my lingerie, and under that, the items I most wish to protect. My fingers move aside bras and panties and slips and the little wood carving of Trusty and a sachet, this one Chanel No. 5, a gift from Adam.

My hand shakes, just a little, as I pull out the framed deed. I sit on the edge of my and Adam's bed and study the signatures, barely legible, of Austin Perkins, the man at the deed office who officially marked the deed to transfer Will's land to me, and of Ray Martin, our witness, and our own signatures.

And for a second I'm back at that place where Will and I knelt, suddenly clasping each other and staring down at a frozen square inch of land in the Alaskan wild, knowing we've done the impossible by making it to this spot, and that our little toothpick flag won't last more than a few days, or maybe hours, to mark our having been there, that it will soon be swept away by ice and snow and wind, but then—in the way that scenes change and fuse and multiply and fade and merge in dreams and memories—I also see us looking up, as if someone has gently tucked a loving hand under our chins and tilted our faces, so we can watch the sky fill with the northern lights, a grand celestial dance of great swaths of tangerine and azure and teal, veils between our momentarily earthbound selves and all that is possible and infinite, rippling and swaying and lifting so that we can feel, just for a second, the enormity of all that lies beyond, waiting for each of us.

"Donna?"

I look up at Adam coming out of the bathroom, bare chested, and my heart surges with love and desire for this man with whom I know I'll spend the rest of my life. He quietly sits down next to me, waiting. Finally, I move so he can better see the frame I'm holding, and at last, I begin.

"This," I say, "is my deed. To my one square inch of Alaska."

Acknowledgments

So many individuals and organizations provided support—practical and emotional—that sustained me on the journey of writing this novel.

First, thank you to my wonderful husband, David, and our beautiful daughters, Katherine and Gwen, for bestowing upon me endless patience when I asked, yet again, "Are you sure I can do this?" by answering without hesitation, "Of course!" I can't begin to describe how much all those long discussions about the novel and your comments on early pages—especially in the early stages before I dared share this work with anyone else—meant to me. Endless love and thanks to all three of you.

Thank you to a lovely book club, the Goddesses, particularly "Supreme Head Goddess" Barbara Heckart, Lee Huntington, Judy DaPolito, and Mary Ann Schenk. These Goddesses might be surprised to learn that the very first flicker of the idea for this book was lit during a book club discussion at Mary Ann's lovely home when they began talking about "square inch deeds in cereal boxes in the 1950s" for some delightful reason (although it had nothing to do with the book we were discussing.) But perhaps, in their infinite wisdom, these Goddesses wouldn't be surprised at all.

Thank you to the Montgomery County Arts and Cultural District for a 2011 Literary Artist Fellowship and to the Ohio Arts Council for a 2012 Individual Excellence Award. Both awards were based, in part, on early chapters of this novel, and both awards enabled me to focus on my work as a novelist. I'm honored to be a recipient of both awards and proud to live in a region and state that supports and celebrates the arts, and understands that the arts ennoble and encourage its citizenry.

Thank you to the Antioch Writers' Workshop for my current role as director and for providing instruction and inspiration to so many writers, including me, over the years.

Thank you to two friends from another book club, the Socrates Café, for providing their comments and insight as lovers-of-books-of-all-kinds about this novel, Peggy Coale and Laurel Kerr.

Thank you to Dr. Gary Nicholson, who provided valuable insight into cancer treatment regimens of the 1950s.

Thank you to a host of wonderful writers and publishing professionals who I am deeply grateful to also know as friends: Ron Rollins, for writing a letter of recommendation for the Montgomery County Arts fellowship; Jeffrey Marks, Nancy Martin, Marcia Talley, Charlaine Harris, for providing excellent advice in querying agents; Carrie Bebris, Trudy Krisher, Judy Clemens, and Sarah Durand McGuigan for both providing advice and reading early chapters. I am especially indebted to Katrina Kittle, Kristina McBride, Becky Morean, Marti Moody, and Heather Webber not only for patting me on the head and wiping my brow when I needed the emotional support of close writer friends, but also for reading not just one . . . but at least TWO versions of the full manuscript and providing invaluable insight. An extra thank you to Katrina for also writing a letter of recommendation for the Montgomery County Arts fellowship and to Marti for providing an introduction to the agency that, in the end, would win my heart.

About that agency . . . thank you to Elisabeth Weed and Stephanie Sun, who not only believed in this story but provided valuable guidance in making it deeper and better. Thank you for also working with Jenny Meyer Literary Agency to find a publishing home for this novel in Germany. Thank you to Denise Roy, who brilliantly edited my novel with the intellectual precision of a surgeon and the heart of one who loves and understands storytelling. I am so delighted and grateful to be working with this amazing, savvy, dedicated publishing team!

And finally, thank you to readers who have followed my work over the years and are now joining me on this new literary venture, and to all new readers, too! I'm humbled and honored that you're coming along on Donna and Will's adventure.